Praise for the Novels of

Karen Marie Moning

DREAMFEVER

"Great detail and nonstop action. *Dreamfever* is fast moving, well-written, and will leave readers wanting more." —DARQUE REVIEWS

"[Karen Moning's] fans will be clamoring for this next installment." —DEAR AUTHOR

FAEFEVER

"Ending in what can only be described as a monumental cliffhanger, the newest installment of this supernatural saga will have you panting for the next. Breathtaking!" —ROMANTIC TIMES

"Erotic shocks await Mac in Dublin's vast Dark Zone, setting up feverish . . . expectations for the next installment." —PUBLISHERS WEEKLY

BLOODFEVER

"Moning's delectable Mac is breathlessly appealing, and the wild perils she must endure are peppered with endless conundrums. The results are addictively dark, erotic, and even shocking." —PUBLISHERS WEEKLY

"Mac is madder and 'badder'—as well she should be in the second Fever tale, and her creator's pacing is running full tilt. Moning brilliantly works the dark sides of man and Fae for all they are worth." —BOOKLIST

"I loved this book from the first page. It sucked me in immediately. . . . More. I want more." —LINDA HOWARD

DARKFEVER

"A wonderful dark fantasy . . . give yourself a treat and read outside the box." —CHARLAINE HARRIS

"A compelling world filled with mystery and vivid characters . . . will stoke readers' fervor for *Bloodfever*, the next installment." —PUBLISHERS WEEKLY

"Clear off space on your keeper shelf—this sharp series looks to be amazing." —ROMANTIC TIMES

SPELL OF THE HIGHLANDER

"Moning's characters are truly loveable; her tales are entertaining, touching, and incredibly hard to put down once begun. *Spell of the Highlander* is another sweeping tale of Highlander romance that longtime fans will treasure and will surely capture the imagination of new fans as well . . . an enchanting tale." —ROMANCE REVIEWS TODAY

THE IMMORTAL HIGHLANDER

"Seductive, mesmerizing, and darkly sensual, Moning's hardcover debut adds depth and intensity to the magical world she has created in her earlier Highlander books, and fans and new readers alike will be drawn to this increasingly intriguing series." —LIBRARY JOURNAL

"All readers who love humorous fantasy romance filled to the brim with fantasy-worthy Highlanders will find Moning's latest to be a sensuous treat." —BOOKLIST

"Nonstop action for fans of paranormal romance." —KIRKUS REVIEWS

THE DARK HIGHLANDER

"Darker, sexier, and more serious than Moning's previous time-travel romances . . . this wild, imaginative romp takes readers on an exhilarating ride through time and space." —*PUBLISHERS WEEKLY* (starred review)

"Pulsing with sexual tension, Moning delivers a tale romance fans will be talking about for a long time."

—*OAKLAND PRESS*

"*The Dark Highlander* is dynamite, dramatic, and utterly riveting. Ms. Moning takes the classic plot of good vs. evil . . . and gives it a new twist."

—*ROMANTIC TIMES*

KISS OF THE HIGHLANDER

"Moning's snappy prose, quick wit and charismatic characters will enchant." —*PUBLISHERS WEEKLY*

"Here is an intelligent, fascinating, well-written foray into the paranormal that will have you glued to the pages. A must-read!" —*ROMANTIC TIMES*

"*Kiss of the Highlander* is wonderful. . . . [Moning's] storytelling skills are impressive, her voice and pacing dynamic, and her plot as tight as a cask of good Scotch whiskey." —*CONTRA COSTA TIMES*

THE HIGHLANDER'S TOUCH

"A stunning achievement in time-travel romance. Ms. Moning's imaginative genius in her latest spellbinding tale speaks to the hearts of romance readers and will delight and touch them deeply. Unique and eloquent, filled with thought-provoking and emotional elements, *The Highlander's Touch* is a very special book. Ms. Moning effortlessly secures her place as a top-notch writer." —*ROMANTIC TIMES*

DREAMFEVER

Books by Karen Marie Moning

THE FEVER SERIES

Darkfever

Bloodfever

Faefever

Dreamfever

Shadowfever (coming January 2011)

THE HIGHLANDER SERIES

Beyond the Highland Mist • To Tame a Highland Warrior

The Highlander's Touch • Kiss of the Highlander

The Dark Highlander • The Immortal Highlander

Spell of the Highlander

DREAMFEVER

A MacKayla Lane Novel

BOOK 4

Karen Marie Moning

DELL
NEW YORK

Dreamfever is a work of fiction. Names, characters, places,
and incidents are the products of the author's imagination or
are used fictitiously. Any resemblance to actual events, locales,
or persons, living or dead, is entirely coincidental.

2010 Dell Mass Market Edition

Copyright © 2009 by Karen Marie Moning, LLC

Bonus material copyright © 2010 by Karen Marie Moning, LLC

All rights reserved.

Published in the United States by Dell,
an imprint of The Random House Publishing Group,
a division of Random House, Inc., New York.

DELL is a registered trademark of Random House, Inc.,
and the colophon is a trademark of Random House, Inc.

"Taking Back the Night" by Neil Dover, copyright © 2009.
From Bloodrush/Machalo Records. Reprinted by permission
of the author.

Originally published in hardcover in the United States
by Delacorte Press, an imprint of
The Random House Publishing Group,
a division of Random House, Inc., in 2009.

ISBN 978-0-440-24440-0

Printed in the United States of America

www.bantamdell.com

2 4 6 8 9 7 5 3 1

Cover design: Eileen Carey
Cover concept: Abdullah Badawy
Cover illustration: Tom Hallman
Book design: Carol Malcolm Russo

Some people are a force of nature.
Like wind or water over stone, they
reshape lives. This book is dedicated
to Amy Berkower.

When I was in high school, I used to hate that Sylvia Plath poem where she talked about knowing the bottom, that she knew it with her great taproot and that it was what everybody else feared, but she didn't, because she'd been there.

I still hate it.

But I get it now.

—Mac's journal

Prologue

Death. *Pestilence. Famine.*

They surround me, my lovers, the terrifying Unseelie Princes.

Who'd've thought destruction could be so beautiful? Seductive. Consuming.

My fourth lover—War? He ministers to me tenderly. Ironic for the bringer of Chaos, creator of Calamity, maker of Madness—if that is who he is. I cannot see his face, no matter how I try. Why does he hide?

He caresses my skin with hands of fire. I char, my skin blisters, bones fuse from sexual heat no human can endure. Lust consumes me. I arch my back and beg for more with parched tongue, cracked lips. As he fills my body, he quenches my thirst with drink. Liquid spills over my tongue, drips down my throat. I convulse. He moves inside me. I catch a glimpse of skin, muscle, a flash of tattoo. Still no face. He terrifies me, this one who keeps himself concealed.

In the distance, someone barks commands. I hear

many things, understand none. I know that I have fallen into enemy hands. I know also, soon, I will no longer know even that. *Pri-ya,* a Fae sex addict, I will believe there is no place, nothing else I would rather be.

If my thoughts were coherent enough to form sentences, I would tell you that I used to think life unfolded in a linear fashion. That people were born and went to . . . what's that human word? I dressed up for it every day. There were boys. Lots of cute boys. I thought the world revolved around them.

His tongue is in my mouth, and it's tearing apart my soul. Helpmesomeonepleasehelpmemakehimstopmakethem-goaway.

School. That's the word I'm looking for. After that, you get a job. Marry. Have . . . what are they? Fae can't have them. Don't understand them. Precious little lives. Babies! If you're lucky, you live a good, full life and grow old with someone you love. Caskets then. Wood gleams. I weep. A sister? Bad! Memory hurts! Let it go!

They're in my womb. They want my heart. Tear it open. Gorge on passion they can't feel. Cold. How can fire be so cold?

Focus, Mac. Important. Find the words. Deep breath. Don't think about what's happening to you. See. Serve. Protect. Others at risk. So many died. Can't be for nothing. Think of Dani. She's you inside, beneath that adolescent thumbs-in-the-pockets, one hip cocked, thousand-yard stare.

I orgasm without ceasing. I become the orgasm. Pleasure-pain! Exquisite! Mind-melting, soul-shredding, the more they fill me the emptier I am. It's slipping, all slipping, but before it goes, before it's gone completely, I get a hateful moment of clarity and see that

Most of what I believed about myself, and life, I derived from modern media, without questioning any of it. If I wasn't sure how to behave in a certain situation, I'd search my mind for a movie or TV show I'd seen, with a similar setup, and do whatever the actors had done. A sponge, I absorbed my environment, became a by-product of it.

I don't think I ever once looked up at the sky and wondered if there was sentient life in the universe besides the human race. I *know* I never looked down at the earth beneath my feet and contemplated my own mortality. I tunneled blithely through magnolia-drenched days, blind as a mole to everything but guys, fashion, power, sex, whatever would make me feel good right then.

But these are confessions I would make if I could speak, and I can't. I'm ashamed. I'm so ashamed.

Who the fuck are you? Someone shouted that question at me recently—his name eludes me. Someone who frightens me. Excites me.

Life's not linear at all.

It happens in lightning flashes. So fast you don't see those lay-you-out-cold moments coming at you until you're Wile E. Coyote, steamrolled flat as a pancake by the Road Runner, victim of your own elaborate schemes. A sister dead. A legacy of lies. An unwanted inheritance of ancient blood. An impossible mission. A book that is a beast that is ultimate power, and whoever gets their hands on it first decides the fate of the world. Maybe *all* the worlds.

Stupid *sidhe*-seer. So sure you had things headed in the right direction.

Here and now—not on some cartoon highway from which I can peel myself, stand up, and magically reinflate, but on the cold stone floor of a church, naked, lost, surrounded by death-by-sex Fae—I feel my most powerful weapon, the one I swore never to give up again—hope—slipping away. My spear is long gone. My will is . . .

Will? What's will? Do I know the word? Did I ever?

Him. He's here. The one who killed Alina. Please, please, please don't let him touch me.

Is he touching me? Is he the fourth? Why conceal himself?

When the walls come tumbling, tumbling down, that's the question that matters. *Who are you?*

I reek of sex and the scent of them—dark, drugging spices. I have no sense of time or place. They're inside me and I can't get them out, and how could I have been such a fool to believe that at the critical moment, when my world fell apart, some knight in shining armor was going to come thundering in on a white stallion, or arrive sleek and dark on an eerily silent Harley, or appear in a flash of golden salvation, summoned by a name embedded in my tongue, and rescue me? What was I raised on—fairy tales?

Not this kind. These are the fairy tales we were *supposed* to be teaching our daughters. A few thousand years ago, we did. But we got sloppy and complacent, and when the Old Ones seemed to go quietly, we allowed ourselves to forget the Old

Ways. Enjoyed the distractions of modern technology and forgot the most important question of all.

Who the fuck are you?

Here on the floor, in my final moments—MacKayla Lane's last grand hurrah—I see that the answer is all I've ever been.

I'm nobody.

1

Dani: 2:58 p.m., November 1

Hey, it's me—Dani. I'm gonna be taking over for a while. Fecking good thing, too, 'cause Mac's in serious trouble. We all are. Last night everything changed. End-of-the-world stuff. Uh-huh, that bad. Fae and human worlds collided with the biggest bang since creation, and everything is a mess.

Fecking Shades loose in the fecking abbey. Ro through the roof with it, screaming that Mac betrayed us. Ordered us to hunt her. Bring her in dead or alive. Shut her up or shut her down, she said. Keep her away from the enemy, because she's too powerful a weapon to be used against us. She's the only one who can track the *Sinsar Dubh*. No way we can let her fall into the wrong hands, and Ro says any hands but hers are the wrong ones.

I know stuff about Mac that she'd kill me for, if she knew I knew. Good thing she doesn't know. I never want to fight Mac.

But here I am, hunting her.

I don't believe she spiked the Orb with Shades. Pretty much everyone else does, though. They don't know Mac like I do. I know Mac like we're sisters. No way she betrayed us.

Seven hundred thirteen of us alive at the abbey at five o'clock last night. Five hundred twenty-two *sidhe*-seers left at last count. Taking Dublin back. Hunting Mac. Kicking every bit of Fae ass we see along the way.

No sign of her yet. But we're headed in the right direction. There's an epicenter of power in the city, reeking stinking nasty Fae as toxic as the fallout plume from a nuclear explosion. We all feel it. Taste it. Practically see the mushroom cloud hanging in the air. We don't even talk to one another. Don't need to. If Mac's still in Dublin, that's where she is, straight ahead. No way any *sidhe*-seer could turn away from this kinda pull. I hope she's nailing their butts with the spear. We'll fight back to back like we did a couple nights ago.

But I've got this sick feeling in the pit of my stomach. . . .

Bull-fecking-crikey! I don't feel sick. I *never* feel sick. Sick is for wusses and wannabes.

Mac can take care of herself. She's the strongest of us all.

" 'Cept me," I mutter, with a swagger and a grin.

"What?" Jo says behind me.

I don't bother answering. They already think I'm cocky enough. I have reasons to be cocky. Uh-huh, I'm *that* good.

Five hundred twenty-two of us closing in. We fight like banshees and can do some serious damage, but we've got only one weapon—the Sword of Light—that can kill a Fae.

"And it's *mine*." I grin again. I can't help it. Fecking A, it's the supercoolest gig in the world to be a superhero. Superfast, superstrong, with a few extra "supers" in me that Batman would trade all his toys for. What everybody else wishes they could do, I can. Behind me, Jo says "What?" again, but I'm not grinning anymore. I'm back to feeling prowly, pissed. Being fourteen—well, I *almost* am—blows. One minute I'm on top of the world, next I'm mad at everybody. Jo says I'm hormonal. She says it gets better. If better means I'm gonna turn into a grown-up, thanks but *not*. Gimme a blaze of glory any day. Who wants to get old and wrinkly?

If the Unseelie hadn't taken the power grids down last night, turning the whole city into a Dark Zone, I'd've come after Mac sooner, but Kat made us hide like cowards 'til dawn. *Not enough flashlights,* she said.

Duh, I'm superfast, I said.

Great, she said, *so you'd have us watch you whiz superfast right through a Shade and die? Smart, Dani. Real smart.*

Pissed me off, but she had a point. When I'm moving like that, it *is* hard to see what's coming at me. With the power grids down, ain't nobody gonna dispute the Shades own the night once it falls.

Who put you in charge? I said, but it was rhetorical and we both knew it, and she walked away. Ro put her in charge. Ro *always* puts her in charge, even though I'm better, faster, smarter. Kat's obedient, dutiful, cautious. Gag me with a spoon.

Crashed and burned cars everywhere we turn. I thought there'd be more bodies. Shades don't eat dead flesh. S'pose other Unseelie do. The city is spooky quiet.

"Slow down, Dani!" Kat yells at me. "You're speeding up again. You know we can't keep up with you!"

"Sorry," I mutter, and slow down. With what I feel up ahead and this stupid sick feeling in my stomach—

"Not *sick*." My teeth clench on the lie. Who the feck am I kidding? I feel sick, sick, sick. My palms and pits are slick with dread. I wipe my sword hand against my jeans. My body knows things before my brain can. Always been that way, even when I was a kid. Used to freak Mom out. It's what makes me fight so good. I know what I'm gonna find up ahead is gonna be one of those things I'll wake up in the middle of the night wishing I could scrape out from behind my eyeballs.

Whatever we're headed for, whatever's throwing all that fallout into the sky, is more Fae power than I've ever felt before, all clumped together in one place. The way we work things, the other *sidhe*-seers close in and pound ass while I do what I've been doing best since Ro took me in when Mom was murdered.

I kill.

We range out like a net. Five hundred strong. Drape ourselves, *sidhe*-seer by *sidhe*-seer, around the epicenter and close in tight. Nothing's getting through us unless it flies. Or sifts.

Aw, crap! Or *sifts*. Some of the Fae can travel from place to place at the blink of a thought—just a hair faster than me, but I'm working on that. I have a theory I been testing. Haven't worked out the kinks yet. The kinks are killer.

"Stop," I hiss at Kat. "Tell 'em all to stop!"

She cuts a hard look my way but bites a sharp command that rips down the line. We're well trained. We move together and I tell her my worry: that Mac's in there, in serious trouble, and if the big-bads throwing off all that power are sifters—which most of the big-bads are—she'll be gone the second we're spotted.

Which means I'm going in alone. I'm the only one who can sneak-attack fast enough to pull it off.

"No way," Kat says.

"No choice, and you know it."

We look at each other. She gets that look grown-ups get a lot and touches my hair. I jerk. I don't like to be touched. Grown-ups creep me out.

"Dani." She pauses heavily.

I know that tone like I know the back of my hand, and I know where it's going: Lectureville on a runaway train. I roll my eyes. "Save it for somebody who cares. Newsflash: It ain't me. I'll go up"—I jerk my head at a nearby building—"to get the lay of things. Then I'm going in. Only. When I. Come. Back. Out." I spit each word. "Can you guys go in."

We stare at each other. I know what she's thinking. Nah, reading minds isn't one of my specialties. Grown-ups telegraph everything. Somebody kill me before I get one of those Play-Doh faces. Kat's thinking if she makes the call against me and loses Mac,

Ro'll have her head. But if she lets *me* make the call and things go bad, she can blame it on headstrong, uncontrollable Dani. I take the blame a lot. I don't care. I do what needs to be done.

"*I'll* go up," she says.

"I need the visual snapshot myself, or I could end up grabbing the wrong thing. You want me coming out with some fe—er, effin' fairy in my hands?" They rip me a new one when I cuss. Like I'm a kid. Like I haven't spilled more blood than they've ever seen. Old enough to kill but too young to cuss. They make a pit bull poodle around. What kinda logic is that? Hypocrisy pisses me off worse than most anything.

Her face sets in stubborn lines.

I push. "I *know* Mac's in there and for some reason she can't get out. She's in major trouble." Was she surrounded? Wounded that badly? Had she lost her spear? I didn't know. Only that she was in way deep shit.

"Rowena said alive or dead," Kat says stiffly. She left "It sounds like she'll be dead soon and our problems will be solved" hanging unspoken.

"We want the Book, remember?" I try reason. Times I think I'm the only one in the whole abbey that's got any.

"We'll find it without her. She betrayed us."

Feck reason. Pisses me off when people jump to conclusions they have no proof for. "You don't know that, so stop saying it," I growl. Somebody's fist is holding Kat's coat collar, got her up on her toes. It's mine. I don't know who's more surprised, her or me. I drop her back on the ground and look away. I've never done anything like that before. But it's Mac in there and I have to get her out, and Kat's wasting my time big-time with total BS.

Her mouth sets with tiny white lines around it, and her eyes take on a look I get a lot. It makes me feel mad and alone.

She's afraid of me.

Mac isn't. One more way we're like sisters.

Without another word, I give my feet the wings they live for and vanish into the building.

From the rooftop, I stare.

My fists clench. I keep my nails real short; still, they gouge blood from my palms.

Two Fae are dragging Mac down the front steps of a church. She's naked. They drop her like a piece of trash in the middle of the street. A third Fae exits the church and joins them, and they stand, imperial guards around her, heads swiveling, surveying the street.

The raw sex they're throwing off blasts me, but it's not like V'lane, who I'm gonna give my virginity to one day.

I'm as obsessed with sex as anybody, but those . . . things . . . down there . . . those incredibly—*fecking A, they hurt to look at; something's wet on my cheeks; are my eyes boiling in their sockets?*—beautiful things scare even me, and I don't scare easy. They don't move right. Storms of color rush under their skin. Black torques slither at their necks. There's nothing in their eyes. *Nothing.* Eyes of pure oblivion. Power. Sex. Death. They reek of it. They're Unseelie. My blood knows. I want to fall on my knees at their feet and worship, and Dani Mega O'Malley don't worship *nothing* but herself.

I wipe my face. My fingers come away red. My eyes are leaking blood. Freaky. Kinda cool. Vamps got nothing on Fae.

I close my eyes, and when I open them again I don't look directly at the things guarding Mac. Instead, I take a wide-angle image of the scene. Every Fae, fire hydrant, car, pothole, streetlamp, piece of trash. I map objects and empty spaces on my mental grid, lock it down tight, calculate margin of error based on likely movement, slap it over my snapshot.

I squint. A shadow moves in the street, almost too fast to see. The Fae don't seem to know it's there. I watch. They don't respond to it. No heads swivel to follow it. I can't focus on it. Can't make out its shape. It moves like I move . . . mostly. What the feck? Not a Shade. Not a Fae. A blur of shadow. Now it's hanging over Mac. Now it's gone. Bright side—if the Unseelie aren't noticing it, they shouldn't notice *me* when I whiz in to snatch her. Dimmer side—what if whatever it is can see me? What if we collide? What is it? I don't like unknowns. Unknowns can kill.

I catch the glint of Mac's spear in a red-robed man's hand. He's carrying it at arm's length from his body. Only Seelie or humans can touch the Seelie Hallows. He's one or the other. The Lord Master?

They have Mac. They have the spear. Don't know if I can grab both so won't try. Would chance it if it wasn't Mac. They hurt her bad. She's bloody everywhere. She's my hero. I *hate* them! Fae took my mother and now they've taken Mac. I refresh my snapshot of the scene right before I let myself go nuts inside, let that ancient *sidhe*-seer place in my head swallow me whole.

Instantly, I'm cool and perfect and detached from everything. I'm the Shit. It's the most massive high in the world!

I zip from one freeze-frame to the next. No in-betweens.

I'm on the roof of the building.

I'm in the street.

I'm between the guards. Lust—*wantneedsexdie*—incinerates me, but I'm moving too fast and they can't touch what they can't see and they can't see me and all I have to do is not cave; hate, hate, hate, make armor from it. Got enough hate to Kevlar all Ireland's Garda.

I grab Mac.

Freeze-frame.

Heart in my throat! Shadow-thing blocks my path! What *is* it?

I'm past it.

Hear Fae shouting behind me.

Then I'm screaming at Kat and the crew to get their asses in there, grab that spear, and kill those bastards.

Mac in my arms, I freeze frames as fast as I can, heading for the abbey.

Dani: November 4

L et me be certain I'm understanding you cor-
rectly," Rowena says tightly.

Her back is to me; her small frame bristles with
anger. Times, Ro seems ancient. Others, she's wicked
spry. It's weird. Her spine's ramrod-straight, her
hands fisted at her sides. Her long white hair is
braided, wrapped regal as a crown around her head.
She wears the formal white Grand Mistress robes
emblazoned with the symbol of our order—the misshapen emerald shamrock—that she's been wearing
ever since all hell started to break loose. I'm surprised she's waited this long to rip me a new one,
but she's been busy with other things.

She took away my sword. It's on her desk. The
blade shimmers alabaster, like light stolen straight
from heaven—*my* light—reflecting the glow of
dozens of lamps arranged in the office to illuminate
every corner, nook, and cranny.

When the Orb exploded on All Hallows' Eve,
freeing the Shades, we were so caught off guard that
the slithery fecks managed to take out fifty-four of

us before we got enough lamps and flashlights on to protect ourselves. As far as we know, they're unkillable. My sword can't touch them. Light's a temporary stay of execution, just drives 'em deeper into whatever dark crevices they can find. Our abbey's been compromised, but we won't give an inch. No way Shades are taking our home and turning it into a Dark Zone. One by one we'll hunt 'em down and force 'em out.

Yesterday, there was one inside Sorcha's boot. Clare saw it happen. Said Sorcha just kind of vanished down into her shoe, clothes collapsed around it. When we dumped the boot upside down on the front steps in the sunshine, a papery husk, jewelry, and two fillings spilled out, followed by a Shade that shattered into a zillion pieces. None of us is putting on our shoes now without shaking the crap out of 'em and shining flashlights deep. I been wearing sandals a lot, even though it's cold. What a way to go: death-by-shoe-Shade. I grin. I have a black sense of humor. You try living my life, see what color yours turns.

I stare at my sword. My fingers curl on emptiness. It kills me to be parted from it.

In a whirl of white robes, Rowena spins and skewers me with a look sharp as an ice pick. I shift uncomfortably. I might make fun of Rowena, call her "Ro," and blather about how cool I am, but— make no mistake—this old woman is someone you wanna tread carefully around.

"You were within killing distance of the Lord Master and three Unseelie Princes and you *did not even draw your sword*?"

"I couldn't," I say defensively. "I had to get Mac. Couldn't risk that she might be killed in the fight."

"Which part of dead or alive did I fail to impress upon you?"

Well, obviously the "dead" part, but I don't say that. "She can track the Book. Why's everybody keep forgetting that?"

"No longer! You knew that the moment you laid eyes on her. Traitor, and now *Pri-ya,* she is of no use to us. Incapable of thought or speech, she can't even feed herself! She'll be dead in days, if she lasts that long. Och, and there you went, discarding the only chance we've ever had at slaying our enemy plus three Unseelie Princes, all for saving the life of a single worthless girl! Who do you think you are to be making such decisions for the lot of us?"

Mac might be *Pri-ya,* but she's not a traitor. I won't believe that. I say nothing.

"Get out of my sight," she shouts. "Get out! Get out! Or I'll throw you out!" Her voice rises and she flings an arm at the door. "Thinking you know what's best—then go! Have a try at it, you ungrateful child! As if I haven't done everything for you a mother would and more! Leave! See how long you survive out there without me!"

I stoically refuse to glance at my sword. No telegraphing for me. Ro catches everything. But if she's serious, I can beat her to the sword, and will.

I look at her and *ooze* neediness and remorse. Cram my eyes full of it. Make my lower lip quiver. We stare at each other.

By the time all the muscles in my face are screaming from holding such a stupid, wussy look, her gaze softens. She draws a deep breath, releases it. Closes her eyes, sighs. "Dani, och, Dani," she clucks, opening her eyes. "When *will* you learn? When you're dead? I have only our best interests at heart. Do you not trust me?"

I'm massively suspicious of that word. It means to accept without question. I did that once. "I'm sorry, Rowena." My voice catches on the words. I hang my head. I want my sword back.

"I can see you have feelings for that, that—"

"Mac," I supply, before she calls her something that really pisses me off.

"But I swear I will *never* ken the why of it." She pauses heavily, and I know it's my cue to begin justifying my existence.

I tell her everything she wants to hear. I'm lonely, I say. Mac was nice to me. I'm sorry I was so stupid. I'm really trying to learn to be the person you want me to be, I tell her. I'll do better next time.

Ro dismisses me but keeps my sword. I deal. For now. I know where it is, and if she doesn't give it back soon, I'll find an excuse for something that needs killing.

In the meantime, I got a lot to do. Because I'm superfast, they have me whizzing all over the county, collecting lamps, bulbs, batteries, a whole list of supplies. The crazy stuff we saw in Dublin hasn't started happening out here yet. We still got power. Even if we didn't, we got backup generators out the wazoo. Our abbey's totally self-sufficient. Own electric, food, water. We got it all.

So far, I haven't spotted a single Unseelie. Guess they prefer the city. More to feed on. Kat thinks they won't go rural 'til they've gorged on urban, so we should be safe for a while, 'cept for those fecking Shades. 'Tween times, I check on Mac. Keep trying to get her to eat. Ro has the key to her cell. Don't know why she needs locking in, since she has all those wards around her and can't seem to walk. If I don't get food in her soon, I'll be requisitioning that key. I can coax her to crawl over to the bars, but I can't force her to eat through them.

Thing I really want to know is: Where the feck is V'lane? Why hasn't he come for Mac? Why didn't he stop the Unseelie Princes from raping her? I call for him as I dart around the countryside, but if he hears me yelling, he doesn't answer to *me*. Guess not to Mac anymore, either.

And Barrons—what's his deal? Doesn't he want her alive? Why have they all abandoned her when she needs 'em the most?

Men.

Dude, they suck.

I dump supplies in the dining hall. Superglue, lights, batteries, brackets. Nobody looks up. *Sidhe*-seers at every table, making more of the cool helmet Mac was wearing the night we fought together. After I snatched her from the princes, Kat and the others went in, kicked ass, snagged Mac's spear and backpack, and found the pink helmet inside.

Now they got an assembly line going that I keep supplied, 'cept it's getting hard to find Click-It lights. I might have to go into Dublin, even though Ro says not to raid stores there.

Since so many of us work as bike couriers for Post Haste, Inc.—that's the front for the international *sidhe*-seer coalition, with offices around the world—most of us already have our own helmets. Just need 'em modified. With Shades in the abbey, everybody's arguing to be first in line for the next one done. I told 'em Mac called it a MacHalo, but Ro forbade anyone to call it that, like it pissed her off Mac thought of it or something.

I whiz into the kitchen, yank open the fridge so hard it tips over catty-corner and I have to right it, then stand there cramming my mouth full of food. Don't know what I'm eating, don't care. I'm shaking. I have to eat constantly. Superspeed drains me. I go for high fat, high sugar. Butter, cream, raw eggs go down fast. OJ. Ice cream. Cake. I keep my pockets stuffed with candy bars and don't go anywhere without my fanny pack. I gulp two sodas and finally stop shaking.

I picked up a couple protein drinks for Mac at the store. I worry she might choke on solid food if she resists. She's gonna eat this time, period.

Cassie says Ro's making rounds. It's time for that key.

I don't cry. I don't remember if I ever cried. Didn't when Mom was killed. But if I was gonna cry, I'd do it when I look at Mac. See, her and me? We'd *die* for each other. Seeing her like this slays me. I drag my feet on the way to her cell, which, for me, means walking like a Joe. I munch a couple more candy bars.

She won't keep her clothes on. Tears 'em off like they burn her skin. Dude, I want to look like her when I grow up. When I brought her here, Ro took her and locked her downstairs in one of the old cells they used back when. Stone walls. Stone floor. Pallet. Bucket for waste. She's not making any, 'cause she's not eating or drinking, but still—it's the principle! She's not an animal, even if she's acting like one. She can't help it! Prison bars for a door.

Ro said it was for Mac's own good. Said the Unseelie Hunters would track her, and the princes would sift in and take her back to the Lord Master, if we didn't put her below earth and surround her with wards. We spent most of the day I brought her back painting symbols all over the abbey, with the Haven looking over our shoulders, telling us what to do. They had pictures. Ro got 'em out of a book in one of the Forbidden Libraries. It was wicked cool! We had to mix blood into the paint. I know, 'cause Ro wanted mine. She didn't want me to tell the other girls. I know a lot of stuff the other girls don't. The walls of Mac's cell are covered with wards, inside and out.

I pass Liz in the corridor on the way to the stairs. She's wearing a MacHalo, blazing like a small sun.

"How is she?" I say.

Liz shrugs. "No idea. Not my turn to be checking on her, and you won't find me down there 'less it is."

When I pass Barb and Jo, I don't ask. Most of the *sidhe*-seers feel the same way as Liz. They don't want Mac here, and nobody's taking any chances. There's no electricity downstairs. Like medieval times. Torches burning in wall sconces. You get the picture.

It'd make me nervous for Mac, 'cept I tossed fifty or so click-on LED lights in her cell and been keeping an eye on the batteries.

"I don't know why you bother," Jo throws over her shoulder. "She spiked the Orb. She flirted with a Seelie Prince. She was asking for it. Fae and human don't mix. That's the whole point of our order—we keep the races *apart*. She got what she was asking for."

My blood boils. I thought I was at the door, about to go down, but I've got Jo flattened against the wall, our noses separated only by the distance forced by the front lights of our MacHalos.

There's that look. Scared of me.

"You should be," I say coolly. "Scared of me. Because if anything happens to Mac, you're gonna be the first person I come looking for."

She shoves me away, hard. "Rowena will take away your pretty sword. Without your sword, you're not so tough, Danielle."

Was she *kidding* me? "It's Dani." I hate that sissy name. I shove her back against the wall.

I can't fecking believe it, but she shoves me *again*. Still got that scared look but defiant, too.

"You might be faster and stronger, kid, but enough of us together could kick your ass, and we're beginning to want to. You take care of a traitor, you start looking like one."

I look at Barb, who shrugs as if to say, "Sorry, but I agree."

Buncha idiots. I whiz off without a backward

glance. Not wasting time or breath on them. Mac needs me.

My first clue something's wrong is I open the door to the downstairs and it's dark. I stand there, stupid for a second. No way all the torches burned out at once. I'm not sensing Fae, and even the weakest *sidhe*-seer among us has range enough to cover the whole abbey.

No Fae around means one of *us* put out the torches. Means we got somebody in our ranks wants Mac dead bad enough to try to outright kill her. *And* expects to get away with it. I punch on my Click-Its, go into superspeed mode, and bingo—I'm at her cell.

It's worse than I thought.

When we brought buckets of paint downstairs, we never got around to carrying the unused gallons back up, and now somebody's gone and dumped black paint all over the floor and splashed it on the walls outside her cell, obliterating the wards.

I toe it with a sandal. It's wet, fresh.

I frown. Something's not making sense. With the torches out—sure, the Shades could get down here. With the wards obliterated, they could even enter the cell—*if* there weren't fifty lights blazing in there with her, but there are. So what's the point? Why make a half-assed murder attempt that has no chance of working?

"Aw, crap," I say, as it dawns on me. Because it's not Shades someone's expecting. It's something bigger and badder, something not afraid of the light.

No way. No way we got *that* serious a traitor in our walls!

I mull the evidence. Brain says, *way*, Dani. Wise up.

Don't want to leave her alone, but I can't guard her without a weapon! Still not sensing Fae. I need forty-five seconds, tops. Gotta risk it.

Freeze-frame!

Moving like I do is cool; 's 'bout as close to being invisible as you can get. People say they feel a rush of wind blasting by that practically blows off their hair. I'm still testing the limits. I like running outside best, 'cause there's less to crash into. Bruises are me.

Point I'm making is, people can't even see me. So a person *touching* me when I'm freeze-framing? Totally out of the question.

I can sort of see what's going on around me, hear a little, too, but it's mostly a blur of movement and noise.

The noise that tips me off, moments before I get freaked out of my skin, is male voices. Angry. Violent. No men are allowed in the abbey.

Ever. No exceptions. The night Mac brought V'lane here, we all 'bout died.

But here they are. Men headed toward me. Lots of them. Gunshots! Fecking A! What kinda idiot brings guns to this kinda war? What would guns kill? Oh, jeez, duh—*us*. Why? Right ahead, coming faster than expected—

AVOID! AVOID! AVOID!

I call on every ounce of speed and agility I got, because something major weird is happening and

something's sort of *in* my space with me, and I'm
having a shit of a time avoiding it, and all the sudden I'm plucked from the air by my elbows and
jammed into a stationary position on the floor, so
hard my teeth rattle.

Plucked.

Me.

Snatched straight out of superwhiz speed. *Forced*
to stop.

I can't deal.

I squeak.

"Dani," a man says.

I gape. Mac never told me what he looked like. I
can't believe Mac never told me what he looked like.
I can't stop staring. "Barrons?" I breathe. It has to be
him. It can't be anybody else. *This* is what she lived
with every day? How did she stand it? How did she
ever say "no" to him about anything? How does
he know who I am? Did Mac tell him about me? I
hope she told him how awesome I am! I'm so embarrassed I could die. I squeaked in front of him.
Mice squeak. He takes up too much space. He
yanked me from midair.

I scramble back, half-freeze-frame speed. I get the
feeling he *lets* me. It chafes, bad.

I look past him and nearly squeak again.

Eight men fan in V formation behind him, pack-
ing weapons from head to toe, draped in ammo, toting what look like Uzis. Big men. Couple of 'em
seem more animal than human. One of 'em looks
like Death himself, with white hair, pale skin, and
hot dark eyes that assess restlessly, incessantly. They
fix on me. I cringe. They all move sleek and strange.

Ooze arrogance like Fae, but they're not Fae. *Sidhe-seers* are plastered up against the walls, trying not to draw attention to themselves. Nobody dead that I can see. I think the gunshots I heard were warnings, sprayed into the air. Hope so. The energy rolling off these dudes is fierce. Whatever Barrons has got—I can't put my finger on it, but on a raw-power graph it's off the fecking charts—they've got, too. Watching this crew stalk down the hall of the abbey makes even *me* feel like peeling out of the way.

One of the men has Ro banded by a forearm, knife at her throat.

I should whiz in and save her. She's our Grand Mistress. She's our highest priority. Thing is, I'm not sure I can make it past Barrons.

"Get out of my abbey!" she's shouting.

"Where's Mac?" Barrons says, soft, making my gaze dart back to him. Soft from him is a surgical knife poised above your jugular. "Has the bitch hurt her?"

If looks could kill! Someday somebody's gonna look at somebody about *me* like that. I'm not about to tell him I'm pretty sure Ro was gonna let her die. "No. She's okay." I clarify a little. "Well, I mean, as okay as she was when she got here."

He gives me a look and says, "Where?" again.

A cold, hard fact just got driven home for me with the doused torches and painted-over wards. I can't keep Mac safe by myself. Even *I* have to sleep sometimes. With the exception of All Hallows' Eve, Barrons has kept her safe.

Still . . . there's no way anything human plucked me out of the air like that. What *is* he? I don't know how much Mac trusts him. "Promise me you won't harm Ro," I say. "We need her."

Something savage moves deep in his eyes. "I'll decide that when I see Mac."

I feel savage all the sudden, too. "Well, where the feck were you when she needed you?" I snarl. "*I* was there."

Without another word, I freeze-frame out.

Only two things I trust in these walls: me, and my sword. If my instincts are spot-on—as they always are—Barrons isn't the only thing headed Mac's way right now.

I'm gonna beat 'em all there.

I let that old, cold *sidhe*-seer place in my head swallow me. I become power, strength, speed, free!

The door to Ro's office splinters.

The sword is mine.

Then I'm in Mac's cell, standing over her. She rolls over like she senses the heat of my body. Clings to my leg. Rubs against me. Makes noises. I pretend nothing's weird. She can't help herself right now. I don't look straight at her. I haven't since I got her out. I don't know a lot about sex, but I do know what's happening to her is no way to learn it. I've been doing a little research. It's got me worried. There's not a single case of a person turned *Pri-ya* coming back from it. Not one. They're mindless animals that do whatever they're told until they die. And *those* were the cases of people turned by Seelie. Never been anyone turned by Unseelie, and Mac got the whammy from three of the most powerful! But Mac's got wicked balls. She'll claw her way back somehow. She has to. We need her.

A Fae sifts in!

Wantneedsexdie blasts me. Hesitation ain't me! I jab my sword into its gut. It looks down. Thing is stunned, disbelieving. We stare at each other. Unbearable perfection. My cheeks get wet like last time I looked at a prince, and I don't have to wipe them to know it's blood. If just looking at it makes my eyes bleed, how did Mac survive three of them *touching* her? Doing things to her? Even mortally wounded, it's forcing me to my knees. I want to let it do anything it wants to me. I want to obey it. I want to call it Master. Ro says they're the equivalent of the Four Horsemen of the Apocalypse, so who's my sword stuck in? Death, Pestilence, Famine, or War? Dude, what a kill! I'd pat myself on the back if it wasn't taking everything I got to keep from pulling my sword out of it and turning it on myself. It's fecking with me. Trying to take me with it. Its iridescent eyes blaze in what I'm pretty sure is its dying attempt to incinerate me. Then we're both falling to our knees: it 'cause it's dead, and me—I'm so fecking embarrassed—'cause I think I just had my first ever orgasm killing an Unseelie Prince. That's wrong. I hate it. I hate that it made me feel that now. It wasn't supposed to be that way.

Then Barrons is in the cell.

Then there's another Unseelie Prince sifting in behind me. The thing is so powerful, my *sidhe*-seer senses pick up on it before it becomes corporeal. I spin, lunge, but I don't get the rush of killing it, because the bastard takes one look *behind* me and vanishes.

I get that. I'm not stupid. It was more afraid of Barrons than of me and my sword.

I whirl to face him, to demand answers, because I'm not letting him take Mac anywhere until he explains a few things, but the look in his eyes shuts me down.

Way to go, Dani, the look says. You're not a kid, say his eyes. You're a warrior, and a bloody fine one at that. His look takes me in, measures me up and down, and reflects me back at myself, and in the glittering black mirror of his gaze, I am one *hell* of a woman. Barrons sees me. He really *sees* me!

When he picks up Mac and turns away, I swallow a dreamy sigh.

I'm gonna give Barrons my virginity one day.

Mac: in the cell at the abbey

I am heat.
I am need.

I am pain.

I am more than pain. I am agony. I am the other side of death denied the mercy of it. I am life that should never have been.

Skin is all I am. Skin that is alive that hungers that aches that needs to be touched to endure. I roll and roll, but it is not enough. It makes the pain worse. My skin is on fire, flayed by a thousand red-hot blades.

I have been on the cold stone floor of this cell for as long as I can recall existing. I have never known anything but this cold stone floor. I am hollow. I am barren. I am empty. I do not know why I continue to be.

But wait! In my stasis is there something? Is this change?

I lift my head.

There is other-than-empty near!

I crawl to it, beg it to make my agony stop.

The other-than-empty tries to put things in my mouth and make me chew. I roll my head away. Resist. Not what I want. Touch me here. Touch me now!

It does not. It goes away. Sometimes it returns and tries again.

Time has no meaning.

I drift.

I am alone. Lost. I have always been alone. There has never been anything but cold and pain. I touch myself. I need. I need.

The other-than-empty comes and goes. Puts things in my mouth that smell and taste bad. I spit them out. Those are not what I need.

I drift in my stasis of pain.

Wait! What is this? Change again? Am I to know something besides agony?

Yes! I know this! He Who Made Me is here! My prince has come. I rejoice. An end to my suffering is at hand.

Wait—what is other-than-empty *doing*?

My prince is . . . no, no, no!

I scream. I hammer other-than-empty with my fists. The other-than-empty is hurting my master with a long shiny thing. He is ceasing to be! Take me with you, I beg! I cannot endure. I am pain! I am pain!

The other-than-empty kneels beside me. Touches my hair.

My prince is gone.

The other made him cease to be!

I collapse. I am grief. I am despair. I am desolation. I am the cliffs of black ice from whence my masters come.

Change again?

Another He Who Made Me has come? Am I to be saved after all? Granted mercy at my master's hands?

No, no, *no*! He is gone, too. Why am I being tortured?

I am agony. I have been forsaken. I am being punished and I do not know why.

But wait . . .

Something looms over me. It is dark and powerful. It is electric. It is lust. It is not one of my princes, but my body arches and steams. Yes, yes, yes, *you* are what I need!

It touches me. I am on fire! I weep with relief. It holds me to its body, crushes me to its skin. We sizzle. It speaks, but I do not understand its language. I am in a place beyond words. There is only skin and flesh and need.

I am an animal. I hunger without conscience, without qualm.

And I have been given a gift to exceed all gifts—my masters must be pleased with me!

Its language is gibberish to my ears, but the flesh recognizes its own.

The creature that holds me now will do more than end my pain. It will fill all that is empty.

It is an animal, too.

4

I am alive. I am so alive. I have never been more alive in my life. I sit, cross-legged, nude, in a tangle of silk sheets. Life is a sensual banquet and I am voracious. I glisten with sweat and satisfaction. But I need more. My lover is too far away. He is bringing me food. I do not know why he insists. I need nothing but his body, his electric touch, the primitive, intimate things he does to me. His hands on me, his teeth and tongue, and most especially what hangs heavy between his legs. Sometimes I kiss it. Lick it. Then *he* glistens with sweat and hunger and strains beneath my mouth. I hold down his hips and tease. It makes me feel powerful and alive.

"You are the most beautiful man I've ever seen," I tell him. "You are perfect."

He makes a strangled sound and mutters something about how I might seriously reconsider that at some point. I ignore it. He says many mystifying things. I ignore them all. I admire the preternatural grace of his body. Dark, strong, he pads like a great beast, muscles rippling. Black and crimson symbols cover much of his skin. It's exotic, exciting. He is large. The first time I almost couldn't take him. He fills me, sates me completely. Until he is no longer inside me and I am empty again.

I push onto all fours and arch my rump invitingly. I know he cannot resist my ass. When he looks at it, he gets a funny look on his face. Savage, his mouth tightens, his eyes harden. Sometimes he looks away sharply.

But he *always* looks back.

Hard, fast, hungry like me.

I believe he is divided in desire. I do not understand that. Desire is. There is no judgment between animals. No right or wrong. Lust is. Pleasure is the way of beasts. "More," I say. "Come back to bed." It took me a while to learn this exquisite thing's language, but when I did, I learned rapidly, although parts of it elude me. He claims I knew it all along but had forgotten it. He says it took me weeks to regain it. I do not know what "weeks" are. He says they are a way of marking the passage of time. I have no care for such matters. He often speaks nonsense. I ignore it. I shut his mouth with mine. Or with my breasts, or other parts. It works every time.

He shoots me a look, and for a moment I think I have seen that look before. But I know I have not, because I could never have forgotten such a divine creature.

"Eat," he growls.

"Don't want food," I growl back. I tire of him making me eat. I reach for him. I am strong. My body is sure. But this fine beast is stronger than me.

I savor his power, when he lifts me on top of him, when he holds me down and fills me, when he's behind me, driving deep. I want him there now. He knows no limits. Though I have drowsed, I have never seen him sleep. Though I demand incessantly, he is always able to please me. He is inexhaustible. "I want more. You. Come here. Now." There goes my rump again. Up.

He stares.

He curses. "No, Mac," he says.

I do not know what "Mac" means.

But I know what "no" means.

And I do *not* like it.

I pout. But it quickly curves into a smile. I know a secret. For a beast of such power, his self-control with me is weak. I have learned this in our time together. I wet my lips, give him a look, and he makes that raw, angry-sounding noise deep in his throat that makes my blood hot, hot, hot, because every time he makes it I know he's just about to give me what I want.

He cannot resist me. It bothers him. He is an odd animal.

Lust *is*, I tell him, again and again. I try to make him understand.

"There's more to life than lust, Mac," he says roughly, again and again.

There is that word "Mac" again. So many words I do not understand. I weary of talk. I tune him out.

He gives me what I want. Then forces me to eat—*boring!* I humor him. Belly full, I am sleepy. I tangle my body with his. But when I do, lust takes me again, and I cannot sleep. I roll on top of him, straddle him, breasts swaying over his face. His eyes glaze and I smile. He traps me beneath him in a smooth graceful roll, stretches my arms above my head, and stares into my eyes. I grind my hips up. He is hard and ready. He is *always* hard and ready.

"Be still, Mac. Bloody hell, would you just be still?"

"But you're not *in* me," I complain.

"And I'm not going to be."

"Why not? You want me."

"You need rest."

"Rest later."

He closes his eyes. A muscle works in his jaw. He opens his eyes. They glitter like arctic night. "I am trying to help you."

I arch up against him. "And I am trying to *help* you help me," I explain patiently. My beast is dense sometimes.

He growls and drops his face in my neck. But he doesn't kiss or nip it. I grunt my displeasure.

When he lifts his head again, he wears a mask of impassivity that does not promise more of what I want. My hands are still trapped in his.

I head-butt him.

He laughs, and for a moment I think I have won, but then he stops and says, "*Sleep,*" in a strange voice that seems to echo with many voices. It pressures my skull. I know what it is. This beast has magic.

I have magic, too, in a place in my head. I push back at him with it, hard, because I want what he has and he will not give it to me. It angers me that he resists, so I push into him, I try to make him do what

I want him to do. With my beast magic, I search for his weakness to use it against him, like he's trying to use mine. Then something gives way, and abruptly I am no longer snug between the pleasure of silk at my back and man at my front but—

I stand in a desert. I am inside my lover's body, staring out from his eyes. I am mighty, I am vast, I am strong. We breathe stiflingly hot night air. We are alone, so alone. A scorching wind gusts across the desert, kicking up a violent sandstorm, blinding us to all but a few feet ahead, driving thousands of tiny, needlelike grains into our unprotected face, our eyes. But we make no move to shield ourselves. We welcome the pain. We become the pain, unresisting. We breathe grains of sand. They burn our lungs.

Others flank us; still we are so alone. What have we done? What have we become? Have they gotten to her? Does she know? Will she denounce us? Turn her face away?

She is our world. Our highest star, our brightest sun, and now we are dark as night. We were always dark, feared, above and beyond any law. But she loved us anyway. Will she love us now? We who have never known uncertainty or fear now know both in what is absurdly the moment of our greatest strength. We who have killed without conscience, taken without question, conquered without hesitation, now question it all. Undone by a single act. The mighty, whose stride has never faltered—we stumble. We fall to our knees, throw back our head, and, as our lungs fill with sand, roar our outrage through cracked and burning lips to the heavens, those mocking, fucking heavens—

Someone is shaking me.

"What are you *doing*?" he is roaring. I am in bed again, between silk and man. I still feel the searing heat of the desert, and my skin seems gritty with sand. He stares down at me, his face white with fury. And more. This beast that does not rattle is rattled.

"Who is she?" I ask. I am no longer inside his head. It was hard to stay there. He didn't want me there. He is very strong and cast me out.

"I don't know how you did that, but you will *never* do it again," he snarls, and shakes me again. "Do you understand?" He bares his teeth. It excites me.

"You preferred her to all others. Why? Did she mate better?"

It makes no sense.

I am a fine beast.

He should hold *me* above all others.

I am here. Now. She is gone. I do not know how I know it, but she has been gone for a very, very long time. Far longer than his "weeks."

"Stay the fuck out of my head!"

Fuck. There's a word I understand. "Yes, please."

"*Sleep*," he orders in that strange, multilayered voice. "*Now.*"

I resist, but he keeps saying it over and over. After a time, he sings to me. Finally, he gets ink and draws upon my skin. He has done it before. It tickles . . . but soothes.

I sleep.

I dream of cold places and fortresses of black ice. I dream of a white mansion. I dream of mirrors that are doorways to dreams and gateways to hell. I dream animals that cannot exist. I dream of things

I cannot name. I weep in my dreams. Powerful arms band me. I shudder in them. I feel like I'm dying.

There is something in my dream that *wants* me to die. Or at least cease living as far as I understand it.

It makes me angry. I will not cease to exist. I will not die, no matter how much pain there is. I made a promise to someone. Someone who is *my* highest star, my brightest sun. Someone I want to be like. I wonder who it is.

I push on through the cold, dark dreams.

A man wearing red robes reaches for me. He is beautiful, seductive, and very angry with me. He calls to me, summons me. He has some kind of hold over me. I want to go to him. I need to go to him. I belong to him. He made me what I am. *I will tell you of she for whom you grieve,* he promises. *I will tell you of her last days. You long to hear.* Yes, yes, although I do not know of whom he speaks, I want desperately to hear about her. Did she have happy days, did she smile, was she brave at the end? Was it quick? Tell me it was quick. Tell me there was no pain. *Find me the Book,* he says, *and I will tell you all. Give you all. Call the Beast. Unleash it with me.* I do not want this book. I am terrified of it. *I will give you back she for whom you grieve. I will give you back your memories of her and more.*

I think I would die to have those memories back. There was a hole. Now there is a hole where the hole was.

You must live *to get those memories back,* another voice growls from a distance. I feel tickling on my skin and hear chanting. It drowns out the voice of the man in red robes. He is fury in crimson, melting into blood, then he recedes and I am safe from him for now.

I am a kite in a tornado, but I have a long string. There is tension in my line. Somewhere, someone is holding on to the other end, and, although it cannot spare me this storm, it will not let me be lost while I regain my strength.

It is enough.

I will survive.

He plays music for me. I like it very much.

I find something else to do with my body that gives me pleasure. He calls it dancing. He sprawls on the bed, arms folded behind his head, a mountain of dark muscle and tattoos against crimson silk sheets, watching me as I dance naked around the room. His gaze is carnal, hot, and I know my dancing pleases him greatly.

The beat is driving, intense. The lyrics apropos, for he has recently taught me that the moment of pleasure is called "orgasm" or "to come," and the song is a cover of a Bruce Springsteen song by someone called Manfred Mann. Over and over it says, *I came for you.*

I laugh as I sing it to him. I play it again and again. He watches me. I lose myself in the rhythm. Head back, neck arched. When I look back at him, he is singing: *Girl, give me time to cover my tracks.*

I laugh. "Never," I say. If my beast thinks to leave me, I will track him. He is mine. I tell him so.

His eyes narrow. He lunges from the bed and is

on me. I exhilarate him. I see it in his face, feel it in his body. He dances with me. I am struck again by how strong and powerful and sure of himself he is. On a predator scale of one to ten, I have enticed a ten. That means I, too, am a ten. I am proud.

Our sex is fierce. We will both be bruised.

"I want it to always be like this," I tell him.

His nostrils flare, obsidian eyes mock. "Try holding on to that thought."

"I do not need to try. I will never feel differently."

"Ah, Mac," he says, and his laughter is as dark and cold as the place of which I dream, "one day you will wonder if it's possible to hate me more."

My beast adores music. He has a pink thing he calls an eye-pod, although it does not look to me as if it was ever a pod for eyes, and with it he makes many sounds. He plays songs over and over and watches me carefully, even when I do not dance.

Some of the songs make me angry and I do not like them. I try to make him stop playing them, but he holds the eye-pod over my head and I cannot reach it. I like hard, sexy songs, like "Pussy Liquor" and "Foxy, Foxy." He likes to play peppy, happy songs, and I am beyond sick of "What a Wonderful World" and "Tubthumping." He watches me, always watches me, when he plays them. They have stupid names and I hate them.

Sometimes he shows me pictures. I hate those, too. They are of others, most often a woman he calls Alina. I do not know why he needs pictures of her when he has me! Looking at her makes me feel hot and cold at the same time. Looking at her hurts me.

Sometimes he tells me stories. His favorite one is about a book that is really a monster that could destroy the world. *Boring!*

Once he told me a story about Alina and said she died. I screamed at him and wept, and I do not know why. Today he showed me something new. Photos of a man he calls Jack Lane. I tore them up and threw the pieces at him.

Now I have forgiven him because I have him inside me, and he's got his big hands on my petunia—I do not know that word, or where it came from!—rump, and he's doing that slow, erotic bump and grind so smooth and deep that makes me purr to the bottom of my toes and kissing me so hard I cannot breathe around it and I do not want to. He is in my soul and I am in his, and we are in bed but we are in a desert, and I do not know where he begins and I end, and I suppose if his peculiar madness is music and photos and stories that chafe, it is a small price to pay for such pleasure.

He comes hard, shuddering. I match him, bucking with each shudder. When he comes, he makes a noise deep in his throat that is so raw and animal and sexual that I think if he merely *looked* at me and made that noise, I might explode in an orgasm.

He holds me. He smells good. I drowse.

He starts with his stupid stories again.

"I do not *care*." I raise my head from his chest. "Stop talking at me." I cover his mouth with my hand. He pushes it away.

"You *must* care, Mac."

"I am so sick of that word! I do not know 'Mac.' I do not like your pictures. I hate your stories!"

"Mac is your name. You are MacKayla Lane. Mac for short. It is who you are. You are a *sidhe*-seer. It is what you are. You were raised by Jack and Rainey Lane. They are your parents and love you. They need you very much. Alina was your sister. She was murdered."

"Stop talking! I will not listen." I clamp my hands to my ears.

He pries them away. "You love pink."

"I despise pink! I love red and black." The colors of blood and death. The colors of the tattoos on his beautiful body that cover his legs, his abdomen, half his chest, and twine up one side of his neck.

He rolls me over beneath him and traps my face between his hands. "Look at me. Who am I?"

There is something I have forgotten. I do not want to remember. "You are my lover."

"I was not always, Mac. There was a time when you didn't even like me. You have never trusted me."

Why does he tell me lies? Why does he seek to ruin what we have? It is now. It is perfect. There is no cold, no pain, no death, no betrayal, no icy places, no terrifying monsters that can steal your will and turn you into something you cannot even recognize and make you feel ashamed, so ashamed. There is only pleasure here, endless pleasure.

"I trust you," I say. "We are the same."

His smile is sharp as knives. "We are not. I've told you that before. *Never* make that mistake. We meet in lust. But we are not the same. Never will be."

"You worry about things of no importance. And you talk too much."

"You got me a birthday cake. It was pink. I smashed it into the ceiling."

I do not know "birthdays" or "cakes," so I say nothing.

"You like cars. I let you drive my Viper."

Cars! I remember those. Sleek, sexy, fast, and powerful, all the things I like. Something nags at me. "Why did you smash this 'birthday cake' into the ceiling?" I wait for his answer and am struck by a violent sense of déjà vu—that I have waited for many answers from my beast, and have gotten few, if any.

He stares down at me. He seems startled that I have asked such a question. I have confused myself with it. I do not ask questions. I have little interest in talk. There is only now. I met my lover the day he became my lover. What do I care of things called cakes and birthdays? Yet I seem to want his answer very much and feel oddly deflated when he does not give me one.

"I am Jericho Barrons. Say my name."

I try to turn my face away, but his hands clamp like a vise on my skull and hold it immobile, preventing me from looking away.

I close my eyes.

He shakes me. "Say my name."

"No."

"Damn it, would you just cooperate?"

"I do not know that word, 'cooperate.' "

"Obviously," he growls.

"I think you make up words."

"I do *not* make up words."

"Do, too."

"Do not."

"Too."

"*Not.*"

I laugh.

"Woman, you make me crazed," he mutters.

We do this often. Get into childish arguments. He is stubborn, my beast.

"Open your eyes and say my name."

I squeeze them shut more tightly.

"It would make my cock hard to hear you say my name."

My eyes pop open. "Jericho Barrons," I say sweetly.

He makes a pained sound. "Bloody hell, woman, I think a part of me wants to keep you this way."

I touch his face. "I like how I am. I like how you are, too. When you are . . . What is that word you used? Cooperating."

"Tell me to fuck you."

I smile and comply. We're back in territory I understand.

"You didn't say my name. Say my name when you tell me to fuck you."

"Fuck me, Jericho Barrons."

"From now on, you will call me Jericho Barrons every time you speak to me."

He is a strange beast. But he gives me what I want. I suppose it will not kill me to do the same.

And so we begin a different way of being. I call him Jericho Barrons and he calls me Mac.

We are no longer animals. We have "names."

* * *

I dream of his "Alina" and wake up weeping. But there is something new inside me. Something cold and explosive beneath the tears.

I do not know what to call it, but it makes me pace. I stalk the room like the animal I am, smashing and breaking things. I scream until my throat is raw.

Suddenly I have new words.

Rage.

Anger. Violence.

I am all the fury that ever was. I could scourge the earth with my grief and madness.

I want something. But I do not know what it is.

He watches me in silence.

I think it must be sex. I go to him. He sits on the edge of the bed and pulls me to stand between his legs.

My hands hurt from hitting things. He kisses them.

"Revenge," he says softly. "They took too much. You give up and die, or learn how to take back. Revenge, Mac."

I cock my head. I try the word on my tongue. "Revenge." Yes. That is what I want.

He is gone when I wake, and I have a bad moment, but then he is there and has brought many boxes and some of them smell good.

I no longer resist when he offers me food. I anticipate it. Food is pleasure. Sometimes I put things on his body and lick them off, and he watches me with dark eyes and shudders as he comes.

He leaves and returns with more boxes.

I sit on the bed, eat, and watch him.

He opens boxes and begins to build something. It is strange. He plays music on his eye-pod that makes me feel uncomfortable . . . young, childish.

"It's a tree, Mac. You and Alina put one up every year. I couldn't get a live one. We're in a Dark Zone. Do you remember Dark Zones?"

I shake my head.

"You named them."

I shake my head.

"How about December twenty-fifth? Do you know what day that is?"

I shake my head.

"It's today." He hands me a book. There are pictures in it of a fat man in red clothing, of stars and cradles, of trees with shiny pretty things on the branches.

It all seems quite stupid to me.

He hands me the first of many boxes. In them are shiny, pretty things. I get the point. I roll my eyes. My stomach is full and I would rather have sex.

He refuses to comply. We have one of our spats. He wins because he has what I want and can withhold it.

We decorate the tree while happy, idiotic songs play.

When we are finished, he does something that makes a million tiny bright lights glow red and pink and green and blue, and I lose my breath like someone has kicked me in the stomach.

I drop to my knees.

I sit cross-legged on the floor and stare at the tree for a long time.

I get more new words. They come slowly, but they come.

Christmas.

Presents.

Mom.

Dad.

Home. School. Brickyard. Cell phone. Pool. Trinity. Dublin.

One word disturbs me more than all the rest of them combined.

Sister.

He makes me put on "clothes." I hate them. They are tight and chafe my skin.

I take them off, throw them on the floor, and stomp on them. He dresses me again, in rainbow colors that are bright and hurt my eyes.

I like black. It is the color of secrets and silence.

I like red. It is the color of lust and power.

"*You* wear black and red." I am angry. "You even wear it on your skin." I do not know why he gets to make up the rules, and I tell him so.

"I'm different, Mac. And I get to make up the rules because I'm bigger and stronger." He laughs. There is power even in such a simple sound. Everything about him is power. It thrills me. It makes me want him all the time. Even when he is dense and troublesome.

"You are not so different. Do you not wish me to be like you?" I yank the tight pink shirt over my head. My breasts pop out, bouncing. He stares hard, then looks away.

I wait for him to look back. He always looks back. He doesn't this time.

"*I have no business looking forward to pink cakes,* isn't that what you said?" I am angry. "You should be happy that I want black!"

His head whips back around. "What did you just say, Mac? When did I tell you that? Tell me about it!"

I do not know. I do not understand what I just said. I do not remember such a time. I frown. My head hurts. I hate these clothes. I strip off my skirt but leave on my heels. Nude, I can breathe. I like the heels. They make me feel tall and sexy. I walk toward him, hips swaying. My body knows how to walk in such shoes.

He grabs my shoulders, holds me away from him. He does not look at my body, only at my eyes. "Pink cakes, Mac. Tell me about pink cakes."

"I don't give a rat's petunia about pink cakes!" I shout. I want him to look at my body. I am confused. I am afraid. "I don't even know what a rat's petunia *is!*"

"Your mother didn't like you and your sister to cuss. 'Petunia' is the word you say instead of saying 'ass,' Mac."

"I do not know *that* word, 'sister,' either!" I lie. I hate the word.

"Oh, yes, you do. She was your world. She was killed. And she needs you to fight for her. She needs you to come back. Come back and fight, Mac. Bloody hell, fight! If you'd just fight like you fuck, you'd've walked out of this room the day I carried you in!"

"I do not want to walk out of this room! I *like* this

room!" I will show him fight. I launch myself at him, a volley of fists and teeth and nails.

I am ineffectual. He is as obdurate as a mountain.

He prevents me from damaging him or myself. We stumble and fall to the floor. Abruptly I am no longer angry.

I sprawl on top of him. I hurt inside my chest. I kick off my shoes.

I drop my head in the hollow where his shoulder meets his neck. We are still. His arms are around me, strong, certain, safe. "I miss her," I say. "I do not know how to live without her. There is a hole inside me that nothing fills." There is something else inside me, too, besides that hole. Something so awful that I will not look at it. I am weary. I do not want to feel anymore. No pain, no loss, no failure. Only the colors of black and red. Death, silence, lust, power. Those things give me peace.

"I understand."

I draw back and look at him. His eyes are deep with shadows. I know those shadows. He *does* understand. "Then why do you push me?"

"Because if you don't find something to fill that hole, Mac, someone else will. And if someone else fills it, they own you. Forever. You'll never get yourself back."

"You are a confusing man."

"What's this?" He smiles faintly. "I am a man now? I am no longer a beast?"

It is all I have called him until now. My lover, my beast.

But I have found another new word: "man." I look at him. His face seems to shimmer and change, and for a moment he is shockingly familiar, as if I have known him somewhere before here and now. I touch him, trace his arrogant, handsome features slowly. He turns his face into my palm, kisses it. I see shapes behind him. Books and shelves and cases of trinkets.

I gasp.

His hands close tight on my waist, hurting me. "What? What did you see?"

"You. Books. Lots of them. You . . . I . . . know you. You are . . ." I trail off. A sign creaking on a pole in the wind. Amber sconces. A fireplace. Rain. Eternal rain. A bell rings. I like the sound. I shake my head. There was no such place or time. I shake my head harder.

He surprises me. He does not push me with words I do not like to hear. He does not shout at me or call me Mac or insist I talk more.

In fact, when I open my mouth to speak again, he kisses me, hard.

He shuts me up with his tongue, deep.

He kisses me until I cannot speak or even breathe, until I do not even care if I ever breathe again. Until I have forgotten that for a moment he was not a beast but a man. Until the images that so disturbed me are singed to ash by the heat of our lust and gone.

He carries me to the bed and tosses me on it. I feel anger in his body, although I do not know why.

I stretch my naked body on the sleek silk, luxuriating in sensation, in the sure knowledge of what is to come. Of what he is about to do. Of what he makes me feel.

He stares down at me. "See how you look at me. Fuck. I understand why they do it."

"Who does what?"

"The Fae. Turn women *Pri-ya*."

I do not like those words. They terrify me. I am lust. He is my world. I tell him so.

He laughs, and his eyes glitter like night sky pierced by a million stars. "What am I, Mac?" He pours his sleek, powerful body over mine, laces our fingers together, and stretches my hands above my head.

"You are my world."

"And what do you want from me? Say my name."

"I want you inside me, Jericho. Now."

Our sex is savage, as if we are punishing each other. I feel something changing. In me. In him. In this room. I do not like it. I try to stop it with my body, drive it back. I do not look at this room in which we exist. I do not let my mind wander beyond the walls. I am here and he is, too, most of the time, and that is enough.

Later, when I am drifting like a balloon, in that happy, free place that is the twilight sky before dreams, I hear him take a deep breath as if he is about to speak.

He releases it.

Curses.

Takes another breath but says nothing again.

He grunts and punches his pillow. He is divided, this strange man, as if he both wants to speak and wants not to.

Finally, he says tightly, "What did you wear to your senior prom, Mac?"

"Pink dress," I mumble. "Tiffany bought the same one. *Totally* ruined my prom. But my shoes were Betsey Johnson. Hers were Stuart Weitzman. My shoes were better." I laugh. It is the sound of someone I do not recognize, young and without care. It is the laugh of a woman who knows no pain, never did. I wish I knew her.

He touches my face.

There is something different in his touch. It feels like he's saying good-bye, and I know a moment of panic. But my dream sky darkens and sleep's moon fills the horizon.

"Don't leave me." I thrash in the sheets.

"I'm not, Mac."

I know I am dreaming then, because dreams are home to the absurd and what he says next is beyond absurd.

"You're leaving me, Rainbow Girl."

5

We're "Tubthumping" again. He makes me dance around the room, shouting: *I get knocked down but I get up again. You're never gonna keep me down.*

He dances with me. We shout the lyrics at each other. Something about seeing this man, this big, sexual, powerful—and, some part of me knows, highly dangerous and unpredictable—man, dancing nude, shouting that he's never going to be kept down, completely undoes me.

I feel as if I am seeing something forbidden. I know without knowing how I know that the circumstances under which he would behave in such a fashion are incalculably few.

Suddenly I am laughing and cannot stop. I laugh so hard I cannot breathe. "Oh, God, Barrons," I finally gasp. "I never knew you could dance. Or have fun, for that matter."

He freezes. "Ms. Lane?" he says slowly.

"Huh? Who's she?"

He stares at me, hard. "Who am I?"

I stare back. There is danger here, in this moment. I do not like it. I want more "Tubthumping" and tell him so, but he turns off the music.

"What happened on Halloween, Ms. Lane?" He fires the question at me, and I now have the strangest feeling he has been asking me this question over and over for a long time but I block it every time he asks it. Refuse to even hear it. And that perhaps there are *dozens* of questions he's been asking me that I have been refusing to hear.

Why is he calling me that new name? I am not she. He repeats the question. Halloween. The word gives me chills. Something dark tries to bubble up in my mind, to break the surface I keep placid and still with sex, sex, sex, and suddenly I am no longer laughing but my body is trembling and my bones are so soft I fall to my knees.

I clutch my head in my hands and shake it violently.

No, no, no. I do not want to know!

Images bombard me: A mob shouting, surging out of control. Rain-slicked, shiny dark streets. Shadows moving hungrily in the darkness. A red Ferrari. Glass breaking. Fires burning. People being driven, herded into hell.

A place of books and lights that falls to the enemy. It mattered to me, that place. I'd lost so much, but at least I had that place.

A gruesome meal. A weapon I both need and fear. People rioting. Trampling one another. A city burning. A belfry. A closet. Darkness and fear. Finally, dawn.

Holy water splashing, hissing on steel.

A church.

I shut down. Walls slam in my heart, my mind. I will not go there. There is/was/will never be a church in my existence.

I look up at him.

I know him. I do not trust him. Or is it me I do not trust?

"You are my lover," I say.

He sighs and rubs his jaw. "Mac, we have to leave this room. It's bad out there. It's been months. I need you back."

"I am right here."

"What happened at the"—he breaks off, his nostrils flare, and a muscle works in his jaw—"church?"

It seems he does not want to hear about what happened at this church any more than I want to know about it. If we are in agreement on this, why does he push?

"I do not know that word," I say coolly.

"Church, Mac. Unseelie Princes. Remember?"

"I do not know those words."

"They raped you."

"I do not *know* that word!" My hands are fists; my nails hurt me.

"They took your will. They took your power. They made you feel helpless. Lost. Alone. Dead inside."

"*You should have been there!*" I snarl, but I have no idea why. I was never at a church. I am shaking violently. I feel like I might explode.

He drops to the floor on his knees in front of me and grabs my shoulders. "I know I should have!" he snarls back. "How the *fuck* many times do you think I've relived that night?"

I beat at him with my fists, hard. I punch him and punch him. "Then why *weren't* you?" I shout.

He does not resist my blows. "It is complicated."

" 'Complicated' is just another word for 'I screwed up and am making excuses!' " I yell.

"Fine. I screwed up!" he yells back. "But I only ended up stuck in Scotland because you asked me to go help the bloody damned MacKeltars!"

"And there you go making excuses!" I stare at him, furious, betrayed, and I do not know why.

"How was I supposed to know? Do I look omni-scient?"

"Yes!"

"Well, I'm not! You were supposed to be at the abbey. Or back in Ashford. I tried to send you home. I tried to get you to go to Scotland. You never do what I tell you to do. Where the fuck was your fairy little prince? Why didn't *he* save you?"

"I do not know those words—fairy, prince." They burn my tongue. I hate them.

"You do, too! V'lane. Remember V'lane? Was he there, Mac? Was he at the church? Was he?" He shakes me. "Answer me!"

When I say nothing, he repeats in that strange multilayered voice he sometimes uses, *"Was V'lane there when you were raped?"*

V'lane failed me, too. I needed him and he did not come. I shake my head.

His grip on my shoulders relaxes. "You can do this, Mac. I'm here. You're safe now. It's okay to re-member. They can never hurt you again."

Oh, yes, they could. I will not remember, and I will never leave this room.

Here there are things that keep the monsters away.

I need those things. Right now.

His body. His lust. Erases it all.

I push him back on the floor, frantic with need. He responds savagely. We explode at each other, grabbing fistfuls of hair, kissing, grinding our bodies together. Rolling across the floor. I want to be on top, but he flips me over and pushes me forward, spreading me. Licks and tastes me until I come and come, then carries me to the bed and covers me with his body. When he pushes himself inside me, in my anger I push, push, push back at him with that magic place inside my head, because I am sick of him stirring up things inside me. It is my turn to stir things up inside him, and

—we are in his body, both of us, and we are killing violently, and our cock is hard while we do it. It never felt good to kill before. It never felt bad, either, but now it exhilarates. Now it is power, it is lust, it is being alive. The children are dead, the woman cold, the man dying. Bones crunch, blood sprays—

He knows I am there. He shoves me out with such violence that it flattens my magic completely. I am awed by his strength. It excites me.

Our sex is primitive.

It exhausts me. I sleep. I do not know who I am anymore.

I thought I was an animal.

I am no longer so sure.

* * *

It's hard to say what makes the mind piece things together in a sudden lightning flash.

I've come to hold the human spirit in the highest regard. Like the body, it struggles to repair itself. As cells fight off infection and conquer illness, the spirit, too, has remarkable resilience. It knows when it is harmed, and it knows when the harm is too much to bear. If it deems the injury too great, the spirit cocoons the wound, in the same fashion that the body forms a cyst around infection, until the time comes that it can deal with it. For some people, that time never comes. Some stay fractured, forever broken. You see them on the street, pushing carts. You see them in the faces of the regulars at a bar.

My cocoon was that room.

After Barrons left—I later realized he often left while I slept—I dreamed.

Some say dreaming is another place we go. That we don't know it as such because it's not a physical realm we recognize. It exists in another dimension, which mankind has not yet discovered and to which it attributes no credence.

I dreamed my life back.

Alina and I playing, laughing, running hand in hand, chasing butterflies with nets, but we don't catch them, because who wants to trap a butterfly in a net? Too fragile, too delicate. You don't want to break their wings. Like sisters and love. You have to be vigilant with precious things. I fell asleep on my watch. I wasn't vigilant. I didn't hear the undercurrents in her voice. I was lazy and ignorant in my happy pink world. A cell phone dropped into a pool. Ripples spreading on the surface. Everything changed forever.

I am grief.

I dream my parents, but they're not. Alina and I were born to others, but I have no memory of them, and I wonder for the first time if someone *took* those memories from me.

I am betrayed.

I dream of Dublin and the first Fae I ever saw and that nasty old woman, Rowena, who told me to go die somewhere else if I couldn't protect my bloodline, then left me alone without offering me the smallest bit of help.

I am anger. I didn't deserve that.

I dream Barrons and V'lane, and I am lust wed to suspicion, and those two emotions together are poison.

I dream the Lord Master, my sister's murderer, and I am vengeance. But no longer hot. I am cold vengeance, the lethal kind.

I dream the Book that is a beast, and it speaks my name and calls me kindred.

I am *not*.

I dream Mallucé's lair. I eat the flesh of immortal beings and I am changed.

I dream Christian and Dani and the abbey of *sidhe*-seers. O'Duffy, Jayne, Fiona, and O'Bannion, the Hunters, and the monsters invading my streets. Then the dreams come darker and faster, blows from a world-class boxer bruising my brain, pulping my heart.

Dublin goes dark! The Wild Hunt! The smell of spice and sex!

I am in the narthex of the church, and there are Unseelie Princes all around me, and they slice me open and rip out my insides and scatter them all over the street, leaving a shell of a woman, a bag of skin and bones, and the horror of it, God, the horror of watching yourself from the outside as everything you know about yourself gets stripped away and demolished, not just the loss of power over your body but power over your mind, rape in the deepest, most hellish sense of the word, but wait—

There's a spark.

Inside that hollowed-out woman, there's a place they can't touch. There's more to me than I thought there was. Something that no one and nothing can take away from me.

They can't break me. I won't cease. I'm strong. And I am *never* going to go away until I've gotten what I came for.

I might have been lost for a while, but I was never gone.

Who the fuck are you?

With an explosive inhalation, I snap upright in bed, and my eyes fly open—like coming alive after being dead and interred in a coffin.

I am Mac.

And I'm back.

PART
11

One of my college Psych professors claimed that every choice we made in life revolved around our desire to acquire a single thing: sex.

He argued that it was a primitive, unalterable biological imperative (thereby excusing the human race our frequent idiocy?). He said that from the clothing a person selected in the morning, to the food they shopped for, to the entertainment they sought, at the very root of it all was our single-minded goal of attracting a mate and getting laid.

I thought he was a jackass, raised a manicured hand, and told him so with lofty disdain. He challenged me to rebut. Mac 1.0 couldn't.

But Mac 4.0 can.

Sure, a lot of life is about sex. But you have to pull up high and look down on the human race with a bird's-eye view to see the big picture, a thing I couldn't do when I was nineteen and pretty in pink and pearls. Shudder. Just what kind of mate was I trying to attract back then? (Don't expect me to analyze Mac 4.0's predilection for black and blood. I get it, and I'm perfectly fine with it.)

So, what's the big picture about our lust for sex?

We're not trying to acquire *something. We want to* feel *something: Alive. Electrically, intensely, blazingly alive. Good. Bad. Pleasure. Pain. Bring it on—all of it.*

For people who live small, I guess enough of that can be found in sex.

But for those of us who live large, the most alive we ever feel is when we're punching air with a fist, uncurling our middle finger with a cool smile, and flipping Death the big old bird.

—Mac's journal

6

I was mad as hell.

I had so many grievances that I didn't even know where to begin listing them.

I was pissed-off walking. Or rather pissed-off sitting, tangled in crimson silk sheets that smelled like somebody'd been having a sexathon.

That would be me.

And that made me even madder.

Just when you think your life has gotten as crappy as it can get, it goes and gets crappier. Gee, Mac doesn't get to have a *choice* about having sex with someone. Good-bye: dating, flirting, and building up to that special romantic moment. Hello: I'm getting screwed senseless, and then, when I've gotten about as low as I can get, I'm getting screwed back to my senses—although I wouldn't in a million years admit any such thing to the man who was no doubt feeling impossibly smug that, by the power of his sexuality alone, he'd rescued me from the mindless state it had taken multiple Unseelie death-by-sex Fae to drag me to, kicking and screaming.

If I knew Jericho Barrons, he was walking around feeling like his dick was the most huge, magnificent, perfect, important creation under the sun.

Which—I winced—I vaguely recalled telling him a time or two.

Well . . . maybe several times.

I yanked the sheets up over my breasts with a snarl. The animal I'd been recently hadn't left me. She was still in me and would be forever. I was glad. I welcomed her feral nature. Pink Mac had needed a good dose of savagery. It was a savage world out there.

I was coldly glad to be alive, glad that I lived another day, no matter the methods by which it had been accomplished. I was also seething, furious at everyone I'd met and everything that had happened to me since the moment I'd left Ashford, Georgia.

Nothing had gone as planned. Not one thing. My sister's murderer was supposed to be a *human* monster that I was going to bring to justice, either via Ireland's Garda or by my own methods. I wasn't supposed to get caught up in a deadly war between the human race and a supernatural, supersexed, immortal, and mostly invisible race, little more than a weapon to be used by whoever could figure out how to manipulate me most effectively. And that was only the beginning of the many, many things that had gone wrong.

Speaking of manipulative bastards . . .

What was the point of Barrons' stamping a tattoo on the back of my skull if he hadn't been able to use it to find me when I needed help the most? What was the point of V'lane embedding his name in my tongue if, at the crucial moment, it wouldn't work? Weren't Barrons and V'lane supposed to be the most powerful, dangerous, brilliant players of all? That was why I'd allied myself with them!

But both had failed me when I'd needed them the most. I'd counted on them. I'd believed Barrons could find me. I'd believed V'lane would instantly appear when summoned. I'd believed Inspector Jayne could help me with certain problems. Those three had been the extent of my diversification.

And who'd saved me?

Dani. A thirteen-year-old kid. A girl.

She'd blasted in, plucked me right out of the LM's grasp, and whisked me to safety.

No, not safety. Not quite.

She'd taken me to Rowena, who locked me in a cell and left me alone, hellishly alone.

To die?

There were memories from the time of my capture by the LM and my early incarceration at the abbey that weren't accessible. They were *in* me. I could feel them, deep, dark, secreted away in a mind that had been impressionable but uncomprehending. They weren't exactly memories, because memory is stored by a brain that functions and mine hadn't during those traumatic hours. More like imprints. Photographs snapped but not understood. Conversations overheard. Things seen. It would take work to dredge them from the muck at the bottom of my psyche.

But I would.

The LM hadn't expected me to ever escape.

Rowena hadn't expected me to live.

"Surprise," I purred. "I did."

I tossed back the sheet and pushed up from the bed. My body felt *good*. It was sleeker, stronger than I remembered it being. I stretched and glanced down, then blinked, admiring myself.

Gone was all softness, save my breasts and butt. My calves, thighs, arms, stomach—all were toned, shaped by smooth, sleek muscle. I flexed a bicep. I *had* one. Long fingernails dug into my palms. I studied them. On Samhain, they'd been cut to the quick.

Just how long had I been having sex with Jericho Barrons? How long did it take to resculpt a body like mine had been into—Savage Me was pleased to note—this much more useful new shape? What had we been doing? Constant sexual gymnastics?

I shut down that thought. I had a few too many memories that weren't remotely blurry, and they gave rise to impossibly conflicting emotions.

Like: Thanks for saving me, Barrons—too bad I'm going to have to kill you for doing those things to me and seeing me like that.

I'd had sex with Jericho Barrons.

Not just sex. Incredibly raw, intensely intimate, completely uninhibited sex.

I'd done everything a woman could do with a man. I'd pretty much worshipped every inch of him. And he'd let me.

Oh, no, much more than that—he'd enthusiastically participated. He'd egged me on. He'd plunged right into my animalistic frenzy with me, met me move for move in that dark lust-crazed cave where I'd been living.

I turned to stare at the big silk-sheeted bed. It was

exactly the kind of bed I'd expect Barrons to sleep in. Sun King ornate, four-postered, draped in silk and velvet; a sensual masculine lair.

There were fur-lined handcuffs on the bedposts. I got knotted up in that memory for a minute before I managed to extricate myself.

My breathing was shallow and my hands were fists. "Oh, yes, I'm going to have to kill you, Barrons," I said coolly. Partly because, for the most minuscule sliver of an instant, while looking at those handcuffs, I'd imagined myself climbing back into bed and pretending I wasn't cured yet.

And I'd thought interacting with Barrons had been difficult before. Since the day we'd met, we'd maintained a careful wall of non-intimacy between us and rarely slipped. I was Ms. Lane. He was Barrons. That wall had been blasted to dust, and I hadn't had anything to say about it. We'd fast-forwarded from formal and testy most of the time to See Mac Bare All/Body & Soul, without a single ounce of relationship progression along the way. He'd seen me at my absolute worst, my most vulnerable, while he'd been in complete control, and I still didn't really know a damned thing about him.

We'd gotten as close as two human beings—well, overlooking the fact that he wasn't one—possibly could. Now, in addition to wondering whether he'd spiked the Orb of D'Jai with deadly Shades before he'd given it to me to give to the *sidhe*-seers and whether he'd sabotaged the ritual at the MacKeltars' on Halloween because he *wanted* the walls down between Fae and human realms, I knew that killing aroused him. Turned him on. I hadn't forgotten *that* enlightening little detail I'd found poking around inside his skull. It cast a harsh new light on the moment I'd watched him walk out of an Unseelie mirror carrying the savaged, very dead body of a young woman.

Had he killed her just for fun?

My intuition wasn't buying it.

Unfortunately, I wasn't sure what my intuition was worth where he was concerned. If there was one thing I'd learned about Barrons, it was that speculating about him was as pointless as tap-dancing on quicksand, with no solid ground in sight.

Speaking of solid ground . . .

I glanced around. I was below it. I can feel belowground in my bones. I hate being there. I hate confined, windowless spaces. Yet, for a time, this space belowground had been my harbor in a brutal storm.

What had happened to Dublin while I'd been *Priya*, clawing my way back to sanity? What had happened to the world?

How was Ashford? Were Mom and Dad okay? Had anyone gotten the Book? What was happening out there with all the Unseelie free? Was Aoibheal, Queen of the Seelie, okay, or had the Unseelie gotten to her, too, on Halloween? She was the only one with any hope of ever reimprisoning them. I *needed* her to be alive. Where was V'lane? Why hadn't he come for me? Was he dead? I felt a moment of pure panic. Maybe he'd tried to rescue me after all and that was one of those confused imprints, and the LM had taken my spear and—

My fingers clenched on emptiness. Oh, God, where was my spear? The ancient Spear of Destiny was one of only two weapons known to man that was capable of killing an immortal Fae. I remembered throwing it away. I remembered it hissing and steaming at the foot of a basin of holy water.

Where had it gone from there?

Was it possible it was still lying there, in the church? Could I be so lucky?

I needed it back.

Once I had it, I could get to work on other things. Like figuring out how the Unseelie Princes had managed to turn it against me at the critical moment. True to Fae lore—which held that the Unseelie couldn't touch any of the Seelie Hallows, and vice versa—they hadn't been able to physically take it from me, but they'd managed to coerce me into turning it on myself, forcing me to choose between stabbing myself with it or tossing it, putting me completely at their mercy.

I not only needed my spear back—I needed to learn how to control it.

Then I was going to kill every Unseelie I could get my Nullifying hands on, slaughtering my way straight up the chain of command, not stopping until I'd taken out all the Unseelie Princes, the LM, and maybe even the Unseelie King himself. And the Seelie, too, with the exception of those I needed to restore order to our world. I was sick of the terrifying, inhumanly beautiful, homicidal interlopers. It had been *our* planet first and, although V'lane didn't seem to think that should count for much, it was all that mattered to me. They were scavengers who'd damaged their own world so badly that they'd had to go find another one—and now they were doing the same thing to ours. They were arrogant immortals who'd created an immortal abomination—the Unseelie court, the dark mirror of their race—and they'd lost control of them on our planet. And who was paying the highest price for all their mistakes?

Me. That's who.

I was going to get tougher, smarter, faster, stronger, and spend the rest of my life killing Fae, if that was what it took to put my world back the way it used to be.

I might not have a spear at the moment, but I was alive and I was . . . different. Something irrevocable had changed inside me. I could feel it.

I wasn't entirely certain what it was.

But I liked it.

I ransacked the room before I left it, looking for weapons. There were none.

Apart from what looked like a hastily plumbed shower in a corner of the room, the rest of it was filled with my belongings that I'd kept at the bookstore.

Wherever we were now, in his efforts to restore my memory, Barrons had gone to some lengths to re-create pretty-in-pink Mac's world. He'd plastered the walls with blown-up pictures of my parents, of Alina, of us playing volleyball with our friends on the beach back home. My driver's license was stuck to a lamp shade, next to a photo of Mom. My clothes were draped all over the place, arranged in outfits, complete with matching purses and shoes. Every shade of pink fingernail polish ever made by OPI was lined up on a shelf. Fashion magazines covered the floor, along with some other ones I really hoped he and I hadn't looked at together. There were peaches-and-cream candles—Alina's favorite—scattered on every surface. There were dozens of lamps in the room and a blazing Christmas tree.

My backpack was nowhere to be found, but Barrons had obviously been counting on me regaining my sanity, because there was a new leather one, crammed with batteries, LED lights, and a MacHalo. He'd used a black helmet to build it. All the lights were black, except two. Guess he figured I'd've graduated from pink if I survived. I still liked pink. I would always like pink. But there wasn't anything pink inside me anymore. I might be back, but I was black Mac now.

There was nothing useful here. I took a quick shower—I smelled like Jericho Barrons from head to toe—got dressed, strapped the MacHalo on my head, clicked it on, and headed for the door.

I was locked in.

It took me less than a minute to kick the door down. I not only had muscle now, I had another useful tool in my new black toolbox: rage.

Barrons seems to plan for everything. I want to be like him.

I was in a basement.

I found the guns in the crates, stacked next to the deafeningly loud generators that were powering the room I'd been living in, next to what looked like a year's supply of gasoline.

There were dozens of crates of guns and twice as many crates of ammo. It seemed a little risky to me to keep so much ammunition next to so much gasoline, but who was I to judge? I was just glad it was all there. I sat on a crate and examined the different guns, finally settling for a semiautomatic with a shorter barrel than the rest. It resembled an Uzi, with a few minor differences.

Before all hell had broken loose on Halloween, I'd been researching guns on the Internet and had been angling to get Barrons, with his unlimited connections, to buy me one. The gun I chose now was a PDW: a personal defense weapon. Perfect for a woman of my size and stature. Highly manageable, highly effective, highly illegal. Able to fire even from a prone position. I intended to practice firing from every position possible. Gunfire might not kill Fae, but I was willing to bet it might slow down the non-sifting kind.

I crammed clips of ammunition into my pack everywhere they'd fit, then filled my boots and the pockets of the new black leather coat I'd found draped over a chair in just my size. It irked me that Barrons had been making fashion choices for me, but not enough to be stupid about it: I needed that coat. I was pretty sure it was winter in Dublin, and it had been cold already in late October.

I wasted a lot of time searching the basement for my spear, because I knew Barrons well enough to know that he'd have requisitioned it, if it'd been possible. When I didn't find it, I ruled out the possibility of it still being at the church. He'd have checked there. Which meant someone else had picked up my spear and backpack. I needed to know who.

I discovered crates of protein bars and loaded up on those, too. Like I said, Barrons plans for everything.

I'm not so sure he planned for one thing, though.

His OOP detector—the one he'd worked so hard to restore to sanity so he could use me some more, tracking down his precious Objects of Power— wasn't hanging around.

"Thanks," I told the empty house, "but I'll take it from here."

Besides, knowing him, he'd probably amped up his brand on the back of my skull, while I'd slumbered nearly unconscious from one of our marathon sex sessions, or put a new, improved one on me somewhere else. I had no doubt Barrons could find me one way or another. He wasn't the kind of— whatever he was—that a woman could lose, if he didn't feel like being lost.

I walked through the silent house, which was crammed with furniture covered with dusty sheets, and stepped out onto the front steps. The house had been built on an elevation with a good view of the neighborhood. I'd spent so much time driving in Dublin, hunting the *Sinsar Dubh,* that I'd gotten pretty familiar with it. I was on the northern outskirts of the city. Dawn smudged the horizon, and the first rays of sun slanted across a sea of gray roofs.

I smiled.

It was the start of a brand-new day.

7

The wards knocked me on my ass the moment I tried to leave the property.

"Ow!" I rebounded like a rubber ball off a brick wall and landed on the lawn. Or, rather, what was left of the lawn, which was dirt. I was in a Dark Zone. It wasn't winter but Shades that had stripped the yard of life. Mother Nature left grass, even in her harshest moments. Shades left nothing. Barrons must have brought me here after they'd already claimed the neighborhood. What better place to hide a weapon from the enemy than deep in their own territory? Especially since he and they seemed to have a tacit agreement to leave each other alone.

I took off my MacHalo—it was light enough that I wouldn't need it again until nightfall, and I suspected the Shades that had devastated this area had moved on to more-fertile ground, anyway—hooked it onto a strap on my pack, and rubbed my head. The wards had nearly split my skull. My molars hurt, even my scalp felt bruised. I hadn't seen that coming. I narrowed my eyes. Faint silver runes glistened on the sidewalk I'd just tried to cross. Wards were sneaky things, often hard to see, made doubly so this morning by a thin coating of frost. But now that I knew they were there, I could discern the telltale shimmer of Barrons' subtle work, vanishing east and west around both sides of the house. Although I knew he was meticulous, I still walked the perimeter, looking for a gap.

There wasn't one.

I decided it must have been an aberration that the wards had repelled me so violently. Barrons warded things *out*. He never warded me in. I stepped onto the lightly iced sidewalk in a different place.

I went flying backward again, teeth vibrating, ears ringing.

I sat up, growling. The *nerve*. If I hadn't been determined to leave before, I was now.

"He has warded me out, as well, MacKayla. Or I would have come for you long ago."

V'lane's voice preceded his appearance. One moment I was glowering at the air, the next at V'lane's knees. For a moment, I kept my gaze fixed there. A woman might feel a little terrified after what I'd been through—not that *I* did, just that some other woman might.

V'lane is Seelie, one of the alleged "good" guys, if any of the Fae can be called that, but he's still a death-by-sex Fae, same as those masters of killing lust that had so recently devolved me into the lowest common denominator. All Fae royalty, whether light court or dark, can turn humans *Pri-ya* with sex. And like his darker, deadly Unseelie brethren— when in his natural high glamour—V'lane is too beautiful for a human to look at directly. I'm no exception. The dark princes had made my eyes bleed. V'lane could, too, if he felt like it.

Since the day I met him, he'd been using his death-by-sex magnetism on me to varying degrees, although I now knew just how "gentle" his coercion had really been compared to what he could have done in his efforts to make me help him track the *Sinsar Dubh*. We'd had an ongoing battle about what form he would assume in my presence, with him always turning on too much sexual charisma and me always insisting he "mute" it.

I raised my gaze to the inevitable perfection of the Seelie Prince's face, bracing myself for the impact.

There was none.

He stood before me with every bit of his death-by-sex Faeness dampened. For the first time since I'd met him, I was able to look directly at him, absorbing his inhuman, incredible perfection without being affected by it. V'lane looked as close to a human male as he could get, in jeans, boots, and a loose linen shirt half unbuttoned. He was apparently unaffected by the frigid weather—or perhaps the cause of it. Fae can affect the weather with their moods. His beautifully muscled golden body was no more perfect than that of any airbrushed model; his long golden hair no longer shimmered with a dozen seductive, otherworldly shades; his flawlessly symmetrical features might have graced any magazine cover. The only aspect of his Fae nature he'd retained were those bottomless, ancient, iridescent eyes. He was still something to see: tawny, sexy man with alien, glowing eyes, but I was not assaulted by a frantic desire to tear off my clothes, I didn't feel a tingle of lust, not the faintest sensation of being weak at the knees.

And he'd done it without my even having to ask.

I wasn't about to thank him. It was the least he could do after what his race had done to *me*.

He studied me while I studied him. His eyes contracted slightly, then widened infinitesimally, which on a human face meant very little but on a Fae's was an expression of astonishment. I wondered why. Because I'd survived? Had my odds really been so low?

"I have been monitoring these wards and sensed the disturbance. I am pleased to see you, Mac-Kayla."

"Thanks for the rescue," I said coldly. "Nice of you to show up when I needed you. Oh, wait," I barked a sharp little laugh, "I remember now. You didn't. In fact, your name crashed and burned when I tried to use it." If he'd never given me his name on my tongue, I wouldn't have been so fearless that night. I'd been lulled into complacency, believing I had a Seelie Prince available at the snap of my fingers to sift in and sift *me* out to instant safety. It had made me feel invincible when I shouldn't have. And when I'd needed him the most, it had failed. Better never to have depended on it at all. I should have kept Dani by my side that night. *She* could have whisked me to safety.

He spread his hands, palms up, and bowed his head in a gesture of subservience.

I snorted. The holier-than-thou Seelie Prince was bowing his head to *me*?

"A thousand apologies could not atone for the

harm my brethren were permitted to inflict upon you. It sickens me that you were—" He broke off, bowing his head even more deeply, as if he couldn't bring himself to go on.

It was a completely human gesture.

I didn't trust it one bit.

"So." I picked myself up off the ground and dusted off my new leather coat. "What's *your* excuse for failing me on Halloween? Barrons said he was stuck in Scotland. Actually, he said it was 'complicated.' Was it complicated, V'lane?" I asked sweetly, as I slung my gun around the back side of my shoulder. It banged into my backpack. I liked the solid, reassuring weight of my weapons and ammo.

He winced at the tone of my voice, not missing the arsenic in the sugar. While I'd been busy being *Pri-ya,* V'lane had obviously been busy expanding his repertoire of human expressions. Still, these expressions were different than that first one. They were too large for a Fae, overblown. Iridescent eyes met mine. "Exceedingly."

I hooked my thumbs in my jeans pockets. "Go on." I smiled. There was nothing he could say that would ever make me trust again in something so mystical and fundamentally flawed as a Fae name embedded in my tongue, but I wanted to see how far he might go to get back into my good graces.

"Aoibheal was my first priority, MacKayla. You know that. Without her, all else is insignificant. Without her, the walls can never be rebuilt. She alone is our hope of reclaiming the Song of Making."

The Fae were matriarchal, and only the Seelie Queen could wield the Song of Making. I knew very little about the Song, just that it was the stuff from which the walls of the Unseelie prison had been forged, hundreds of thousands of years ago. Roughly six thousand years ago, when the Compact had been negotiated between our races, apportioning shares of the planet, Aoibheal had jury-rigged an extension of those ancient walls to separate Fae and human realms. Unfortunately, her tampering had weakened the prison walls, enabling Darroc the Lord Master to bring them *all* crashing down on Halloween.

So why didn't Aoibheal just sing them back into existence?

Because in typical Fae infighting fashion, the Unseelie King had killed the long-ago Seelie Queen before she'd been able to pass on her knowledge to the next one. Aoibheal, latest in a long succession of queens to rule with diminished power, had no idea how to sing the Song of Making. They needed me—OOP detector extraordinaire—to find the one remaining clue to re-creating the Song: the *Sinsar Dubh*, a deadly book that contained all the dark magic of the Unseelie King. The king had been close to discovering it when his mortal concubine killed herself, and he'd abandoned his experiments that had created the dark half of the Fae race.

"And only I can find the Book she needs to do it," I said coolly. "So who's expendable?"

His eyes narrowed minutely and he glanced sideways. Pink Mac wouldn't have even noticed it. I wasn't her anymore. My spine snapped straight, and I went nose to nose at the ward line with him. If I could have reached through it and grabbed him by the throat, I would have. "Oh, God, you actually thought that through and decided it was *me*! You *knew* I was in trouble and didn't help me!" I snarled. "You believed I would survive it! Or was it that you figured I'd be even easier to use if I was *Pri-ya*?"

His iridescent eyes blazed. "I could not be in two places at once! I was forced to choose. The queen would not have survived the night. It was imperative she survive."

"You son of a bitch. You *knew* they were *coming for me*."

"I did not!"

"Liar!"

"By the time I learned what they'd planned, it was too late, MacKayla! Despite my powers, I failed to foresee how dangerous Darroc had become. None of us foresaw it. We believed the walls would weaken further on Samhain, we even believed more of the Unseelie would escape, but we did not believe Darroc could succeed in bringing the walls down completely. Not only did he accomplish the unthinkable, he managed to block *all* Fae magic as thoroughly as he demolished your human grids. For a time that night, not one of us could sift. Not one of us could change form. Not *one* of us could draw upon the birthright of our magic. I was forced to carry my queen to a new hiding place on *human*"—he sneered the word—"feet."

"While I lay on my human ass and your *fairy*"—I sneered the word—"brethren fucked my brains out and nearly killed me."

"But failed, MacKayla. But *failed*. Remember that. You are queenly in your own right."

"So the end justifies the means? Is that what you think?"

"Do they not?"

"I suffered," I gritted. "Horrible, unspeakable things."

"Yet you stand here now. Toe to toe with a Seelie Prince. Impressive for a human. Perhaps you are becoming what you need to be."

"What doesn't kill me makes me stronger? That's what you think I should take away from this?"

"Yes! And be glad for it."

"Let me tell you something." I fisted my hand in the collar of his shirt. "What I will be glad for is the day the last one of you is *dead*."

He went oddly, completely still.

I shook him. He didn't budge.

I blinked, then got it. He was frozen. I'd Nulled him. Nulling is a rare *sidhe*-seer talent and, according to Rowena, I'm the last Null alive. I can freeze a Fae with the mere touch of my hands. I can turn it on or off at will, the same way Fae Princes can control their lethal eroticism. I hadn't even been thinking about Nulling, but apparently my hostility toward his race in general had come across as intent to Null. Since he was already frozen, I punched him a few times, indulging my rage at all things Fae.

Then I focused on my *sidhe*-seer center and forced it to relax.

A muscle worked in his perfect jaw. Oh, yes, he'd been brushing up on his human gestures. "Punching me was not necessary."

Oops. I'd forgotten they were only frozen when I

Nulled them, not oblivious. Oh, well. "But it sure felt good."

"Well done, MacKayla," he said tightly.

"For freezing you? I've done it before."

"Not that." He looked down at my hand.

I looked down at it, too. Then past it, to my feet.

I was over the ward line. I'd stepped right through it without even realizing it. Not only that, I was holding a Seelie Prince by the collar and I wasn't remotely aroused. No matter the form V'lane had donned in the past, I'd never stood so close to him without having to battle the irresistible impulse to have sex with him, right then and there, even when he'd been toned down as far as—according to him—he could go.

I leaned into him, pressed myself against his perfect Fae body. He molded to me instantly, slid his arms around me, dropped his face to my hair. He was hard, ready.

I felt nothing.

I drew back and looked up. There was that minute contraction and widening of his eyes again. Astonishment. Why? What had astonished him when he'd first seen me? That I had recovered from being *Pri-ya*? Or something more—a thing virtually inconceivable to him?

I stretched on my toes, pulled his head down, and kissed him. His response was instant and held every bit of one hundred and forty thousand years of sexual expertise—but not one ounce of that elusive, deadly death-by-sex Fae quality.

I pushed back and stared at him. I could feel intense sexual arousal rolling off him, but no more so than I would coming off any man. There went that muscle in his jaw again. Was it possible he *wasn't* muting himself? I'd heard that if you took certain poisons but didn't die, you acquired immunity. Had I drunk enough Poison de Fae? "Unmute yourself," I demanded.

"I. Am. Not. Muted."

Did he ever sound pissed! "You're lying." Could it really be true? Had everything I'd gone through made me immune to Fae sexual compulsion?

"No, MacKayla."

"I don't believe you." I would not be lulled into stupidity again, into believing something that wasn't true, so it could be used against me.

"I would not have believed it, either. No human has ever come back from being made *Pri-ya*, and, although I am pleased that you have recovered from what was done to you, I am not pleased that I must now compete for you with no glamour, without the glory of my birthright. They were Unseelie, MacKayla, the foulest of the foul, the darkest of my race, the abominations. I am Seelie, and we are vastly different. I had hoped that one day, when you trusted me, you would let me share with you the ecstasy of being with one like me. With no pain, MacKayla, and no price. Now that can never be. You have no idea how exquisite the experience might have been and now never will."

"Bullshit," I said. Games within games. That was all my life was anymore. Was he lying just so he could ambush me when I least expected it?

"You suffered the full, undampened power of

three Unseelie Princes. They were inside you. It is impossible to predict all it might have done to you."

"Four," I snarled. "And don't remind me where they were. I'm acutely aware of it."

His eyes narrowed to slits and sparked with inhuman fire. "Four? There were four? Who was this fourth? Was it Barrons? Tell me!"

I flinched. The thought had never occurred to me. The fourth one who had kept himself concealed from me had been the fourth Unseelie Prince. Hadn't he? The fourth was Fae. Wasn't he? All my *sidhe-seer* abilities had been completely deadened from eating Unseelie flesh the night before, to gain Fae-heightened strength to escape the riots and make it to safety. In all honesty, I couldn't swear the fourth was Fae. I could only say he'd been intensely sexual.

Why had he kept his face hidden? All I'd ever seen of him was a glimpse of skin, muscle, tattoo.

Tattoo.

"It couldn't have been Barrons. He was in Scotland that night."

V'lane's anger iced the air. The temperature dropped so sharply that my next inhalation burned my lungs. "Not the entire night, MacKayla. The Keltar ritual to maintain the walls between realms was sabotaged. The circle of stones in which the sacred rites have been performed since the day the Compact was negotiated between my queen and your human Keltar was destroyed, supplanted by a Fae realm. Barrons was last seen at midnight on Samhain. He could easily have been in Dublin before dawn."

Ouch! Then why hadn't he come for me immediately? Why hadn't he tracked me by the brand he'd stamped at the base of my skull and saved me? For that matter, how long *had* it taken for him to rescue me from my hell at the abbey? My memory of those early days was badly blurred. "Barrons doesn't hang out with the Unseelie or the LM. They don't like him any more than you do."

"Indeed." V'lane's iridescent eyes were mocking.

"Remind me," I said with acid sweetness, "why is that, again?" He'd never told me, and I didn't think he would now. But I would find out, one way or another. I was going to find out *everything*, one way or another.

I had to consider what V'lane was saying. In my unpredictable, frequently inexplicable world, I had to consider everything. Not only did Barrons have some kind of agreement with the Shades, he knew a tremendous amount about the never-before-seen-by-humans-because-they'd-always-been-incarcerated Unseelie half of the Fae race. He was much older than a human could be, and I'd recently caught him stepping out of the Unseelie Silver he kept in his study at the bookstore, carrying a woman who'd been brutally killed.

What possible reason might Barrons have to turn me *Pri-ya*, then bring me back? For the opportunity to play the hero? To storm in and save the day, in hopes of securing my blind faith once and for all? Not only hadn't it worked, but why wouldn't he just keep me *Pri-ya* and use me? He could have stopped in his efforts to restore my mind halfway through, left me hanging in a mentally impaired yet functional *Pri-ya* state indefinitely, and I'd have done anything he'd asked, to keep getting sex. I'd have traipsed all over the world, hunting the Dark Book, slave to his every command.

But he hadn't. He'd brought me *all* the way back. Freed me.

"What does Barrons want, MacKayla?" V'lane said softly.

Same thing as V'lane and everyone else I'd met since I'd arrived in Dublin: the *Sinsar Dubh*. But neither Barrons nor I could touch it. I could track it, and he believed I had the potential to get my hands on it eventually, with the right training.

I didn't believe Barrons had been the fourth. That wasn't his way. But might it have been his idea of "the right training"? How far would Barrons go to get what he wanted? He was mercenary to the core, constantly pushing me, trying to make me tougher, stronger. Trying to make me what I needed to be in order to do what he wanted me to do.

I was now immune to death-by-sex Fae. I could walk through wards. I was more powerful in ways that could have been accomplished only by putting me through something that would either kill me or make me stronger. A proving ground: die or evolve.

It was too awful for me to contemplate. "Maybe the fourth was you, V'lane. How do I know it wasn't?"

My skin frosted. When I shivered, crystals of ice fell in a small snowstorm to the sidewalk. "I was with my queen."

"So you say."

"I would never harm you."

"You constantly manipulate me sexually."

"Only to a pleasurable limit."

"According to who?"

His face tightened. "You do not understand my race. Seelie and Unseelie do not suffer the other to exist. We do not consort. Even now we battle, as we did before, so long ago."

"So you say."

"How can I set your mind at ease, MacKayla?"

"You can't." I could trust no one. Rely on nothing but myself. "I don't know who the fourth was that day, but I *will* find out. And when I do . . ." I reached for the comfort of my gun and smiled coldly. By Fae weapon or human, I would have revenge.

"Ah, yes, you have changed." V'lane's eyes narrowed, and he studied me. "Could it be?" he murmured.

"What?" I demanded. I didn't like the way he was looking at me. Fascination in a Fae's eyes is never a good thing.

"Behold me. I believe you can." Was that grudging respect in his voice? He shimmered and was suddenly something else.

I'd seen a vision similar to the one he showed me now that morning at the church, when the three Unseelie Princes had circled around me, morphing from shape to shape. My brain hadn't been able to process what I'd been seeing, and I'd guessed it was a complex state of being that had more dimensions than humans could comprehend.

Unlike the Unseelie Princes, however, V'lane didn't continue moving from form to form. He adopted a static one. At least, I think it was static. It wasn't change. Stasis and change are how the Fae define everything. For example, if a human dies—

or, as they say, "ceases to exist"—they don't perceive the loss of life at all, they merely perceive "change." They're cold bastards.

My eyes could see V'lane, but my brain couldn't define him. We've invented only words we've had need of, and we've never seen anything like this. Energy—but multidimensional? I don't understand the first thing about dimensions, just the little I learned in school about space, time, and matter. My mind strained to grasp what was before my eyes . . . expanded . . . nearly tore itself in two trying to reconcile the image with some frame of reference I understood. I couldn't find one, and the more I searched and failed, the more frantic I felt, which in turn made me keep trying to find one, which in turn made me more frantic. It was a backfeed loop, escalating quickly. *Stop fighting it,* I told myself, *stop trying to define and simply see.*

The strain eased. I stared.

"You apprehend me in my true form. Mortals cannot do so and retain a unified mind. It fractures. Well done, MacKayla. Was it not worth it? Would you not do it all over again?"

Bile rose in my throat. At the cost of a piece of my soul? That's what he thought? That if I'd been given the choice, I would have *chosen* to go through what had happened on Samhain? That I would have chosen Dublin falling, the walls coming down, the Unseelie getting freed, being raped and turned into an animal that'd had to be rescued first by Dani, then by Barrons? "I would never have chosen it!" It wasn't just me who had suffered. How many humans had been slaughtered that night and since?

He was back in his human form. "Really? For such power? You are immune to me—a Fae Prince. Impervious to sexual glamour. You can gaze upon my true form without your mind fracturing. You can walk through wards. I wonder what else you can do now. What a creature you are becoming."

"I'm not a creature. I'm a human and proud of it."

"Ah, MacKayla, only a fool would still call you human now." He vanished, but his voice lingered. "Your spear is at the abbey . . . Princess." Laughter danced on the air.

"I'm not a princess, either," I snapped, then frowned. "And how do *you* know where my spear is?"

"Barrons approaches." The words were nearly indistinguishable from the chilly morning breeze. A breath of sultry warm air, in sharp contrast to the frigid wintry day, gusted down my shirt and caressed the tops of my breasts.

I yanked my coat shut and buttoned it. "Stay out of my clothes, even as the hot air you are, V'lane."

More laughter. "Unless you wish to see the one that exploited you at your weakest, perhaps even made you so, go southeast, MacKayla, and quickly."

A snapshot from late last night flashed behind my eyes: me, nude, straddling Barrons' face.

I went.

Certain dates are stuck in my head, permanently scarred there.

July 5: the day Alina called my cell phone and left a frantic message that I ended up not hearing until weeks later. She was murdered mere hours after she placed that call.

August 4: the afternoon I stumbled into a Dark Zone for the first time and ended up on the front steps of Barrons Books and Baubles.

August 22: the night I had my first skull-splitting encounter with the *Sinsar Dubh*.

October 3: the day Barrons fed me Unseelie to bring me back to life and I experienced the intoxicating effects of dark Fae power.

October 31: yeah, well, enough said. It had been an insane few months.

Today I had no idea what the date was, so I couldn't etch it into my memory just yet, but I knew I would never forget a single detail of it.

The entirety of Dublin had been devoured by Shades, turned into a wasteland. If there was another person alive in the city besides myself, they were in deep hiding.

I walked for hours through eerily silent districts. Not one blade of grass remained, not a shrub, bush, or tree. I knew I shouldn't waste time, especially if Barrons was nearby, but I needed to see this.

I collected snapshots of the city like bricks, and I stacked and mortared them into a wall of determination: I would live to see this affront to humanity undone.

What few newspapers were left on the stands were dated October 31, the last day Dublin had functioned. The city had fallen that night and never gotten back up.

Storefronts were bashed in, windows broken out.

There was glass everywhere, cars abandoned, some on their sides, others burned.

The worst part of it was the dried husks—I quit counting after a while—blowing down the streets, tumbleweeds of human remains, that part of us that Shades find indigestible.

I would have wept, but I didn't seem to have tears left in my body. I gave the bookstore wide berth. I couldn't bear to see if it had been destroyed. I preferred to keep my second-to-last image of it in mind, the way it had looked the afternoon of Halloween: Everything in its place, waiting for me to return, push open the door, pick up the mail, straighten the magazines people were always riffling through, start a fire, curl up on the chesterfield with a good book, and wait for that first customer of the day.

Every streetlamp I passed had been smashed, many ripped right out of their concrete bases, twisted and flung, as if by raging giants. Shades have no physical form, so I assumed some other caste of Unseelie must have done this to ensure that, if we somehow managed to get our grids back up and running, there'd be no lamps to route the power to.

Almost as bad as the husks—I cringed every time I stepped on one and it crunched beneath my feet— were the piles of clothing, cell phones, jewelry, dental devices, implants, and wallets. Each was a sacred burial mound in my mind.

Still, it didn't keep me from picking up a few things.

An open switchblade caught the cold morning light, and my attention. I suspected its owner had been trying to stab the unstabbable when the Shade devoured him. "I'll put it to good use," I told the pile of black leather topped by a necklace of metal skulls. "I promise." I retracted the blade and slid it into my boot.

My next scavenged prize was a chunk of living Unseelie flesh I found flopping in the street. I had no idea where it had come from, how or why, but it sure might come in handy. Ingesting Fae flesh not only made the average human able to see the Fae—including the innately invisible Shades—as well as any *sidhe*-seer, it also bestowed superstrength and heightened senses, the ability to dabble in the black arts, and miraculous healing powers.

I used my new switchblade to dice it, then stopped in a ransacked drugstore, where I pilfered baby-food jars, washed them out, and presto—I had a new stash of Unseelie sushi, if I needed it. Assuming, of course, I got into a situation dire enough that I would A: be willing to sacrifice my *sidhe*-seer talents, which seemed to be growing by leaps and bounds; B: let myself be vulnerable to my own spear again, which I fully intended to have back by the end of the day, come hell or high water; and C: ever be willing to put any part of anything Unseelie in my mouth again. I'd had more than my unwilling fill.

I shuddered. Interestingly, I seemed to have been cured of my burgeoning addiction to eating Unseelie flesh. I eyed the baby-food jars and their squirming contents with revulsion.

Still, weapons are weapons, and all weapons are good weapons.

A short time later, I was in a slightly dented Range Rover Sport. I'd swept the husks from it, trying not to look too hard at the tiniest husk as I'd unbelted and gently placed the car seat, along with a fluffy pink teddy bear and a shirt that said *I ♥ Daddy*, beneath a leafless oak tree.

I headed for the abbey, mostly alongside the road because so much of it was clogged with abandoned cars. I munched a couple of protein bars as I drove and paused periodically at petrol stations and convenience stores, stocking the back of the Rover with water, food, batteries, and, at one of my stops, plastic containers of gas I'd discovered already pumped, much to my mixed emotions. I needed it and was grateful for it. But there'd been no way to miss the pile of rugged work pants, hip implant, Irish fisherman's sweater, and boots next to the three containers. Had a father come out, too close to dusk, for gas to keep his family's generator running? Did they still wait somewhere, cowering in the darkness?

About an hour after I'd left the city, I saw the strangest thing. Initially, from a distance, I mistook it for a very large, very low-flying bizarre plane. But as I drew closer, I could see that it was an Unseelie Hunter and some other kind of Fae that I'd never seen before locked in battle, beating air with their massive wings, tearing at each other with teeth and talons.

Were Unseelie fighting themselves, or was this a Seelie fighting an Unseelie? Were the Hunters once again keepers of Fae law, as they'd been an eternity past?

I didn't know, I didn't care. I just wanted to pass

unnoticed beneath their radar. Hunters hunt *sidhe-seers*. Was I giving off a betraying scent? It was too late to go back and I *needed* to go forward, so I held my breath and muttered prayers to every deity I could think of that the Fae were too engrossed in their fight to look down.

One of the pagan gods must have heard me, because I passed beneath them without incident, holding my breath and watching as the battle vanished to a pinpoint in my rearview mirror. I sucked down air greedily and pretended my hands weren't shaking. "My kingdom for a spear," I muttered.

About thirty minutes from the abbey, I got another surprise: Dirt gave way to wintered grass.

For whatever reason, the Shades had stopped here.

Perhaps it was the farthest they'd gotten and they were hunkered in a dark culvert or had slithered beneath a fallen tree for the day, where they impatiently awaited the night to resume eating their way toward the abbey. Perhaps the soil in this part of the country didn't taste good, salted with so many centuries of *sidhe*-seers living on it. Perhaps Rowena and her merry band had done something to halt their progress. Who knew? I was just glad to see something besides dirt.

The next surprise came so quickly, I had no chance to react.

One moment I was driving parallel to a road so narrow that only a whopping-good sport would call it two-lane, on a wintry Irish day, and the next I was—

Beneath the triple canopy of a lush tropical rain forest, driving on the surface of a dark, glassy swamp, throwing up a splash of foam in my wake, and I had no idea how it had happened or, more important, *why* I wasn't sinking. I know cars. All kinds. They're my passion. The Range Rover Sport has a curb weight of roughly 5,700 pounds. I should have sunk like a stone. I looked out my window. Nothing but more water beneath the eerily colored surface.

I blinked. What had just happened? Giant trees surrounded me, sprouting things from their trunks that looked like brilliant orchids mated to octopuses. Birds the size of my Rover paddled around the trees, leathery wings folded on their backs. Periodically they stabbed the water with their beaks, tossed back their heads, and swallowed. They had very large, very sharp beaks.

"V'lane?" I said incredulously. But this didn't stink of V'lane. V'lane did "seductive" when he sifted me. Not "disturbing" and "potentially lethal," although those two phrases certainly did spring to mind when he was around.

Still, being sifted seemed to be the only possible explanation for how abruptly my surroundings had shifted.

A hummingbird glided by. It was the size of a small elephant. Its long, pointed beak was proportionate. In my world—not that many people know it: They mistakenly "ooh" and "ah" over the sweet, delicate little sugar-water drinkers—hummingbirds are carnivores. They accept the sugar water we offer them only in order to fuel their hunt for meat.

I was meat.

I jammed my foot down on the gas, skidding on the water, dodging trees, birds, and vines. I didn't look behind me to see if anything was giving chase. I just drove.

Abruptly, I was back in Ireland, a dozen feet from slamming into a tree.

I pumped the brakes, skidded on dead grass, and stopped much too close to bark. I sat for a moment, gasping.

After seeing that freaky Fae sky battle, I'd thought I was ready for anything. I was wrong.

I got out, walked around to the back of the Range Rover, and stared at where I'd just been.

It took me about twenty seconds to figure out how to see it.

If I narrowed my eyes and slanted a look very casually sideways, like I was peeking, I could see the sliver of Fae reality—almost as if it were trying to hide, the better to ambush me—spiking through our own.

If human air was clear glass, Fae air was slightly thicker, slightly wavy, and slightly off-color.

I remembered Samhain night, watching from the belfry as Fae and human realms had competed for space in a world with no walls.

Apparently we'd lost a few of those battles.

It infuriated me. It was one more danger I had to watch out for. Dark Zones were bad enough. Now I had IFPs: Interdimensional Fairy Potholes screwing up my roads, lurking around, looking all innocuous and benign, waiting to blow out the tire or break the axle of the unwary traveler, stranding them in a no-man's-land with alternate laws of physics, hostile life-forms, and no discernible rules of the road.

I got back into my Rover and slammed the door.

I resumed driving, this time watching the terrain ahead much more closely.

What other surprises might this day bring?

I considered the shocks I'd already faced: Barrons doing . . . well, that thing he'd done in order to drag me back to reality; the discovery that I was immune to wards and the deadly sexual allure of Fae Princes; Shades taking over half of Ireland; Fae sky battles; and now IFPs.

I'd never have believed the most disconcerting shock of my day was yet to come.

8

I made one last stop about twenty miles from the abbey, where I got out and played with my new gun, taught myself to load and fire it.

It took me less time to get over my initial gee-what-if-I-drop-this-thing-and-blow-my-own-head-off? than I expected.

The gun felt *good* in my hands, solid and comforting, just like every weapon I've ever picked up. I think it's somehow coded into my *sidhe*-seer DNA. We were born to protect, to fight. The blood knows. I suspect our bloodlines have been manipulated for a long time. Centuries, perhaps millennia.

I resumed driving toward the abbey, passing through dozens of wards. Rowena certainly was keeping her little flock busy, gadding about, etching protective runes and whatnot. I wondered what else she was keeping them so busy with that they didn't have time to consider mutinying, which, in my opinion, they should have done years ago. Like, say, *before* they lost the Dark Book that this whole stupid war was about, because somebody sure must have fallen asleep on *her* watch to let that happen.

Oh, yes, I had a few bones to pick with the not-so-Grand Mistress.

I parked my Rover in front of the stone fortress of the abbey, got out, locked it—they were my supplies, and nobody was taking them—and marched to the door. I left my pack and MacHalo in the car but brought my gun. I was rather surprised the old woman wasn't waiting out front, arms crossed, glasses perched on her nose, magnifying the intellect and ferocity in those sharp blue eyes, with a band of *sidhe*-seers gathered behind her, denying me entrance. We've never been on the best of terms, and I had no doubt that our relationship, if you could call it that, was worse now than it had been before.

Frankly, I didn't give a damn.

The door was locked. I fired a quick burst of bullets at the handle with my favorite new toy and kicked it open.

The entry hall was empty. Could it be that no one was expecting me? I'd passed through all those wards, setting them off. I frowned. Or *had* I set them off?

If I could pass through wards now, was it possible I did it without tripping them? That certainly could come in handy. Still, I'd just let loose a round of automatic gunfire. Surely that had alerted someone.

When the attack came, it blasted me from nowhere, hit me like a brick wall, and I went sprawling on my ass for the third time that day. It was getting old. Something yanked at my gun and pummeled me like a speed boxer.

Then a face blurred into view and I gasped, and she gasped, then she stopped hitting me and grabbed me and hugged me so tight I thought my spine was going to snap.

"Mac!" Dani cried. "You're back!"

I laughed and relaxed. I loved this kid. "Have I told you you're the Shit, Dani?"

She rolled off me and bounded to her feet. "Nope. Never. I woulda remembered it. But you can say it again, if you want. And you can tell everybody else, too. I wouldn't mind a bit." Cat eyes gleamed in her gamine face.

"You're the Shit, Dani." I got up and slung my gun back over my shoulder. We stood and smiled for a moment, absorbed in being happy to see each other.

Then we spoke at the same time:

"You okay, Mac?"

"What *happened* to you, Dani?"

"You first." She looked me up and down admiringly. "Dude, you look awesome. Love the coat. What you been doing? Weight training or something?"

I blushed. Then I rolled my eyes at myself. Toting automatic weapons and still blushing? I needed to get over that fast.

"Dude!" she said reverently. "With Barrons? You been having *sex* this whole time? S'that how he got you back from Nympholand? I was so worried when you didn't come back. Guess I shouldn't a been. I couldn't find you anywhere. Where'd he take you? I been hunting all over Dublin for you every chance I could duck under Ro's radar. Which wasn't

often," she said sourly, then immediately brightened. "You gotta tell me everything! Everything!"

I wrinkled my nose. "Where did this 'dude' thing come from?"

She preened. "Don't I sound more like you? I been watching a lot of American movies. I been practicing."

"I liked you better when every other word was a cussword. And I'm not telling you anything. Not today, not ever. All you need to know is, I'm okay now. I'm back."

"You had sex with Barrons and you aren't going to tell me *one thing* about it?" She looked incredulous. "Nothing? Not even one tiny little detail?"

Oh, God. She was so thirteen. What was I going to do with her? "Nothing. Ever."

"You suck."

I laughed. "Love you, too, Dani."

She grinned. "I saved you."

"Big-time. And I owe you big-time."

"You can pay me back by telling me about sex."

"If you've been watching so many movies, honey, you know more than enough."

"Not about . . . you know . . . *him*."

I gave her a sharp look. She sounded breathless. Gone was all mischief; she looked positively doe-eyed. Dani—tough, punk Dani—looked like she'd gone soft at the knees. I was flabbergasted. "You've got a crush on Barrons now? I thought it was V'lane you were so crazy about."

"Him, too. But when Barrons came and pulled you out of here, *dude*, you shoulda seen the way he looked at you!"

"I'm not a dude. Lose it." I was *not* going to ask. "So, how did he look at me?"

"Like it was his birthday and *you* were the cake."

At least he hadn't smashed this one into the ceiling. It seemed Barrons had finally gotten his cake and eaten it, too.

I winced. I refused to entertain that metaphor further. Barrons-thoughts were far too complicated for me to deal with. Especially any that involved eating the cake. Later I might get around to asking Dani about my earliest, confused days at the abbey. Now I had other priorities. "My turn. What happened to you?" Everywhere that skin was visible on the fiery-haired teen, she had bruises. Her forearms were especially bad. Two fingers were splinted. One eye was black and blue and swollen nearly closed, her lip was busted, and both cheeks sported the yellowish-purple blossoms of healing contusions.

She glanced around edgily.

I tensed instantly. "What? Is somebody coming?"

"You never know 'round here anymore," she muttered, and looked around again. Although the hall was empty, she lowered her voice. "Been trying to get into the Forbidden Libraries. Hasn't been working so well."

"By doing what? Blasting into the doors at high speed?"

She shrugged. "Sort of. Mostly I been falling down. No big."

"It's a big to me. It doesn't look like superhealing is one of your strengths. Try to be more careful with yourself, okay?"

She gave me a quick, startled look. "Okay, Mac."

Had everyone at the abbey left her alone for so long that a mere expression of concern for her well-being startled her? "I mean it. Quit banging yourself up unless it's absolutely necessary."

"I hear and obey, Big Mac." She flashed me an outrageous grin.

Big Mac. It was like a fist to my heart. Alina had called me Baby Mac. Sometimes Junior. I'd called her Big Mac. It was an inside joke with us. "Why'd you call me that?"

"Movies. American stuff. McDonald's. You know."

"Don't call me Big Mac and I won't call you . . . Danielle." I took a guess and knew by her instant sour look I'd guessed right. "Deal?"

"Deal."

"Where's my spear?"

She stiffened again, glanced around again, and dropped her voice even further. "Don't know," she said softly. "But we picked it up that day at the church. Kat brought it back. Hasn't been seen since. I kinda thought she'd arm one of us with it. She hasn't."

My lips thinned. I knew why. Rowena was carrying it herself.

"I think so, too," Dani said, and I looked at her sharply. "Nah, I just know the way you think. We're alike that way. We see things the way they are, not the way folks want us to believe they are or how we *wish* they were."

"Where is the old witch?"

Dani gave me a glum look. "Right now?"

I nodded.

"Behind you."

9

I whirled, bringing my gun up sharp and hard.
And there it was: my biggest, most disconcerting
shock of the day. Far more shocking than expanding
Dark Zones, sky battles, and Interdimensional Fairy
Potholes.

There stood Rowena, decked out in high Grand
Mistress garb—the robes of the order that had been
founded for the express purpose of hunting and
killing Fae—arm in arm with a Fae. The Fae that had
just sifted her in behind me.

It was no wonder Dani had been looking around
nervously.

And no wonder V'lane had known my spear was
at the abbey.

He was at the abbey.

All cozy with Rowena. Sifting her around, apparently.

I lowered my gun and glared at V'lane. "Is this a
joke? Do you think this is funny? Why didn't you
just sift me here to begin with, if you were coming
this way?"

Rowena's nose could have pointed more sky-ward only if she'd been lying on her back. "As the spear is no longer your possession, nor is this Fae Prince. He has seen the light you fail to see. He aids *all sidhe*-seers now, not just one."

Oh, really? We'd see about that. Both the spear and the prince. "I was talking to V'lane, old woman, not you."

"He doesn't answer to you."

"Really?" I laughed. "You think he answers to *you*?" Only a fool would think a Fae Prince answered to anyone. Especially when one needed one.

"Are you fighting over me, MacKayla? I find this . . . attractive." V'lane tossed his golden head. "I have seen this in humans before. It is called jeal-ousy."

"If that's what you think, you have a problem in-terpreting subtle human emotions. It's not called jealousy. It's called 'you're pissing me off.' "

"Possessiveness."

"My ass."

"Is far more shapely than last I saw it."

"She's been working out." Dani snickered.

"You have no business looking at it," I said.

"But Barrons does?" The temperature in the room dropped sharply.

My breath frosted the air. "We are not talking about Barrons." We were never going to talk about Barrons.

"I'd like to talk about Barrons," said Dani.

"You chose," V'lane said coldly.

"I chose *nothing*. I was out of my mind. Is that

what this is about, V'lane? Barrons? You sound jealous. Possessive."

"He does," Dani agreed.

"Haud your whist!" Rowena snapped. "The lot of you! For the love of Mary, can you not see the world is falling apart around you, yet you stand here, bickering like children? You"—she stabbed a finger at me—"a *sidhe*-seer, and you"—she actually poked V'lane in the arm, and he looked startled that she'd done it—"a Fae Prince!" She glowered at Dani. "And don't even get me started on *you*. You think I don't know what you've been doing to bruise yourself so badly? I'm Grand Mistress, not grand fool. Enough, all of you!"

"Haud your whist yourself, old woman," I told her flatly. "I'll bicker while the world falls apart if I feel like it. I've done more good and less damage than you. Who had the *Sinsar Dubh* to begin with— and lost it?"

"Don't be pushing your nose into doings you can't begin to understand, girl!"

"Then help me understand them. I'm all ears. Where—no, *how*—were you keeping the Book?" That was what I wanted to know most. The secret to touching it, to containing the *Sinsar Dubh*, was the key to harnessing its power. "What happened? How did you lose it?"

"You answer to me, *sidhe*-seer," she spat, "not the other way around."

"In whose warped fantasy?"

"While at my abbey. Now might be the time to take a careful look around you." It was a threat.

I didn't need to. I'd heard the other *sidhe*-seers

crowding close while we were arguing. The hall was large, and from the hushed murmurs, I guessed several hundred were behind me. "What have you done since the walls came down, Rowena?" I demanded. "Have you found the Book yet? Have you accomplished anything that might restore order to our world? Or are you still lording your power over a band of women who would do better with a little power of their own? You squeeze the heart out of who and what they are with your rules and regulations. You tie them down when you should be helping them learn to fly."

"And getting them killed?"

"In any war there are losses. It's their choice. It's their birthright. We fight. And sometimes we pay terrible prices. Believe me, I know. But as long as we breathe, we get back up and fight again."

"You brought us the Orb spiked with Shades!"

"You don't believe that," I scoffed. "If you did, you'd have killed me when I was *Pri-ya*, unable to defend myself. I'll bet the very fact that I got turned *Pri-ya* is what convinced you that I wasn't allied with the Lord Master." I shrugged. "Why turn a turncoat? There's no need."

"There are spies within spies."

"I'm not one of them. And I'm staying right here, in your abbey, until you see that."

She blinked. I'd startled the old woman. I wasn't angling for an invitation. I was staying with or without her permission. Openly or in hiding. I didn't care which. There were two things within these walls I needed: my spear and answers, and I wasn't leaving without both of them.

"We don't want you here."

"I didn't want my sister to be murdered. I didn't want to find out I was a *sidhe*-seer. I didn't want to be raped by Unseelie Princes." I listed my grievances but kept it brief. "In fact, I haven't wanted a single thing that's happened to me in the past few months. Fact is, I really don't even want to be here myself, but a *sidhe*-seer does what needs to be done."

We stared at each other.

"Would you agree to supervision?" she said finally, very tightly.

"We can discuss that." Discussing is where it would end. I would take all her BS under advisement. Before I discarded it. "How's the Book hunt going, Rowena?" I knew the answer. It wasn't. "Has anyone spotted it lately?"

"What do you propose?"

"Give me the spear and I'll go out hunting it."

"Never."

" 'Bye, then." I walked past her, toward the door.

Behind me, *sidhe*-seers exploded. I smiled. They were frustrated. They were tired of being caged and accomplishing nothing. They were primed for a little pre-mutiny meddling, and I was primed to meddle.

"Silence!" Rowena said. "And you"—she snapped at my back—"stop right there!"

The hall went still. I paused at the door but I didn't turn. "I won't go out hunting it without the ability to defend myself." I paused and bit my tongue hard before adding, "Grand Mistress."

The silence stretched.

Finally, "You can take Dani, with the sword. She will defend you."

"Give me the spear and she can come, too. And you can send any of your other *sidhe*-seers you want, as well."

"What's to keep you from walking away, from turning your back on us the minute I give you the spear?"

I whirled. My hands fisted and my lips drew back. Later, Dani would tell me I'd looked half animal, half avenging angel. It impressed even *her*, and the kid is tough to impress.

"I care, that's what," I snarled. "I drove out here through a wasteland. I saw the piles and husks everywhere. I looked in the baby's car seat before I took it out of the Rover. I know what they're doing to our world, and I will either stop them or die trying. So get the feck off my back—where you've been since the night you met me—and wake up! I'm not the bad guy. I'm the good guy. I'm the one who can help. And I will, but on my terms, not yours. Otherwise, I'm out of here."

Dani stepped past Rowena and joined me. "And I'm going with her."

I looked at her, my lips rounded on "no," then I caught myself. What rights had I just argued for? Dani was old enough to choose. In my book, old enough to kill is old enough to choose. I think hell has a special place for hypocrites.

Kat stepped forward from the crowd. Of all the *sidhe*-seers I'd met, the quietly persistent gray-eyed brunette who had led the small group in the attack on me at Barrons Books and Baubles (BB&B) the day

I'd inadvertently killed Moira seemed the most levelheaded, open-minded, and firmly fixed on the long-term goal of ridding our world of the Fae. She and I had met several times, attempting a tentative partnership. I was still open to one if she was. In her mid-twenties, she had the unassuming quiet confidence of someone much older. I knew she had influence over the others, and I was interested to hear what she had to say. "She's a tool, Grand Mistress. And, like it or not, she may be our most useful yet."

"You no longer blame her for spiking the Orb?"

"She can stay and help us get rid of the blimey fecks if she's so innocent."

"Language," Rowena said sharply.

I rolled my eyes. "Oh, for crying out loud, Rowena. It's a war, not a congeniality contest."

Somebody snickered.

"Wars need rules!"

"Wars need to be won!" I fired back, to a satisfying chorus of murmured assents.

"What say you to a vote?" Kat proposed.

"Fine," Rowena and I both snapped in unison, and looked at each other with distaste. I could tell that she didn't believe for a moment I might win, or she wouldn't have agreed to it. I wasn't sure I would, either, but I figured high emotions and years of dissatisfaction with her rule gave me nearly even odds. Kat had a large following among the *sidhe*-seers, and she was arguing for me. Even if I lost, at least I'd know who I could count on my side.

Kat turned to face the hall, crammed to overflowing with *sidhe*-seers in the doorways. "It's being left up to us, so think it through well and call it: Does she stay, or does she go? If you're after her staying, raise your right hand and hold it high while I take your tally."

It was a tight vote.

I won by a narrow margin.

I committed to memory the face of every woman who voted against me.

"What the feck is V'lane doing here?" I demanded, the moment Dani and I were alone.

It was hours before we were. Rowena had decided to push me a little in front of the other *sidhe*-seers after I'd won the vote, to see if I'd bend. She instructed me to clear no less than a dozen Shades from the abbey before I ate or slept, in order to earn my keep.

I'd bent for her this time.

Not only did I enjoy tracking the Shades and driving them out into the late-afternoon light—I'd been watching them long enough as my neighbors at the bookstore that I knew all the places they liked to hide—but I've learned to choose my battles. I understood the importance of throwing a few of the smaller fights, to keep my competition off balance, underestimating me. Rowena would believe I was fully cooperative, right up to the moment her ranks rebelled and overthrew her. I had no intention of staying in the abbey long. I was here for my spear, answers, and to incite a riot among the Grand Mistress's followers. Wake them up to their calling. Get them to ditch the old woman and become all they could be.

"He showed up the day Barrons took you," Dani said. "You shoulda seen it! When he heard you were gone, he went ballistic."

"The Fae don't go ballistic, Dani." Impassive, they rarely showed emotion. Not even V'lane's recently acquired reactions could be construed as "ballistic."

Her eyes got big. "Dude, he iced Rowena."

"You mean turned her into a block of it?" Dani was so full of slang it was hard to know what she meant sometimes. Since Rowena was alive, I figured she had to be speaking literally.

Dani nodded. "From the neck down. Left her head un-iced so she could talk. Then threatened to flick her with his fingernail so she could watch herself shatter. It was wicked cool."

"Why?"

She shrugged. "He was überpissed that Ro let you go. I told him nothing coulda stopped Barrons, but that just seemed to piss him off more. Said he'd been stuck guarding the queen and couldn't get to you. I think he planned to do what Barrons did, and when he learned Barrons beat him to it by a few hours, he totally melted down. I thought he'd ice us all."

"Why is he still here? And after that little trick, how did he get to be such buddies with Rowena?" I tried not to think about what might have happened if V'lane had gotten to me first. It didn't seem to me that sex with another death-by-sex Fae would have done anything but *kept* me *Pri-ya*. I could hardly imagine V'lane telling me stories of my childhood or showing me pictures of my family to help bring me back.

Dani grinned. "Easier to show you." She moved toward me so quickly that she blurred out of sight and was gone.

Then *I* was gone, too, or, rather, the hallway we'd been standing in was gone, and I couldn't make out anything but blurs of motion and noise. I could feel Dani's hands on my shoulders. She was whizzing me somewhere at an extreme rate of speed.

I banged my elbow on something that grunted. "Ow!" I said.

Dani snickered. "It helps if you keep your elbows tucked in."

"Watch where you're going, kid!" someone yelled.

"Oops, sorry," Dani muttered.

Something slammed into my hip. "Ow," I said again. I heard someone curse; it faded quickly.

"We're almost there, Mac."

When we stopped, I scowled at her and rubbed my elbow. It was no wonder she was bruised all the time. "Let's just walk the next time, okay?"

"Are you kidding me? S'the coolest thing in the world to move like I do! I'm not usually so clumsy, but there are more people out of their rooms 'cause you're here and they're all talking 'bout you. I know these halls by heart. I can do 'em in my sleep, but the fecking people get in the way."

"Maybe you could persuade them to start signaling their turns," I said dryly. "You know, like you do when you're bicycling around as couriers."

Her face lit up. "Think they would?"

I snorted. "Doubt it. We're not exactly their favorite people." I glanced around. We were in a huge room filled with a U-shaped conference-table arrangement and dozens of chairs. "Why did you bring me here, and what—"

I broke off, staring past her at the enormous maps covering the walls.

After a moment, I turned slowly.

"We call it the War Room, Mac. S'where we keep track of things."

The entire room was wallpapered with maps, hung from ceiling to floor. There were notations everywhere, with Post-it notes stuck on some areas and enlarged inserts taped to others. Some of the cities bore the *Sidhe*-Seers, Inc. (SSI) emblem of the misshapen shamrock, our oath to See, Serve, and Protect.

"Where's the key?" What did all these symbols and notes stand for?

Dani saw where I was looking. "The shamrocks show the headquarters of the foreign branches of Post Haste, Inc. Ain't no key. Ro won't let us write it down. Room's majorly warded."

"We have *that* many *sidhe*-seer offices?" I was incredulous. There were more of us worldwide than I'd ever have guessed. SSI had obviously been global for a long time. Our "war" had also gone global while I'd been out of it. The Unseelie hadn't stayed in one place once they were freed. They'd ranged out over the entire planet and, according to what I was seeing on the maps, certain castes seemed to prefer certain climes. There were drawings and notes scribbled everywhere. It would take days for me to absorb it all. I walked around the room slowly. "What are these?" I pointed to two areas close together, which were marked off with brown slash marks.

"Wetlands. There's a caste of Unseelie that's nuts about swamps, and they take you down as fast as Shades. We don't go near them."

"And these?" Squares, heavily outlined in bold black marker.

Dani flinched. "Some of 'em 've been rounding up kids, really young ones. They keep 'em for a while before they . . . do things with 'em. We try to find where and break 'em out."

I inhaled sharply and kept walking. I stopped when I reached a column of dates, with numbers written next to them that had been crossed out dozens of times.

The most recent date was January 1.

The number next to it was a few *billion* shy of the nearly seven billion it should have been.

I pointed a finger and didn't even try to pretend it wasn't shaking. "Is this date and number telling me what I think it's telling me? Is *that* how many of us are left on this planet?"

"By our estimates," Dani said, "total world population has been reduced by more than a third." It was one of the few complete, well-spoken sentences I'd ever heard pass her lips. I looked at her sharply and caught a split second of a completely different Dani—a geeky, smart thirteen-year-old abandoned by everyone she'd ever trusted or loved, in a world gone mad. It was so quickly masked by an insouciant grin that I wondered if I'd really seen it at all. "Dude. Pretty intense, huh?" Her green eyes sparkled.

"Dude me one more time and you're Danielle forever." I looked back at the maps. I was never going to be able to sleep tonight. A third of our world's population was *dead*. "How long was I . . . out of it? What's the date?"

"January seventh. And, sorry, it just slips."

"What does this have to do with V'lane?" Keep talking, I told myself, so you don't melt down. We'd lost a third of our planet's population! More than two billion people were dead! They'd been dying the whole time I'd been a mindless animal. The guilt was crushing.

I followed the maps around the room, looking for Georgia, feeling sick inside. The state had two inky spots smudged on it, one over Savannah and one over Atlanta, both of which were only a few hours from Ashford, Georgia, my hometown. Most of the spots on the maps were over major cities. "What are the dark smudges?" I asked tightly, afraid I knew.

"Dark Zones." My face must have betrayed my thoughts, because she added hastily, "V'lane checked on your folks. He says they're okay."

"Recently?"

She nodded. "He keeps watch. Says he does what he can."

I drew a deep breath, the first since I'd laid eyes on the maps. "How did the Shades spread so quickly?" I demanded. "How did they even get overseas? Is the power out everywhere in the world?"

"V'lane says initially other Unseelie were helping 'em, 'til they decided the Shades were chewing up their new playground too fast. Now he says Unseelie are fighting each other for territory. Some of 'em are even trying to get the power back up, to keep the Shades out."

I remembered the sky battle I'd seen, wondered what it had been about.

"One time when I went into Dublin looking for you, I saw humans walking with Rhino-boys, going down into a boarded-up bar. Didn't follow, 'cause it freaked me out so bad. They were girls, Mac. Dunno if they were *Pri-ya*, but they didn't look like it. Looked like they went 'cause they wanted to." Her lambent gaze clouded. "Mac, I think Unseelie are the new vamps to some fecked-up groupies out there."

"Does V'lane know all this? Are the Seelie *doing* anything about it?" I was horrified. I knew my generation. We had a world of opportunities for instant gratification at our fingertips, with few or no censors, and most of my friends hadn't had a daddy like mine, who said things like, *Don't confuse intensity of emotion with quality of emotion, baby,* when I'd gotten tangled up with class heartbreaker Tommy Ralston. The more he'd hit on my girlfriends, the harder I'd worked to keep him. It was like I was addicted to whatever made me feel most intensely, even though it was hurting me. *Pain is not love, Mac. Love makes you feel good.* I missed my dad. I needed to see my parents. See with my own eyes that they were all right.

"V'lane says they're trying to stop the worst of the Unseelie," Dani said, "but they can't kill each other, 'cause they don't die and we got the sword and the spear. V'lane says the Seelie want 'em back, but so far none of 'em have tried to take 'em from us. He says it's just a matter of time, though."

Chaos. It was complete chaos. Unseelie free, fighting Seelie, fighting one another, acquiring human groupies like Mallucé's band of Goth worshippers. I wouldn't be at all surprised if Mallucé's cult had simply converted allegiance to the latest, greatest exotic danger in town.

A third of the world population gone!

All because we'd failed to keep the walls up on Halloween. Because *I'd* failed. I closed my eyes and rubbed them, as if it might somehow rub the horrifying reality of a world with a third less people right out of existence, or at least out of my mind.

"At first, we had no clue what was going on anywhere. No phones or text messages. No email. No Internet. No TVs or radios. S'like living in the Stone Age. Well, maybe not that bad," she allowed with a grin, "but you get the picture. Then V'lane offered to help. Said he could sift around, gather intel, find out what was going on, carry messages, take Ro places. After he iced her like that, she didn't trust him one bit. Not that she ever trusted him. But it was an offer she couldn't refuse."

"What about the *Sinsar Dubh*? I take it no one's gotten their hands on it yet?"

She shook her head.

"Has anyone seen it recently?"

She shook her head again. "I think that's the real reason Ro let you stay, and would have even if they'd voted against you. Just woulda pushed you 'round harder. Her and V'lane been swapping information, bartering with each other. She told him what I told her I saw in the street the day I rescued you—"

"I wondered how V'lane knew about that." I might have found his knowledge of the Unseelie Princes incriminating, except both V'lane and Barrons *always* seemed to have the inside scoop on everything. It no longer surprised me.

"—in exchange for him telling her what you'd learned about how the Book was moving around. That you were targeting it by tracking the worst crimes. But now there's so much violence everywhere, and no newspapers or TV, so there's no way to find the fecking thing."

I thought about that and smiled. "Except for me." I was even more important now.

Dani grinned back. "Yup. I figure we're the two most kick-ass weapons she's got."

"But she's still keeping the sword from you, isn't she, Dani? Doling it out when she feels like it?"

Dani's expression soured and she nodded.

It was time for some meddling, and Dani was definitely primed. "Doesn't it seem wrong to you that the two most powerful *sidhe*-seers in this abbey aren't armed at all times? Don't you think, since you're superstrong and superfast, you *deserve* to carry the sword? I bet even your hearing is superheightened, isn't it? That's why you heard me come in today, when no one else did, isn't it?"

She nodded.

"You're amazing, Dani. You're hands down the most valuable asset Rowena has. And look at me—not only can I track the Book, I can Null the bastards. Freeze them, shut them down cold while we kill them. Remember the night we fought together?" It had been exhilarating. I wanted to do it again. I wanted to do it every night, until the night was ours again. I wanted to be out there prowling, hunting them like they hunted us. I wasn't willing to be afraid any longer. It was time for them to be afraid of *me*.

Her eyes narrowed, her lips parted on a sharp breath, and she nodded again. Her sword hand was clenching and unclenching, like mine did when I didn't have my spear and I thought about Fae. I wondered if I got that almost-not-quite-human look on my face sometimes, too.

I didn't need to see a window to know that night was falling. I could feel the approach of twilight in my bones, as surely as I imagined a vampire must. No matter how heavily warded the perimeter of the abbey was, without my spear I felt like I was missing an appendage: the most important one. I might be immune to death-by-sex Fae glamour—though I wouldn't trust that completely until I'd tested it on some other Fae besides V'lane—but they could still capture me if they came in force. And if turning me *Pri-ya* wouldn't work this time, they could just torture me to make me do what they wanted. I wasn't immune to torture. Pain bothered me. A lot. I needed my spear. Now.

"Dani, you and I were *made* for those weapons. Nobody else can use them like we can! Nobody else is as strong or has as many abilities. By keeping the spear and sword, Rowena makes *all* of us vulnerable. How dare she sit in her study with both of the only weapons that can kill the Fae, leaving the whole abbey unprotected? She's too old to use them! If a Fae got past the wards, she'd be worthless in a fight. We'd be sitting ducks. She knows the Seelie want the Hallows back. That it's just a matter of time. Shouldn't those weapons be in the hands of the two *sidhe*-seers most capable of defending and keeping them? And isn't that us?"

"What are you thinking? You wanna go talk to her together? Gang up on her? Tell her she *has* to give us the weapons?" Dani looked thrilled by the idea.

I snorted. "Talk? Hardly. Rowena needs a little wake-up call. We don't work for her. We don't answer to her. We work *with* her. By choice. Or not at all."

Fear battled with savage glee in the adolescent's face. "You know there's no going back if we do this," she said breathlessly.

"Who wants to go back?" I said coolly. "I want to go forward. And if you're always looking over your shoulder, worrying about the next step you're taking, you can't. Hesitation kills."

"Hesitation kills," Dani echoed like a battle cry, and punched the air with her fist. "I'm in, Mac."

10

There are moments in my life when I feel like I'm exactly where I'm supposed to be, doing exactly what I'm supposed to do. I pay attention to them. They're my cosmic landmarks, letting me know I'm on the right path. Now that I'm older and can look back and see where I missed a turn here and there, and know the price I paid for those oversights, I try to look sharper at the present.

Tonight was one of those perfect moments: speeding into Dublin in a well-stocked Range Rover beneath a moon so bright and full that I could have driven without headlights if I'd wanted to, with Dani at my side, armed with the Sword of Light, and me holding the Spear of Destiny. It felt like heaven in my hand, the weight of it, the breadth of it, the way it fit my palm so perfectly.

Getting the sword hadn't been difficult, but I hadn't expected it to be. Truth was, Dani could have taken it anytime she'd wanted. She knew all of Rowena's hiding places, and blasting down doors is one of her specialties. Rowena had controlled her by simple fear of repercussions, and Dani—thirteen and treated like an outcast so much of the time— was starved for what little approval and attention she got.

Now she had *my* approval and attention, and it was unconditional. Or at least not predicated on her being subservient to me. I would never do that to her.

The spear had been trickier. As we'd figured, Rowena was carrying it. I never expected to be able to take it stealthily. I just wanted to take it and get out fast. And for that—plus about a zillion other reasons—I'd needed Dani.

I had her slam us both into Rowena at high speed. While I kept the old woman busy trying to get untangled from me on the floor, Dani stayed in high-speed mode, patted her down, snatched the spear from a pouch the old woman had sewn into her robes, grabbed me again, and whizzed us both out.

Rowena's shouts had roused the entire abbey. We'd fled into the night, followed by cries of "Traitors, traitors!"

"We can never go back to the abbey, Mac." Dani looked simultaneously exhilarated and as young and lost as I'd ever seen her. I remembered being a teenager and didn't envy her a bit. Emotions ran so high and changed so quickly, it was hard to know which end was up.

I laughed. "Oh, we're going back, Dani. I need things there." Answers. Lots of them. Tomorrow I would begin working on how to get into the Forbidden Libraries and putting together my own troops of *sidhe*-seers.

"They'll never take us back, Mac. We ganged up

and defied Rowena. We're outcasts. Forever." She sounded as miserable as she did proud.

"Trust me, Dani. I've got a plan." I'd been fleshing it out while I was tracking Shades and driving them outside. "They'll take us back. I promise." More important, I planned to take *them* with *me*. But I needed to make a big statement first. I needed to show them how it could be. I knew what the other *sidhe*-seers wanted the most and I could give it to them, and that was the key to motivating any pack to follow a leader. Standing in the hall while they voted, I'd felt it in my blood. They were sick to death of menial tasks, of being corralled and ordered about, tired of seeing the world fall apart on their watch while they did the only thing Rowena would let them do: gather what survivors they could find and teach them to do what the pathetic and defeated did—hide.

What they wanted most of all was to hunt and kill Fae. And why wouldn't they? They'd been born to do it!

During her time as Grand Mistress, Rowena had tried to civilize them, circumscribe them, organize them, but she'd only been polishing their surfaces, changing nothing where it counted, because deep inside every *sidhe*-seer was a hunter, bred to kill Fae, stalking, snarling, waiting with bated breath for the opportunity to do it. Beneath the skin of even the most timid *sidhe*-seer was a different creature entirely. Case in point? See pink Mac go black.

I was going to invite them out to play.

I was going to give them the opportunity they'd been jonesing for, show them what we could do together. Having only two weapons wasn't the most desirable situation, but there were ways to work with it. If I could motivate five hundred *sidhe*-seers to fight and capture as many non-sifting Fae as possible, Dani and I could focus solely on killing them, instead of having to waste time hunting them ourselves. On our own, Dani and I might be able to take out a hundred a night, but if the Fae had already been captured and rounded up, we could kill a thousand in a few hours! Maybe more. And that was if every *sidhe*-seer at the abbey managed to find and capture only two apiece!

There was no doubt that Dani and I would be better than the other *sidhe*-seers at capturing the Fae and that pretty much *any sidhe*-seer could stab them, but I was never letting my spear go again. I would tell the other *sidhe*-seers the same thing I'd told Dani: We needed to keep the weapons because we were the only two who could protect them if the Seelie came for them. I would never let any of them know what I knew: that V'lane could take both weapons away from us at any time if he felt like it.

I shoved that thought away and turned to another I was still mulling over. If we began feeding Unseelie flesh to normal humans, we could turn every man, woman, and child into a fighter and arm them with the ability to defend themselves. It sickened me to think of billions out there that couldn't even see the Shades.

"Are the Unseelie projecting glamour?" I asked Dani. "I mean, are they making themselves invisible to the average human?"

She shook her head. "V'lane says concealment is the Seelie way of things. He says Unseelie get off on human fear. They ain't hiding nothing. The Shades are still invisible to normal folks 'cause that's their natural state, but people can see all the other castes, far as we know."

So, other humans could see their death coming, unless it was by Shade. They just couldn't do anything about it. But if they were fed Unseelie, they would gain superstrength, like Mallucé, Derek O'Bannion, Fiona, and Jayne, and be able to fight back. We could capture far greater numbers, and wouldn't it be worth it, even if it changed those who ate it on some fundamental level? I wasn't sure exactly what changes it caused or how long-term they might be, but I didn't feel worse for it. Fear of my own spear had been the greatest drawback. Wasn't the survival of our race and our world the most important thing, no matter the means by which it was accomplished? In a "Your Pure Human Genes" or "Your Life" contest, I'd come down firmly every time on the side of life.

"IFP, Mac!" Dani exclaimed. "Dead ahead!"

I veered sharply, skidding around it. It was a small one, the circumference of a carnival calliope. We'd seen three so far. She'd laughed when I told her what I'd christened them. They were easier to see at night. When headlights hit them, they shimmered with thousands of what looked like tiny dust motes dancing on the air. The first—the swamp I'd driven through earlier today—had shimmered pale green; the last two had been silvery. I wondered if their color had anything to do with the landscape inside and what dangers they held, if perhaps similar colors came from similar parts of Fae realms. I made a mental note to begin recording as much as I could about them in my journal. I thought I might organize scouts. Pick half a dozen and send them out to learn everything they could about the Interdimensional Fairy Potholes. Were they gates to Faery? Was there some way to use them to our advantage?

It was quarter to eleven by the time we arrived in Dublin. We worked our way past abandoned wrecked cars, parked near Temple Bar, and got out, MacHalos blazing, weapons in hand.

My *sidhe*-seer senses were picking up a tremendous number of Fae in the city. I sensed *thousands* of them, spread out in all directions. Why so many? The city was eerily quiet and appeared to be devoid of human life. Wouldn't Unseelie want to be wherever the most humans were gathered? It didn't seem as if any were left here at all.

"Are you sensing a ton of Fae, Dani?" I asked.

"Uh-huh. S'part of the reason I kept coming in. Looking for you and trying to figure out what was going on. Was kinda freaky alone, though. I think Dublin's, like, their official headquarters or something."

I stared into the shadows, searching the night for Shades, glancing from dark alley to darker lane.

Dani didn't miss it. "I think most of 'em are gone, Mac. Last time I saw one of the creepy fecks in here was more than a month ago, and it was a really small one. I think they ate their way out and just kept going. Only ones I see anymore are in the abbey with us."

I was still keeping my MacHalo on. She made no move to take hers off, either. "Where's the boarded-up bar you said you saw?" We'd start there. Kill everything that was Fae. Try knocking sense into any humans stupid enough to be found there. "You know what to do if we get surrounded," I reminded her.

"Grab you and get out fast," she said with a grin. "Don't worry, Mac. I got your back."

Like I said: It was one of those perfect moments. We fought for hours, racking up the kills. With each Unseelie we "exterminated," I felt stronger, more charged, more determined to track and destroy the last one, even if it took until my dying breath.

Dani and I punched and stabbed and sliced our way down the dark Dublin streets. Drunk on our own sheer kick-ass glory, we made up a song that would one day become the anthem of *sidhe*-seers around the world. But we didn't know that. We only knew that shouting it kept us pumped up, feeling invincible.

> *We're taking back the night!*
> *Let there be light.*
> *We're not afraid anymore.*
> *You took what was mine*
> *And now it's time*
> *For you and me to settle the score.*
> *We're taking back the night!*

"Shh!" Dani suddenly hissed.

I froze, mid-lyric and mid-stab, dying Rhino-boy stuck on my spear, tusked mouth working soundlessly.

I couldn't hear a thing, but I don't have heightened senses unless I've eaten Unseelie, and thanks but no. I'll survive with what gifts I have.

"Pull your spear out," she whispered.

I did, and the next thing I knew, I was being whizzed down alleys so fast and jerkily that I wanted to puke. I will *never* understand how Dani can stand moving like she does.

Then we were still and she was pointing. "Look up, Mac!"

I looked, and shivered. With all the Fae in the city, I'd not been able to distinguish castes. I harbored a special hatred for this one: Unseelie Hunters.

Since time immemorial, they have hunted and killed *sidhe*-seers. Enforcers of Fae law and punishment, mercenary to the core, they work for whoever pays them with whatever it is they want most at the moment. They flip sides constantly. They have telepathic abilities and can get inside your skull and twist you up on yourself. To make matters worse, they chill you to the bone and look like the devil himself, come for your soul.

Two enormous Hunters were circling in the sky, a few blocks from the river Liffey. Twice the size of any I'd seen in the past, they were blacker than night, with great leathery wings, forked tails, talons as long as my spear, and eyes that blazed like furnaces from hell. They were clawing air, talons forward, screaming at something in the streets the way I imagined dragons must scream, churning black ice crystals into the air with every flap of those deadly black sails.

"D'ya fecking believe it?" Dani breathed. "Are they *nuts*?"

She didn't mean the Hunters. She meant whoever was down in the streets, shooting at them.

I could see holes being punched in their great wings and healing almost instantly, bullets dropping to the street below. I could hear the *rat-a-tat-tat* of automatic gunfire.

It was doing nothing much but pissing them off. A lot.

Whoever was doing it was going to get themselves killed!

I looked at Dani, and she nodded. "Better go save their ass," she agreed, and reached for me.

I stepped back. "Thanks, but it's only a few blocks. I'll walk."

I turned.

She grabbed my shoulder and we were there in a heartbeat. I was really going to have to loot a drugstore for Dramamine, because when she let me go again, I could only stand bent over, battling the overwhelming urge to puke on a pair of shiny black shoes.

Momentarily incapacitated was no way to arrive at the scene of potential danger. Superspeed was worse than being sifted. Sifting was smooth. Superspeed was a horse and carriage on a rutted road, at jet speeds, with no shocks.

I looked up from the shoes and blinked. For a moment, words eluded me.

"Ms. Lane. Good to know you're alive. I'd begun to wonder."

Turning to the uniformed troops behind him, Inspector Jayne snarled, "Fire!"

11

It seemed a lifetime ago that the tough-talking, burly inspector standing before me had picked me up, dragged me off to the Garda station, and interrogated me for the murder of his co-worker and brother-in-law, Inspector Patrick O'Duffy. At least half a lifetime must have passed since I'd opened his eyes to the Unseelie that had invaded Dublin by sneaking bits of their immortal flesh into his dainty sandwiches the afternoon I'd invited him to the bookstore for tea.

Then I'd taken him on a sightseeing tour and forced him to confront what was happening to his city, for the dual purposes of enlisting his aid in tracking the Book and getting him off my ass. After that, we'd spoken only whenever he had a tip about the Book's location, and very curtly at that, until the day he picked me up off the street again and shocked me by asking me to make him my special "tea" one more time. I hadn't seen that coming. I'd expected him to close his eyes and mind to the impossible-to-explain, like most people do. He had surprised me.

I eyed him speculatively. When his men paused between rounds, I said, "Are you still eating Unseelie?" Or was he just going after the ones he could see?

Dani made a choking sound. "Eating *Unseelie*? *Eating* it? Are you fecking kidding me? It's goopy, and some of 'em ooze green stuff and they have . . . like . . . *pus*-filled things in 'em! Ugh. Just fecking ugh!" She stuck her tongue out and shook her head violently. "Ugh!" she exploded again.

I shrugged. "Long story. Tell you later."

"Need-to-know basis. Don't." She made a retching sound.

"You get used to it," Jayne told her. To me, he said, "I've been eating it since the day I asked you to feed it to me."

"You never came back for more."

"And be dependent on you? What if you weren't around when I needed it?" He snorted. "I never let it wear off, because if I did, I wouldn't have been able to see them to kill them to get more. Vicious cycle. Had the wife prepare it for breakfast every day. Now with the lot of them showing themselves, it's not the problem it once was. My men eat it. Wife feeds it to our kids in sandwiches. Fire!"

The men resumed shooting. Screams of fury filled the night sky.

The noise was deafening. When it finally stopped, I snapped, "What are you doing? You can't kill them! You're just pissing them off!" I could feel their anger—dark, deep, ancient. I could feel more than that, too: a cunning patience born of eternity, the unflappable certainty that they would outlive this nuisance in the streets below that dared offend. We were nothing. We were dust already, death waiting to happen. They were outraged that we had the audacity to even gaze upon them without being on our knees, worshipping, praying to them, begging for their permission to breathe.

I learned a few months ago that telepathy with Hunters goes both ways, at least for me. They can get in my head, but I can get in theirs, too. And they don't like that one bit. Even now I could feel them both pressing at me, trying to decide what I was that made me . . . different. Guess I wasn't as notoriously well known among Unseelie as I'd expected after my abduction by the LM and his Unseelie Princes.

"Good!" Jayne said. "Because they're pissing *me* off. They're in my city, and I'll not be tolerating it. They think I'll be making it easy for them to hover over my streets? Spy on us? Track down our survivors? We're showing them otherwise, aren't we, now? They're not taking one fecking more of mine!"

He turned back to his group of fifty or so crisply uniformed and helmeted men and issued a quiet command. Four of them broke off, moved down the street, and began setting a massive gun on a tripod. Most of his men were armed with dated-looking semiautomatics, a few with tommy guns—the only ones that seemed to be having any impact on the Hunters. When Jayne shouted "Fire" again, they raised their guns in tight unison and sprayed bullets at two of the Unseelie's most fearsome.

A smile tugged at my lips.

Jayne was deliberately provoking the Hunters.

Pissing them off because they'd pissed him off.

My smile grew. When I'd reluctantly fed this man

Unseelie, I'd never have foreseen this moment. How perfect. How right. We needed him, here in the streets, seeing that those who survived continued to do so. This man would never stop serving his city and his people, even though his pay had been terminated months ago. He was police/protector to the core.

Delighted by the serendipity of it all, I laughed.

Jayne glanced at me sharply, and for a moment his grim expression was tinged by a smile. The admiration must have shown in my eyes, because he said, "It's what we do, Ms. Lane. We're the Garda."

"Feck the Garda," one of his men shouted. "We're the Guardians! A new force for a new world!"

"Hear, hear!" the men cried.

I nodded appreciatively. The Guardians. I liked that. "It's good to see you, too, Jayne," I murmured. "Especially like this." What an unexpected boon. The Hunters were pushing at me more insistently now. I sent the only message necessary upward and didn't need to use one ounce of telepathy to do it.

I raised my spear, shook it threateningly. It shimmered alabaster in the light from my MacHalo. Following suit, Dani thrust her sword into the air.

The Hunters hissed and reared back with such sudden violence that the vortex caused by the flapping of their great dark wings sucked the litter on the streets into the air and lifted the lids off trash cans. Bits of debris stung my face and hands. Lids clanged into the brick buildings, bouncing from wall to wall.

We will hunt you until the end of time, sidhe-*seer. We will eradicate your line.*

I was pretty sure it already had been, except for me, but couldn't have replied if I'd wanted to. I was on my knees, clutching my head. It was an awkward feat, wearing a MacHalo and holding a spear.

They'd surprised me.

These Hunters weren't just bigger. They were something else, too. Weren't all of them the same? When the Unseelie King had done his experiments and created his dark race, had he made variations on his themes? Were some of the same castes more deadly and powerful than others? The bastards had nearly split my skull with their threat. I hadn't been prepared for it. I was going to have to regard every Fae I encountered, from this moment on, as a wide-open possibility, unpredictable in any but the most basic ways. It pissed me off. A knife *should* be a knife. How was I supposed to live in a world where a knife could be a grenade? I was going to have to make no assumptions. Ever. Expect the unexpected.

I might be on my knees outside, but I wasn't inside. I sought that dark cave where I'd so recently been an animal. *Try, you fuckers,* I blasted them.

They screamed again. I heard the pain in it, and smiled.

Trash-can lids clattered to the pavement. Debris battered my head and shoulders. The night stilled.

The Hunters were gone.

I lifted my head and watched two winged silhouettes fly past the moon. It was an eerie sight. Even more eerie, the moon had a crimson tint around the edges, like a halo of blood.

Was the juxtaposition of Fae and human realms changing them? Were the dimensions bleeding to-

gether, altering each other? What would our world
be like in a few more months? A few more years?

I pushed up from my knees to find Jayne staring
at my spear.

"Those are the weapons you spoke of at our tea,"
he said. "The ones that can kill the Fae."

I inclined my head. I didn't like the way he was
staring.

"We've never tried to bring down one of those
devil-dragons."

"Hunters," I told him. Ironic and fitting that he'd
singled out his Fae equivalent to harass. "They're
enforcers of Fae law. Although they're Unseelie,
they work for both courts, depending on who pays
best."

I saw a flash of amusement in his dark eyes, then
it was gone, and he was staring fixedly at my spear.

My fingers tightened around it.

"We know we can't cage them like the others we
capture. They're too big. But with that spear, we
could kill them where they fell."

"Cage them? You're caging Unseelie? How?"

"Took us some time to sort it out. When you
opened my eyes to what was happening, I opened
my mind to the old legends. We Irish are steeped in
them. I kept stumbling across lore that said the Old
Ones couldn't abide iron. I decided that if were-
wolves hated silver and vampires hated holy water
and garlic, and those things could harm them, perhaps iron could harm a Fae."

"Does it?" I asked.

"To some degree. It seems to interfere with their
power. Enough of it can trap and hold some of them

where they are. The more pure the iron, the better. Steel doesn't work so well." He slipped his close-fitting helmet from his head and showed me the inside. "We coat them with iron. We lost a few good men before we learned what your so-called Hunters could do."

"Iron keeps the Hunters from being able to project into your head?" I'd be altering my MacHalo the moment I could get my hands on some!

"Not entirely. It dampens it, makes it survivable. We all heard what you heard. Just not as painful. But we've gotten pretty used to them trying to feck with us. We're wearing iron everywhere. Around our necks, in our pockets. It's what we make our bullets from."

"Feckin' brilliant!" Dani exclaimed. "Mac, we need iron!"

Jayne glanced at my spear, then at Dani's sword. "Do you know how much good we could do with one of your weapons?" He searched my face. "It's not like we're looking to leave you unarmed. The two of you could share the sword."

"No," Dani and I snapped at exactly the same moment. I tensed. I didn't need to look at Dani to know she hovered on the verge of superspeed, a heartbeat from whizzing us out of there.

"Ms. Lane, we're all in this together."

"Not that together."

"Look at us. We're capturing hundreds of Fae a week. Locking up the ones that can't pull that vanishing-into-thin-air trick. Now, there's a lethal move for you," he said bitterly.

"They call it sifting," Dani told him.

He cursed. "Well, those sifters come back and kill my men. They either sneak in behind us or track us, like they're playing with us. They'd think twice if they knew we had a way to kill them. You have two weapons that can. You can't tell me that's fair."

"What the feck is fair, Jayne? Is it fair that I got dragged into this to begin with?"

"We all got dragged into this," he growled.

Touché, I thought. "We can work something out," I offered. "We'll kill them for you." The more Fae dead, the happier I'd be.

"Some of them will still get away. Unless you're saying you'll hunt beside us. Be there to bag the buggers the moment we take them down."

"I can't. I'm hunting something else, and without it none of this will ever end."

His eyes narrowed. "Would that be the Book I was helping you track?"

"If I don't find it, Jayne, we'll *never* be able to drive them from our world, and I'm afraid the longer the walls are down, the more screwed up things are going to get. Maybe irrevocably."

He measured me coldly. Finally he said, "I should barter with you. Demand favor for favor. But it's not my way. I care more that people survive than I care for vengeance. You might take a lesson from that. Your Book is still in Dublin."

"It's not *my* Book," I hissed. When he'd called it that, my spine had iced with violent chills. As if somehow it was. Or wanted to be. Or I was having some hint of a premonition of things to come. I shook it off. So, the *Sinsar Dubh* was still being spotted in Dublin. That explained why so many Fae were here.

We were all hunting it. I wouldn't have thought it would be so difficult to find. It had been months since the walls had come down. Didn't it *want* to be found by Unseelie? Weren't they kin? What did it want in this city? It was a huge world out there, with countless countries and opportunities for chaos and destruction. Yet it remained in Dublin. Why?

"It took one of my men a few weeks ago on his way home to his family. Would you like to know what it did then, Ms. Lane? After it hitched a ride home to his wife, kids, and his mother?"

I kept my head perfectly still and said nothing. I wasn't about to ask. I knew what happened when the Book took over a human. I'd seen so much carnage in the last few months that I was running out of room in my head for more gory images. "I'm sorry," I said, knowing it wasn't enough. I understood him wanting one of the Hallows. I could even have made a really good case for it myself, in his shoes. A kinder, gentler Mac would care. A nicer me would share.

I wasn't, and I wouldn't.

"It's unfortunate there aren't more weapons to go around," I told him with complete sincerity, but it didn't change a thing. I had enough to worry about, and I had plans in the works that were every bit as good or better than Jayne's. I'd meant it when I said we could work something out. We could stop by once a week, wherever he and his men were keeping the Fae caged, and kill them all for him.

"I'd prefer it not end this way," he said softly, and sliced air with a hand gesture. His men closed in around us.

Dani moved to stand next to me, shoulder to shoulder. I imagined that to them we looked like two young girls, huddling close, daunted by such a show of armed manpower.

"So would I," I said just as softly. "Never try to take from me, Jayne. Never make that mistake. What's mine is mine. You really don't know what you're messing with."

"I don't want to 'mess' with you at all, Ms. Lane. I'm merely looking for a little teamwork."

"I've already got my team, Jayne." I looked at Dani and nodded.

Her face lit up and she grinned. "Tuck in your elbows, Mac."

I poked them out, the better to bruise a few ribs along the way. I got a gratifying chorus of grunts, heard guns clatter to the pavement.

They didn't even see us go.

"We need iron, Mac," Dani said as we moved down the street, back at normal speed again. We'd put a huge chunk of the city behind us in a matter of seconds. Her mode of transportation, nauseous as it made me, was worth its weight in gold.

I nodded absently, still mulling over the Jayne encounter. I regretted that it had ended on a note of animosity. I wanted every front in the battle for our planet united, with no cracks any Fae could slip through.

"We need more than iron." I was busy making a mental list to scribble in my journal later. Between high school and college, my dad had made me take a Franklin Planner course. He said it would help me get control of my life. I told him I *had* control of my life: sun, friends, fashion, marriage one day. *That's not enough for you, baby,* he said.

I argued; he bribed. I took the course, let Daddy spend a fortune on pink flower-covered calendar pages, doodled on them until I got bored, and shelved it.

What a brat I'd been.

One of the primary tenets of the course was that highly successful leaders kept journals, morning and night, in order to stay tightly focused on their goals. I was going to be a highly successful leader.

"I don't have a gun, Mac. I need a gun." Dani had turned to face me and was walking backward, bounding from foot to foot, a thousand watts of hyper energy, gobbling a candy bar. I was surprised her auburn hair wasn't crackling with static electricity from frantic friction with the pavement.

I laughed. "All weapons are good weapons, is that it?"

"Aren't they?"

Watching her was like watching a Ping-Pong ball bounce back and forth: *zing-zing, zing-zing.* I liked the way she thought. "I've got a plan."

"You said you'd make them take us back at the abbey. Is this part of it?"

"You bet." I eyed her speculatively. "Just how super is your superhearing? If there was somebody really stealthy nearby, could you hear him before we stumbled on him?"

Her eyes narrowed. "How stealthy?"

"Very."

She gave me a suspicious look. "We talking Jericho Barrons stealthy?"

I frowned. "How do you know how stealthy he is?"

"I saw him the day he busted you out. The nine of 'em were all the same. Oozing whatever it is he oozes."

I opened my mouth. Closed it. Tried to wrap my brain around what she'd just said. Then, "Nine?" I said. "Eight other men like Barrons? As in *exactly* like him?"

"Well, they weren't ninetuplets or nothing, but yeah. He had eight other . . . whatever they are with him. Big men. Badasses. Major show of force, breaking you out. Ro never woulda let you go." She was bouncing from foot to foot so rapidly, she was becoming difficult to focus on.

"I don't remember that! How come I didn't see them? I mean, I know I was . . . out of it, but—"

"He didn't let any of 'em near you. It was like he didn't even want 'em to see you. None of 'em was human, that's a fact."

I sucked in a sharp breath. "You know that? How?"

Her face was too blurred to see, but I heard the scowl in her voice. "He grabbed me out of superspeed. Like it was no effort at all. Nothing human could do that."

"Barrons was able to stop you?" I said incredulously.

"Snatched me right outta the air."

"How could he even move fast enough to get to you in the first place?" I exclaimed. Was there *anything* the man couldn't do? Most of my plans relied heavily on Dani's superspeed.

" 'Zactly what I thought."

I tried to focus on her but couldn't. It was giving me a headache. "Would you slow down?" I said, exasperated. "You're impossible to see."

"Sorry," said the smudge of long black leather coat, MacHalo lights, and luminous sword. "Happens when I get excited or upset. Pissed me off that he could do it. Hang on." She was visible again, tearing open another candy bar.

"So, there are eight others like Barrons." I tried to wrap my mind around the fact. Where had they been all this time? What were they? What was *he*? Another caste of Unseelie no one knew about? "You're absolutely certain? It's not possible they were normal men?"

"No way. They moved weird. Way weirder even than Barrons, like he's the civilized one of the lot. It was creepy. I didn't pick up Fae, but I sure didn't get no human read off 'em, either. And some of their eyes were way fecked up. Nobody wanted to get near 'em. *Sidhe*-seers plastered against the walls, trying to stay as far outta their way as possible. One of 'em had a blade to Ro's neck. All toting Uzis, storming in there, not taking shit from nobody. You could tell they were Death walking if anybody even blinked wrong. The girls couldn't stop talking about it. They were pissed, but . . . well, they were kinda fascinated, too. Shoulda seen the way those dudes looked. The way Barrons looked. *Dude*," she said reverently, then glanced at me, alarmed. "I mean, *man*, you shoulda seen it. Don't call me Danielle, I hate that name."

There were eight other . . . beings . . . like Barrons

out there. I could barely deal with one. Who and what were they? Of all the things I'd learned today, this one rattled me the most. I'd considered him an anomaly. One of a kind. He wasn't. I should have expected the unexpected.

Eight others like him. At *least* eight others, I amended. Who knew? Maybe he'd only brought a limited number with him. Maybe there were dozens more. And he'd never told me about them. Not one word.

Any reservations I might have entertained about the plan I'd been working on since encountering Jayne vanished.

"You're right, Dani," I said. "You need a gun. In fact, we need a lot of guns. And I know just where to find them."

12

It was nearly dawn by the time I parked the school bus in front of the abbey.

I hated giving up the Range Rover, but I needed larger transport. I'd found the bright blue bus, with its dented sides, peeling paint, and lethargic transmission, outside a youth hostel. Dani and I had packed it with crates of guns and Unseelie corpses.

I was bone-tired. I'd been up for twenty-four hours straight, and they'd been crammed full. I didn't expect to get much sleep before moving on with my plans, but I hoped to snatch an hour—at least—of silence and the opportunity to clear my mind, so I could sort through all that had happened, all I'd learned.

"The Dragon Lady's library's in the east wing, Mac," Dani said, as she headed off toward the kitchen. "Ain't been used in years." She wrinkled her nose. "It's dusty but cool. I sleep there times they're blaming me for something or I just don't feel like dealin'. Most of the east wing's empty. I'll hook up with you after I eat. Du—*man*, I'm fecking starved!"

As she sped off, I shook my head and smiled. She'd told me that as long as she kept eating, she could go days without sleep. She was constantly testing her limits. I wondered what I might have been like if I'd grown up knowing what I was. I imagined I would have pressed my limits, too. Probably been a lot more useful than I felt now. I envied her stamina. I had no such gift. Lack of sleep had eroded my patience and left me raw. I was in no shape to make a rousing join-up-with-me-*sidhe*-seers-and-let's-kick-some-Fae-ass speech. I rubbed my eyes. I couldn't stretch out on a comfy sofa soon enough.

I entered the abbey through a side door and hurried toward the east wing. Halfway there, I realized I was being followed.

I smiled tightly but made no move to acknowledge her. I wasn't about to get into an argument with the Grand Mistress in the middle of a corridor, where all the other *sidhe*-seers could burst from their rooms at the sound of raised voices and chip in their two cents' worth before I was ready to deal with it. If she wanted a fight, she was going to get it on my terms, on my turf. I made a mental note to find out what Dani knew about wards. It would be too perfect if I could block Rowena from the east wing and secure my own little space in her abbey. Otherwise, I was never going to feel safe.

I followed Dani's directions down dimly lit corridors. I was surprised Rowena didn't stick closer to me with my blazing MacHalo. Although I refused to turn and acknowledge her, no glare of light competed with mine casting shadows on the stone walls, which meant she couldn't be carrying more than a couple of flashlights. We had no idea how many Shades were still in the abbey. The old woman had balls.

I stepped into the library and moved from one lamp to the next, turning them all on. I was pleased to see a plush brocade sofa where I could grab a catnap.

As soon as I got rid of Rowena.

"Not now, old woman," I tossed over my shoulder coldly. "I need sleep."

"Funny. You didn't seem to need so much a few days ago."

I felt the blood drain from my face. I wasn't ready for this confrontation. I might never be ready for it.

"In fact, sleep was the *last* thing on your mind," he said tightly. He was angry. I could hear it in his voice. What was *he* angry about? I was the one who'd been through the emotional wringer.

My hands curled into fists, my breathing grew shallow. I trusted him no more today than I had two months ago.

"Fucking was all you wanted."

It was what I wanted right now, too, I was horrified to realize. His voice worked on me like an aphrodisiac. I was wet and ready. I had been since he began speaking. For two months, I'd been trapped in a Fae-induced sexual frenzy, having constant, incredible sex with him, while listening to his voice, smelling his scent. Like one of Pavlov's dogs, I'd been conditioned by repeated stimuli to have a guaranteed response. My body anticipated, greedily expected pleasure in his presence. I inhaled, caught myself straining for the scent of him, forced it back out, and closed my eyes, as if maybe I could hide behind my own lids from an ironic truth: V'lane and Barrons had swapped roles.

I was no longer sexually vulnerable to the death-by-sex Fae Prince.

Jericho Barrons was my poison now.

I wanted to punch something. Lots of somethings. Starting with him.

"Cat got your tongue? And what a lovely tongue it is. I know. It licked every inch of me. Repeatedly. For months," he purred, but there was steel in the velvet.

I locked my jaw and turned, bracing myself for the sight of him.

It was worse than I expected.

I was nearly flattened by erotic images. My hands on his face. *Me* on his face. Me backing up to him. Me straddling him, my I'm-a-Wanton-Pink fingernails long and sexy as I wrapped both hands around his big, long, hard ... yeah.

Well.

Enough images.

I cleared my throat and forced myself to focus on his eyes.

It wasn't much better. Barrons and I have wordless conversations. And right now he was reminding me, in graphically lush detail, of everything we'd done in that big Sun King bed of his.

He'd especially enjoyed the handcuffs. I had as many memories of his tongue as he had of mine. He'd never offered turnabout as fair play, even though I'd asked plenty. I'd never understood why.

We'd both known nothing so flimsy could hold whatever he was. Now that I was clearheaded again, I understood. Even if it was only illusory, he was not a man to tolerate dominance. It was all about control with him. He never relinquished it. And that was a huge part of what chafed so badly, burned like salt in an open wound. I'd been completely out of control the entire time we'd spent in that room. He'd seen my most raw, bare, vulnerable self, yet he'd never shown me anything of himself that I hadn't had to rip from his head against his will.

He'd never lost control. Not once.

You told me I was your world.

"It wasn't me. I was an animal." My heart pounded. My cheeks burned.

You never wanted it to end.

"Why are you being such a jackass, slamming me in the face with my own humiliation?"

Humiliation? That's what you call this? He forced a more detailed reminder on me.

I swallowed. Yes, I certainly remembered that. "I was out of my mind. I'd never have done it otherwise."

Really, his dark eyes mocked, and in them I was demanding more, telling him I wanted it to always be this way.

I remembered what he'd replied: that one day I would wonder if it was possible to hate him more.

"I had no awareness. No choice." I searched for words to drive my point home. "It was every bit as much rape as what the Unseelie Princes did to me."

His glittering gaze went flat black, opaque as mud,

the images died. Beneath his left eye, a tiny muscle contracted, smoothed, contracted again. That minute betrayal was Barrons' equivalent of a normal person having a hissy fit. "Rape isn't something—"

"You walk away from," I cut him off. "I know. I get it now. Okay?"

"You crawl. You were crawling when I found you."

"Your point?"

"You walked away from me. Stronger for it."

"Point?" I gritted. I was tired, impatient, and I wanted the bottom line.

"Making sure we're on the same page," he clipped. His eyes were dangerous.

"You did what you had to do, right?"

He inclined his head. It was neither nod nor negation, and it pissed me off. I was sick of nonanswers from him.

I pressed. "You made me capable of walking again the only way you could. It had nothing to do with me. That's what you're saying, right?"

He stared at me, and I had the feeling our conversation had taken a wrong turn somewhere, that it could have gone a completely different way, but I couldn't think of how it might have or where it had strayed.

He brought his head down, completing the nod. "Right."

"Then we're on the same page. Same paragraph, same sentence," I snapped.

"Same bloody word," he agreed flatly.

I felt like crying and hated myself for it. Why couldn't he have said something nice? Something that wasn't about sex. Something about *me*. Why had he come in here all stalking and shoving in my face that we'd been in each other's skin? Would it have killed him to show a little kindness, some compassion? Where was the man who'd painted my nails? The one who had papered the room with pictures of Alina and me? The one who had danced with me?

Means to an end. That was all it had been for him.

The silence lengthened. I searched his eyes. There wasn't a single word to be found in them.

Finally, he gave me a faint smile. "Ms. Lane," he said coolly, and those two words spoke volumes. He was offering me formality. Distance. A return to the way things had been, as if nothing else had ever passed between us. A façade of civility that made us able to work together when we had to.

I'd be a fool not to accept it.

"Barrons." I sealed the deal. Had I ever told this enigmatic, cold man that he was my world? Had he really demanded I say it, over and over? "Why are you here? What do you want?" I was exhausted, and our little run-in was swiftly depleting my last stores of energy.

"You might start by thanking me." There was that dangerous look in his eyes again, as if he felt taken advantage of. *He* felt taken advantage of? I was the one who'd been at her weakest, not him.

"For what? For finding something else that was so important to do that it took you all the way from midnight on Samhain 'til *four days later* to come for me? I'm not going to thank you for saving me from something you failed to save me from to begin with." I'd asked Dani on the way back to the abbey when he and his men had broken me out. She'd said late in the evening on November 4. Why? Where had he been, and why not with me?

He lifted a shoulder, shrugged, grace and power in an elegant Armani suit. "You look fine to me. In fact, you're better than fine, aren't you? You walked right through my wards, without a word. Didn't even leave a note by the bedside. Really," he mocked, "after all we shared, Ms. Lane." He gave me a wolf smile, all teeth and promise of blood. "But do I get any thanks for doing the impossible and bringing you back from being *Pri-ya*? No. What do I get?" He eyed me coldly. "You steal my guns."

"You snooped in my bus!" I said indignantly.

"I'll snoop anywhere I damned well please, Ms. Lane. I'll snoop inside your skin if I feel like it."

"You just try," I said, eyes narrowing.

He moved forward in one swift, violent lunge but caught himself and locked down hard.

I mirrored the move, without conscious thought at all, as if our bodies were connected by puppet strings. Lunged forward, froze. Fisted my hands at my sides. They wanted to touch him. I looked down. His hands were fisted, too.

I uncurled my hands and crossed my arms.

He crossed his at exactly the same moment.

We both practically flung them down at our sides.

We stared at each other.

The silence lengthened.

"Why did you take my guns?" he said finally.

His question snapped me fully awake again. I was dangerously tired. "I needed them. Figured it was the least you could give up after all the sex you got," I added, with flippancy I didn't feel.

"You think you can steal from me? You're out of control, Rainbow Girl."

"Don't call me that!" She was dead. And if she wasn't, I'd have killed her myself.

"And you know it."

"*You're* the one who's out of control," I said, just to irritate him.

"I'm *never* out of control."

"Are, too."

"Am—" He broke off and looked away. Then, disbelievingly, "Bloody hell, have you learned nothing?"

"What was I supposed to learn, Barrons?" I demanded. My temper, already a frayed rope, snapped. "That it's a sucky world out there? That people will take everything from you that matters, if you let them? That if you want something, you'd better hurry and get it, because odds are somebody else wants it, too, and if they can beat you to it they will? Or was I supposed to learn that it's not only okay to kill but sometimes it can be downright fun? *That* was a real kicker to find inside your head. Want to talk about it? Share a little intimacy with me? No? Didn't think so. How about this: The more weapons, knowledge, and power you can get your hands on, *any way you can,* the better. Lie, cheat, or steal, it all comes out in the wash. Isn't that what you think? That emotion is weakness and cunning priceless? Wasn't I supposed to become like you? Wasn't that the point?" I was shouting, but I didn't care. I was furious.

"That was *never* the point," he snarled, moving toward me.

"Then what was it? What the bloody hell *was* the point? Tell me there was some kind of point to all this!" I snarled back, stepping toward him.

We charged each other like bulls.

An instant before we collided, I shouted, "Did you help the LM turn me *Pri-ya* just to make me stronger?"

His head snapped back, and he stopped so suddenly that I slammed into him, bounced off, and sprawled on my ass. On the floor. Again.

He stared down at me, and for a split second I saw a completely unguarded look in his eyes. No. He hadn't. Not only hadn't he, this . . . man, for lack of a better word . . . who enjoyed killing, was horrified by the thought of it.

A terrible tension inside me eased. Breath came more easily.

I stayed on the floor, too drained to get back up. There was another of those long, strained silences.

I sighed.

He took a deep breath. Released it.

"I would have given you the guns," he said finally.

"I should have asked for them," I admitted grudgingly. "But then you probably would have spiked them with something deadly, same way you did the Orb, and I'd have gotten blamed for that, too," I couldn't resist adding.

"I didn't spike the Orb. I bought it at an auction. Somebody set me up."

He said it with such a complete lack of heat that I almost believed him.

There was another long silence.

He slid a bag from his shoulder, dropped it at my feet. It was my backpack.

"Where'd you get that? I didn't see it in the room when I left, and I hunted for it." I'd wondered where it had gone.

"Found it here at the abbey while I was waiting for you to get back."

I frowned. "How long have you been here?"

"Since late last night. I spent all day yesterday trying to find you. By the time I tracked you here, you'd left again. Easier to wait for you to come back than waste time tracking you again."

"Doesn't your trusty little brand work?" I rubbed the base of my skull where he'd stamped his mystical tattoo. The one that had failed me when I'd needed it.

"I can sense your general direction, but I can't get a solid lock on you. Haven't been able to since the walls came down. It's working more like a compass than a GPS, now that Fae realms have splintered ours."

"IFPs. I call them Interdimensional Fairy Potholes."

He smiled faintly. "Funny girl, aren't you?"

We lapsed into another uncomfortable silence. I looked at him. He looked away. I shrugged and looked away, too.

"I wasn't—" I began.

"I didn't—" He began.

"How charming," V'lane cut us off. His voice arrived before he did. "The very portrait of human domestic bliss. She's on the floor, you're towering over her. Did he strike you, MacKayla? Say the word and I'll kill him."

It annoyed me to think V'lane might have been hanging around, invisible, eavesdropping on us. I gave him a sharp look when he appeared. My hand slipped instantly inside my coat, searching for my spear, holstered beneath my arm. It was gone. V'lane never let me keep it in his presence, but he always returned it when he left. I hated that he had the power to take my weapon. What if he didn't give it back? What if he decided to keep it for his race? Surely he would have taken the spear and the sword months ago, if he'd wanted them. He'd give it back this time, too, I thought coolly. Otherwise the almighty Book detector would tell him to piss off.

"As if you could," said Barrons.

"Perhaps not. But I do enjoy thinking about it."

"Bring it on, Tinker Bell."

I stood up.

V'lane laughed, and the sound was angelic, celestial. Although he no longer affected me sexually, he still packed that otherworldly punch. Regal, larger than life, he would always be too beautiful for words. He was dressed differently than I'd ever seen him, and it suited his golden perfection. Like Barrons, he wore an elegant dark suit, crisp white shirt, and blood-red tie.

"Get your own fashion adviser," Barrons growled.

"Maybe I decided I like your style."

"Maybe you thought if you were more like me, she'd fuck you, too."

I flinched, but my reaction was nothing compared to V'lane's.

I was frozen for a moment, stiffer than the Tin Man without oil. I gave a full body shudder, and ice tinkled to the floor. I stepped forward, leaving my frosty casing behind. The entire library—furniture, books, floor, lamps, walls—glistened with a thin sheet of ice. The bulbs popped, one after the next.

"Stop it," I snapped, breath frosting the air. "Both of you. You're tough guys. I get it. But I'm tired and fed up. So say whatever you came here to say, without all the posturing, then get the hell out."

Barrons laughed. "Good for you, Ms. Lane."

"Bottom-line it, Barrons. Now."

"Get your things. We're going back to Dublin. We have work to do. The *sidhe*-seers didn't save you. I did."

"It was Dani who rescued me."

"You would have died here if not for me."

"I would have saved her," said V'lane.

"Bottom-line it, V'lane. And mop up your mess." The ice was melting. "I'm not cleaning up after either of you. And fix the lamps. I need light."

The lamps glowed again. The library was dry. "The Book was spotted recently. I know where and can sift you about, hunting it. You can track it much more quickly with me than with him."

"And you'll report to the Grand Mistress on our progress?" I said dryly.

"I aided Rowena only to pave the way for us to continue the moment you were able. I answer to you, as always, MacKayla. Not her."

"*After* your queen," I said bitterly. "The one you chose to stay with instead of rescuing me."

"You were first to me," Barrons said. "There was no queen in front of you with me."

"Right. No queen—just four days," I reminded. "I don't believe it took you that long to find me. Care to tell me where you were the whole time? What *did* come before me?"

He said nothing.

"I didn't think so."

I crossed the room and moved to stand by the fireplace. It was the old-fashioned kind, made for logs, with no gas hookup. V'lane's temper tantrum had left me chilly. It had been a cold night in Dublin, and this unused wing was minimally heated. I missed my bookstore fires. I wanted comfort. "Make me a fire, V'lane."

Flames crackled and popped from white-barked, fragrant-smelling logs before I'd even finished speaking.

"I will provide for all your needs, MacKayla. You have but to ask. Your parents are well. I have seen to it. Barrons cannot give you what I can."

I rubbed my hands together, warming them. "Thank you for checking. Please continue to do so." At some point, I wanted to see them, if only from a distance. Even if the cell towers had been up, I wasn't sure I could have spoken to them right now. I was no longer the daughter they'd known. But I was the daughter who loved them and would do everything in my power to protect them. Even if that meant staying away, so none of my enemies could follow me there.

I turned around. V'lane was on my right, Barrons at my left. I was amused to see that a sofa, four chairs, and three tables had appeared in the twenty-five feet between them. V'lane had rearranged furniture while my back was turned. As if a little furniture would stop Jericho Barrons. He could move lightning-fast, and there was no love lost between these two. For the umpteenth time, I wondered why. I knew neither of them would ever tell me.

Still, there might be a way . . .

In the meantime, while I stockpiled my flagging energy for the attempt, I said, "Bring me up to speed. What happened at the Keltars' on Samhain?"

"The ritual to maintain the walls failed," said Barrons.

"Obviously. Details."

"We used dark magic. We tried everything. The Keltar come from a line of Druids that have long been walking a fine line. Especially Cian. Dageus and Drustan made the first attempt. When that failed, Christian and I took our turn."

"What exactly did your 'turn' constitute?"

"Don't ask, Ms. Lane. This time just leave it. It was the only thing we could have done that might have worked. It didn't. It's no longer relevant."

I dropped the subject. I'd get more detail from Christian than I'd ever get from Barrons, and I planned to see him as soon as possible. He was an integral part of my plans for the future.

As if he'd read my mind, Barrons said, "Christian is gone."

I jerked. "What do you mean, gone?"

"Missing. He disappeared when the Fae realm

supplanted *Ban Drochaid,* the white stones where the Keltar perform the ritual. He was in the circle when it happened."

"Well, where did he go?" I demanded, looking from Barrons to V'lane.

"If we knew that, he wouldn't be missing," Barrons said dryly.

"Impossible to say," said V'lane, "although we have been searching. My queen is deeply distressed to have lost one of her Keltar Druids at such a critical time. His uncles, too, seek him."

"He's been missing for two months?" I was horrified. Where was the young, sexy Scotsman? Don't let him be in Faery, I thought, being made *Pri-ya*! He had just the kind of extraordinary good looks that appealed to the Fae. I hated asking the next question. "Do we know if he's alive? Does either of you have some mystical way of determining that?"

They shook their heads.

I sighed heavily and rubbed my eyes. Damn. Christian was the only man I'd met since arriving in Dublin that I'd actually trusted—well, more than anyone else, at least—and now he was gone. I refused to believe he was dead. That would be giving up on him. I would never give up on any of my humans.

Not only did I like him, I needed him. He was a walking lie detector. His ability to discern truth from fiction was a talent I'd been itching to put to use. And it was these two standing in this very room that I'd wanted to test it on. I narrowed my eyes. How very convenient for both of them that he'd disappeared when he had.

I was worried for Christian. I was disappointed that I'd lost the opportunity to force some answers.

But I hadn't lost *all* my opportunities.

"Get your things," Barrons said. "Let's go. Now."

"MacKayla comes with me," said V'lane. "You cannot protect her parents. You cannot sift. She will not choose you."

There was enough testosterone in the room for an entire army of men, and I wasn't immune to it. Even without glamour, V'lane was more seductive than any human male alive. And Barrons—well, the body remembered and reveled in every moment of it. The two of them turning it up at the same time made it a little hard to breathe.

I looked from one to the other, considering my options. They watched in silence, waiting for me to make my choice.

I stepped toward Barrons.

His dark gaze glittered with triumph. I could feel the smugness rolling off him, nearly as strong as the sexual charge he was throwing my way.

"Think hard and fast," V'lane hissed. "It would be unwise to alienate me, MacKayla."

I *was* thinking hard and fast.

I closed my hand around Barrons' forearm. He could not have looked more pleased if I'd just gazed up at him with doe eyes and told him he was my world.

I locked my hand down, dug my nails into his flesh, and held on.

His eyes narrowed, then flared, and then I was no longer seeing him at all, because I'd pushed, pushed, pushed violently, stabbed myself brutally deep into his mind with the special *sidhe*-seer talent that had fully wakened in his bed.

I wanted answers. I wanted to know why there was so much animosity between these two. I wanted to know who to trust, who was not the better man but at least the slightly less-bad one.

I pushed, seeking any breach I could exploit, and suddenly I was—

In Faery!

It had to be. The scenery was impossibly lush, the colors too rich, vivid, so full of tone they had texture, like that first beach V'lane had taken me to months ago, where I'd played volleyball with Alina, when he'd given me the gift of seeing her again, if only in an illusion. But this was no beach—this was the Fae court!

Brilliantly colored silk chaises were scattered around a dais. Trees sprouted leaves and flowers of incomprehensible color and dimension. The breeze smelled of jasmine and sandalwood and some other scent that I imagined heaven—if such a place existed—would smell like.

I wanted to look around. I wanted to see the queen on her dais, but I couldn't turn my/our gaze toward it because I was a passenger in his head, and I was—

Inside Barrons' body.

I was strong.

I was cold.

I was mighty, and they didn't even know just how mighty I was.

They didn't recognize me, the fools.

I was danger.

I was everything they should fear, but they'd lived so long that they'd forgotten fear. I would teach them.

I would remind them.

I was with a Fae Princess, buried deep inside her. She throbbed around me. She was energy, she was empty, she was sex that devoured. Her nails were on my shoulders, clawing. I was more pleasure than any of her princes could ever be. I was full. I was inexhaustible. It was why she'd sought me. Word had spread, as I'd meant it to, and, bored, jaded, she'd come for me, as I'd known she would.

I'd spent months at court, in her bed, watching, learning, studying the Seelie court. Seeking answers. Hunting the bloody damned Book.

But now I was bored, and I'd learned all there was to know from them, because they were fools who drank again and again from a mystical cauldron to make themselves forget. As if forgetting eradicated the sin.

I needed them to remember.

They couldn't.

But I could make them remember fear.

V'lane was watching me, as he'd been watching me from the moment I'd taken his princess, waiting for her to be his again, certain she would; after all, they were immortal. They were gods. They were invincible. Waiting for that moment when I was no longer her protected plaything so he could destroy me.

GET OUT OF MY HEAD!

I dug my nails into Barrons' arm and cried out.

He was fighting me. Resisting. He'd shoved me out of the princess's body, sent me tumbling, end over end, from his memory at the Fae court.

I was on the fringes of his mind, reeling from the unexpected ejection.

I gathered myself, forged myself into a missile of sheer will, and fired back at the blockade he'd erected. I'M NOT DONE YET!

I ricocheted off a smooth black wall and knew instantly it was impenetrable. He was stronger than me. I couldn't get through it. I would end up ramming myself to death on it if I tried.

But I wasn't about to admit defeat. I harnessed the velocity of that ricochet like a boomerang, made a last-minute course adjustment, and veered sideways.

Whatever was behind that wall would remain concealed, but I could get something else. I knew I could.

And suddenly there I was again, standing—

At Fae court, looking down at the princess—

Barrons slammed a wall up in front of me. But not fast enough.

I blasted through it.

I was Barrons and she was on the ground and I was laughing—

He slammed up another wall but didn't get it reinforced fast enough.

I toppled it.

The bitch was dead.

He slammed one more wall up. Too little, too late.

I shattered it right out of existence.

Every Fae in the queen's court was screaming, fleeing for their lives, because the unthinkable had happened.

One of their own had ceased to exist.

One of their own had been killed.

By me/Barrons/us.

I was choking, sputtering, trying desperately to breathe, and I realized with horror that it wasn't the

Barrons/Mac persona that was choking. It was my *body*.

I pulled back, yanked back, stumbled back, ripped myself from Barrons' mind. It wasn't easy to untangle us.

His hand was on my throat.

Mine was on his.

"What the *fuck*?" V'lane exploded. It was the most human sentence I'd ever heard him utter. He'd been watching us but had no idea what had happened.

Our battle had been a private one.

Barrons and I stared at each other.

We released each other's throats at the same moment.

I backed up a step.

He didn't. But then, I hadn't expected him to.

"You really *can* kill V'lane!" I exclaimed. "That's why he won't let you near him. You can *kill* him. How?"

Barrons said nothing. I'd never seen him so still, so silent.

I whirled on V'lane. "How?" I demanded. I was shaking. Barrons could kill Fae. It was no wonder the Shades left him alone. "Did he have the spear or the sword?" But I knew in my bones that it had been neither of those weapons. The wall he'd thrown up had shielded the answer. Whatever weapon he'd used, it was not one I knew.

V'lane said nothing.

"What does he *have* on you?" I cried, exasperated.

"Decide, Ms. Lane," Barrons said, behind me.

"Choose," V'lane agreed.

"Go to hell, both of you! New world. New rules. New me. Don't call me. I'll call you."

"To call me, you will require my name back," V'lane said.

"So it can fail me again when I need it?"

"It failed only during that brief time when all magic was down. Such a moment is impossible to sustain. Darroc will not attempt it again. He does not need to. He achieved his end."

"I'll think about it," I said. And I would. All weapons. Good.

Something clattered to the floor at my feet. It was a cell phone.

I didn't turn. "What's that for? Duh, no towers, remember?" I mocked.

"It works," said Barrons. He paused heavily, the better to emphasize his *coup de grâce*. "It always did."

My breathing stopped. What he was saying was not possible. I spun, searched his eyes. "The power was down! My call to Dani was disconnected. I never got service back!" I knew. I'd kept checking all night.

He moved toward me so quickly, I didn't see him coming and had no chance to react. His body was pressed to mine, his lips were against my ear.

I leaned into him and inhaled. I couldn't help myself.

He whispered, "O ye of little faith. Not for *IYD*."

It was the number he'd programmed into my cell, which stood for *If You're Dying*.

"But you didn't even *try*."

His tongue touched my ear. Then he was gone.

13

I sat on the edge of the sofa, rubbing my eyes. I needed sleep in the worst way, but I suffered few illusions that I was going to get any.

My encounter with V'lane and Barrons had left me too wired for words, and soon the abbey would be waking up, and I'd have a whole new set of challenges to face.

I stroked the glittering beauty of my spear.

True to form, V'lane had returned it when I'd demanded he leave. After reassuring myself with its comforting weight, I tucked it back into my shoulder holster.

I toed my old backpack over by the strap and dug around in it for my journal. I was surprised to find it. I thought someone would have confiscated it. I figured it was a pretty safe assumption both Rowena and Barrons had read it.

I rubbed the embossed leather cover, grateful to see it again, as if it were an old friend. Since Alina had been killed, I'd filled three notebooks with feelings, speculations, and plans. At first, I'd begun keeping a journal as a sort of tribute to her, a way to somehow connect to her memory.

Then I'd learned I could pour my grief into its pages, instead of hurting my parents with it. Finally, I'd discovered what my older sister had known all along: that it was an invaluable tool for sorting thoughts, clarifying and refining them, and planning future action.

God, I missed her! What I would give to sit and talk with her again! To hug her and tell her that I loved her. Since her death, I'd realized how few times I told her what she meant to me. I'd always assumed she knew, that we'd have decades together, planning each other's weddings, having baby showers, sending our children off to school together, taking pictures at their proms: a lifetime of sisterhood. I steeled myself. No time for emotion. When this was all over, I would wallow in grief. I would make V'lane give her back to me again, in Faery. I would grant myself the balm of illusion. When all this was over, I would deserve it.

I flipped to a fresh page and began making notes of everything I'd learned recently. If something happened to me, I wanted to leave as detailed a record behind as possible for the next idiot who tried to do something about the mess we were all in.

- I can walk through wards. All of them? Or just certain ones?
- I'm immune to Fae glamour. Must test this on a Fae besides V'lane.
- Barrons can kill Fae. How? V'lane won't tell me. Why?

- Christian is missing. Is he alive?
- The Keltar ritual failed. What did they try and what went wrong? Must learn more about Druid magic. Is it possible I can do Druid magic, too? V'lane said once that I had only begun to discover what I was. Like Dani, I need to test my limits.
- Jayne is leading a civilian army that he's trained to eat Unseelie, protecting Dublin. There are still people in the city. Where? Should we try to move them out, to a safer place?
- Iron has some kind of effect on the Fae. What does it do, and does it work the same on every caste? How effective a weapon?

I made a second column on the page, a to-do list:

- Form troop to investigate IFPs.
- Form troop to collect iron to make weapons and bullets.
- Form troop to figure out <u>how</u> to make weapons and bullets.
- Get into the Forbidden Libraries. Find out: What is the Haven's prophecy, and who are the current members? What are the five?

Someone had been sending me pages of Alina's journal. From her notes, I'd learned that in order to do whatever it was my sister had been trying to do (I assumed stop the Book and drive the Fae from our world), she'd learned there was a prophecy known to the Haven—which was the *sidhe*-seer's High

Council—that said we needed three things: the stones, the Book, and the five.

I knew what the stones were: four bluish-black rune-covered rocks that, according to Barrons, could either translate parts of the Dark Book or "reveal its true nature." Barrons had two of them in his possession. V'lane had the third or knew where it was. I had no idea where to find the fourth.

I knew what the Book was, too. That was easy.

Unfortunately, I had no idea what the five were.

I hoped the prophecy might clear things up, and I figured the best place to look for any prophecy about *sidhe*-seer matters was in Rowena's Forbidden Libraries, which was why I was so determined to secure a foothold at the abbey. I didn't care how much I pissed off Rowena. It was the support of the *sidhe*-seers I wanted.

I added a more immediate, personal goal to my to-do list:

- Take Dani into Dublin tonight and try to track down Chester's and Ryodan.

IYCGM was *If You Can't Get Me* on the cell phone Barrons had given me. I'd called it once. It was answered by a man named Ryodan, and we'd had a very cryptic, Barrons-like conversation. I was willing to bet my last pair of clean panties—and I was dangerously low on them—that Ryodan was one of Barrons' eight. Both Barrons and Inspector O'Duffy had mentioned talking with the mysterious Ryodan at a place called Chester's. I'd been meaning to track him down for months, but I'd been distracted by one crisis after another.

I had no idea what or where Chester's was or if it even still existed in the rubble that was Dublin, but if there was an opportunity to find one of the eight men who'd stormed the abbey with Barrons to free me, I wasn't about to pass it up. Any man who knew Barrons, any man Barrons trusted to cover his back, was someone I wanted to have a nice, long face-to-face talk with.

On the panties note:

* Loot store tonight for new underwear.

A lot. Doing laundry wasn't something I saw my-self having time for in the near future. I raked a hand through my hair. My nails were long against my scalp. They weren't all that had grown. I'd seen the reflection of my hairdo in a window last night. The cut was still good, but I had an inch of blond roots that made me look like a skunk.

* Loot store for hair dye and manicure kit.

I planned to grab more clothes while I was at it. Whether it should matter or not, people responded to outer appearances and were motivated to certain behaviors by them. A well-groomed, attractive leader was much more influential than an unkempt one.

I made a third column: long-term major goals that would hopefully be accomplished short term, be-cause our world was changing drastically, much too fast. These were the critical ones. They *had* to happen.

- Figure out how to contain the <u>Sinsar Dubh</u>!

I nibbled the tip of my pen. Then what? During my first encounter with V'lane, he'd made it clear he felt there was only one option, that there was no one else who could be trusted with it.

- Take the <u>Sinsar Dubh</u> to the Seelie Queen so she can re-create the Song of Making to rebuild the walls and reimprison the Unseelie?

I worried about that one. It wasn't in my blood to trust anything Fae, but I wasn't exactly flush with alternatives. I could drive myself crazy wondering what to do with the *Sinsar Dubh* once I'd gotten it. I decided to focus on one impossibility at a time. Get the Book, then figure out the next step.

I crossed out the last bullet and wrote another one:

- <u>Kick their fecking Fae asses off our world!</u>

I liked that one. I underlined it three times.
O ye of little faith . . . you didn't even try.
I winced, closed my journal and my eyes. Since Barrons had left, I'd been trying not to brood over his parting comment. For the past twenty-four hours, while I'd been running around half of Ireland, I'd been replaying the events of Halloween in

the back of my mind, indulging myself in an exercise in futility, torturing myself with all the choices I might have made that night that could have yielded a different outcome.

Then Barrons had gone and fired the real killer at me: I'd had a way to reach him the whole time, right there in my backpack.

I opened my eyes, pulled out my cell, and thumbed through the three numbers that had been preprogrammed into the phone when he'd given it to me. I pressed the first one—Barrons' cell number. I knew it wouldn't ring. It rang, startling me.

I disconnected quickly.

Mine rang.

I flipped it open, snarled at Barrons, "Just testing," and immediately disconnected. How in the world were these cell phones working? Was service back up in certain areas?

I changed my settings to *private* and dialed my parents' number so they wouldn't know it was me, reserving the right to hang up if they answered and I couldn't bring myself to speak. It didn't go through. I tried The Brickyard, where I'd bartended back home. No connection. I tried a dozen other numbers, with no success. Apparently Barrons had some kind of special service.

I thumbed up *IYCGM* and pressed it.

"Mac," a male voice growled.

"Just testing," I said, and hung up.

I scrolled to *IYD*.

My phone rang. It was *IYCGM*. I answered it.

"I wouldn't if I were you," Ryodan said.

"Wouldn't what?"

"Test the third one."

I didn't bother asking how he knew. Like Barrons, he was on top of my every thought. "Why not?"

"There's a reason it's called *If You're Dying*."

"What's that?"

"So you use it only if you're dying," he said dryly.

Also, like Barrons, I could go around in circles with him forever. "I'm going to call it, Ryodan."

"You're better than that, Mac."

"Better than what?" I said coolly.

"Lashing out because you hurt. He's not the one who hurt you. He's the one who brought you back."

"Do you know what his idea of bringing me back *was*?" I snapped.

There was a smile in Ryodan's voice. "I volunteered for the job. He didn't seem at all touched by my offer." The smiled faded. "Don't lose yourself in anger, Mac. It's gasoline. You can burn it as fuel, or you can use it to torch everything you care about and end up standing on a scorched battlefield, with everybody dead, even you—only your body doesn't have the good grace to quit breathing."

Deep inside, his words resonated. I was straddling a fine line and I knew it. But there was a part of me that *wanted* to go over the edge. *Wanted* to scorch the battlefield. Just to watch the damned thing burn.

"Stay focused, Mac. Keep your eyes on the prize."

"What the bloody hell *is* the prize?"

"We work together. Take back our world. We all win."

"What are you, Ryodan?"

He laughed.

"What are the *nine* of you?" I pressed. He said nothing. "I'm going to call it," I threatened. " 'Bye now." I didn't hang up.

He stopped laughing. "I'll kill you myself, Mac."

"No, you won't."

"Woman," he said, and his voice was suddenly so hard and cold and ancient-sounding that the fine hair at the nape of my neck lifted and prickled all the way down my spine, "you don't know the first thing about me. The Mac that would call *IYD* when she's not dying isn't the Mac I'll protect. Choose carefully. Choose wrong, and it will be the last choice you ever make."

"Don't you threaten—" I held the phone away from my ear and stared at it disbelievingly.

He'd hung up. On *me*. The only one who could track the Book. This season's MVP! And I hadn't even gotten around to asking him what Chester's was and where to find it!

My hair gusted, raised straight up in the air around my face in a tangle. Sheets flapped on the furniture. The flames of the fire flared, crackled, then nearly went out.

Dani stood in front of me, guzzling orange juice and cramming her mouth with what looked like Little Debbie cakes.

"We got trubs, Mac. Ro's at the bus, and so's half the abbey. Shit's hittin' the fan big-time. S'time to go," she mumbled around a mouthful. She sniffed the air and looked crestfallen. "Dude, they were *both* here? Why'n't'cha call me?"

If Ro and half the abbey were at the bus, "trubs" were troubles. I was exhausted. I was wired. I was as ready as I was going to be. I stood and shoved my cell phone into my pocket. "You have superhearing. Why didn't you hear them?"

"S'not *that* good."

My eyes narrowed. "You really can smell that they were here?" What I'd give for her supersenses.

She nodded. "I'm gonna give one of 'em my virginity one day." She preened.

I was momentarily dumbstruck. I couldn't begin to enumerate all the things that were appalling about that possibility. "We *so* have to talk," I finally managed. I added pointedly, *"Danielle."* Her gamine grin faded and I hated to see it go, so I added, "I don't know why you don't like it. It's such a pretty name." I knew why. Her toughness was all she had.

"Ow. Sorry I duded you. Man." She held out her hand.

"No, thanks, I'm walking."

She snickered, grabbed my arm anyway, and we were gone.

14

It was complete chaos, and Rowena wasn't having an ounce of success taking control of the situation.

When Dani stopped, I headed straight for the front of the bus. Biting back the urge to puke, I climbed up on the bumper and hauled myself onto the hood, where I stood, looking down.

Hundreds of *sidhe*-seers stared back at me, with expressions ranging from disbelief that we'd dared return, to curiosity and excitement, to fear and blatant distrust.

If I'd been an attorney like my daddy, the bus would have been my opening argument and—filled to overflowing as it was with dead Unseelie and automatic weapons—it would certainly be swaying the jury. The *sidhe*-seers had opened the doors and begun unloading it. Guns were piled on the lawn, between dead Fae. I doubted they'd ever seen so many of our enemy up close and personal, sequestered as Rowena kept them. They couldn't seem to take their eyes off them, poking at them with their toes, turning this way and that, examining them.

Initially, I'd planned to fill the back of the Range Rover with dead Unseelie heads, to show the *sidhe-seers* what effect a mere two of us could have in a single night out on the town. But then we'd learned about iron, and raided Barrons' stash of guns, and we'd had to swap rides.

Dani blew the bus horn to silence the crowd. When a few short bursts did nothing, she laid on it, making it impossible to hear. Finally, there was silence.

Rowena pushed from a small cluster of *sidhe-seers*, moved to the front of the bus, and glared up at me. "Get down from there this instant," she demanded.

"Not until I've had my say."

"You have no right to a say. You stole the spear and sword and left this entire abbey unprotected last night!"

"Oh, please," I said dryly, "like it's being protected with you keeping the Hallows to yourself, doling them out on rare occasions. What could *you* do if the Fae came for them? And we didn't steal them. I took back what was mine to begin with and gave Dani what should have been hers all along. Then we put them to the use they were meant for—killing Fae." I gestured behind me. "In case you didn't notice, a *lot* of Fae."

"Return them to me now," Rowena demanded.

I shook my head. "Not a chance. Dani and I did more last night to strike at our enemy than you've ever let these women do, and not because they can't but because you won't permit it. We're supposed to See, Serve, and Protect. You told me we were born for it. That in the old days, when we arrived at a village, they feasted and offered us the finest of all they had, because we were their honored, revered guardians. We protected them. We lived and died for them. You don't let these women be guardians. You've made them afraid of their own shadows."

"I obviously have a higher opinion of them than you do. You will get down from there this very instant. You do not lead these women. You never will."

"I'm not trying to lead them. I'm showing them their options." It was a lie, but a white one, and my heart was in the right place. I *would* lead them. One way or another. I raised my eyes from Rowena and addressed the crowd. "Does your Grand Mistress. encourage you to explore your heritage? Does she help you hone your skills? Does she tell you anything about what's going on? Or does she keep things all hush-hush with her secret council?" I paused heavily to emphasize what I was about to say next. "Do you know that iron *hurts* the Fae? That there are civilian troops—your average everyday *humans* in Dublin—who are actively hunting the Unseelie, doing our job, protecting the people who are still alive, shooting them with bullets of iron? Dani and I ran into a battalion of fifty last night. They were firing at the Hunters, driving them out of our city, while you slept behind the walls of this abbey. While you hid in safety, abandoning them to their fate. Is that who you are? Is that who you want to be?"

There was a moment of stunned silence, then a deafening cacophony of voices. Dani laid on the horn again. It took a full minute to silence them this time.

Kat stepped forward. "*How* are humans hunting them? They can't see them."

"Most of the Fae no longer hide behind glamour, Kat. You'd know that if she ever let you leave. They feel invincible, and why wouldn't they? There are no *sidhe*-seers getting in their way, stopping them. But we can change that."

"If we start hunting them, won't the Fae just start concealing themselves with glamour again?"

I nodded. "Sure, it'll get more dangerous. And we'll need every special *sidhe*-seer talent we've got."

"Then the humans will no longer be able to fight them," she worried. "They won't be able to reinforce us." Fear underscored her words, and I understood it. How could a mere few hundred *sidhe*-seers with only two weapons hope to defeat an army of Unseelie?

I wanted to know what Rowena knew, so I watched her carefully when I told Kat, "Humans have found a way to open their eyes and see the Fae as we do."

The crowd gasped. When Rowena's expression didn't change at all, I knew it was just one more weapon, like the sword and the spear, that she'd withheld from the women. "You knew!" I exploded. "You knew all along! And in the past two months, you never *once* considered using it to help defend our planet!"

" 'Tis old lore, and forbidden," Rowena hissed. "You've no idea of the consequences!"

"I know what the consequences are if we *don't* do

it! We'll lose our planet, piece by piece! Two billion are already gone, Rowena. How many more will you let die? How many lives do you consider expendable? It was *our* duty to protect the *Sinsar Dubh*! We didn't. Now it's our duty to fix this mess!"

"You knew there was a way to make the average human safer and you didn't tell us?" Kat stared at Rowena. "All those families around the countryside that we've promised to protect and have lost, we could have taught to protect *themselves*?" Her eyes filled with tears. "For the love of Mary, Rowena, I lost my Sean and Jamie! I could have made them able to see the Unseelie? They could have defended themselves?"

"What she's *not* telling you," Rowena spat, "is that in order to see them, they must eat the living, immortal flesh of the dark Fae."

Sidhe-seers gasped; some made choking noises. I understood that perfectly. Even when I'd been battling a growing addiction to it, it had still been revolting.

"What she's *not* telling you," Rowena continued, "is that eating it has unspeakable consequences! It's addictive, and once a human begins they can't stop. It changes the person. What would you expect cannibalizing the flesh of our dark enemy to do? It corrupts their very soul! Och, and is that the sentence you would have inflicted upon your innocent brothers, Katrina? Would you have seen them damned rather than dead?" Her voice rose, strong with fury. "What she's *not* telling you, and should be if we're discussing dark secrets being withheld, is that it was *she* who taught these humans to eat it, and *she*—"

"Who has eaten it herself," I announced, before she could. "And you *can* kick the addiction. I did." Score one for Rowena. As I suspected, she'd read my journal. I tried to rapidly mentally review it, to anticipate where else she might try to pull the rug out from under me. I'd poured my heart and soul into those pages. "Rowena says it changes you. I'm not so sure about that. Judge for yourself whether I'm 'damned,' " I told them. "Judge for yourself whether the humans in Dublin who are fighting *our* war for us are truly any different for having done what was necessary to survive. Or continue blindly taking Rowena's word for things. If I'm so damned, why am I the only *sidhe*-seer out there on the front lines doing something?"

"Hey." Dani was suddenly on the hood of the bus, beside me. "What am I? Chopped liver?"

"Surf and turf," I assured her. "Top-shelf whiskey."

She grinned.

"Because she wants the Book herself," Rowena accused, "that's why she's out there. So she can take power for herself."

"Oh, balls," I scoffed. "If that were true, I would have allied myself with the Unseelie long ago. The LM would never have had to turn me *Pri-ya*."

"How do we know you're not still?" Rowena demanded.

"I can walk," I said dryly. *"Pri-ya,"* I told the women, "is a terrible thing to be. But not only did I recover from it, I've acquired some kind of immunity to sexual glamour. V'lane no longer has any death-by-sex Fae impact on me now."

That got their attention.

"Look, you can face what's out there and get stronger for it, or you can stay behind these walls and take orders until our planet is beyond saving. You want to talk about damned? Our entire race is, if we don't do something about it!"

The women exploded again and turned to one another, talking frantically. I'd definitely stirred them up. I'd given them more information in a few short minutes than their Grand Mistress had in years. I'd made them feel more empowered than she'd ever let them feel.

Rowena gave me an icy look and turned to study her protégées.

She made no move to silence them, nor did I. I preferred they work themselves up even more. Then I would cut in and tell them my plans. Form troops and assign tasks.

Rowena was looking at me again.

I suspected she wanted to address the crowd, but I wasn't about to help her silence them. I would blow the horn in a few minutes and give my closing, rousing mutiny speech.

What happened next happened so quickly that I couldn't stop it.

Rowena slipped a whistle from the pocket of her robes and blew on it sharply, three shrill bursts. The crowd instantly fell silent, obviously trained to the sound. Then she was speaking, and it was too late for me to stop her without seeming argumentative and petty. I would have to let her have her say, then turn it against her when she was done.

"I've known most of you since birth," she said. "I've visited your homes, watched you grow, and brought you here when it was time. I know your families. I have been a part of your everyday struggles and triumphs. Each of you is as my own child."

She favored them with a gentle smile, the very portrait of a loving parent. I didn't trust it one bit. I wondered if I was the only one who saw the disturbing image of a cobra, smiling with human teeth.

"If I have erred, it is not that I have not loved you enough but that I have loved you *too* much. I have wanted, as any mother would, to keep her children safe. But my love has prevented my daughters from becoming the women they could and should be. It has prevented me from leading you as I must. I have erred but will no longer. We are *sidhe*-seers. We *are* humanity's defenders. We were born and bred to battle the Fae, and from this day forward, that is what we will do." All softness in her demeanor abruptly melted away. She snapped straight, suddenly seemed a foot taller, and began firing orders.

"Kat," she barked, "I want you to handpick a group and put them to work determining how we can use iron as a weapon. Catch a few Unseelie. Test it on them. Devote a second group to locating the most common sources of it and collect it, with all haste." She waved a hand at the bus behind her. "We have guns enough for all of us!" she shouted triumphantly, making it sound as if the triumph were hers. "I want iron bullets to go around!"

I gritted my teeth.

"Learn how to make them," she ordered. "Set up a smithy in the old ways if we must. Select a third group to scout Dublin, and, Katrina—you have proved yourself again and again a worthy and valuable leader—I want you in charge of this group yourself."

Kat glowed.

I seethed.

At this point, I knew the wisest thing for me to do was stay silent. But it wasn't easy. There were a dozen biting comments I wanted to make. Reminders that *I'd* brought the guns, *I'd* found out about iron, *I'd* been the one advocating battle when their precious GM had been blindly and insistently against it. But I could read the mood of this crowd, and at the very root of it was an adage as old as time: Better the devil you know than the one you don't know. Especially if the devil you *do* know is about to give you what you wanted anyway.

I couldn't compete with that. I was the devil they'd known for only a few short months. And my press hadn't exactly been good. Not with Rowena in charge of the media.

The Grand Mistress' voice soared in volume. "I want to know the numbers of Fae in the city, so we can begin planning how and when to attack." She raised her small hand into the air and made a fist. "Today is the dawn of a new order! No longer will I allow my love for you to blind me as it has in the past. I will lead my daughters proudly into battle, and we will do what we were born to do. We will remind the Fae that *we* drove them from our world and forced them to hide for six thousand years. We will remind them why they feared us, and we will drive them from it again! Sidhe-*seers, to war!*"

The crowd exploded into cheers.

Beside me, Dani said, "What the feck? How'd she do that, Mac?"

I looked at Rowena and she looked at me and we had an entire conversation in a glance.

Child, did you really believe you could take them from me? her fierce blue glare mocked.

Touché. Watch your back, old woman.

She'd won, for now.

But it wasn't a complete loss. Although Rowena was taking the credit for it, at least the *sidhe*-seers were getting to do everything I'd wanted them to do, short of exploring IFPs, and that could wait. I might have lost the war, but I'd won a few of the battles. My first attempted coup had failed. My next one wouldn't.

"Politics, Dani," I muttered. "We've got a lot to learn." Nothing had been easy for me in Dublin. I no longer expected it to be, nor would I waste time complaining when it could be put to better use moving forward.

"Uh-huh," she agreed glumly. "But I still ain't giving her back my sword."

Rowena turned her cobra smile our way. "Kat, it's long past time I bestowed this honor upon you," she said. "You will lead us to victory carrying the Sword of Light. Dani, give it to Katrina. The sword is now hers."

Five seconds later, I was on my hands and knees in the middle of a rocky field, vomiting the remains of the protein bar I'd eaten an hour ago. I'd never been on such a bumpy, horrible ride in my life. "What *was* that?" I groaned, wiping my mouth with the back of my hand. "Hyperspeed?"

"I *said*," Dani snapped, "I ain't giving her back my sword!"

I looked up at her standing over me—skinny elbows poking out, fists at her waist, fiery red hair flaming in the sunlight—and nearly laughed. The kid was a total wild card. But our disappearing act was going to have consequences. Left to my own devices, I would have stood my ground longer. I would have offered cooperation, protection, and tried to sell them on it, same way I'd tried with Jayne. If that had failed, I'd have had Dani whiz us out of there. But I would have tried first, and the trying would have spoken volumes to some of the girls. It was too late now. I had no doubt Rowena was exploiting the situation for all it was worth. Making us out to be complete traitors. Turning our backs on the entire order.

I rubbed my eyes. I was too tired to think. I needed rest. Then I would figure out how to salvage the things I needed salvaged. It wasn't that I minded being an outcast. I'd been feeling that way ever since I'd arrived in Dublin and had gotten downright comfortable with it. Alone, I had a lot less to worry about. But to accomplish my goals, I needed at least some of the *sidhe*-seers on my side.

"Did ya see her face?"

"How could I? All I saw was a big blue blur of bus as we whizzed past it, then nothing."

"Was she ever wicked pissed! She really didn't think I'd do it," Dani said wonderingly, and I could tell she herself hadn't been entirely sure she'd do it.

Until she did, there was a chance Rowena might forgive her. Blame it all on me and take her back into the fold. There wasn't any more. Dani was *persona non grata*. There was no going back from this one.

"It *was* goin' good, wasn't it, Mac? I mean, I wasn't just imagining it? The girls were listening to us and liking us?"

I nodded.

"Man, it went bad really fast."

I nodded again.

We looked at each other for a long moment.

"Dude," she said finally, "I think we're outcasts."

"Dude," I agreed, with a sigh.

15

At ten-thirty that night, I was back in Dublin and headed for 939 Rêvemal Street.

I was pretty sure I'd found Chester's.

There were three listings in the phone book under that name: a barbershop, a men's clothing store, and a nightclub.

I'd opted for the nightclub because the advertisement had suited the voice of the man I'd spoken to on the phone. Upscale, classy, with a touch of the risqué, as if anything one might want was available for purchase there, if one had the right currency, walked the walk, and talked the talk.

I caught a glimpse of my reflection in a passing window and smiled. I was walking the walk. My hair was jet and a little wild. I'd moussed it and let it do what it wanted. My lipstick was red and glossy and matched my nails. I was wearing black leather from head to toe, not for the statement it made but for the practicality of it. With the right kind of leather, you can sponge off just about anything. Fabric isn't blood-repellent.

There was energy in my step and fire in my eyes. I'd finally gotten some much needed sleep. Dani and I had holed up in a deserted house on the outskirts of Dublin until late afternoon, then headed out for food and supplies. It had felt strangely intimate and uncomfortable, occupying the residence of someone who'd either died in the riots on Halloween or fled Dublin, but we needed somewhere to stay and it seemed pointless not to take advantage of one of the tens of thousands of unoccupied homes.

Since both my MacHalos were back at the abbey, our first stop had been a sporting-goods store, where we built two new ones and stuffed backpacks with flashlights and batteries. Although the Shades seemed to have left Dublin, I wasn't taking any chances.

Then we'd gone to the mall, where I dyed my hair in a public restroom, washed up, and changed. Dani had headed off for an electronics store, where I later found her sprawled in front of a computer, next to a small mountain of battery packs and a pile of DVDs. I toed a few of the DVDs out. My eyes widened. I glanced quickly at the computer screen. Fortunately for her, it wasn't one of them. "Watch any of that porn," I growled, "and I'm going to kick your petunia."

She looked up. "Wicked-cool outfit, Mac!" Then she scowled. "I hunt and kill things. What does it matter what I watch? These eyeballs seen it all, dude." She somehow managed to swagger while cross-legged on the floor.

"I don't care how tough you think you are. You're thirteen and there are limits. You're not watching this stuff. And if you are, you'd better hide it from me, because if I catch you, there's going to be hell to pay."

She shoved the computer from her lap and bounded to her feet. "That's ridiculous," she spat, green eyes sparking. "I watch things die every day but I can't watch people feck? You're not the boss of me." She grabbed her pack and began walking away.

"Those aren't just people fecking, Dani. Those are hard-core."

"So?" she sneered over her shoulder. "What were you a few days ago?"

"It wasn't like that."

"So you gonna tell me what it *was* like? Being *Priya* was all poetry and roses?"

There had been moments that had felt startlingly like that. Not with the Unseelie Princes. But later with Barrons. I crammed that thought into the padlocked box in my head where I keep all those things I can't deal with. Soon I was going to have to sink the thing in concrete to keep it shut. "I'm not telling you not to watch people having sex, although I wish you'd wait a few years. I'm telling you to make better choices. Watch the soft-core stuff, the ones that show sex as something good."

"Mac," she said flatly, "get a grip. The world sucks. Ain't no good left in it."

"There's good everywhere. You just have to look for it." I nearly choked on my words. I sounded just like my daddy and was surprised I still believed what I'd said, after all I'd been through. Looked like the rainbow wasn't entirely black.

She whirled on me, cheeks flushed, eyes furious. "Really? What? Name some of those good things for me, will you? Why don't you tell me about 'em? I got a great idea. Let's make a list. Let's write down all the wonderful things in the world. 'Cause I been looking really hard lately, and I ain't been seeing a fecking one!" Her hands were fisted and she was shaking.

It had taken me until I was twenty-two to be carved by tragedy. How old was Dani when its razor-sharp teeth drew first blood? She'd told me her mother was killed by the Fae six years ago, which would have made her seven at the time. Had she watched it happen? Was that how long she'd been with Rowena? What had the ruthless old woman been doing to her all that time? "What happened to you, Dani?" I said softly.

"You think you have the right to just *ask* me that? Like I'm gonna peel myself open and let you poke around inside me? Like you can pour me out like some little teapot, 'cause you're dangling me by my handle?"

"I'm not dangling you by any handle, Dani."

"You're trying to! Trying to force me to spill my secrets! Dump 'em all over the place so once you know 'em you can throw me away like a piece of trash, same as the Unseelie Princes did to you! Like some stupid fecking stupid fecker that shouldn't have even been fecking born!"

I was stunned by the intensity of her reaction, baffled by the direction our conversation had taken. "I'm not trying to pry into you, and I would never throw you away. I care about you, you prickly little pain-in-the-butt porcupine. So buck up and deal with it. I worry about what you'll become. Enough to fight with you about it. And I'm telling you, choose better movies, eat your vegetables, floss, and treat yourself with respect, because if you don't, nobody else will. I *care*!"

"You wouldn't if you knew me!"

"I *do* know you."

"Leave me alone!"

"Can't," I said flatly. "You and me. We're like sisters. Now get a grip on the teen angst and let's get moving. I need you tonight, and we've got a lot to do." It had always worked whenever Daddy did it to me: made me *do* something, to keep my mind off wallowing in whatever emotion I felt like I was going to die from at the moment.

She stared at me, eyes narrowed, lips drawn in a snarl, and I got the impression she was on the verge of freeze-framing out. I wondered how my parents had survived me. I wondered what she was really so upset about. I wasn't stupid. There was subtext here. I just couldn't figure out what it was. I was about to begin tapping a foot when she finally turned around and began walking.

I followed her in silence, giving her the chance to cool off.

The fabric of her long black leather coat eventually relaxed and creased between her shoulder blades. She took a few deep breaths, then said, "Sisters forgive each other a lot, don't they, Mac? I mean, more than most people?"

I thought of Alina and how she'd fallen for the worst villain in this epic mess, even inadvertently helped him gain power. Of how she'd waited until it was too late to call me. Recently I'd begun to realize my sister had made some hedgy decisions. Like not telling me what was going on as soon as she learned about it and trying to handle it all herself without asking for help. Strength wasn't about being able to do everything alone. Strength was knowing when to ask for help and not being too proud to do it. Alina hadn't called in all the reinforcements she could, and she should have. I wouldn't make the same mistake. Still, regardless of anything she'd done or failed to do, it didn't change how much I loved her, and it never would. Nothing could.

"Like fighting over what movies to watch," Dani clarified, when I didn't answer immediately.

I was about to reply when she muttered, "I thought you'd think I was cool for watching 'em."

I rolled my eyes. "I *already* think you're cool. And, honey, sisters forgive each other everything."

"Really, truly everything?"

"Everything."

As we walked out of the electronics store, I caught a glimpse of her face in the mirror above the door.

It was bleak.

My Dublin no longer existed.

Smashed, broken were the brilliant neon signs that had illuminated the buildings with a kaleidoscope of colors. Long gone were the colorful, diverse people that had filled the streets with boisterous camaraderie and endless craic. Wrecked were the façades of the hundreds of pubs of Temple Bar. The quaint streetlamps were twisted pretzels of metal, and no music spilled from open windows or doors. It was silent. Too silent. All animal life was gone, down to the crickets in the soil. Not one motor hummed. There were no heat pumps kicking on and off. You don't realize how much white noise the world makes until it suddenly stops, making it sound like prehistoric times.

This new Dublin was dark and creepy and . . . still not dead. The once-bustling Irish city was now *undead*. You could feel the life in her, lurking in the dark wreckage, but it was the kind of life you wanted to drive a stake through.

Given the number of Fae I could sense in the city—so many that it was impossible to separate them out until we were almost on top of them—we encountered surprisingly few Unseelie on the streets. I wondered if they were holding the equivalent of a convention or political rally somewhere for the great LM—freer and leader of the bastard half of the Fae race. Nor did we see Jayne, so I supposed he was off terrorizing Hunters in another part of the city.

Over the course of the twenty or so blocks that we walked—"like a Joe," as Dani called it, because I wasn't about to come face-to-face with Ryodan for the first time feeling like I wanted to puke on his shoes—we encountered four Rhino-boys (why did they always travel in pairs?) and an awful slithering thing that was nearly as fast as Dani. I took the RBs, she got the snake.

We were at the cross streets of Rêvemal and

Grandin when I saw her. If my senses hadn't been so fuzzed with Unseelie static from too many on one channel, I might have picked up one of the sifting caste ahead and reacted better.

At first, I couldn't believe my eyes. In my defense, from behind I thought it was *him*—they looked so similar—but I knew it couldn't be, because Barrons and I had killed him. Then I thought he must not have been a singularity. Some of the Unseelie castes have countless numbers, like the Rhino-boys, while others are the only of their kind given dark birth by the Unseelie King, perhaps because even *he* considered them abominations. I had a bad moment, contemplating the horror of hundreds or even thousands of this type of Unseelie loose on the world, and in that moment I forfeited the element of surprise. I must have made some small sound, because she suddenly turned, nine feet of leprous body topped by a long, squished face that was all ravenous mouth. In a blink of an eye, she assessed and dismissed me.

I was the wrong gender.

Dani got kudos for trying. She freeze-framed, but I could have told her not to bother. This one sifted. I knew because its male counterpart had once sifted down a street at me and, if not for Barrons, would have killed me.

The Unseelie vanished into thin air, leaving Dani standing a block down the street from me, sword drawn back, seething at having lost her kill. "What the feck was that, Mac?" she said. "I never seen one before. You?"

"Barrons called it the Gray Man. We killed it. I

thought it was one of a kind, but we just saw the Gray *Woman*."

"What's her specialty?" Dani looked morbidly fascinated. I'd been that way once. Obsessed with all the terrible ways I might die at an Unseelie's hands. Or claws. Or hundreds of sharp-toothed mouths, like Alina.

"They have a taste for human beauty. Barrons says they destroy what they can never have, devour it like a delicacy. They cast a glamour of physical perfection and choose the most attractive humans to seduce. They feed off them through touch, leeching their beauty through the open sores in their hands until they've stolen all there is to steal, leaving their prey as hideous as they are."

They didn't kill their victims but left them alive to suffer, and sometimes returned to visit them, drawing some sick sustenance from their horror and misery. I'd watched the Gray Man feed twice. He'd been especially terrifying to me because, for years, I'd shamelessly used my looks to my advantage, flirting for better tips, batting my eyelashes at a traffic cop, feigning sultry-blond stupidity to get my way. Before I'd come to Dublin, I thought my looks were pretty much the only power I had, and losing them would have made me feel worthless.

"Barrons says the victims inevitably commit suicide," I told her, "because they can't face living, looking like they do."

"We'll bag the bitch," Dani said coolly.

I smiled, but it faded quickly. We'd arrived at our destination, and I stared, spirits sinking. I wanted answers and I'd been counting heavily on getting some here, but 939 Rêvemal was a complete disappointment.

A few months ago, Chester's elegant granite, marble, and polished-wood façade would have drawn the upper crust of the city's bored rich and jaded beautiful, but, like the rest of Dublin, it had been brought to its knees on Halloween, and the once-sophisticated three-story building was a wreck. Stained-glass windows crunched beneath our boots as we skirted riot debris. Marble entry pillars were deeply scored by gash marks that looked as if they'd been made by something with talons of steel. Lavish French-style gas lamps had been ripped from the sidewalk and tossed in a twisted pile, blocking the club's entrance, as if whatever Unseelie was responsible had held some special hatred for the place.

The club sign dangled by cables in front of the pile. It had been smashed to bits. The front and sides of the building were heavily covered with graffiti. Between the lamps and the club sign, there was no getting into the building through the front door.

And no reason to.

Chester's was as deserted as the rest of the city.

I punched my palm with a gloved fist. I was sick of dead ends and nonanswers. "Let's go hunt the Gray Woman. She's got to be around here somewhere," I growled.

"Why?" Dani looked at me blankly.

"Because I'm frustrated and pissed off, that's why."

"But I ain't ever been in a club," she protested. "I even dressed for it."

"That isn't a club, Dani. It's a destroyed building."

"There's all kinds of stuff happening here!"

"Like what? Shades having a party inside all that rubble?"

She laughed. "Aw, man, I forget you're deaf! You can't hear the music. It's got a cool beat, different from most I've heard. I been listening to it for blocks now. Down, Mac. We gotta go down."

Dani was right: The music *was* different. But as I would soon find out, it wasn't the only thing different about Chester's. In fact, nothing was normal. The club would shift all my paradigms and slam home the many changes the world had gone through while I'd been otherwise . . . occupied.

The entrance to the club was now around back: an inconspicuous battered metal door in the ground that looked like a forgotten cellar entry. If Dani hadn't been able to hear the music, I would have walked right past the place and never suspected a thing.

The door creaked as it opened on a narrow black maw. I sighed. I hate being underground, but somehow I keep ending up there. I unhooked the MacHalo from my pack, punched on all the lights, and strapped it on my head. Dani did the same, and we descended the ladder in a blaze of light, opened a second trapdoor, and descended a second ladder. We found ourselves in the middle of an industrial foyer of sorts—tastefully decorated in the height of urban chic—facing tall double doors.

I still couldn't hear any music. The doors had to be seriously thick. I flexed the *sidhe*-seer place in my head, wishing I had some idea what to expect, but the channel was still full of static, just louder.

Dani slanted me a narrow-eyed look. "Don't you kinda think there'd be guards or something?"

"I think making it through the Dublin night alive and figuring out where this place is might be all the guards it needs," I said dryly. I shoved at the door. It didn't budge. "That and getting the door open." I slipped off my MacHalo and strapped it, still blazing, onto my pack. I tousled my hair to get rid of hat-head.

Dani joined me, and together we shoved open the door and got our first look at Chester's.

I love you so much you must kill me now . . .

The music was so loud, the bass vibrated my bones. They were playing Marilyn Manson's "If I Was Your Vampire," but it had been rerecorded to a completely different beat—a little dreamier, a little darker, a thing I wouldn't have thought possible.

I stood in the doorway and stared.

Here was the new Temple Bar. Gone underground.

Chester's: slick, chic, the height of urban sophistication married to industrial muscle. Chrome and glass, black and white. Coolly erotic, basely sexual. Manhattan posh wed to Irish mob.

Everything's black, no turning back . . .

The place was huge, the tables packed. The tiered dance floors were crammed with hot bodies. It was standing room only. I was astonished to see that so many humans had survived and were still in Dublin—partying, at that. Under other circumstances, it might have been a pleasant surprise.

These so weren't other circumstances.

Dani grabbed my arm. It would bruise. "Un-fecking-real," she breathed.

I nodded. I'm a *sidhe*-seer. To me, things are simple: There are two races—human and Fae. I work with V'lane because I have to in order to save my people. I'll work with the Queen of the Fae for the same reason. But it's programmed into my genes, coded into my blood, that these two races were always intended to live separately, and it's my job to keep things that way.

Chester's was a *sidhe*-seer's nightmare.

It was crammed with Fae and humans—mingling.

No, it was worse than that. They were socializing.

Oh, who was I kidding? Young, attractive humans by the dozens were flirting outrageously with Unseelie. On one of the dance floors, half a dozen girls were licking a Rhino-boy's sharp yellowed tusks with pretty pink tongues. His beady eyes gleamed; he was grunting like a pig and stamping a hoof.

On another dance floor, a blonde had pulled up her shirt and was rubbing her bare breasts against a tall, dark, faceless Fae, while two other women tried to push her away so they could have their turn.

In a booth, a shirtless male waiter, showcasing his chiseled abs with heavily oiled skin, was caressing the . . . uh . . . udders of a thing I'd never seen before and hoped I wouldn't again.

Beside me, Dani stiffened. "Ew. Just *ew*! That's disgusting." She made a gagging noise in the back of her throat. Then she snickered. "Sure gives a

whole new meaning to the phrase 'I gave her the finger,' don't it?"

"What? Where?"

She pointed.

A woman was sucking erotically on the tip of a
Rhino-boy's stumpy finger—which he'd given to
her by cutting it off his hand.

I inhaled sharply, as the reality of what was going
on here smacked me between the eyes. Humans
weren't just cozying up to the newest exotic big-bad
because it was something different and exciting.

As Dani had feared, Unseelie were the new vamps.

My generation has an incurable, bottomless obsession with the undead. The heavily romanticized
version, of course: the defanged fangbanger, not the
real deal, which is *really* dead and *really* kills you.

As I watched, the woman bit down hard and
began chewing with an expression of near-religious
ecstasy.

These humans were eating Unseelie—not to fight
them off and reclaim our world, but for the rush
of it.

Unseelie flesh—the new drug.

"They're trading sex for the high," I said flatly.

"Looks like," Dani said. "Let's just hope those
skanks can't get knocked up."

The thought was too awful to contemplate.

A young Goth-girl with feverishly bright eyes approached. "You better hurry! The song's almost
over!"

"So?" Dani said.

Goth-girl looked her up and down. "Not a bad

idea. Gangly and awkward might just intrigue. They like experimenting."

I didn't have to look at Dani to know her hand had gone inside her long coat to her sword. "Easy, Dani," I said softly. "You're not."

But the girl was already going on, vapidly intense. "You two must be new. They play it once a night, and while it's playing you can try to persuade one of them to choose you. Otherwise, you aren't allowed to approach them. Competition's fierce. It can take weeks to get one to notice you."

"Choose you for what?" I encouraged.

"Where've you been all this time? To make you immortal like them. If you eat enough sanctified flesh, you become immortal, too. Then you get to go to Faery with them!"

I narrowed my eyes. Did eating Unseelie really change you? Or were the dark Fae capitalizing on a lie? I was inclined to believe the latter. Mallucé had eaten it constantly, long-term, and had never become immortal. "How much is enough?" I fished.

She shrugged. "I don't know. Nobody knows yet. It keeps wearing off. But we will. I've had it four times! It's incredible! And the sex—OMG! *See you in Faery*," she chirped brightly, and dashed off, and I didn't have to hear anyone else say it—although I would hear it so many times over the next few months that I'd want to kill somebody—to realize I'd just heard one of the many strange new buzz phrases in this strange new world.

"This is worse than an IFP," Dani muttered. "I feel like I'm stuck in an IFCF."

I raised a brow.

"Interdimensional Fairy Cluster Fuck," she said sourly. "Don't they see what's happening? Don't they know the Unseelie are destroying our world? Don't they see we're gonna die out if we don't stop them?"

Apparently they didn't care. I needed a drink. Badly. Pushing through the crowd, I headed for the bar.

16

A heavily industrialized version of Trent Reznor's "Closer" was playing by the time I grabbed a bar stool and barked at the bartender's back that I needed a shot of top-shelf whiskey and make it fast.

I want to feel you from the inside . . .

Due to recent experience, I had a far greater understanding of the darker half of the Fae race than I'd ever wanted. I knew the emptiness that drove them. I'd been food for their bottomless hunger.

Chester's was full of the Unseelie King's abominations, and humans were welcoming them, competing to get noticed by them, willing to let them "feel them from the inside" if that was what it took to get their fix, seduced by the promise of heightened strength and senses and the temptation of immortality. I'd never understood why anyone would want to live forever. It had always seemed to me that death lent life a certain poignancy, a necessary tension.

"Maybe two billion of us *needed* to die," I muttered. I was in a foul mood.

"I'll take one, too." Dani hoisted herself onto a stool beside me.

"Nice try."

"You ever gonna let me grow up? Or you gonna be like everybody else?"

I looked at her, then amended my original order to two shots of Macallan, one-hundred-proof. Daddy had done the same thing to me at her age. Tough love.

Shot glasses clinked on the polished chrome bar top, accompanied by a deep "Hey, beautiful girl."

My gaze jerked to the bartender and I did a double take. It was the dreamy-eyed boy that I'd first met while scouring a museum for OOPs and had later been surprised to find working with Christian at Trinity College's ALD, the Ancient Languages Department. My first impulse was pleasure that he'd survived. It was squelched by suspicion. Coincidences make me nervous.

"Small world," I said coolly.

"Big enough." He flashed an easy smile. "Most of the time."

"New job?"

"City changes. Jobs, too. You?"

"Unemployed. Nobody buying books." They were all out hunting one.

"Different look. Going dark, beautiful girl?"

I touched my hair.

"More than the 'do."

"Enough to survive."

"Hard to say when enough's enough."

"Look who's working where."

"Look who's drinking where."

"I can handle myself. You?"

"Always." He gave me another of those smiles and moved down the bar, tossing glasses, pouring high, fast, and flashy.

Beside me, Dani choked, spit, wheezed, and began to cough uncontrollably. When I patted her back, she jerked away and skewered me with a glare. "What are you trying to do? Kill me?" she squeaked, when she could speak. "That's petrol! Who would wanna drink that?"

I laughed. "You develop a taste for it."

"I think I mighta been born with all the tastes I need!" She pilfered a handful of cherries from across the bar, crammed them in her mouth, and hopped down from her stool. "Grown-ups are weird," she said darkly.

"Where do you think you're going?"

"Take a look around."

I didn't like the idea and told her so.

"C'mon, Mac, I'm superfast and superstrong. Nobody can touch me. I'm the one should be worried about leaving *you* alone, slowpoke."

Put that way, she had a point.

"Gimme room to breathe, Mac."

She was fidgeting from foot to foot, and the look in her eyes said she was about to whiz off whether I said okay or not. I had a sudden unwanted understanding of Rowena: How do you mother a kid who's faster than you, stronger than you, and quite possibly smarter? "Don't go far, and not for long, deal?"

"Deal."

"And be careful!" Wind ruffled my hair. She was already gone.

"Who's the kid?" The dreamy-eyed boy was back. A shot clinked to the chrome counter. I tossed it back, grimaced, gasped. Fire exploded in my gut.

"Friend."

"Good to have in times like these."

"How'd you find this place?"

"Same way as you, I imagine."

"Doubt it."

"Ever find Christian?"

He was referring to the day I'd called the ALD dozens of times, hunting for the young Scot. I'd been worried sick because Barrons had "Voiced" me into revealing that the Keltars were spying on him, and I was afraid Barrons was going to hunt Christian down and hurt him. "Yes." I didn't see any point in telling him I'd lost him again, perhaps permanently.

"Seen him lately?"

"No. You?"

"No. I'd like to."

"Why?" Suspicion was me.

"Friends—good to have in times like these."

"What do you think of this place?" Why was he here? Another pretty boy in search of immortality?

"Life and death, beautiful girl. Been about it since the beginning. Will be 'til the end."

"What's your poison? You want to live forever, too?"

"I'd take some peace and quiet. A beautiful girl." He laughed. "A good book."

"Man after my own heart. I love a good book, too." In the mirror above the bar, something caught my eye. I tensed. In a booth behind me, the Gray

Woman was holding hands with the well-muscled, gorgeous waiter who'd earlier been flirting with the udder-thing. I could see both what she was and what she was making him see. To him, she was a Fae Princess, inhumanly beautiful, mind-numbingly sexual, gazing at him with rapt adoration.

Only I could see the open, oozing lesions with which she caressed him, with which she was sucking his life away, leaving rotting teeth, rheumy eyes, parchment-thin gray skin. She was making short work of him. He wouldn't last the hour.

My hand went to the shoulder holster beneath my coat.

"Watch yourself, beautiful girl," the dreamy-eyed boy said softly.

I tore my gaze away from the mirror and stared at him. He was eyeing my coat, watching my hand move beneath it. He couldn't possibly know what I was reaching for.

"What are you talking about?"

He looked behind me. "They're here, and . . . well, you'll figure it out."

Big hands bit down on my shoulders. There were two men behind me. I could feel them. Big, electric, powerful men.

"Pull that thing out," a man growled, "we'll take it from you and never give it back. First rule of house: This is neutral ground. Second rule of house: Break a rule, you die."

"Get your hands off me," I gritted.

"We have the kid. You want to see her again, get up."

My eyes narrowed. *How* had they gotten Dani? "There's no way you—"

"We're faster."

"Like Barrons?"

There was no answer.

Well, I'd found my eight, or at least two of them. And they had Dani. Sighing, I stood and glared up at the Gray Woman in the mirror, but she didn't notice, too busy serving herself off her waiter's well-muscled platter. My blood boiled. He was no longer remotely good-looking. Barrons had told me the Gray Man rarely took so much that his victims died. Apparently the Gray Woman had larger appetites. I revised my estimate: He had another ten minutes, at most.

The dreamy-eyed boy was reflected in the mirror below them. I stared. He didn't look the same in the mirror. He was . . . blurred around the edges and . . . wrong, very wrong. I shivered, struck by a soul-deep chill. I tried to bring his reflection into focus. The harder I tried, the blurrier he became. The blurred shape cleared, gave me a sharp look. "Don't talk to it, beautiful girl. Never talk to it."

I gaped. "*Her*, you mean? The Gray Woman?"

"It." He spat the word with such revulsion that I flinched.

I looked down from the mirror at the real thing, not the reflection, and suddenly I could breathe again. He was a boy. A handsome, dreamy-eyed boy. Not something I wanted to run screaming from. "What 'it'?"

He stared at me blankly. "I didn't say anything."

"Now," the man behind me growled impatiently. "Move."

They escorted me up a wide chrome staircase, to the top floor of Chester's. Behind a chrome balustrade, dark-glass walls lined the entire circumference of the upper floor, smooth, without doors or handles.

I glanced from one of my escorts to the other. They hadn't spoken a word since they'd closed their hands around my upper arms and begun steering me through the crowd. Nor had I. I could feel what they were made of: leashed violence. Both looked to be in their early thirties, heavily muscled. The man on my left had hands that were badly scarred. They were massive men. There was something about their eyes that made me decide keeping my mouth shut until I had a better understanding of my situation was the wisest course of action.

I glanced down as we topped the open-tread stairs. The waiter was on the floor, dead. The Gray Woman was already looking around for a new toy. My hands fisted. We walked along the wall of darkened glass until an indefinable characteristic in the featureless surface must have indicated a door, because the man on my right placed his palm to the glass. A panel slid aside, revealing a large room constructed entirely of two-way glass, cornered by metal girders. You could see everything going on outside it. The perimeter of the ceiling was lined with small screens fed by countless security cameras. Here were the guts of the club. Nothing happened anywhere in Chester's that wasn't seen here.

"Brought her like you said, Ry."

They pushed me inside. The panel slid closed behind me with a soft hiss. The room was dark but for the glow of LCD panels. I took a step to catch my balance. For a moment I thought I was falling, but it was an illusion created by the floor, which was also made of two-way glass. It was so dim in the room that all I could see were outlines: a desk, a few chairs, a table, and a man standing across the room, his back to me. Everything beneath the room, however, was clearly visible. It made each step feel like a leap of faith.

"Glass houses, huh, Ryodan?" The first time I'd ever called *IYCGM* on my cell phone, Ryodan had berated me, told me people who lived in glass houses shouldn't throw stones, implying my goals were no loftier than Barrons'. Now here he stood, surveying his world from inside one. Did he consider his own goals so pristine? I narrowed my eyes. There was another room beyond the one in which we stood, even darker. Whatever lurked in its shadows, he was watching it intently.

After a moment he said, without turning, "Why did you come, Mac?"

"Why are you feeding humans to the Unseelie?"

"There is no force at my club. Only desire. Mutual."

"They don't understand what they're doing."

"Not my problem."

"They're dying. Somebody needs to wake them up to reality."

"They're in love with dying."

"They're misguided, confused."

"Not my problem."

"You could do something about it!"

"So I should?" he said. "Does that seem a friendly crowd down there to you? It trembles on the verge of another riot, yet you would have me play moral adviser. Men have been crucified for less. I've seen enough train wrecks to know when the rails are locked and the brakes have failed. It's all train wrecks down there, Mac. Only one thing holds my interest now. Potential. Barrons thinks you have it."

His tone made it plain. "But you don't," I said flatly.

"You worry me."

"You worry me, too." I took a few more steps into the room. I wanted a better look at him. I wanted to know what he was watching. Like Barrons and my escorts, Ryodan was tall, well built. I wondered if it was a requirement to be whatever they were: no wimps allowed. He wore dark pants and a crisp white shirt, sleeves rolled up on thickly muscled forearms. A silver cuff, identical to Barrons', glinted at his wrist.

"Everyone seems to think you're the solution, don't they?" he said.

I shrugged. "Not everybody." Rowena didn't.

"Has it occurred to you that you might be the problem?"

"What do you mean?"

"Why do you think you keep having so many brushes with the Book, when everyone else who's searching for it never gets a glimpse of it? Even Darroc, your illustrious master, can't get close to it. Word is it's been taking its own—Unseelie—

chewing them up and spitting them out. But nobody who really wants it can find it. Except you."

"I'm an OOP detector," I reminded him. "I'm the only one who can sense it. There's potential for you."

"Indeed. Potential for what? Has it occurred to you that perhaps you don't keep finding the Book— *it* keeps finding you?"

"What are you saying?"

"What do you think the Book wants, Mac?"

"How should I know? Death. Destruction. Chaos. Same as the rest of the Unseelie."

"What would you want if you were a book?"

"I'm different, and that's easy. I'd want to *not* be a book."

"Maybe you're not so different. Maybe it wants also to not be a book."

"It has other forms. It's the Beast, too."

"Has the Beast ever harmed anyone? Don't you think it would if it could? Isn't that its nature?"

I studied his back, pondered his words. "You're saying the Beast is only glamour. That like any Fae, it creates illusion."

"What if its only true form is a book? One that can't walk, or talk, or move, or do anything on its own?"

"Are you saying you think it takes people over just to have a body?"

He glanced up at the LCD screens above his head. "I don't know what I think. I consider everything. You watch them long enough, you see what they want. Unseelie hunger, like starved prisoners, for whatever it is the Unseelie King brought them into existence lacking. What if the Book is after corporeality? A movable form it can use with autonomy? A body it can keep and control? A life of its own?"

"Then why would it kill the people it takes?"

"Maybe it doesn't. Maybe, like dolls, they break. Or maybe some part of them manages to regain control for a few moments and stop what the Book is doing to them the only way they can. Or maybe it's biding time, waiting for just the right moment. Maybe it has the Fae ability of prognosticating possibles, delicately shaping events to achieve certain ends. Has the Book ever spoken to you?"

"Yes."

"Barrons said it called you by name."

I'd never told him that. He must have heard it speak to me that night. I'd thought it spoke only in my head. "So? I don't know how it knew my name." He liked the "maybe" game. I could play it, too. "Maybe it knows everybody's. I don't know what you're getting at, but the Book repels me. I can barely get close to it. I'm too good and it's too evil."

"Really." He could not have said it more dryly.

"What do you mean, 'really'?" I said defensively.

"Good and evil are merely opposite sides of a coin, Mac. Get tossed in the air enough, it's easy to come down on the wrong side. Maybe the Book knows something about you that makes you different. Makes it want you. Makes it think if you flipped sides, you'd be worth more to it than any of the rest of us."

What he was saying didn't make sense. And it was creeping me out. "Like what? And if that was the case, then why wouldn't it have taken me already? It's had plenty of chances."

"Darroc bided his time, waiting for the perfect moment. Maybe you're not primed to flip yet. Eternal life breeds eternal patience. If you lived long enough, you might feel that if today amuses, today is good. All sense of right or wrong, all morality, all value, might cease to exist."

With the exception of two compartments to hold everything: stasis and change—the classic Fae attitude. Of course, immortality *would* do that. "So you think the Book is amusing itself, waiting for the right moment to pounce? Wake up. There's never going to be a right moment for it to pounce on me."

"Arrogance, like anger, is often a fatal flaw."

"Darroc lost me. He didn't get what he wanted. I'm still standing. And I'm still fighting. And I will *never* flip sides," I said coldly.

"You're still standing because of that one, Mac." He nodded at the room he was staring into. "Don't forget it. Never seen anything like her, and I've seen a lot."

I moved to stand beside him, peered into the room. Up close, I could discern shapes. Dani was in the middle of four men, spinning ceaselessly, sword up, snarling.

"You hurt her, I'll kill you," I told him. No matter that he was a foot taller than me and twice my mass.

"She said the same about you."

Suddenly Dani went into hyperspeed, then they all disappeared, and then there was Dani again, surrounded by four men.

"She hasn't stopped trying to get out since I put her in there. I wonder how long she could survive."

Not very long without food, but I wasn't about to tell him that. I looked up at him.

He turned his face to mine, looked down. Handsome, chilling man. His eyes were the clearest I'd ever seen. This was a man that suffered no conflicts with himself. He had no problems being what he was.

We stared at each other. "Black looks good on you," he murmured. "Has Barrons seen you like this?"

"Eternal patience," I murmured back. His tie was loosened, and in the open collar of his white shirt his neck was a skein of scars, with a long, wicked-looking one stretching up the left side from shoulder to ear. I didn't need a nurse to tell me he'd healed from a wound, long ago, that would have killed most men. How long ago? "Does today amuse, Ryodan?"

His lips curved. He looked back at Dani and, after a moment, nodded. "It does. More than it has in recent . . . years."

"She's thirteen."

"Time will remedy that."

"You worry me, Ryodan."

"Back at you. Bit of advice, Mac. Life's an ocean, full of waves. All are dangerous. All can drown you. Under the right circumstances, even the gentlest swell can turn tidal. Hopping waves is for the weekend warrior. Choose one, ride it out. It increases your odds of survival." He watched Dani for a moment, then said, "There are rules in my house."

"Your buddies already told me the first two. Neutral ground. Break a rule you die."

"No killing Fae inside my club. In my walls means under my protection."

"I just watched one of your *protected* Fae kill a human."

"If they're stupid enough to be here, they're stupid enough to die."

"Does that mean I can kill humans, too?" I said sweetly. There were two in particular who had just caught my eye. Derek O'Bannion, the younger brother of the Irish mobster I'd killed after I stole the Spear of Destiny from him, and current right-hand man to the Lord Master, was crossing the dance floor beneath my feet. Accompanying him was Fiona, the woman who used to run Barrons Books and Baubles, until she'd tried to kill me; then Barrons had fired her.

Now I just needed the LM himself and a few Unseelie Princes to have all my enemies in the same place.

"Special rules for you, Mac. You don't get to kill anything in my club, Fae or human. Your fight is outside these walls. And if Barrons' belief in you is unfounded, there won't be anyplace you can hide. Every last one of us will come after you."

I didn't dignify his threat with a response.

He knocked on the glass and made a gesture with his left hand. Three of the men disappeared. Dani blinked out. Then suddenly there she was again, and one of *his* men had her sword pointed at her throat.

"If you ever come into my club carrying again, we'll take your weapons and never give them back. Clear?"

"As the floor beneath my feet."

17

I felt like the Queen of Standoffs, hostility and tension everywhere I turned. Always venturing, never gaining.

Last night I'd realized I wasn't the only one with trust issues. None of the players on Dublin's board trusted anyone else. I'd made the mistake of assuming—since Barrons had chosen Ryodan to be my backup support—that when I went to see him he would be, well, supportive.

Not only wasn't he, he'd impugned my motives at the deepest level, questioning my fundamental character. He'd made it out like the Book might be after *me,* drawn by something kindred. I was about as far from evil as the North Pole was from the South. "Throwing stones, my ass," I muttered. There he'd stood in his glass house, letting Unseelie prey on humans, and he accused *me* of having moral issues.

I was in a horrible mood. Dani and I had pretty much slunk back to "our" house after getting tossed out of Chester's by four of Ryodan's "men."

Dani's eyes had been feverishly bright and she'd been spitting fury, but, beneath the pale-faced bravado, I'd glimpsed fear. I understood. Just when I thought I'd finally become a halfway decent power on the board, traded my pawn in for a rook or a knight, some king or queen came along to remind me how ineffectual I was.

I was getting damned sick of it.

I'd lie awake on the couch—sleeping in a stranger's bed had seemed weird—stewing, until nearly dawn. Then I slept like the dead for a few hours and woke to feel the wind ruffling my hair as Dani paced: *zing-zing, zing-zing.*

I swung my legs over the edge of the couch and sat up, eyeing the blur. Although being at the abbey had been bad for Dani in many ways, Rowena and the girls had kept the gifted teen occupied constantly. She had too much energy, intelligence, and angst to leave to her own devices for long.

When I asked her to go spy at the abbey, to find out when Rowena planned to send the girls in to scout Dublin, she looked relieved at the prospect of something to do.

"Nobody'll even know I'm there," she promised, grabbing her sword and coat and slinging her backpack over a shoulder. "When do you want me back?"

"Just make sure it's before dark."

After she left, I contemplated the fireplace morosely. The house we were squatting in, like the rest of Dublin—except for Chester's, which I assumed was powered by an entire room of underground generators—had no electricity or gas. Not only was it dark, it was freezing. And—of course—it was raining outside. I tugged the comforter that I'd pilfered from the bedroom more snugly around my shoulders and sat, teeth chattering. I'd have given my eyeteeth for a cup of coffee. Where was V'lane when I needed him? I considered the pile of logs and tried to decide where the prior owner might have stashed matches.

I heard the kitchen door open. "What did you forget, Dani?" I called.

A silhouette stepped into the doorway between the kitchen and living room. "I had begun to think the child would never leave," said a deep, musical voice.

I don't have Dani's hyperspeed—but I achieved something close to it. One moment I was sitting on the couch feeling sorry for myself, the next I was plastered back against the far wall, spear drawn.

In that moment, I faced a harsh truth: I might have a serious hate on, I might even be stronger than I'd ever been before, but I still wasn't strong *enough*.

I still needed allies.

I still needed Barrons' tattoo, and I still needed V'lane's name on my tongue, even though neither could be completely relied upon. I needed Jayne and his men, and I needed the *sidhe*-seers. And I hated needing anyone.

"Brought you coffee, MacKayla," said the Lord Master, stepping into the room. "I hear you like it strong and sweet, with a lot of cream."

"Where'd you hear that?" I was shaking. I bit my tongue hard enough to draw blood, focused on the pain, and stopped shaking.

"Alina. She talked about you a great deal. But she pretended you were her friend, not her sister. She hid you from me. Think about that when you remember her. Why did she conceal your existence unless she sensed, from the very beginning, something about me was not to be trusted? But she chose me anyway. Loved me anyway."

"She didn't love you. And you're lying. You must have found her journal and read it."

"And she wrote in her journal how you took your coffee? Pitiful rationale, MacKayla."

"You took a lucky guess. Get out of my house." I eyed my gun, which was lying on the floor next to the couch. I should have grabbed it, too, but his voice had sent me flying off the sofa, all instinct and no intellect. The only reason I had the spear was because it had been on my lap when he walked in. Although the Lord Master had once been Fae, the Seelie Queen had punished him by turning him mortal. He was now merely human, pumped up on Unseelie. Could I kill him with a gun? I was more than willing to try. I doubted he'd let me get close enough with the spear. I was surprised he'd come this close without a sifting Fae standing next to him.

"Sit down and drink your coffee. And put that spear away." He glanced at the fireplace, murmured a few words, and flames leapt from the cold logs.

"How did you do that? You're not Fae."

"Fae isn't the only game in town. Your illustrious benefactor taught me well."

"V'lane?" I said.

"No."

Something inside me went very still. "Barrons?"

"He taught me many things. Including Voice. *Kneel.*"

"Kiss my ass."

"I said *kneel before me now.*"

I sucked in a sharp breath. Layered voices resonated around the room, pushing at me, trying to invade my mind, make his will mine. It was Voice as strong as Barrons had once used on me.

I smiled. It was an annoyance, nothing more. It looked like I'd found that place inside me that Barrons had sent me hunting for, where I had the strength to resist Voice. Too bad I still didn't understand what it was. I had no idea how to *use* Voice, but it no longer worked on me. I was free. It was another of the things that had changed in me. One more power. "No," I said. I took a step toward the couch and my gun.

"Look out the window." It was a warning. "Touch that gun, they sift."

I looked, and jerked. "Dani."

"She's almost as impressive as you. If she could sense the Book, I wouldn't need you. But she can't and I do, so you and I are going to come to terms, one way or another. Sit, sheathe the spear, forget anything so stupid as shooting me, and listen."

I would never have obeyed, but beyond the window, out in that cold, rainy day, two Unseelie Princes were holding Dani between them.

Her cheeks were running with blood, and she was shivering violently. She wasn't cold. She wasn't even getting rained on. I guessed the UPs didn't like being wet. She was shivering with heat. Lust. The destroying kind.

Her sword gleamed alabaster, forgotten in a muddy puddle on the dirt lawn. I knew they couldn't possibly have touched it. Somehow they'd made her throw it away, same as the LM had done to me.

I was seriously beginning to think I'd gotten the short end of the stick. That all *sidhe*-seers had. What good were we, with all our limitations? We just kept getting shoved around.

I pushed a chair in front of the window so I could keep a constant eye on her. I had no idea what I'd do if the princes did anything other than restrain her as they were now, but I'd do *something*. They were in static form, clothed. They'd better stay that way. I was looking at two of the princes who'd turned me inside out. Who'd very nearly taken my soul from me. One day I would kill them, if it was the last thing I did. I was wise enough to know today was not that day. "Talk," I said tightly.

He did. I sipped my coffee—irritatingly, it was good—while the Lord Master told me a story about being thrown out of Faery for defying the queen, for attempting to return their race to the Old Ways when the Fae had been worshipped as the gods they were, instead of living like sheep alongside puny mortals.

He told me how she'd stripped him of his Fae essence and turned him mortal, about finding himself alone in our world, human and fragile. He'd been cast naked, unarmed, and without human currency into the middle of Manhattan, in a subway station. He'd barely survived those first few minutes, had been attacked by a group of mocking, cruel humans wearing leather and chains, sporting shaved heads and hammering fists.

He told me how for a time he'd been out of his mind, horrified by a body that felt pain, that *needed* to eat, drink, and make waste, how he'd discovered germs and been terrified of death after so many hundreds of thousands of years of not even being able to comprehend it. He'd wandered with no place to rest, no money or understanding of how to care for his finite, weak shape that required so many things and caused so much misery. He—a god—was reduced to scavenging through human trash for sustenance to keep his body alive. He'd had to kill to seize clothing, had to scrounge like an animal. He'd studied his new environment, determined to find a better way to survive so he could then do *better* than merely survive.

He wanted revenge.

"You see," he said, "you and I aren't so different, are we? Both after the same thing. You, however, are misguided."

"And you aren't?" I snorted. "Give me a break."

He laughed. "Perspective, MacKayla. Yours is skewed." Bit by bit, he told me, he'd clawed his way from the bottom.

When he'd finally learned to satisfy his base requirements, he made a startling discovery: His new form felt more than mere need. The ennui and dispassion of immortality began to melt away. The fear of death awakened unexpected facets of his nature. Emotion stirred in him sensations that being Fae never had and never could. Madness was replaced for a time by sheer lust, but finally his head had cleared. His existence under control, he began to seek power on the human plane, pursuing his agenda.

Fae knowledge and hundreds of thousands of years of existing had given him a distinct advantage. He knew where to look for the things he wanted and how to use them when he found them.

He'd discovered two of the Silvers at an auction house in London, risked Cruce's terrible curse, and found his way into Unseelie, where he'd made a pact with the mercenary Hunters to help him regain what was rightfully his and had been wrongfully taken from him: his essential Fae nature.

He trained with a warlock in London, from whom he stole precious copies of pages torn from the *Sinsar Dubh*, which he'd then traded to Barrons in exchange for a crash course in the Druid arts at which Darroc had excelled, gifted as he was with Fae intellect and understanding of the cosmos.

"Why didn't Barrons just take the pages from you?"

"We pursued a common agenda for a time. He doesn't kill anyone he thinks might prove useful in the future."

Mercenary to the core. Sounded like the man I knew. "What is he?"

"Consider instead what he is not. He is *not* the one that hunted me down for what I did to you. Doesn't that tell you enough, MacKayla? You are a tool to him. His tool works again. He is satisfied."

"How did pages get torn from the *Sinsar Dubh*?" I

changed the subject swiftly. If I ignored the knife he'd just driven through my heart, maybe it would go away.

He shrugged. He had no idea. They'd served their purpose. Now he needed the real thing. He'd continued collecting power wherever it could be found. The Hunters taught him to eat lesser Unseelie, to protect his fragile mortal existence.

"Why would they help you?"

"I promised them freedom. And I gave it to them." He was an Unseelie hero, he told me, and soon the Seelie would recognize him as such, too. Yes, he had disobeyed his queen. So had many others, who'd never been punished so harshly. Had the crime he'd committed merited a death sentence? There were other Seelie who felt as he did, who wanted a return to the Old Ways. His only crime had been trying to bring about what many of them secretly longed for. He should have been rewarded for standing up for his brethren. Even humans resisted doling out such a horrific punishment, and their blink-of-an-eye lives were so comically short they were worthless. He'd lost *eternity*, for a single broken rule. He wanted it back. Was that so wrong?

I made a hand gesture when he paused.

"I have not seen that one before," he said.

"Miniature record player, playing 'My Heart Bleeds for You.' I should care about this why? You made me *Pri-ya*." I narrowed my eyes, studying him. Had he been the fourth? Had this monster touched me?

"*You* made you *Pri-ya*. I gave you other options. You refused them."

"Do you really think the Unseelie will continue to obey you now that they're no longer imprisoned?"

"I freed them. *I* am their king now."

"So, what's keeping one of them from killing you and going after the Book, himself?"

"They're too drunk on freedom to see beyond the moment. They feast. They fuck. They don't think."

"You never know. One of them might snap out of it. Rulers get toppled all the time. Look at what you were trying to do to your queen."

"I have Cruce's amulet. They fear it."

"How long do you expect that to last? You're not even Fae."

"I will be again, as soon as I get the Book."

"Assuming one of them doesn't kill you first."

He waved a dismissive hand. "The Unseelie do not wish to rule. After an eternity in hell they wish only to be free to indulge their hungers." His face went hard and cold as marble. "But I will not explain my race to a mere human."

At that moment, I could clearly see the icy, imperious Fae he'd once been and would be again, given half a chance. He claimed to have been changed by his experience with mortality. If, indeed he had—and there was plenty of doubt in my mind on that score—I could too easily see him changing back, in a heartbeat. "You're pretty 'mere' yourself right now, bud. Cannibalizing your own race. I've heard the Seelie court has a special, horrific punishment for that."

"Then you'd better hope they don't find out about you, MacKayla," he said coolly.

We stared at each other a long moment, then he

tossed his long hair and flashed me a smile meant to charm. In another time and place, had I not known who and what he was, it probably would have worked. He was a beautiful, cultured, powerful man, and the jagged scar on his face made him all the more intriguing. I imagined Alina must have found him utterly fascinating when they'd first met. There wasn't anything remotely like him in Ashford, Georgia.

As if he'd somehow picked up on my thoughts of her, he said, "I came to Dublin because I learned the *Sinsar Dubh* had been sighted in the city. That was when I met your sister."

I went still inside. I wanted to hear about Alina, even if it came from him. I was starved to know about my sister's last days.

"How did you meet?"

He'd walked into a pub where she was sitting with friends. She looked up, and he felt as if everyone else in the bar had melted away, just vanished into the background, leaving only him and her. She'd later told him she felt the same thing.

They'd spent the afternoon together. And the night. And the next and the next. They'd been inseparable. He discovered she wasn't like other humans, that she, too, was struggling with a new state of being she didn't understand and had no idea how to handle. They learned together. He'd found an ally in his quest for the Book, in his quest to restore his Fae nature. They'd been fated for each other.

"You lied to her. You pretended you were a *sidhe-seer*," I accused. "She'd never have helped you otherwise."

"So you say. I think she might have. But she was skittish, and I was unwilling to take chances. She made me feel things I did not understand. I made her feel things she'd longed for all her life. I set her free. The way she laughed." He paused, and a faint smile curved his mouth. "When she laughed, people would turn to stare. It was so . . . Humans have a word. Joy. Your sister knew it."

I hated him for having heard her laugh, for knowing she knew joy, for ever having touched her, this monster who'd arranged to have me raped, body and soul, and my eyes must have burned with it, because his smile faded.

"I told you the truth. I did not kill her, which means someone else walking around out there did. You are so certain I'm the villain. What if your real villain is closer to you than you think?"

"I'm going to bottom-line this again: You made me *Pri-ya*." I spat, then fished. "You set four Unseelie Princes on me."

"Three."

I stared. I knew there'd been a fourth. "*You* were the fourth?"

"That would have served no purpose. I am not Fae at the moment."

"Then who was the fourth?" My hands fisted in my lap. Being raped was bad enough. Being raped and not knowing if your fourth rapist was someone you knew was even worse.

"There was no fourth."

"Not believing a word you say."

"The fourth Unseelie Prince was killed hundreds of thousands of years ago, in battle between the queen and king. That *child*"—he shot a glance out the window—"killed another when I tried to reclaim you at the abbey."

A memory from my fractured state of consciousness surfaced sharply: Lying on the cold stone floor, believing salvation was at hand. A flame-haired warrior. A sword. I remembered. It was a shameful memory. I'd wanted to kill Dani for killing my "master." And I was still mad at Dani for killing the prince—but for an entirely different reason: *I* wanted to be the one to kill the bastards.

"The princes want revenge. They want me to let them have her. They are mine to command."

I stared at him, not missing the threat but still trying to digest that there was no fourth prince. How could the LM not have known a fourth was there? *Was* there a fourth, or had I imagined it?

"What has Barrons tried to make of you, Mac-Kayla? And V'lane? A tool for their purposes. They're no different than me. My methods have merely been more direct. And more directly effective. Everyone is trying to use you." He glanced out the window. "If not for her interference, I would have succeeded. I would have had the *Sinsar Dubh* by now and been back in Faery."

"Leaving our world a complete mess."

"What do you think Barrons would do? Or V'lane?"

"At least *try* to put the walls back up."

"You're so certain?"

"You're just trying to make me doubt everyone."

"If you obtain the *Sinsar Dubh* for me, MacKayla,

I will reclaim the Unseelie and restore order to your world."

Not a word in there about restoring the walls. "And give me my sister back?" I said dryly.

"If you wish. Or you may come visit us in Faery."

"Not funny."

"I did not intend it to be. Whether you wish to believe it or not, she mattered to me."

"I saw her body, you bastard!"

His lids half dropped, his mouth tightened. "As did I. It was not done by me or at my direction."

"She told me you were coming for her! That she was afraid you wouldn't let her out of the country! She wanted to come home!"

His lids lifted. He looked startled. On a human face, I would have called his expression pained. "She said that?"

"She was crying on the phone, hiding from you!"

"No." He shook his head. "Not from me, Mac-Kayla. I do not believe she thought it was me. She knew me better than that. Yes, she'd found me out. Discovered what I was. But she didn't fear me."

"Stop *lying* to me!" I lunged to my feet. He'd killed her. I *had* to believe that. In the huge sea of unknowns that had become my existence, there was one certainty, and it was my life raft. The Lord Master was the bad guy. He'd killed Alina. That was my absolute. My unwavering truth. I couldn't let go of it. I couldn't survive in a state of complete paranoia.

He reached into his coat, took out a photo album, and tossed it on the couch. "I expect you to give this back to me. It is mine. I came in peace today," he said, "and offered you one more chance at an alternative to war between us. The last time you refused me, you saw what I did. Three days, MacKayla. I will come for you in three days. Be ready. Be willing." He glanced out the window. He reached into his coat again and this time pulled out the amulet on its thick gold chain. It glowed at his touch. He looked at it for a moment, then at me, as if debating testing it. I was a *sidhe*-seer and a Null, impervious to Fae magic. Would it work on me? Expect the unexpected, I reminded myself. I could make no assumptions.

"I will let you keep the child, today. She is a gift from me to you. I can give you many, many gifts. The next price I call due will not be . . . as you say . . . refundable." He rapped sharply on the window and nodded.

The princes were gone.

Dani slumped into a puddle of mud.

The LM vanished.

"They made me throw away my sword, Mac," Dani said, teeth chattering.

I dabbed gently at the blood on her cheeks. "I know, honey. You told me." Seven times in the past three minutes. It was *all* she'd said since I helped her up from the puddle, dug out a metal teapot, opened two bottles of water, heated it over the fire the LM had left burning, and began cleaning her up.

"Dunno how you survived," she said, and began to cry.

I wiped at her cheeks some more, pushed at her

hair, fretted and fussed like my mom and Alina had fretted over me whenever I wept.

She didn't cry pretty. She cried like a storm breaking loose, a storm that had been brewing for a long time. I suspected she was crying for things I knew nothing about and might never know. Dani was an intensely private person. She cried like her heart was breaking, like her soul was in those tears, and I held her, thinking how strange life was. I'd thought I was fully engaged in life back in Ashford, Georgia, 100 percent invested.

I'd had no idea what life or love was.

Life didn't explode in the sunshine and pretty places. Life took the strongest root with a little bit of rain and a whole lot of shit for fertilizer. Although love could grow in times of peace, it tempered in battle. Daddy told me once—when I'd said something about how perfect his relationship with Mom was—that I should have seen the first five years of their marriage, that they'd fought like hellions, crashed into each other like two giant stones. That eventually they'd eroded each other into the perfect fit, become a single wall, nestled into each other's curves and hollows, her strengths chinking his weaknesses, her weaknesses reinforced by his strengths.

I began telling Dani about my parents. About what life had been like growing up in a happy home in the Deep South. About magnolia-scented days and sultry heat, slow-paddling fans and pool parties. She stilled in my arms. After a while, she stopped crying and leaned back on the couch, staring at me

like a stray cat with its nose pressed to the window
of a restaurant.

When she took off for the abbey, I carefully
tucked the photo album the LM had tossed on the
couch into my backpack, unopened. I knew without
cracking the cover I was going to need time to pore
over the pictures, a luxury I didn't have now.

I headed off into the gray drizzly day for Barrons
Books and Baubles.

18

I detoured past Chester's on the way there, hoping the Gray Woman might be in the vicinity. I was going to spend a lot of time loitering in the streets outside Ryodan's club. "Inside his club" might be under his protection, but that didn't mean the surrounding area wasn't free range.

I walked quietly, tensed for battle, prepared to slam my palms into the hag: Null and stab her and do a victory dance on her gruesome body. But the only Unseelie I encountered on the way to the bookstore were Rhino-boys. Half a dozen of them. And what they were doing confounded me so thoroughly that I ended up walking down the cobbled street, spear sheathed, hands in my pockets, staring at them while they stared at me. I think we all had big what-the-fucks plastered all over our faces. It's kind of hard to tell with those beady eyes and tusks, but I know I did.

They were rewiring the streetlamps and carefully resetting them in the sidewalks. They were sweeping up debris. They were replacing bulbs. They had brooms and jackhammers, wiring materials, wheelbarrows, and concrete.

I was supposed to kill them. That was what I did, what I was made for.

But they were putting Dublin back to rights.

I *wanted* Dublin back to rights. Did this mean they were working to restore the power, too?

"Are you doing it to keep the Shades out?" I shook my head at the oddity of having just initiated a conversation with a Rhino-boy. I would have wondered if my day could get any stranger, but my days *always* get stranger.

"Pigs," one of them grunted, and the rest of them agreed, snorting. "Eat everything. Leave nothing for the rest of us."

"I see." I decided I would let them finish cleaning up the block first and kill them on my way back. Hands in my pockets, I resumed walking.

"Pretty girlie-girl, want to live forever?" one of them grunted at my back. They all snorted and snuffled as if at some inside joke. Like, duh, maybe eating them in exchange for sex really *didn't* give you immortality, just some new, never-before-heard-of Fae STD. "Got something you can suck on, girlie-girl."

Ew. "Not a chance," I said coolly.

They should have let me go. I would have let them go. But Rhino-boys aren't the brightest bulbs in the box. I heard hoofed feet shuffling, moving toward me. Their bribe hadn't worked, so they were switching tactics to brute force. They'd picked the wrong woman to mess with. I hate Unseelie.

"Think twice," I warned.

I suspect Rhino-boys have a hard enough time thinking once.

A few moments later, the six of them were dead and I was walking toward BB&B, thoroughly pissed that I'd had to kill them before they finished wiring the lamps.

The last look I'd gotten at the bookstore was late in the afternoon on that hellish Halloween that would forever be burned into my memory as the second-worst night of my life. All the exterior lights had been broken out. I wasn't sure what to expect as I turned down the street I'd once considered my "way home."

I stopped, stared, and smiled faintly. Of course.

On a street of heavily damaged and looted buildings, BB&B alone stood untouched. The elegantly restored façade of the Old World four-story brick building was immaculate. The spotlights mounted on the front, rear, and sides, which had been broken out last I saw it, were now replaced. The brightly painted shingle proclaiming BARRONS BOOKS AND BAUBLES had been rehung perpendicular to the building, suspended over the sidewalk on an elaborate brass pole, and it creaked as it swung in the drizzly breeze. The sign in the old-fashioned green-tinted windows glowed soft neon: CLOSED. Amber torches in brass sconces illuminated the deep limestone archway of the bookstore's grand alcoved entrance. Ornate cherry diamond-paned doors, nestled between limestone columns, gleamed in the light.

I wondered if the bookstore meant something to

him, that he'd gone to such lengths. Did it hold sentimental value? Or was it merely his possession, his statement to the world in general that nothing and no one would ever take what was his?

I stepped into the alcove, tried the door. It was unlocked. I pushed it open.

I never tire of my first glimpse of my shop. Once you get past the immediate sense of spatial distortion—as if you've opened the door of an old-fashioned phone booth only to find the Library of Congress inside—you notice that luxury and comfort have never gone so effortlessly hand in hand.

The main room is about eighty feet long by sixty feet wide and vaults five stories to a muraled ceiling. On the second, third, fourth, and fifth floors, bookcases line each wall from base to cove molding. Behind elegant banisters, catwalks permit access, while ladders slide on oiled rollers from one section to the next.

But it's the first floor I spend so much time on, with its freestanding bookcases crammed with all the latest, greatest reads standing tall on polished wood floors scattered with plush rugs. Two seating cozies, fore and aft, boast opulent yet comfy chesterfield sofas and brocaded chairs topped by soft throws, centered around my beloved respite from the Dublin rain and cold—fancy enameled gas fireplaces.

I glanced at my well-stocked magazine rack (sadly out of date) and my cashier's counter. I smiled at the old-fashioned register with the tiny silver bell that tinkled whenever the drawer popped open.

I moved to the counter.

A note was propped on the register.

Welcome home, Ms. Lane.

"Arrogant, overconfident jackass." Keys lay on the counter beside it.

I wondered what car he'd left me this time. I was reaching for the keys when, out of the blue, emotions bombarded me, intense and confusing. They were accompanied by a barrage of memories: the day I'd stumbled into this place, my anxiety at being lost, meeting Barrons for the first time, my naïve conviction that he was exactly the kind of man I would never date.

"And we *haven't* dated." I crushed the note in my fist. Just had completely uninhibited raw sex. Months of it.

I closed my eyes, more memories of this place crashing over me: the night I'd seen the Gray Man devour a woman's beauty and had rushed here for answers, with no idea what was wrong with me but already suspecting it was permanent; the night I'd accepted his offer of a fourth-floor bedroom overlooking the back alley and moved in; the day my daddy had come looking for me and I'd realized I could never go home to Ashford until the madness in Dublin was over and I'd either succeeded or didn't care because I'd be going home the same way as Alina, in a box; the night I'd given Barrons a birthday cake, then eaten it alone, after it had splatted from the ceiling.

I inhaled his scent. He was near, a few feet away. Lust nearly buckled my knees. He was a tireless lover. There was nothing off-limits with him.

"Ms. Lane."

I fisted my hands in my pockets and opened my eyes. He stood across the counter, eyes dark, features impassive.

"Barrons."

"It's a Hummer."

"Alpha?" I said hopefully.

His obsidian gaze mocked. *Would I waste my time with anything less?*

"Dani's moving in," I told him.

"Dani's going back to the abbey."

"Then I am, too."

"I hear you're not welcome there."

"I will be soon. I have plans. And I need her."

"You need me," he said flatly. "I thought you'd have figured that out by now."

I had. I kept getting knocked down. And I kept getting back up again, a little stronger each time. But I still wasn't strong enough. One day I would be. Until then, Barrons was the only one that scared all my enemies away. If *IYD* really would have worked on Halloween, he definitely guaranteed me the highest odds of survival. I was done hopping from swell to swell, trying to avoid the tidals. Right or wrong, good or bad, I'd chosen: Barrons was my wave. But there was no way I was living alone with him. I needed a buffer, and my buffer needed a place to live, too.

"What's wrong with Dani staying here?"

"She's in more danger at your side."

"I don't think she'll go. She has a mind of her own."

"Then figure out how to convince her it's best for both of you."

"It might take a few days." According to the LM, I had only three, anyway. "Give me that much, at least." Once she was here, I'd work on keeping her here. And put her to work with her superhearing and other senses at figuring out what was under his garage and how to get us down there. He might be my wave, but he wasn't my surfboard. Knowledge and usefulness were all that stood between me and the riptide.

He studied me for a moment, then nodded tightly. "Forty-eight hours. Keep the kid under control and out of my way. And there are new rules. One: Stay away from Chester's. That means a ten-block radius. Two: You share all pertinent information with me *without my having to ask*. Three: Keep the kid away from my garage. Four: If you try to force yourself into my head, I will force myself into your pants."

"Oh! That's *total* bullshit!"

"Tit for tat." His gaze dropped to my breasts, and I had a sudden, much-too-detailed memory of yanking my shirt up while he'd watched them pop out, jiggling. "Or would that be tit for tit?"

"There's no need to be rude."

"I can think of endless needs to be rude."

"Keep them to yourself."

"Such a different tune you whistle now."

"You sound angry, Barrons. Frustrated. What's wrong? You get a little addicted to me?"

His lips drew back, baring his teeth. I'd felt them on my nipples. I could almost feel them there now.

"We fucked, Ms. Lane. Even cockroaches fuck. They eat each other, too."

"Same page, Barrons."

"Same bloody word," he agreed.

Oh, yes, here we were, working together again. All was well—or at least back to normal—at Barrons Books and Baubles.

"I really get to live at Barrons'? With, like, *Barrons*?" Dani exclaimed, bounding from foot to foot backward as we walked through Temple Bar. We were on our way to intercept the *sidhe*-seers. Dani had learned that a group of several dozen, led by Kat, was coming into the city tonight, to scout it out.

"No," I said dryly, "with, like, the LM and his minions."

"I'm living with Barrons! Holy fecking shit! Way cool!"

"Doesn't it bother you that we have no idea what he is or whether he's good or bad?"

"Nope. Not a bit." Her eyes sparkled.

I snorted. She was completely serious. I wished I could be so uncomplicated. But I couldn't. Right and wrong, good and bad mattered to me. Blame it on my parents. They endowed me with a massively inconvenient sense of ethics.

"We're almost there, Mac. I hear 'em dead ahead." She cocked her head, then her eyes widened. "Aw, Ro's gonna be wicked pissed! She told 'em not to fight, no matter what! Just to suss out what's goin' down and how many are where. We gotta hurry, Mac. It don't sound like it's goin' good!"

I didn't have time to brace myself for the rough ride. Her hand was on my arm, and we were gone.

Dani slammed us to a stop, directly in the middle of the fight. It was huge, messy, and filled the street from one end of the block to the next. Dani loves the action. Unfortunately, she forgets that the rest of us aren't as fast as she is. She arrived with her sword drawn, perfectly at ease moving in hyperspeed mode, but it took me a moment to fumble my spear from my shoulder holster. In that moment, I got slammed in the back of my head so hard that I saw stars, and brackets from my MacHalo went flying in three different directions. Snarling, I spun around and drove my spear into an Unseelie's . . . head, I think. It had three roundish things on its shoulders with dozens of slits that spewed icy, stinging liquid as it fell.

Then the fight became a blur of motion, of spinning, kicking, Nulling, and stabbing. I glimpsed Kat's wide eyes, her terrified face. I had no doubt this was her first fight and it had come out of the blue.

Between Unseelie, I caught glimpses of other *sidhe*-seers. They were trying desperately to hold their own. Most of the time, the gifts inside us are dormant, but the presence of Fae and especially of engaging in battle slams them awake. I could see they were in that special *sidhe*-seer state—stronger, faster, tougher, more resilient—but it wasn't enough. There was too much fear in their eyes.

Fear translates to hesitation, and hesitation kills.

If you've ever been behind someone on an on-ramp who's trying to merge onto a highway but is scared to do it, going too slow, stopping and start-ing, and growing more uncertain by the minute, you know what I mean. There you are, hemmed in by traffic, trapped behind rampant indecision, and you know that if they don't get their act together and merge, *you're* going to end up getting hit.

That's how the *sidhe*-seers were fighting. I cursed Rowena for not training them better, for sheltering them so completely that their gifts were a hazard to their own health and mine. Dani and I moved to-gether, back to back, slicing and stabbing our way through the mob of Unseelie.

"Help me!" I heard Kat scream. I glanced wildly toward the sound. She was trapped between two large winged things with sharp talons and teeth that looked horrifyingly like raptors.

I assessed, I acted.

Later, I would puzzle over my decision. Wonder what temporary insanity had possessed me. But I knew they couldn't touch it and she could, and I knew she was dead otherwise, and nobody was dying on my watch if I had anything to say about it.

"Kat!" I yelled. When she looked, I drew back my arm, tossed my spear at her, and watched it go fly-ing, end over end.

Her eyes widened in astonishment. She lunged into the air, snagged the spear, landed lightly on the balls of her feet, and took them both out in one smooth ricochet of motion, left to right.

It was beautiful. If I'd had a remote, I'd have hit *replay* a dozen times.

And there I stood, without a weapon.

Then I had a leathery appendage in my face that probably should have broken my nose but didn't, and I was under attack and lost sight of Kat and my spear. I slammed my palms into my attacker, Nulling it. While it stood, frozen, I retreated into my mind, into that special *sidhe*-seer place. Without my spear, I was in deep shit and I needed more power.

Abruptly, the street faded and I was inside my own head, staring down into a huge black pool. Was this the source of what made a *sidhe*-seer, this vast obsidian lake? I'd never seen it before when I'd gone poking around. Was I so much stronger now that I could see more clearly, probe more deeply?

Power radiated from its dark depths, crackled in the air of the cave in which I stood. I could feel something in the water, waiting in the darkness.

What lay concealed beneath the surface knew everything, could do everything, feared nothing. It was waiting for me. To call it forth. To use it as my birthright.

But doubt as vast as the thing's watery habitat immobilized me.

What if whatever I summoned from those ancient depths wasn't a part of me at all but something else entirely?

If it *was* me, I could use it.

But if by some bizarre twist of events—and no events were too bizarre to consider in my day-to-day existence—there was something down there that *wasn't* me, *it* could use *me*.

I didn't trust myself. No, I didn't trust that *sidhe*-seer place.

Why would I? I hadn't even known it existed until a few months ago. Until I knew more about what it was and wasn't, I wasn't calling forth any unknowns. My current skills would have to suffice.

I shook my head sharply and I was in the street again, with a raptor thing about to take a bite out of me.

I ducked.

Its head flew to the side and its body slid to the cobbled stone, leaving Dani standing where it had been, grinning at me. "Pull your head outta your arse, Mac."

We moved into pattern: I Nulled, she killed.

I don't know how long I fought without my spear. But it was long enough to give me a taste of what I was asking of my sisters-in-arms. I cursed Rowena for sending them into Dublin without guns, without iron bullets. I would never let them be such walking targets.

I kept looking for Kat but couldn't find her in the mess. Without my spear, I felt naked, exposed. I felt wrong.

I slammed my palms into a tall, beetle-bodied Unseelie with a thick, many-plated carapace. It didn't freeze. I drew back my fist, and suddenly there was another hand around mine, and when I drove it forward, Kat and I sunk the spear in its armorlike hide together.

As it crashed to the pavement, I glanced over my shoulder.

Kat smiled, nodded, and let go of the spear, leaving it in my hand. Then she turned her back to mine and moved into pattern with me, as I had with Dani.

Although she wasn't a Null, she had a wicked uppercut, and we made a great team. Dani paired off with another *sidhe*-seer, and the battle raged on.

Later, we sat on curbs, leaned against buildings, and sprawled on the sidewalks, dirty, splattered with disgusting variations of Unseelie blood, exhilarated, and exhausted.

"What happened?" I asked Kat. "How did you get stuck in the middle of so many of them?"

She flushed. "We've grown accustomed to having Dani with us, we have. She hears what we can't. I think they must have begun following us the moment we entered the city, drawn by our hats"—she tapped her MacHalo—"or perhaps the noise of the bus. They gathered more as we went, biding time, looking for a tight spot to close in. If you hadn't happened along . . . well. It's glad we are that you did."

I assessed the carnage. There were several hundred Unseelie dead in the street. "We did good. With guns and a plan, we could do better."

Kat nodded. "May we speak plainly?"

I inclined my head.

"Your differences with the Grand Mistress hurt us all."

"Then she should wise up and see reason."

"Her differences with you hurt us, too," Kat said pointedly. "War is no time for a coup. Continue fighting each other and you'll end up destroying the kingdom you're after ruling."

There was a chorus of murmured assents in the street.

"I'm not trying to rule. I'm just trying to help."

"You're both trying to rule. And we're telling you both to stop. We've been talking since you and Dani left. We want you back. We don't care if you keep the weapons. But we're not willing to trade Rowena's guidance for yours. We want you both. If you agree to team up, we'll help you in whatever way we can and make Rowena accept it, too. The way we see it, neither you nor Rowena can force us to accept either one of you. But we're willing to bet we can force you two to work together for the greater good. That *is* what you both say you're after, isn't it?"

"I'm not living at the abbey, Mac!" Dani bounded to her feet. "You *said* I could live with Barrons."

I looked from Dani to Kat, considering her words. She'd made a point, and I was feeling a little ashamed of myself. I *had* made it personal with Rowena. I'd tried to divide and conquer, and now was not the time to be dividing loyalties over anything. We had enough problems as it was.

My whole goal in sending Dani to the abbey today was to find out when the *sidhe*-seers were coming in, so I could take them into battle, pump them up on victory, and regain a foothold in the abbey. Kat was offering it to me, hand outstretched. Five hundred *sidhe*-seers could force Rowena to co-operate with me, and all I'd have to do was bite my tongue a lot.

"I'm convinced, Kat. Convince Rowena."

"But you *said*," Dani exploded.

I sighed. I wanted my buffer. But Barrons had a point, too. It wasn't just about me. "I need you where you're safest, Dani. After the Unseelie Princes took you today, I'm afraid that's not with me."

Sidhe-seers gasped. "You were taken by the Unseelie Princes, Dani? What? How? Where did they take you? What happened?"

Suddenly Dani was the center of attention. Preening, she began to tell them all about it.

I watched the show—Dani knew how to dazzle and loved doing it—smiling faintly, feeling sad.

I wasn't ready to give her up.

Or face the rest of the night alone with Barrons. I'd rather fight another blockful of Unseelie.

I looked at Kat. "We'll meet you at the abbey in the morning. If the old woman behaves, so will I. You have my word."

She gave me a level look, then her gaze dropped to the spear strapped to my thigh. "I don't need your word, Mac. You gave me something else tonight that said it all."

19

MacKayla."
We were a block from the bookstore when
V'lane's voice slid out of the darkness, an orchestral
variation on an erotic dream. The Fae have extraordinary voices, melodious and rich. The notes vibrate
under your skin, sleek and sensual against the tips
of your nerve endings. If the Song of Making really
is a song, I'm not sure a human could survive hearing it.

I used to have what I would have called a normal
sex drive. Some of my friends were beyond obsessed with it, though. I guess they thought it would
fill the void of purposelessness so many in my generation are afflicted with while trying to find our
place in the world.

But being *Pri-ya* changed me, left me with a voracious awareness of all things sexual. Or maybe sex
with Barrons did it—I don't know. All I know is that
I'm far more attuned to erotic nuances than I used
to be. The Seelie Prince's murmur was a full-body

caress, and I appreciated it for a moment before shrugging it off.

"V'lane!" Dani exclaimed.

He laughed, and if I hadn't been immune to death-by-sex Fae glamour, I would have been in serious trouble. He was putting on the seduction, beautiful golden Fae radiating pure sexual heat. I've begun to think it's simply part of his nature, that he can't help it any more than some men can prevent themselves from oozing testosterone. I think some males of both species just have *more*.

Dani wasn't immune. Her eyes were feverishly bright, her skin flushed, her lips parted. I caught a glimpse in that moment of the woman she would become. "Stop it, V'lane. Leave her alone."

"I do not believe she wishes me to. Who better to awaken her to the shape and texture of Eros? Set the bar, so to speak."

"Uh-huh," Dani said thickly. "I'd like that."

"I don't care what you believe or what she wishes, and you will *not* be setting the bar. She's going to have a normal life." At least, as close to normal as I could make it. "Dani, get inside the bookstore. I'll join you in a few minutes."

"But I don't wanna—"

"*Now,*" I said.

She glared.

"I bet Barrons is there," I dangled. To V'lane I said, "Dampen yourself so she can shake the thrall."

He lifted and dropped one shoulder.

Dani made a soft sigh, as if abruptly released from some inner tension she wasn't entirely glad to be free of, then glanced from V'lane to the bookstore and back again, as if trying to choose between a banana split and a fudge sundae. Then, "Fine," she said, and flashed out. At the door, she tossed a saucy grin over a shoulder and said, "Take your time, Mac. Me and Barrons, we got stuff to talk about."

I bit back a snort of laughter, remembering my own teen crushes. They'd been nightmares of awkwardness and nervous tension. Of feeling gauche, too clumsy for words, and needy. I trusted that Barrons would deftly deflect her hero worship. It was only with me that he was a constant jackass.

I watched until she was safely inside and the door closed behind her. Although there were no indications the Dark Zone that had once neighbored BB&B still existed, I didn't trust those shadow-filled streets beyond the bookstore.

I looked back at V'lane. He was studying me intently.

"You have been battling. Are you well, MacKayla?"

"I'm fine." My reflexes had been dynamite tonight. Even though I took a few crushing blows, I'd managed to duck or pull back at the last minute and minimize the impact every time. I didn't even feel bruised anywhere. No cuts. No contusions. I felt fantastic. I loved this sleeker, stronger me.

The floodlights on the top of BB&B flashed on. The street was suddenly blindingly bright. I had no doubt Barrons was about to step outside.

V'lane shot the bookstore a beautifully imitated look of disgust, then his arms were around me and we were gone.

* * *

We reappeared, high in the dark night sky.

He was holding my hand.

I made the horrific mistake of glancing down briefly. I yanked my gaze back up again. I was standing on nothing. Black air beneath my feet.

Why wasn't I falling?

As soon as I thought that, I began to fall. I lunged at him, wrapped my arms and legs around him, and clung for dear life.

His arms cradled me instantly. "I should have done this long ago, MacKayla," he purred. "Be at ease. I will not let you fall. Look down."

"That's a definite not." I had no idea how high up we were, but it was cold. I squeezed my eyes shut. "Are we just hanging in the sky? Floating here?" This distressed me tremendously. I'm quite certain we were created with feet because we're *supposed* to walk on the surface of the planet. Key word there being "surface": not above it, not below it.

"You would feel safer in one of those conveyances that frequently plummet?"

"Not that frequently."

"All that is required to end a mortal life is one such fall, yet you assume the risk. Humans are irrational and foolish."

"This irrational, foolish human wants her feet on the ground."

"I have a gift for you, MacKayla. I have . . . what is that word . . ." He trailed off, and I was startled to realize there was a teasing note in his voice. "Ah, I have it," he said lightly. "Labored. I have *worked* to give you this gift. I have not merely waved my fairy wand and made it so."

He was teasing. I wasn't sure what disconcerted me more: hanging in the night sky or listening to V'lane tease. The LM claimed that he was changed by exposure to humans. Was V'lane?

"This is the best way to present my gift."

"I looked down when we got here. Lots of dark space. I think I saw stars."

"The stars are above us. Look again." His tone made it clear he was going to keep us hanging here all night if I didn't do what he said.

Sighing, I opened my eyes, took a hasty, panicked look down, and squeezed my eyes shut again. Then I realized what I'd just seen and my eyes flew open again. We were several thousand feet up and city lights glittered far below.

City lights! We were above a brilliant aura that could only be a major metropolitan area. "I thought the power was out everywhere!" I exclaimed.

"I have been working with other Seelie to see it restored," he said with pride.

"Where are we?"

"Beneath us is your Atlanta. On the coast, the lights of Savannah." He pointed. "There, Ashford. I told you I would keep your parents safe. When Barrons beat me by a mere matter of minutes in saving you, I turned my efforts to saving those who matter most to you. Barrons has still never spared them a thought. The Dark Zones that swallowed the cities nearest your home, threatening to spread, have been eradicated. Power is restored. Even now humans learn to defend themselves. My gift to you is your Georgia back."

I stared down at the lights, then at him. "Could you do this for the whole world?"

"Much of our power stems from our ability to manipulate dimensions beyond yours, but the fabric of the human dimension is . . . viscous, thick; the laws of your physics are not as . . . bendable as ours. This alteration required much time, cooperation with other Seelie and many humans."

In V'lane-speak, that translated to a no. He'd done this for me and would do no more.

"Your parents are safe. Would you like to see them?"

I swallowed against a sudden lump in my throat. Mom and Dad were down there. One of those glittering lights beneath me, a mere sift away. They'd always been a mere sift away, but somehow, in Dublin, with four thousand miles between us, it had been easier to keep that fact blocked from my mind so I wouldn't be tempted. So I wouldn't hurt, or worry, or risk exposing their existence to my enemies, I'd crammed Mom and Dad into my padlocked box, with all my other forbidden thoughts. Was that what Alina had done with us, too?

I caught my breath. I shouldn't. I knew better.

"Take me to the street outside The Brickyard," I said. "I'll walk from there."

I was here and I couldn't resist. I wanted to see my world again. I wanted to walk the oak- and magnolia-lined streets of my hometown. I wanted to stand outside my house and look up at my bedroom window. I wanted to see if I could find any trace of the girl I'd once been in these streets or if she'd been completely swallowed up by a dark Fae dream. I didn't dare risk being seen, so I would have to stay to the shadows, but I've gotten good at that lately.

I lightly touched down, my boots settled on pavement.

There was The Brickyard, on its large lot, tucked between two antebellums. The lights were on inside and out. Nothing had changed. I hurried up the walk, peered into a window.

Oh, how wrong I was! Everything had changed. Ashford's police force, firemen, the mayor, and about a hundred townspeople were inside, and I didn't need to crack a window to know they were discussing strategy. The walls were down and the whole world knew it now. If there'd been national newspapers up and running, the headlines would be about nothing else. The Fae were visible, and here were the grassroots efforts of my town to protect itself. I wanted to march in and help. Educate. Take up arms and protect.

"Your place and purpose are not here, MacKayla."

I forced myself to turn away, melt, like a thief, into the night.

It was warm for January in Ashford, but that wasn't so unusual. I've spent Christmases in ice storms. I've spent them in shorts and a T-shirt. Tonight was a jeans and tee night.

As I walked, I inhaled deeply. There was nothing blooming this time of year, but I swear the Deep South always smells of magnolias, wild azaleas, sweet tea, and somebody frying chicken somewhere. In a month, pansies would bloom all over the town—Ashford was nuts about pansies—followed by jonquils and tulips.

I was home. I smiled.

It was safe!

No Shades, no Unseelie, lights on everywhere.

I spun in a delighted circle in the middle of the street.

How I'd missed my world! How lost I'd felt so far away!

It all looked exactly the same. It felt as if I'd never left. As if three blocks down and two blocks over, I'd find Mom, Dad, and Alina playing Scrabble, waiting for me to get home from night class or work to join them (and get my petunia trounced, because Alina and Dad knew words that any reasonable person would have agreed shouldn't be words at all, like "ort" and "quod"—really, who *knew* words like that?), and we'd laugh and I'd worry about what outfit to wear tomorrow and go to sleep with nothing more troubling on my mind than whether my petition to OPI to unretire my favorite shade had been heard. (It had, and they'd sent me a pretty pink-and-gold certificate conferring upon me the title of honorary OPI affiliate, which I'd hung with great pride next to my vanity, where I did my hair and makeup. Oh, the trials and tribulations of a sheltered youth.)

There was the Brooks' house, proud white Southern columns at the top of a grand circular drive. There was the Jennings' place, with its romantic turrets and loads of white lattice accents. I walked the streets, drinking in the sights. I'd always thought Ashford had such rich history, but it was really very young, only a few centuries, compared to Dublin's millennia.

Then I was outside my house, standing in the street, sick with anticipation.

I hadn't seen Mom since August 2, the day I'd left for Dublin. My last glimpse of Dad had been on August 28, when I'd dropped him at the Dublin airport and sent him back home. He'd flown over to find me, determined to take me back to Ashford with him. But Barrons had Voiced him, coerced him into not worrying about me, planted who-knew-what kind of commands inside my dad's head to get him to leave and not come back. I both hated and appreciated that Barrons had done it. Jack Lane is one seriously strong-willed man. He'd never have left without me, and I'd never have been able to keep him safe.

I moved silently up the walk. A dozen feet from the front door, a mirror appeared, suspended in the air in front of me. I shivered, as if someone had walked over my grave. Mirrors are no longer simple things to me. Since the night I stared into the Silver that Barrons keeps in his study at BB&B and watched the twisted, dark creatures moving around inside it, looking at my own reflection has been unsettling, as if all mirrors are suspect and something dark and horrifying might materialize at any moment behind my shoulder.

"In case you were considering being seen," V'lane cautioned, stepping into view behind my shoulder.

I looked at myself.

The moment I'd seen our house, I regressed in my mind to the curvy, pretty girl who'd raced down our front walk for the cab so many months ago, long blond hair swinging, short white skirt showcasing perfect golden legs (when was the last time I'd shaved?), manicure and pedicure meticulously enameled, purse and shoes matching, jewelry in theme.

I stared at myself now.

I was a wild woman, dressed from head to toe in black leather. There was slimy green goop in my tangle of midnight curls. I was stained with vile-smelling Unseelie body fluids. My nails were ripped to the quick, and I was toting a black leather back-pack full of lights and ammunition, wearing a bat-tered bike helmet, and carrying a semiautomatic weapon. He'd made his point.

"Make it go away," I said stiffly.

The mirror vanished.

I didn't belong here. Nothing good could come of my presence. Sure, I could ask V'lane to make me pretty and clean with glamour and drop in for a visit, but what would I say? What could I hope to ac-complish? And wouldn't every minute that I re-mained here potentially invite unsavory attention my parents' way?

After all I'd been through, after all I'd seen, I still couldn't come home.

There was a whole world out there in trouble. My mom and dad were safe. I felt a sudden rush of grat-itude toward V'lane and turned to him. "Thank you," I said. "It means the world to me that you pro-tected them."

He smiled, and I think it was the first real smile I'd ever seen on his face. It was blinding. "You are welcome, MacKayla. Shall we go?" He held out a hand.

I would have taken it, *should* have taken it, but just then I heard voices.

Cocking my head, I listened. My heart constricted. It was Mom and Dad. They were on the screened lanai that overlooked the pool in back of our house. Dense bushes at each side afforded privacy from our neighbors.

I could go press myself into the holly branches and, shielded from their gaze, catch a glimpse of them. I was starved for a glimpse of them.

I slipped off my MacHalo, dropped my backpack and gun. "In a moment," I whispered. "You stay here. I'll be back."

"I deem this unwise."

"Not your decision. Back off."

I slipped into the shadows near my home.

"We've been over this again and again, Rainey," my dad was saying.

I wedged quietly into the bushes and stared hungrily.

Mom and Dad were sitting on white wicker chairs on the lanai. Mom was sipping wine, and Dad was holding a glass of bourbon. I hoped he wasn't drinking too much. There'd been a bad time after Alina had died when he'd slurred too often for my comfort. Dad's not a drinker, he's a doer. But Alina's murder had fried us all. I absorbed my mom's face greedily. Her eyes were clear, her face gently lined and beautiful as ever. My heart swelled with emotion. I ached to touch her, hug them both. Daddy looked robust and handsome as ever, but there was more silver in his hair than I remembered.

"I know it's dangerous out there," my mom said. "But I can't stand this not knowing! If I just knew for certain she was alive."

"Barrons said she was. You were here when he called."

Barrons had called my parents? When? How was his phone working? Damn, I wanted his service provider!

"I don't trust that man one bit."

Neither do I, Mom. And I slept with him. My face heated. *Sex* and *Mom* are two thoughts that don't fit comfortably in my head at the same time.

"We have to go to Dublin, Jack."

I silently willed a thousand "no"s in my mom's direction.

Dad sighed. "I tried to go back. Remember?"

I blinked. He had? When? What had happened?

Mom pounced on it. "My point exactly, Jack. You believe that man hypnotized you, planted blocks in your mind that prevented you from bringing her home, forced you to leave, and is somehow keeping you from going back—you couldn't even get on the plane, you got so sick—but the moment you left the airport you were fine. Three times you tried to go! Yet you accept his word that our daughter is okay?"

You could have knocked me over with a feather. My dad *knew* Barrons had done something woo-woo to him and actually believed it possible? Daddy didn't believe in woo-woo things. It was *he* who'd taught me an abject rejection of all things paranormal. And he and my mother were calmly sipping their drinks, discussing this stuff?

"We can't go over there now. You heard what the scouts told Officer Deaton. Fae reality has gotten mixed up with ours. The few airplanes that have taken off have either come crashing down in flames or disappeared."

"What about a private charter?"

"What good will it do if we die trying to get to her?"

"We have to do something, Jack! I need to know she's alive. No, I need more than that. We have to *tell* her. You should have told her then, when you were there, when you had the chance."

Told me what? I pressed deeper into the shrubs, all ears.

Dad rubbed his eyes. I could tell by the look on his face that he and Mom had been having this conversation a lot lately. "We promised we'd never talk about it."

I nearly beat the bushes with frustration. Talk about *what*?

"We made other promises we broke," Mom said pointedly. "That's what got us into this situation to begin with."

"What would you have had me tell her, Rainey?"

"The truth."

Come on, Daddy, spill it.

"What *is* the truth? One person's truth is another person's—"

"Don't play attorney with me, Jack. I'm not the jury and this isn't your opening argument," Mom said dryly.

He opened his mouth and closed it, looking sheepish. After a moment he said, "Mac was having enough problems dealing with Alina's death. There was no way I was going to tell her about some crazy Irish woman and an even crazier prophecy. Our baby'd been battling depression for months. She had enough on her plate."

Prophecy? Mom and Dad knew about the prophecy? Did *everyone* know about the blasted thing but me?

"What you heard all those years ago when you went digging for Alina's medical records doesn't seem so crazy now, does it?" Mom said.

Dad took a sip of bourbon. He exhaled and seemed to deflate. "Christ, Rainey, fifteen years passed. Perfectly normal."

"She ranted about fairies. Who wouldn't have thought she was crazy?"

I'm not sure Dad even heard her. He tossed back the rest of the glass in one swallow. "I let Alina do the *one* thing I promised the adoption people I'd never let either of them do," he said roughly.

"*We* let her do it," Mom said sharply. "Stop blaming yourself. I let her go to Ireland, too."

"You didn't want to. I pushed."

"We both made the decision. We've always made the big decisions together."

"Well, this was one decision you weren't there to help me make. When I was in Dublin with Mac, you still weren't talking to me. I couldn't even get you on the phone."

"I'm sorry," Mom said after a long pause. "The grief . . ." She trailed off, and my stomach knotted.

She was getting that look in her eyes again. That one that had bruised my heart every day until I'd run away to Dublin.

Daddy looked at her hard, and right before my eyes, he changed. I watched him inflate again, shake off his own emotions, and puff himself up for her. Become her man. Her rock. I smiled. I loved him so much. He'd dragged Mom kicking and screaming from grief once before, and I knew I could rest easy that he would never let grief steal her from him again. No matter what happened to me.

He stood up and stalked over to her. "What would you have had me say, Rainey?" Dad said loudly, jarring her, keeping her from slipping inward. " 'Baby, I'm sorry to tell you this, but according to some ancient prophecy, there's something wrong with you and you're going to doom the whole world'?" He snorted, then laughed. "Laugh with me, Rainey. Come on!" He pulled her to her feet. "Not our girl. Not a chance. You know it's bogus."

I gagged. Hand to my mouth, I staggered backward and nearly fell. There was something wrong with me? I was going to doom the whole world?

"Their mother gave them up because she believed it," Mom fretted.

"That's what the crazy lady *alleged*," Dad said firmly. "She didn't have a single shred of evidence. I interrogated her thoroughly. She'd never seen this supposed 'prophecy' and couldn't point me in the direction of anyone who had. For Christ's sake, Rainey, it's a country that believes in leprechauns, rainbows, and pots of gold! Can I rest my case?"

"But there *are* fairies, Jack," Mom persisted. "The crazy woman was right about that. They're here, now, in our world, destroying it."

"Circumstantial. One accurate prediction doesn't make an entire prophecy."

"She said one of our girls would die young and the other would wish she was dead!"

"Alina almost died when she was eight, remember? But she didn't. *That's* young. Just because she died in her twenties doesn't mean anything else the woman said is true, and it certainly doesn't mean anything's wrong with Mac. I think the Fae are far more likely to doom our world than any human is. Besides, I don't believe in fate, and neither do you. I believe in free will. All the advice I gave her, all the love and wisdom you showered on her, that's what she has now, and I believe it's enough. I know our daughter. She's as good as they come."

He reached for her hands and pulled her into his arms. "Babe, she's alive. I know she is. I can feel it in my heart. I knew when Alina was dead. And I know Mac's not."

"You're just saying that to make me feel better."

He gave her a faint smile. "Is it working?"

My mom punched him lightly. "Oh! You!"

"I love you, Rainey. I almost lost you when we lost Alina." He kissed her. "I won't lose you now. Maybe there's some way to get into contact with Barrons again."

"If only I knew for certain," Mom said.

He kissed her again, then she was kissing him back, and I was feeling strangely embarrassed, because my parents were pretty much making out.

Still, watching them was comforting. They had each other, and there was a love between them that would withstand anything. Alina and I had always intuited, with no small wry pique, that, although our parents adored us and would do anything for us, they loved each other more. As far as I was concerned, that was the way it should be. Kids grow up, move on, and find a love of their own. The empty nest shouldn't leave parents grieving. It should leave them ready and excited to get on with living their own adventure, which would, of course, include many visits to children and grandchildren.

I took one last long look and went to join V'lane.

He moved into step beside me in silence and offered his hand, but I shook my head.

I picked up my stuff, went to the mailbox, and pulled the LM's photo album out of my backpack. I looked through it for a few moments until I found the perfect picture of Alina, standing in front of the arched entry at Trinity College. She was smiling, openmouthed on a laugh. I smiled back.

I turned it over and scrawled on the back:

She was happy.
I love you, Mom and Dad.
I'll be home as soon as I can.
Mac.

20

Y ou may find you have need of me, MacKayla,"
said V'lane, as we materialized in the street outside BB&B.

I'd been thinking that very thing. There was no
disputing that V'lane was the fastest elevator in the
building. Dani was great on the ground but not
across oceans. Sifting was an invaluable tool. Even if
V'lane appeared only half the times I called him, it
would be better than nothing. I would never count
on him again, but I would use him if I could.

"I cannot always be checking to see if you do.
When my queen does not have me occupied with
her tasks, I am busy battling with other Seelie
against our dark brethren. They do not consider
your earth enough. They seek to wrest our court
from us, as well. My queen is in ever-increasing danger, as is my home." He turned me in his arms, tilted
my face up, and ran a gentle finger over my lips.

I looked up at him. I was still numb from seeing
Mom and Dad, from the conversation I'd overheard.
I wanted him to give me his name back, and quickly,

so I could drag myself inside, shower, and crawl into a warm, familiar bed. Pull the covers up over my head and try with all my might to fall asleep instantly, so I wouldn't have to think anymore.

Doom the whole world.

No way. Not me. They had the wrong person, wrong prophecy. I shook my head.

He misinterpreted it. "It is a gift," he said stiffly.

Wounded, proud prince. I touched his face. He'd given me my mom and dad, my whole town, the entire state of Georgia back. "I was shaking my head at something I was thinking, not your words. Yes, I'd like to have your name, V'lane."

He gave me that brilliant smile again, then his mouth was on mine. This time, when he kissed me, the unpronounceable Fae name slid sweeter than tupelo honey across my tongue and pooled there, warm and delicious, filling my mouth with a feast of taste and sensation beyond description before melting into the meat of it. Unlike the other times he'd implanted his name in my tongue, it felt natural, unobtrusive. Also unlike those times, I wasn't battered by an erotic attack, forced into orgasm by his touch. It was an extraordinary kiss, but it invited without invading, gave without taking.

He drew back. "We are learning from each other," he said. "I begin to understand Adam."

I blinked. "The first man? You know about Adam and Eve?" V'lane didn't seem the kind to study human creation myths.

"No. One of my race that chose to become human," he clarified. "Ah, Barrons comes growling." He gave the startling equivalent of a human snicker and was gone. I reached instinctively for my spear. It was back in the holster. I frowned. I'd forgotten to check. Had it ever been gone?

I turned. "Growling" was a mild word for it. Barrons stood in the doorway, and if looks could kill, I'd have been flayed alive in the street.

"One would think you'd have gotten all the Fae shoved in your mouth you could stand, Ms. Lane."

"One would think that I'd gotten all the *male* shoved in my mouth that I could stand. One day I'm going to *choose* to kiss a man. Not because I'm being raped and not because I'm being scraped up off a street named *Pri-ya* and not because I'm being given the mystical equivalent of a cell phone with all the usual cell phone service problems but because I bloody well *want* to!"

I pushed past him. He didn't move an inch. Electricity sizzled where our bodies brushed.

"Tomorrow night. Ten o'clock. Be here, Ms. Lane."

"I'm fighting with the *sidhe*-seers," I tossed over my shoulder.

"Call it an early night. Or find somewhere else to live."

At noon the next day, Dani, all the other *sidhe*-seers at the abbey, and I were gathered in one of their enormous cafeterias, seated around tables, listening as Rowena addressed the crowd, and, oh, did the woman know how to sway sentiment!

The canny GM was the consummate politician. I listened, committing her tactics to memory. Analyzing the words she chose, how she strung them together, how she played emotion for everything it was worth.

Yes, she said, she would put aside her differences with the young rogue *sidhe*-seer who'd never been properly trained and whose sister had betrayed the entire world by helping her lover—the villainous Lord Master—free the Unseelie to kill billions of people around the globe, including two hundred of our own. Yes, she would agree to do whatever they felt must be done to win the most important battle humankind had ever faced. She could not in good conscience step aside or take off the robes she'd been wearing for *forty-seven years*—more than twice as long as the rogue *sidhe*-seer had even been alive—but she would extend her hand in welcome, if that was what her beloved daughters felt was imperative she do, despite numerous and compelling arguments to the contrary.

After her little speech, I could see doubt on some of the women's faces again, so I stood and delivered mine. Yes, I would put aside my differences with the old woman who'd turned me away the first night she'd ever met me, without even asking my name, who'd told me in no uncertain terms to go die somewhere else and leave her alone—when it had been obvious I was a *sidhe*-seer in desperate need of help. Why hadn't I been one of her "beloved daughters" that night? Was it my fault I'd been raised with no idea what I was? Why hadn't she taken me in?

But I would forgive her and, yes, I would work with the woman who'd withheld the weapons that could kill Fae, refused to let the *sidhe*-seers do the job they'd been born to do, and run a constant slander campaign against my sister, whose greatest mistake was being seduced by a Fae-turned-human with hundreds of thousands of years of experience creating illusions and seducing women.

Who among us might *not* have fallen under such circumstances? They'd met V'lane. If they wanted to throw stones, now was the time to do it, or never. Alina had ultimately seen through the Lord Master's act and had paid with her life. Again, where had Rowena been when my sister was struggling to understand what she was? How had Alina and I gotten lost in the *sidhe*-seer shuffle, abandoned to a life with no training?

I was eager to do as Kat suggested, I told them, excited to work together toward common goals, putting the needs of the *sidhe*-seers first. From this moment forward, I vowed, I would speak no ill of the Grand Mistress, provided she did the same of me.

I sat.

She would cooperate, Rowena said from her podium, despite that I'd continually proven myself unreliable and dangerous, allying myself with the likes of V'lane.

"Excuse me, so did you," I pointed out.

"Only for the greater good."

"You wouldn't allow me to be part of the greater good. You denied me welcome here."

Kat stood. "Stop putting us in the middle! Grand Mistress, we must lay aside our differences. Do you not agree?"

Rowena was still a moment, then nodded tightly.

"Full cooperation?" Kat pressed.

Rowena studied the gathered assembly in silence. I knew the precise moment she acknowledged that she'd lost too much ground with her flock to gain it back here and now. Either the two of us would pull the cart together, or the cart was going to leave us behind. "Yes," she said tightly.

"Great." I shot to my feet. "So, where was the Book being kept, how was it being contained, and how in the world did *you* lose it?"

The roar in the hall was deafening, as I'd expected it to be. This, after all, was the question that had been bandied about these walls in whispers and secrecy for more than twenty years.

I dropped back to my seat, curious to see how she would extricate herself. I had no doubt she would.

"Wicked cool, Mac," said Dani, grinning. "I think we've got her now."

I knew we didn't. Rowena was too clever to be trapped that easily.

When the crowd finally quieted, she informed us with humble gravity that unfortunately such matters were not within her span of authority to discuss. That although I seemed to believe she was solely in charge, the abbey had always been run as a democracy, governed by the Haven, and all her actions and choices had to be approved or rejected by them, particularly in matters of such delicacy and danger. She must meet with the High Council, present our questions, and obey their dictates. Unfortunately (and conveniently for her, I noted dryly), some of them were not in-house at the moment. But as soon as they were . . .

"Blah, blah, blah, blah, blah," I muttered. "By the time she gets around to telling us anything, the Unseelie will have killed a billion more humans." No matter. I was back in the walls of the abbey. It was time to go to work on plan A. This meeting had been plan B.

I looked at Dani. "You said you'd been trying to get into the Forbidden Libraries. Do you know where all twenty-one of them are?"

Her eyes sparkled.

21

Dani knew her way around the abbey's endless maze of stone corridors as well as any *sidhe-seer* in the first five circles of ascension, she told me proudly. There were seven circles of ascension in total, with the seventh being the Haven itself. Kat and her crew were in only the third. She herself was subject to no such limits, Dani confided smugly. Rowena had set her apart from such matters, as her own personal charge.

"So Rowena told you where all the libraries are?" That just didn't sound like the GM I knew.

Well, no, Dani hedged, not exactly. So, okay, maybe she'd learned most of what she knew about the abbey before Rowena and the other women figured out that a soft breeze meant she was near, when she'd still been able to snoop freely. What did it matter? She knew, and that was more than any of the others knew! It had taken her years to track down the libraries, and she still wasn't certain of a couple because she couldn't get down those corridors, but the way she figured it, they *had* to be libraries, because what else would Rowena be hiding?

"Place is huge and deadly weird, Mac," she told me. "There's parts of the abbey don't make sense. Wasted space where you think something should be but ain't."

I wanted to see *all* those places, but right now I needed to focus on the libraries. I'd barely slept last night. The conversation I overheard between my parents had played like a stuck record in my head. *Baby, I'm sorry to tell you this, but according to some ancient prophecy, there's something wrong with you and you're going to doom the whole world. . . .*

I'd been anxious to get my hands on the prophecy before. Now that it was supposedly about me, I was desperate. I wouldn't believe it was about me until I saw it with my own eyes, and even then I probably still wouldn't, unless it spelled out my entire name and said something as indubitably incriminating as: *Beware of that evil MacKayla Lane; she's a piece of work. Gonna doom the whole world, that wench.*

I snorted. Absurd. Had Alina learned any of this? Was that why she'd kept me so far away? Not just for my own good but because she'd learned something about me that made her afraid to get me involved, for the world's sake?

"Nah," I said derisively.

"Is, too," Dani defended. "I can show you 'em."

I snapped back to the present. "Sorry, I was thinking out loud. I believe you, and I want to see those places. But first the libraries."

We wound down one corridor after the next. They all looked the same to me. The abbey was huge.

Without Dani, I might have wandered for days, trying to find my way around. Before I came to the abbey the first time, I'd researched it and learned that the enormous stone fortress had been constructed on consecrated ground in the seventh century, when a church originally built by St. Patrick in 441 A.D. had burned down. That church had been built to replace a crumbling stone circle some claimed had, long ago, been sacred to an ancient pagan sisterhood. The stone circle had been predated by a *shian*, or fairy mound, that had allegedly concealed within it an entrance to the Otherworld.

Translation: This specific spot of earth, this precise longitude and latitude, had been a place of great importance, sacred and protected, as far back as records went and—I had no doubt—even further. Why? Because a book of unspeakable power had been trapped beneath it for thousands and thousands of years?

The abbey was plundered in 913, rebuilt in 1022, burned in 1123, rebuilt in 1218, burned in 1393, and rebuilt in 1414. It was expanded and fortified each time.

It was added on to in the sixteenth century and again extensively in the seventeenth, sponsored by an anonymous wealthy donor who completed the rectangle of stone buildings, enclosing the inner courtyard and adding housing—much to the astonishment of the locals—for up to a thousand residents.

This same unknown donor bought the land around the abbey and turned the enclave into the self-sustaining operation it was today. If I ever had

the time to act instead of always being so busy re-
acting, I wanted to find out who that unknown
donor was.

I glanced at my watch. It was three P.M., and my
schedule was tight. I was supposed to meet the
sidhe-seers in Dublin at seven, then Barrons at ten,
for who knew what purpose. Further hampering my
appointment calendar was the LM's threat to return
for me in three days, which put an uncomfortable
squeeze on, because I couldn't decide what day that
was going to be. Was he counting all day yesterday,
which meant he would return on Saturday morning? Or had he meant to begin counting on Friday,
which meant he would return Sunday? Maybe he'd
meant to allow me three full days and planned to
come back on the fourth. It was all irritatingly
vague. Not only had he threatened me, but he'd not
even given me a specific date and time for my impending . . . whatever.

I planned to discuss it with Barrons tonight. He
was my wave. I was counting on him to keep the LM
from making good on any threats.

Back to my time crunch. "Take me to the corridors
you're barred from, Dani. What's keeping you out?"
I envisioned thick stone walls blocking them off,
maybe vault doors with combinations as long as pi.

I couldn't have hoped for a better answer.

She gave me a sour look. "Stupid fecking wards."

Dani knew where eighteen of the libraries were.
There were three places in the abbey she'd never
been able to get near. The first spot she took me to,

wards were etched in the stone floor at ten-foot intervals along the length of the hall, vanishing
around a corner.

I sauntered down the warded corridor, barely
even flinching, while Dani hooted triumphantly behind me. I turned the corner, passed through another few wards, and came to a tall, ornately carved
door.

The door wasn't as easy to get through. It was
loaded with wards and strange-looking runes. I
tried the handle. It wasn't locked, but the moment I
touched it I suffered the horrifying sensation of
falling from a great height and instantly felt I was
being watched/vulnerable/targeted in someone's
crosshairs, an instant away from a bullet in the back
of my head.

I snatched my hand away, and the feelings vanished.

I took a deep breath and tried the knob again. I
immediately felt as if I'd been stuffed into a small
dark box underground and had only moments before I suffocated!

I snatched it back.

I was breathing shallowly and shaking but standing in the hall, perfectly fine.

I peered at the runes on the door and suddenly realized what they were. Since I'd come to Dublin, I'd
become a voracious reader of books on the paranormal, devouring articles on topics ranging from
Druids to vampires to witches, looking for facts in the
fiction and answers in the myths. These were repelling runes! They worked by amplifying the innate
fears of whoever tried to cross them.

The third time I grasped the knob, my body was covered with fire ants, biting viciously, and I remembered how, at seven years old, I thought the silky red dirt of the hill would be fun to play in. I'd been terrified of them ever since.

It's not real.

I braced myself and forced the knob to turn, while the ants shredded the flesh of my fingers away.

The door opened and I stumbled through, choking down a scream, on the verge of clawing my skin off.

All sensation stopped the instant I crossed the threshold.

I looked back. The wood of the threshold was also engraved with repelling runes.

I was through! I was in one of the Forbidden Libraries!

I glanced around eagerly. It wasn't particularly impressive. Not compared to BB&B. The room was small, windowless, and, despite a number of dehumidifiers, musty. Between shelves and tables filled with books, scrolls, and collectibles, dozens of lamps blazed. Rowena was taking no chances with Shades getting into her precious libraries.

I moved into the room and began searching the tables first, while Dani stood watch far down the corridor. As I'd feared, there were no card catalogs in the Forbidden Libraries. Even though the room was small, a thorough search could take days.

Ten minutes later, Dani yelled, and I hurried out into the hall, jerking as I crossed the spelled threshold, to find a mob of *sidhe*-seers pushing and shoving at the ward line.

Kat stood in the front of the mob. "Rowena said you managed to pass through some of her wards and were in forbidden archives. She sent us to stop you."

Well, that answered one of my questions. I'd wondered—now that I could move through wards at will—if I still tripped them when I did. I was surprised Rowena hadn't come herself.

"To stop me, you'd have to be able to cross the ward line, and"—I glanced down at her toes, on the edge of the line of nearly invisible symbols—"it doesn't look to me like you can."

"I can get past most," Barb said, shoving past her. "You're not so hot. Jo can, too." She turned around. "Where'd Jo go?" She looked at Dani. "Wasn't she just here?"

Dani shrugged. "She left."

"We're not after stopping you, Mac." Kat's usually solemn gray gaze danced with excitement. "We're after helping you search."

I broke the ward lines with chewing gum—yes, chewing gum. Wards are delicate things, easy to deface if you can touch them.

In order to touch them, you have to be able to pass them, which usually makes touching them a moot point, but in this case I needed to scrub the ward's power away to let my sisters-in-arms through.

In most cases, all that's required to undermine a ward is to break its continuity, to interrupt the

design and short-circuit the flow of energy it gener-
ates. Sometimes, if you break one badly, you turn it
into something else, but I didn't know that then and
my luck held that day.

Although I could deface the wards on the door, I
could do nothing about the repelling runes carved
into it and into the wood of the threshold. Each
sidhe-seer that stepped across it had to face her personal demons.

They all made it, I was proud to see.

I left them in the library, dozens of sets of willing
hands carefully turning ancient pages, delicately
unwinding thick scrolls, picking up statues and
opening boxes and looking for anything we could
use.

Dani and I moved on to the next library. Gaining
access wasn't as easy this time. Again there were
multiple ward barriers, but each was of increasing
density and intensity. I passed through the first
ward with relative ease, the second with a grunt.
The third generated a small shock and made my
hair crackle. I marked each one with a lipstick from
my pocket as I passed through, so Dani could follow me.

The fourth had me gritting my teeth, cursing
whoever had placed these ancient designs. Rowena?
I wanted to learn.

I made the mistake of trying to barge through the
fifth to get the discomfort over with quickly and
slammed into it like a brick wall. I bounced off and
went sprawling.

Dani snickered.

I tossed my hair from my eyes and glared up at her.

"Dude. Happens to me all the time."

I stood and warily approached the ward line. It *wasn't* a simple ward line. There were layers of wards, shimmering, one on top of another. To date, the only wards I'd seen were silvery delicate-looking things.

These wards had a bluish tint, sharper lines, and more-complex shapes. Now that I was paying careful attention, I could feel the slight chill they threw off. The pages in the Book of Kells had nothing on the intricacy of these designs. Knots became fantastical creatures, morphed into incomprehensible mathematical equations and then back into knots again. I knew nothing of wards. Where was Barrons when I needed him?

I spent ten minutes trying to get through it. If I ran at it, it bounced me off. If I tried to press slowly forward, it simply didn't yield, as if there genuinely was a wall there that I just couldn't see.

"Try blood," Dani suggested.

I looked at her. "Why?"

She shrugged. "Sometimes when Ro needs fierce wicked mojo, she uses blood. Some of the wards we placed around your cell had my blood in 'em. I figure since you can cross most of 'em, your blood might do something. If not, you can try mine."

"What do I do with it?"

"Dunno. Drip some on the wards."

After a moment's consideration, I decided it couldn't hurt. (The day would come when I would discover I was wrong about that. Adding blood to some wards is even more stupid than throwing gas on a fire and, in some cases, actually transmutes them into living guardians. Take it from me, *never* indiscriminately drip your blood on wards of unknown origin!) I reached into my boot for my switchblade. "Stay back, in case something goes wrong," I told her.

I held out my hand, palm up, as close to the ward barrier as I could get without being repelled, and made a shallow slice. Ow.

Blood welled.

I turned my hand over to drip it on the floor.

Nothing dripped. I turned my hand back over. There was no wound.

I sliced my palm again, this time more deeply. "Ow!" Blood welled. I turned it over. Nothing dripped. I frowned. Shook it. Squeezed my hand into a fist.

"What'cha doin', Mac?"

"Hang on a sec." I turned my hand back over. There was no cut.

Setting my jaw, I turned my palm to the floor, kept it down, and sliced fast, hard, and deep. Blood dripped. Good for me. It stopped. I sliced again, deeper. It dripped again, and a thin rivulet ran into the edge of the symbols.

The designs hissed, shivered on the stone floor, and steamed, before eroding where my blood had touched them.

I was able to step across the barrier, although not without difficulty.

"Come on, Dani." We weren't through the storm yet. I could feel things up ahead.

Worse things.

There was no reply.

I turned around. There was a stone wall behind me. "Dani?" I called. "Dani, can you hear me?"

You are not permitted here. You are not one of us.

I whirled back around. A woman stood in the corridor, blocking my way. She was blond, beautiful, with icy eyes.

"Who are you?" I demanded.

Leave now or suffer our wrath.

I took a step forward and instantly felt excruciating pain. I staggered back. "I need to get into the library. I'm just looking for answers."

You are not permitted here. You are not one of us.

"I heard you the first time. I just want to look around."

Leave now or suffer our wrath.

I tried reasoning with her, only to realize that, despite the crushing pain that slammed me every time I tried to take a step forward, the woman was nothing more than the mystical equivalent of a recorded message.

No matter what I said, she repeated the same two things, over and over. No matter how many times I tried to push forward, pain drove me back.

There was no doubt in my mind that these impenetrable wards protected invaluable secrets. I *had* to get through.

I had other tools at my disposal. I opened my mouth and released V'lane's name.

He was there before I'd even finished speaking, smiling—for a split second.

Then he doubled over in pain. His golden head snapped back.

He actually hissed at me like an animal.

And vanished.

I gaped.

I looked back at the woman.

You are not permitted here. You are not one of us.

There was no way forward that I could see at the moment. I didn't have any Unseelie flesh on me to try eating, to see if it would make me immune enough to the pain to continue on. Then again, after what I'd just seen happen to V'lane, I wasn't sure if having temporary Fae running through my veins would help or hinder.

I wasn't completely surprised to discover the stone wall behind me was an illusion.

Still, forcing my way through it hurt like hell.

22

"The LM came to see me yesterday," I said, as I stepped through the front door of Barrons Books and Baubles. The exterior lights of the handsomely restored building were set to low, bathing the street and alcoved entrance in a soft amber glow. The interior lights were equally low. It appeared Barrons no longer considered the Shades much of a threat.

I couldn't see him, but I knew he was here. I'm attuned to even the faintest whiff of Jericho Barrons now. I wish I wasn't. It makes me remember a time when we danced, and he laughed, and I had no cares in the world but to be . . . a fine beast. To eat, sleep, and have sex.

Ah, the simple life.

I tensed. There was an Object of Power, or several, somewhere in the bookstore. It was one kick-ass powerful one, or an assortment of lessers. I could feel it in my stomach. I could sense it, a cold fire in the dark pit of my brain. OOPs no longer make me feel sick. They make me feel . . . alive.

"He said you're the jackass who taught him Voice," I continued. "Funny how you forgot to mention that when you were trying to teach me."

"I forget nothing, Ms. Lane. I omit."

"And evade."

"Lie, cheat, and steal," he agreed.

"If the shoe fits."

"You have absurd priorities." He stepped from the shadows between bookcases.

I looked him up and down. Once before I'd seen Jericho Barrons wearing jeans and a T-shirt. It's like sheet-metaling a W16 Bugatti Veyron engine—all 1,001 horsepower of it—with the body of a '65 Shelby. The height of sophisticated power sporting in-your-face, fuck-you muscle. The effect is disturbing.

He had more tattoos now than he'd had a few days ago. When I'd last seen him wearing nothing but a sheen of sweat, his arms were unmarked. They were now sleeved in intricate crimson and black designs, from bicep to hand. A silver cuff gleamed on his wrist. There were silver chains on his boots.

"Slumming, huh?" I said.

You should talk, said those dark eyes, as they swept my black leather ensemble.

"What's absurd about my priorities?" I evaded. None of my concern what he thought of my outfit. "You hated my rainbows, now you don't like my leather. Is there anything you like on me?"

"The LM, as you call him, sent his princes to rape you and may possibly have raped you himself, and you only now mention that he . . . what? Came calling? Did he bring you flowers? And the answer is skin, Ms. Lane."

I wasn't about to acknowledge his last words. "No flowers. Just coffee. Wasn't Starbucks, though. I'd give my eyeteeth for a grande latte from Starbucks."

"I wouldn't so blithely offer up my eyeteeth. You never know when you might need them. For a woman who was gang-raped recently, you certainly seem blasé."

"Oh, please, Barrons, how much more can I lose?"

"Never wonder that."

"Why did you teach him? Do you realize that inadvertently, perhaps even vertently—"

"Not a word, Ms. Lane."

"—you might have helped him kill my sister?"

"You're stretching."

"Am I? What else did you teach him?"

"A few minor Druid arts."

"In exchange for what?"

"What did Darroc say? Did he promise you your sister back again?"

"Of course."

"And did you tell your rapist you'd think about it?"

"He said he was coming back for me in three days. And that I'd better be willing."

"But you," Barrons said softly, stepping closer, "ah, my dear Ms. Lane, *you* think you have nothing more to lose. When do these three days expire?"

"That's what really pisses me off. I don't know. He was annoyingly vague."

Barrons looked at me, then a faint smile curved his lips, and for a moment I thought he might laugh.

"The nerve. Threatening you and not being precise about it."

"My sentiments exactly."

The faint smile was gone. His face was cold. "You will not leave my side again."

I sighed. "I was pretty sure you'd say that."

"Do you want him to take you again?"

"No."

"Then you won't be stupid. You won't go dashing off into danger at precisely the most inopportune moment for some seemingly noble cause, only to get abducted by the villain, through no fault of your own, because you *had* to do the honorable thing; after all, aren't some things worth dying for?" he said dryly.

I cocked my head. "I didn't know you read romances."

"I know humans."

"Ha. You finally admit you aren't one."

"I admit nothing. You want truths from me? See me when you look at me."

"Why did you smash the birthday cake I got you into the ceiling?"

"You were trying to celebrate the day I was born. Come, Ms. Lane. I have something to show you."

He turned and moved into the rear of the store without looking back to see if I was following.

I followed. Major OOPs, dead ahead.

"Who'd you have to kill to get the third one?" I stared. Three of the stones necessary to "reveal the true nature" of the *Sinsar Dubh* glowed an eerie bluish-black on the desk in his study.

He looked at me. *Do you really want to know?* his dark gaze mocked.

"Scratch that question," I said hurriedly. "V'lane has the fourth, right?" On that note, I wondered where V'lane had gone and why. What had happened to him in that warded corridor? Why had he hissed at me, and what had caused him pain? I'd expected him to sift in shortly after it had happened and either explain or be seriously ticked off at me.

I believe so.

"But we don't know where."

Not at the moment.

"Quit talking without talking. You have a mouth; use it." I resented the implied intimacy of our wordless dialogues.

"I *was* using my mouth a few days ago. So were you."

"Quit reminding me," I growled.

"I thought we were past unnecessary pretenses. I stand corrected."

I moved toward the desk, both drawn and repelled by the power the rune-covered stones were throwing off. I recognized the one I'd stolen from Mallucé's lair. It was the smallest of the three. The second was twice its size, the third even larger. They had sharply hewn edges, as if they'd been chiseled with great force from some substance with vastly different chemical composites and universal laws than anything on our world. Arranged in close proximity to one another, each of the three emitted a delicate crystalline chiming sound of different duration and pitch. The sound was hauntingly beautiful. And intensely disturbing. Like wind chimes from hell.

"You said that if all four were brought together, they would sing a Song of Making. *The* Song? Or a lesser one? *Are* there lesser songs?"

"I don't know."

I fidgeted. Barrons admitting to ignorance disturbed me as much as the sound coming from the stones.

I reached out to touch one of them. As my hand passed above it, its banked glow flared so bright it hurt my eyes. I drew my hand back.

"Interesting," Barrons murmured. "Are you up for an experiment?"

I looked at him sharply. "You want to try to corner the Book with three." To study it, see how it might react and if anything further would be revealed.

"You game?"

I considered it a moment, remembering what had happened the last time he and I had gone chasing the Book.

The thing had abruptly changed course and headed straight for us. It had gotten Barrons in its thrall. It had gone for Barrons, not me. There was nothing wrong with me. I was fine. I was the same Mac I'd always been. Daddy himself had said that I was as good as they came. Everybody knew how wise Jack Lane was. "Sure," I said.

While he gathered the stones and began wrapping them in velvet cloths, I stared at the Unseelie mirror. It had been standing right beneath my nose in his study for months, but I'd never once sensed its Fae presence and that it was part of a vast network of Unseelie Hallows. It was closed now, masquerading as a perfectly normal mirror.

"How does it work?" I asked.

He continued wrapping the stones in silence.

"Oh, come on," I said impatiently. "It's not like I'm trying to pry into your head to uncover any of your precious secrets. The Fae are screwing up my planet and I'm going to kick their asses off it. All knowledge, like weapons—good. So, spill."

He didn't look up from what he was doing, but I could see a faint smile playing at his lips.

"Sometimes I think you refuse to tell me things just to irritate me."

"But you *never* do anything just to irritate me," he said dryly.

"Not when it involves something that might be important. What if I get trapped somewhere with no escape but a Silver? I wouldn't even know how to use it."

"You think you've got the balls to step into one of those things?"

"You might be surprised," I said coolly.

"Not if you do everything like you fuck."

I wasn't going to let him discombobulate me by bringing up sex. "I want to learn, Barrons. *Teach* me. If I knew a fraction of what you know, my odds of surviving would be way higher."

"Perhaps you'd no longer want to."

"Would you just cooperate?" I said, exasperated.

"I do not know that word," he mocked in falsetto.

"I'm trying to arm myself so I *can* fight like I fuck," I snapped. "But you refuse to help." I *hated* it when he reminded me of when I'd been *Pri-ya*.

"I was beginning to wonder if you were ever going to say that word again, Ms. Lane. Time was, you had no reservations. 'Fuck me, Jericho Barrons,' you'd say. Morning, noon, and night."

There are two kinds of verbal honey a Southern woman can slather on her words when she feels like it: the kind that attracts flies, melts men's hearts, and firms up all their other parts, or the kind that makes a man want to curl up and die. I employed the latter. "I didn't know getting you to talk was so easy, or I'd have said it five minutes ago. Fuck you, Jericho Barrons."

He raised his head and laughed, teeth flashing white in his face. I dug my nails into my palms.

"The Silvers," he said, when he'd stopped laughing, "once numbered in the tens of thousands, but some say they're now infinite. Fae things tend to—"

"I know. Take on a life of their own. Change, evolve in strange ways."

"When the Seelie King first made them—"

"*Un*seelie King," I corrected.

"He was Seelie first. And quit interrupting me if you want me to keep talking. When the *Seelie* King first made them, they formed a network of absolute precision and predictability. It was a brilliant invention. They were the Fae's first method of travel between dimensions. Entering one of them instantly deposited you in the Hall of All Days."

"What's the Hall of All Days?"

"The Hall is . . . well, think of it as an airport, the main arrival and departure point of the entire network. It's lined with mirrors that connect to mirrors on other worlds, in countless other dimensions and times. One can stand in the Hall, examine the individual glasses, and choose from hundreds of thousands of places to go. It was the Fae version of a . . . quantum travel agency."

"V'lane told me the king originally created the Silvers for his concubine, not for other Fae at all. He said the king created them so she could live inside the mirrors, never aging, and have other worlds to explore until he found a way to make her Fae like him." I wondered again what had happened to V'lane earlier this afternoon. Even though I knew I couldn't count on it, I felt a little naked without his name in my tongue.

"Did he also tell you that when the queen felt the power of the king's creation spring into existence, she demanded to know what he'd done, and that, to allay her suspicions because she hated his concubine so much, he had to pretend he'd made the Silvers as a gift for *her*?"

"V'lane said the king gave the queen only part of them."

"Unfortunately, he had to give the queen the nexus that contained the Hall of All Days. His concubine got only a small portion of what he'd made for her, sealed off from the rest. To compensate, he built his concubine the fantastical White Mansion, high on a hill, a house of infinite rooms, terraces, and gardens. He made that part of the Silvers accessible only through mirrors that hung in his own private chambers."

"So there are two separate parts to the Silvers." This was a lot to absorb. "One is a collection of possibly infinite mirrors that connect to other dimensions, worlds, and times, from the main 'airport' in the Hall of All Days. The other is a sealed-off smaller network that's where the concubine lived. I guess once she died, that part was never used again," I mused. The Silvers were fascinating stuff. I couldn't imagine being able to step inside a mirror and instantly be transported to some other world or time.

"V'lane told you a lot." Barrons sounded irritated.

"He tells me more than you do. Makes me wonder who to trust."

"Motto to live by: Never trust a fairy. Did he tell you *how* the king's concubine died?"

"He said she hated what the king had become so much that she left him the only way she could. By ending her own life."

"Did he bother pointing out that everything the king had done, he'd done for her? Did she think of that before she decided to kill herself? Did it ever occur to her that sometimes a willingness to turn dark for someone else might just be a fucking virtue?"

"It doesn't sound like he went dark for her. It sounds like he was ticked off that she was going to die and willing to do anything to keep her."

"Perspective, Ms. Lane. Get some."

The Lord Master had said the same thing. "You think the concubine should have appreciated that her lover turned into an obsessed jackass and overlooked the horrific results of his experiments? Maybe if instead of spending all his time—wasn't it tens of thousands of years she waited?—trying to make her live forever, he'd just loved her for the mortal lifetime she had, she'd have been happy!"

Barrons looked at me sharply. "The Silvers are a mess now," he continued abruptly. "There's nothing predictable about them."

"Because Cruce cursed them. Who exactly is Cruce?" I kept hearing his name, but that was all. I didn't even know whether he was Seelie or Unseelie. "And what was the curse?"

"Irrelevant. He's dead." Barrons placed the stones in a black leather pouch covered with delicately glistening runes and tied it with a leather drawstring. The moment he sealed the bag, the chiming ceased and the stones fell silent. "But his curse will never die. It corrupted the Silvers irrevocably. What was once an easily navigated network is now a place of complete chaos. Now some Silvers take you to the Hall, but others don't. Worlds and dimensions fractured and are splintered with IFPs. Some of the main mirrors shattered, others sprang into existence where they were never supposed to be. Many of the two-way Silvers in the Hall are now one-way tickets to wastelands. The looking glasses themselves changed, casting illusory reflections. The Hall of All Days collided with the concubine's realm, with parts of Faery, and some of it even crashed into the Dreaming."

"The Dreaming!" I exclaimed. "There's actually a Fae realm with that name?"

"It doesn't belong to the Fae. The Dreaming is far older and belongs to no one. It's where all hopes, fantasies, illusions, and nightmares of sentient beings come to be or go to rest, whichever you prefer to believe. Complicating things further, Cruce's curse caused tears in the walls of the Unseelie prison, and now the Silvers connect to the prison, as well."

"Well, then, why haven't the Unseelie escaped before?"

"Some have. But the Unseelie prison is so enormous that few discovered the rifts in the walls, and the Silvers are so impossible to navigate that only a handful ever managed to find their way into your world. One could stay lost inside the network of the Silvers forever. They're no longer a realm of the present, but hold the residue of the past. Some say they're also projections of all the possibles, that they really have become the Hall of *All* Days that have ever been and ever will be. There are no assurances. The Fae avoid them completely."

"But not you. And not the LM."

"There are ways—Druid arts that can seal off portions of the Silvers if used wisely, affording a degree of control over temporary transport within a limited space. Depending on the Silver you have to work with, it is not without . . . discomfort. The cold in some of them is difficult to bear."

I knew that. I'd seen him step from it, coated with crystals of iced blood. I'd felt the gust of icy soul-numbing air. "And you killed the woman you carried out of the Silver why?" My voice was spun sugar on a knife's edge.

"Because I wanted to." He matched my sugary lightness of tone. "Didn't expect that, did you, Ms. Lane? Not only an answer but an incrimination, in your book. Come," he said, and his dark gaze glittered with sudden impatience. "The night won't last forever."

"What's the Unseelie prison like?" I wanted to know if it was the cold place I sometimes went to in my dreams. If so, how could I possibly know of it?

"Multiply the chill in my Silver by infinity."

"But what does it look like?"

"No sun. No grass. No life. Just cliffs and cliffs of ice. Cold. Darkness. Despair. The air reeks of it. There are three colors there: white, black, and blue. The fabric of the place lacks the necessary chemical compositions for any other colors to exist. Your skin would be as white as bleached bones. Your eyes, dull black. Your lips, blue. Nothing grows. There is only hunger without sustenance. Lust without satisfaction. Pain without end. There are monsters there that have no desire to leave, because they are such monsters."

"How do you know all this?" I asked as we headed out back to, I assumed, select an incredible car from Barrons' incredible collection.

"Enough. Tell me, Ms. Lane, if you could go back to the day Alina was leaving for Trinity and stop her, would you?"

"Absolutely," I said without hesitation.

"Knowing that this would all play out anyway? The Book was already loose. This was going to happen whether or not she came to Dublin. Just a different variation on the same destructive theme. Would you have kept her in Ashford to keep her alive, never learned what you are, and most likely died in complete ignorance at the hands of some Fae?"

"Isn't there a third option?" I said irritably. "What's behind door number three? Haven't you ever seen *Let's Make a Deal*?"

He gave me a look.

Obviously not.

"What are we driving tonight?" I asked, as I reached for the doorknob.

23

I am *not* riding that." There were times when I had
to put my foot down with Barrons. This was one
of them.

"Shut up and get on."

If I'd shaken my head any more violently, my neck
would have snapped.

"On. Now."

"In your dreams."

Our "ride" was a Royal Hunter.

Barrons had somehow gotten a Hunter to land in
the alley between BB&B and the garage—one of
those terrifying beasts whose primary purpose
was to eradicate my kind from the face of the earth.
Admittedly, it was one of the smaller ones—the size
of a narrow two-story house rather than a five-
story apartment complex—and it wasn't throwing off that massively deadly feel of the ones Jayne
had shot at, but still, it was a Royal Hunter, the
caste responsible for murdering countless *sidhe*-
seers for thousands of years. And he expected me to
touch it?

I hadn't sensed it because it was somehow . . . dampened.

It crouched there, blacker than pitch, looking all Satanic, with leathery wings and fiery eyes, horns and a forked tail. Its labored exhalations puffed gusts of smoke down the alley into what used to be the biggest Dark Zone in the city. The space between the bookstore and the garage was twenty degrees colder than the rest of the night.

I reached inside my coat for my spear.

"Don't you dare," said Barrons. "It's under my control."

We stared at each other.

"What did you have to offer a Hunter to get it to do this? How *does* one mercenary pay another?"

"You should know. How are your precious principles lately?"

I scowled at him. After a moment, I released my spear.

"It can cover the city far more quickly than we can in a car. Your . . . IFPs, as you call them, don't bother it, making it the wisest choice of transport."

"I'm a *sidhe*-seer, Barrons. It's a Hunter. Guess what Hunters hunt? *Sidhe*-seers. I am *not* getting on it."

"Time is short, Ms. Lane. Move your ass."

I poked mentally at the Hunter to glean its intentions, expecting to encounter a roiling pit of homicidal *sidhe*-seer thoughts.

There was nothing but a wall of black ice. "I can't get to its mind." I didn't like that one bit.

"And tonight it can't get to yours, so leave it alone and do as I say."

I narrowed my eyes. "You can't control a Hunter! Nobody can!"

His dark gaze mocked. "You're afraid."

"I am not," I snapped. Of course I was. The thing might be suspiciously dampened and seemingly oblivious to my presence, but fear of it was in my blood. I'd been born with a deep-seated subconscious alarm. "What if it shakes us off as soon as it gets us up there?" I might not bleed like I used to, but I was pretty sure my bones were as easily broken as the next person's.

Barrons walked around to the front of the Hunter. Flames leapt in its eyes when it saw him. It sniffed at Barrons, and some of the heat seemed to die. When Barrons withdrew the pouch containing the stones from his coat, the Hunter pressed its nostrils to it and seemed to like the scent. "It knows it would be dead before it could," he said softly.

"It's never going to let me on it with my spear, and I'm not giving it up," I prevaricated.

"Your spear is the least of its concerns."

"Just how am I supposed to hold on?" I demanded.

"They have loose skin between the wings. Grab it like a horse's mane. But put these on first." He tossed a pair of gloves at me. "And keep them on." They were of strange fabric, thick yet supple. "You don't want to touch it with bare skin." He assessed me. "The rest of you should be fine."

"Why don't I want to touch it with bare skin?" I asked warily.

"On, Ms. Lane. Now. Or I'll strap you onto the damned thing."

It took me a few tries, but a few minutes later I was on the back of an Unseelie Hunter.

I understood why he'd given me the gloves. It radiated such intense cold that if I'd touched it with my bare hands and there'd been any moisture on them at all, they would have frozen to its leathery hide. I shivered, grateful for my layers of leather clothing. Barrons mounted behind me, too close and electric for my comfort.

"Why does it like the smell of the stones?"

"They were chiseled from the walls of the Unseelie King's fortress. It's the equivalent of your pecan pie, fried chicken, and fingernail polish," he said dryly. "Smells like home."

The Hunter gave a blast of smoky air, filling the alley with the acrid stench of brimstone. Then it unfurled its wings and, with one massive pump of those leathery sails, lifted off and flapped darkly into the night, showering crystals of black ice onto the streets below.

I caught my breath and stared down, watching as the bookstore grew smaller.

We rose higher and higher into the cold, dark night sky.

There was Trinity College and Temple Bar!

There was the Garda station and the park. There was the Guinness Storehouse, with the platform where I'd stood looking down the night I realized I'd fallen in love with this city.

There were the docks, the bay, stretching to the ocean's horizon.

There was the hated church where my world had fallen apart. I tipped my head back and looked up at the stars, rejecting both vision and memory. The moon was brilliantly white, brighter than it should have been, rimmed with that same strange bloody aura I'd seen a few nights ago.

"What's with the moon?" I asked Barrons.

"The Fae world is bleeding into yours. Look at those streets north of the river."

I looked away from the crimson-edged moon to where he was pointing. Wet cobblestones glistened a delicate lavender hue of neon intensity, traced by silvery cobwebs of light. It was beautiful.

But it was wrong and deeply disturbing, as if there was more than mere color to those stones. As if some microscopic, lichenlike Unseelie life-form was growing on our world, staining it, transforming it as surely as Cruce's curse had mutated the Silvers.

"We have to stop things from changing," I said urgently. At what point would the changes become permanent? Were they already?

"Which is why one would think you wouldn't waste time arguing when I procure the most efficient mode of travel." Barrons sounded downright pissy.

I glanced down at my "mode of travel," at the inky, leathery skin fisted in my gloved hands.

I was riding an Unseelie Hunter! Had any *sidhe-seer* in the history of humankind ever done such a thing? Dani was never going to believe it. I watched wisps of fog pass its satyrlike head, crowned with lethally pointed ebony horns. I felt the play of tension in its hide as it flapped its massive wings. I studied the city beyond them.

It was a long way down.

"You *do* know Inspector Jayne shoots at these things," I said, worried.

"Jayne is otherwise occupied at the moment."

"You can't know everything." Now I was the one who sounded pissy.

He gave the Hunter's hide a little pat, like one might give a horse.

It reared into an attack pose, craned its neck around, shot a flaming look of banked hatred over its shoulder, and snorted a thin tendril of fire from one nostril in unmistakable rebuke.

Barrons laughed.

I have to admit, aside from the cold and Barrons being much too close, I enjoyed the ride. It was an experience I would never forget. It's funny how, when things seem the darkest, moments of beauty present themselves in the most unexpected places.

Dublin was still without power, but it had been so for months, and wind and time had carried all smog and pollution out to sea. No smokestacks puffed, no cars emitted fumes. There was no halo of city lights competing with the brilliant moonlight. The city had been swept clean. It was the world the way it used to be, hundreds of years ago. The stars twinkled as sparklingly visible in the Dublin night sky as they did in rural Georgia.

The river Liffey split the city down the middle, its many bridges dissecting the long silvery path, all the way to the bay.

To the north, Jayne's men were otherwise occupied indeed, battling a horde of Unseelie I'd never seen before, just a few blocks from the alley where my sister had died. Grief welled, but I slammed it down so hard and fast into my padlocked box that I barely felt it.

On the south side, we passed silently above my sister *sidhe*-seers over and over. MacHalos blazing, led by Kat and Dani, they scouted the streets, doing what damage they could.

Dani had hated my going off without her tonight and had argued fervently that her superstrengths might well be necessary in a pinch. She'd been far more piqued than mollified by my reminder that Barrons was faster than she was.

We flew for hours, circling, circling. It was nearly four in the morning by the time I finally sensed the *Sinsar Dubh*.

The second I did, there went my head—a killer pounding at my temples, spreading to encompass my skull in an ever-tightening vise.

"Got it," I said tightly, pointing in the general direction.

The Hunter took us down. We skimmed rooftops as I tried to target its precise location. Tops of church spires and smokestacks passed a dozen feet beneath us. The lower we got, the more intense my pain grew and the colder I felt. Teeth chattering, shivering with misery, I guided him: *Left; no, right; no, turn here, yes, there. Hurry, it's getting away. Wait, I can't feel it. There it is again.*

Abruptly, the *Sinsar Dubh* stopped. We overshot it by five city blocks and had to circle back around. Hunters don't corner like Porsches.

"What's it doing?" Barrons demanded.

"Besides killing me? Don't know." Didn't really care at the moment. "Are you sure we need to do this?"

"It's merely pain, Ms. Lane, and of finite duration."

"*You* try functioning with your head split open and someone stirring your brains. Isn't there some Druid spell you could do that would help?"

"I lack both tattoo implements and the time. Besides, I'm not certain it would work, and although you recently demanded I dress you in crimson and black, I have no desire to see you wearing it permanently."

"And the reminders just keep coming," I muttered, and rolled my eyes. The motion, coupled with my nausea, nearly made me throw up.

"Only because you seem to keep forgetting who saved your ass."

Unfortunately, not the many things he'd done to it.

The Hunter drew in its wings and dropped to the ground in silence. I slid off its leathery back and hit the pavement, puking.

"Where is it?" Barrons was demanding before I'd even finished.

I wiped my mouth with the back of my hand. "Dead ahead. Three blocks?" I guessed.

"Can you walk?"

I nodded and gagged from the movement but didn't throw up again. I hadn't eaten since lunch, so there was nothing left to throw up. I took perverse comfort in the pain. Obviously I wasn't the one who was going to doom the world. If I was so bad, the

Book would have liked me, wanted me to come closer, not repelled me. Ryodan was wrong. The *Sinsar Dubh* didn't want anything to do with me.

We closed in, Barrons stalking, me stumbling. Behind us, the Hunter lifted off, vanishing in a sudden snowstorm of black ice.

"And there went our ride," I said sourly. As awful as the *Sinsar Dubh* inevitably left me feeling, there was no way I'd be able to make the long trek back to the bookstore. I hoped the stones would succeed in corralling it—even without the fourth—and maybe diminish the pain it was causing me.

"It'll be back when the Book is gone. It insisted on maintaining a certain distance."

I didn't blame it one bit. I just wished I could do the same.

Two blocks away, with the Book firmly fixed on my radar, my pain vanished abruptly, for no apparent reason. The *Sinsar Dubh* was still dead ahead.

I stood up straight for the first time since we'd landed and took a deep, grateful breath.

Barrons stopped walking. "What is it?"

"I don't hurt anymore." I turned to face him in the middle of the deserted street.

"Why not?"

"Got me."

"Postulate."

I gave him a look that said, *Postulate this*.

"I don't like it," he growled.

I didn't, either. But at the same time, I did. I hate

pain. I've always known I would make a terrible torture victim. If someone pulled *one* of my fingernails off, I'd spew the beans like a geyser.

"But you still sense it?"

I nodded.

"Did you eat Unseelie?" he accused.

"Duh, OOP detector here. Can't track if I eat it."

"Yet you feel no pain at all?"

"Not an ounce." In fact, I felt great. Energized, charged, ready for anything. "So?" I prompted. "Are we going to stand here all night or do something?" Free from agony, I was ready to tackle it head-on.

He assessed me, his expression tight. After a moment, he said, "We abort. We're pulling out." He turned and began walking away.

"Are you kidding me?" I snapped at his back. "We're here. We found it. Let's see what those stones can do!"

"No. Move it. Now."

"Barrons, I'm fine—"

"And you shouldn't be." He stopped and turned to glare at me.

"Maybe I've gotten stronger. I'm immune to a lot of Fae glamour now, and I can walk through wards. Maybe it just caught me off guard, and my body adjusted after a few minutes."

"And maybe it's playing with us."

"Maybe this is a prime opportunity to learn something about it."

"Maybe it's got you in its thrall, and you don't even know it."

"Maybe we could stand here all night debating

the maybes, or we could put your plan into action and see what happens! You're the one who thought it up to begin with. Don't wuss out on me now." I turned my back and began marching in the opposite direction, toward the *Sinsar Dubh*.

"Stop this instant, Ms. Lane!"

"What happened to fear-nothing-take-no-prisoners Barrons? Should we go cower somewhere?" I flung over my shoulder.

A moment later, we were shoulder to shoulder, marching for it together.

"You're impossible," he growled.

"Pot, meet kettle," I said sweetly.

"Take this." He handed me one of the stones, wrapped in velvet. Even inside the thick black covering, it glowed blue-black as soon as I touched it. He looked at me, hard, his gaze unfathomable.

"What am I supposed to do with it?"

"We're coming up on O'Connell. I'll circle around to the opposite side of the intersection and close in behind it. I want to triangulate it precisely with the stones. The moment you have both the Book and me in your sight, place your stone on the east corner of the intersection. I'll position the other two where they need to be."

"What do you expect to happen?"

"Best-case scenario? We contain it. Worst case? We run like hell."

24

I headed down the street after Barrons left, certain we were on the right track. It occurred to me
that maybe the stones we were carrying were the
reason I was no longer feeling any pain. Maybe, as
we'd gotten closer, they had erected some kind of
protective barrier. They'd been created to harness
and contain the Book. Why wouldn't they shield
whoever was carrying them from its harmful effects?

I hurried to the intersection and stood on my appointed corner, waiting.

And waiting.

The Book was moving *very* slowly, as if out for a
leisurely stroll.

"Come on. Move, damn you." Was a Fae or a
human carrying it? The city hummed with Fae static,
making it impossible to get a lock on any channel.

As if it had heard me, the Book began moving
more quickly, heading right where we wanted it.

Then, suddenly, it was just . . . *gone*.

"What the—" I spun in a circle, my radar on high,

searching, testing the night. I couldn't pick up a thing. Not even a faint tingle.

I glanced back down the street. Barrons was no-where to be seen.

I didn't like this one bit. We shouldn't have split up. That was always when bad things happened in the movies, and that was exactly what I felt like at the moment: the ingénue, standing on a horror set. No lights, alone in a city of monsters, with an an-cient, sentient receptacle of pure evil somewhere in my immediate vicinity but no longer detectable by me, and with no clue what to do next.

I turned in a circle, stone in one hand, spear in the other.

"Barrons?" I hissed urgently. There was no reply.

Just as suddenly as it had disappeared, the Book was back on my radar. But it was *behind* me now!

I called for Barrons again. When there was still no answer, I tucked my spear under my arm, whipped out my cell phone, and punched up his number.

When he answered, I told him it had moved and where.

"Wait for me. I'll be right there."

"But it's moving. We're going to lose it. Head east." I thumbed End and took off after the Book.

I was rushing toward it, trying to catch up, when the Book suddenly stopped, and I could feel that I was closer to it than I'd initially thought. *Way* closer. All my readings on the thing were wonky tonight.

I froze.

It was just around the corner, maybe twenty feet away from me.

If I walked to the edge of the building and poked my head around it, I would see it.

I could feel it there, perfectly still, pulsing with dark energy. What was it doing? Was this its idea of cat and mouse? Was it . . . amused?

It began moving again. Toward me.

Where the hell was Barrons?

It stopped.

Was it trying to spook me? If so, it was working.

What if Ryodan was wrong? What if the Beast *did* have substance and could shred me? What if whatever was carrying it had a gun and could blow my head off? I was afraid if I retreated, the Book might take it as a sign of weakness, in the way a lion can smell fear, and come after me for all it was worth.

I put on my best bluster and took a step forward.

It moved, too.

I flinched. It was all the way to the corner now.

What was carrying it? What was it doing? What was it planning? Not knowing was killing me.

I was a *sidhe*-seer. I was an OOP detector. This was what I was made for.

I set my jaw, squared my shoulders, marched to the corner, and came face-to-face with a pure psychopath.

He smiled at me, and I really wished he hadn't, because his teeth were chain-saw blades that whirred endlessly behind thin lips. He gnashed them at me and laughed. His eyes were black-on-black, bottomless pools. Tall and emaciated, he smelled of dead things, of coffins with rotting lining, of blood and insane asylums. His hands were white and fluttered like dying moths. His palms had mouths, whirring with silvery blades.

Beneath one arm was tucked an utterly innocuous-looking hardcover.

But it wasn't the *Sinsar Dubh* that held me riveted.

I stared at the psychopath's face.

It had once been Derek O'Bannion.

I had the spear and O'Bannion had been eating Unseelie, so stabbing him would maybe kill him. But if I killed him, what would the *Sinsar Dubh* turn its full attention to next?

Me.

Abruptly, he stopped laughing and yanked the Book out from beneath his arm. He held it with both hands at the farthest possible distance from his body, and for a moment I thought he was offering it to me.

We were so close that, if I'd wanted to, I could have reached out and taken it. I wouldn't have reached out and taken it for anything in the world.

Then he jerked and spun the volume around, as if the text—if there was anything inside it that remotely resembled text—was upside down and unreadable.

From his mouth came the whine of metal grating on metal, and he opened and closed his lips as if trying to form words, but nothing came out.

For an instant, I glimpsed whites around his pupils. Was that horror in his eyes? Had he just ground out "Help" with those metal teeth? I wanted to run. I couldn't stop looking.

Then his eyes were pure black again, and his

body was jerking convulsively, as if he was being ordered to perform and resisting every step of the way.

His fingers closed on the edges of the Book, and it was no longer an innocuous hardcover. Before my eyes it had morphed into the massive, ancient, deadly black tome with intricate locks, and they were all falling away, and the book was opening in O'Bannion's hands, and I knew that whatever was left of Derek O'Bannion inside the psychopath did not *want* the Book to open. It wanted nothing more than to die without ever having glimpsed so much as a single page. Not even one line.

Yet he was being forced to open it.

His fingers began to burn, then his hands were ablaze and he was screaming.

The flames licked up his arms, spread down his chest and legs, and engulfed his face, and suddenly Derek O'Bannion flared white-hot and erupted into ash that exploded ten feet in every direction.

I scrubbed frantically at myself, clawed ash from my hair, and spit it from my lips.

An icy gust scattered all trace of what had been O'Bannion.

The *Sinsar Dubh whumped* to the pavement at my feet.

Open.

25

Growing up, I knew my parameters.

I was pretty enough that one of the class jocks would always ask me to prom, but I'd never score the quarterback.

I was smart enough to squeak into college, but I'd never be a brain surgeon.

I could lift my own aluminum-framed bike off the ceiling rack in the garage, but I couldn't budge my dad's bike that he'd had since law school.

There's comfort in knowing your limits. It's a safety zone. Most people find theirs, get in it, and stay there for the rest of their lives. That's the kind of life I thought I was going to live.

There's a fine line between being stupid and knowing you have to test your limits if you want to do any real living at all.

It was a line I was poised on very delicately at the moment.

The *Sinsar Dubh* lay open at my feet.

I'd avoided looking at it since the moment it hit

the pavement. *Don't look down, don't look down* was my mantra.

Merely opening it had incinerated O'Bannion.

If I gazed into its naked pages, what would it do to me?

I half whispered, half hissed Barrons' name, then was struck by the absurdity of what I'd just done. Did I think if I didn't make much noise, the Book wouldn't notice me?

Hello! It had noticed me. In fact, I was its sole focus. It had been playing with me since the moment I'd appeared on its radar tonight.

Because I was *me*? Or did it play any person who stumbled near?

"Barrons," I shouted, "where the hell are you?"

My only reply was an echo bouncing off brick buildings on the eerily silent street.

I kept my gaze fixed straight ahead and tried to find the thing at my feet with that *sidhe*-seer center of my mind.

Got it!

But it was . . . inert.

I wasn't getting any reading off it at all. Because of the stone in my hand? Because it was conning me in the same way it conned everyone? By masquerading as nothing of consequence at all?

It was entirely too possible. There were too many unknowns. I was wrong. I wasn't poised between stupid and testing my limits. *Miles* of uncharted stupid stretched on both sides of the line on which I stood.

I had to back away, a straight and narrow path

down that line. Taking great pains not to fall off on either side.

I would wait for Barrons. Take no chances.

I took a step back. Then another. Then a third, and my heel caught on something solid, and I stumbled and began to go down.

It was base instinct to try to balance myself by reaching out with both hands and looking at the ground.

"Shit!" I snapped, and yanked my gaze back up.

But it was too late. I'd seen the pages. And I couldn't not look again.

I dropped to my knees and knelt before the *Sinsar Dubh*.

I knelt before it because, on its ever-changing pages, I'd glimpsed the blond, icy-eyed woman who had earlier stood sentinel, forbidding me entrance to one of the Haven's most important libraries. I'd seen her moving from one scene within the Book to the next.

I needed to know who she was and how to get past her. I needed to know everything the Book knew about her. *How* did it know her?

You needed *to know,* Barrons would mock later; *isn't that what your Eve told Adam when she plucked your apple?*

It's not my *apple,* I would counter. *You tried to pluck it, too. Aren't we all after the same thing, thinking we "need" something the Book has in its pages? I have no idea what tempts you, but something does. Tell me, Barrons, come clean: Exactly how long have you been hunting it, and why?*

He wouldn't answer, of course.

Like I said, miles of stupid on both sides of that line.

But kneeling in front of it right now, I was absolutely certain I was on the verge of an epiphany. That truly useful, liberating knowledge was minutes—no, mere seconds away. Knowledge that would give me control over my life, power over my enemies, that would shed light on the mysteries I was unable to solve, show me how to lead, how to succeed, grant me whatever I wished for most.

As I searched those two constantly changing pages, I was tormented by the drone of an insect at my ear.

I swatted at it incessantly, but it refused to go away. I was busy. There were things here I needed to know, just beyond my comprehension. All I had to do was let go, quit worrying. Learn, absorb, be. And everything would be all right.

After a time, the buzz became a whine. The whine became a shout. The shout a bellow, until I realized it wasn't an insect at all but a person roaring at me.

Telling me about myself. Who I was. Who I wasn't. What I wanted.

What I *didn't* want.

"Walk away!" the voice thundered. "Get up, Mac. Haul your ass out of there *now*! Or I'll come kill you myself!"

My head snapped back. I stared down the street.

I narrowed my eyes, squinted. Barrons came into focus.

There was an expression of horror on his face. But

it wasn't directed at the Book open at my knees, and it wasn't directed at me.

It was focused on whatever was *behind* me.

Chills iced my spine. What made Jericho Barrons feel horror?

Whatever it was, it was breathing down my neck. Now that I'd been jarred from the trance I was in, I could feel it, malevolent, mocking, beyond amused, laughing, right behind my ear.

"What are you?" I whispered, without turning.

"Infinite. Eternal." I heard the sound of chain-saw blades, felt a gust of breath that smelled of oil, metal, and decay hot on my cheek. "Without parameters. Free."

"Corrupt. An abomination that should never have been. Evil."

"Sides of a coin, Mac," it said in Ryodan's voice.

"I'll never flip."

"Maybe something's wrong with you, Junior," it said, soft and sweet, in Alina's voice.

Barrons was trying to move toward me, hammering his fists on an invisible wall.

I turned my head.

O'Bannion crouched behind me, his emaciated body pressed to mine, the scent of death surrounding us, those awful chain-saw blades an inch from my face.

He gnashed his teeth at me and laughed. "Surprise! Gotcha, didn't I?"

I didn't have to look back to know the Book wasn't lying on the pavement.

It never had been.

I hadn't actually seen a thing. It had all been illusion, glamour. Which meant the *Sinsar Dubh* had somehow skimmed my mind and plucked from it the images it believed would draw me in, keep me occupied. Some part of my brain must have been thinking about the woman, wondering how I would get past her tomorrow.

It had shown me a glimpse of what I wanted to see, then kept me busy hunting for more with elusive, sketchy images, all promise, no substance.

While in reality it had been crouching behind me, doing . . . what? What had it been up to while I'd been staring into pages that weren't there?

"Learning you. Tasting you. Knowing you, Mac." O'Bannion's bladed hand caressed my arm.

I shook it off.

"Sweet. So sweet." O'Bannion's breath was on my ear.

I gathered my will, lunged to a half crouch, and dragged myself down the pavement, away from it.

"I SAY WHEN WE'RE DONE!"

I was crushed to the street, flattened with pain, and I realized the stones hadn't been protecting me, nor had any change in my strength or abilities. The *Sinsar Dubh* had released me from my pain and could return it any time it chose.

It chose now.

It soared over me, rising, stretching, transforming into the Beast, telling me, in graphic detail, what I could do with my puny little stones that only a fool would believe could contain, could dampen, could ever hope to even brush the greatness of something as limitless and perfect as *it*. It lacerated me with red-hot blades of hatred and cold black blades of despair.

Agony screamed inside my skin.

I couldn't fight. I couldn't flee.

I could only lie there whimpering, immobilized by pain.

When I came to, it took me a moment to figure out where I was.

I blinked in the low light and remained motionless, performing a rapid physical assessment of myself.

I was relieved to realize I was experiencing no current pain—it was all residual. My head was one massive bruise. My bones felt as if they'd been crushed, splinted, and had barely begun to heal.

Internal check completed, I turned my attention to my surroundings.

I was in the bookstore, propped on my favorite chesterfield sofa before the fire in the rear conversation area. I was iced to the bone, wrapped in blankets.

Barrons stood in front of the fire, a tall, powerful shape surrounded by flame, his back to me.

I exhaled with relief, a tiny noise in the large room, but Barrons whirled instantly, a sound rattling deep in his chest, guttural, animal. It made my blood run cold.

It was one of the most inhuman sounds I'd ever heard. Adrenaline erased my pain. I rose up on all fours on the sofa, like some wild thing myself, and stared.

"What the fuck are you?" he snarled. His dark eyes burned ancient and cold in his face. There was blood on his cheeks. Blood on his hands. I wondered if it had come from me. I wondered why he hadn't bothered trying to wash it off. I wondered how long I'd been out. How had I gotten back here? What time was it, anyway? What had the Book done to me?

Then his question penetrated. I pushed the hair from my eyes and began to laugh. "What am I? What am *I*?"

I laughed and laughed. I couldn't help it. I held my sides. There might have been an edge of hysteria in it, but after all I'd been through, I figured I was entitled to a little lunacy. I laughed so hard I couldn't breathe.

Jericho Barrons was asking *me* what *I* was!

He made that sound again, like a rattlesnake—a giant one—was shaking a warning tail in his chest. I stopped laughing and looked at him. The sound chilled me the same way the *Sinsar Dubh* did. It made me think that Jericho Barrons' skin might be a slipcover for a chair I never wanted to see.

"Kneel, Ms. Lane!"

Shit. He'd Voiced me!

And it was *working*!

I crashed off the sofa in a tangle of blankets and landed on my knees, gritting my teeth. I thought I was immune to Voice! The LM's hadn't worked on me! But then, Barrons is better at everything.

"What are you?" he roared.

"I don't know!" I shouted. I didn't. But I was sure beginning to wonder. V'lane's comment that night at the abbey had been haunting me with increasing frequency: *They* should *be afraid of you,* he'd said. *You have only begun to discover what you are.*

"What does the Book want from you?"

"I don't know!"

"What was it doing to you while it kept you there in the street?"

"I don't know! How long did it keep me there?"

"Over an hour! It turned into the Beast and eclipsed you. I couldn't fucking get to you! I couldn't even fucking see you! *What was it doing?"*

"Learning me. Tasting me. Knowing me," I gritted. "That's what it said. Stop Voicing me, Barrons!"

"I'll stop Voicing you when you can *make* me stop Voicing you, Ms. Lane. *Stand up.*"

I pushed to my feet on trembling legs, residual pain in every ounce of my body. I hated him at that moment. There was no need to kick me when I was already down.

"Fight me, Ms. Lane," he growled, without the aid of Voice. *"Pick up the knife and cut your hand."*

I glanced down at the coffee table. An ivory-handled knife with a wicked, jagged blade shimmered in the firelight. I was horrified to find myself reaching for it. I'd been here before. This was exactly how he'd tried to train me in the past.

"Fight!"

And just like in the past, I kept reaching.

"Bloody hell, look inside yourself! Hate me! Fight! Fight any way you can!"

My hand stopped. Pulled back. Moved forward again.

"Cut yourself deep," he hissed in Voice. *"Make it hurt like hell."*

My fingers closed around the hilt of the knife.

"You're a natural victim, Ms. Lane. A walking, talking Barbie doll," he sneered. "See Mac's sister get killed. See Mac get raped. See Mac get fucked. See Mac get crushed in the street by the Book. See Mac dead on top of the trash heap out back."

I sucked in a sharp, pained breath.

"Pick up the knife!"

I raised it jerkily in my hand.

"I've been in your skin," he taunted. "I know you inside and out. There's nothing there. Do us all a favor and die so we can start working on another plan and quit thinking maybe you'll grow the fuck up and be capable of something."

Okay, *enough!* "You don't know me inside and out," I snarled. "You may have gotten in my skin, but you have *never* gotten inside my heart. Go ahead, Barrons, make me slice and dice myself. Go ahead, play games with me. Push me around. Lie to me. Bully me. Be your usual constant jackass self. Stalk around all broody and pissy and secretive, but you're wrong about me. There's something inside me you'd *better* be afraid of. And you can't touch my soul. You will *never* touch my soul!"

I raised my hand, drew back the knife, and let it fly. It sliced through the air, straight for his head.

He avoided it with preternatural grace, a mere whisper of a movement, precisely and only as much as was required to not get hit.

The hilt vibrated in the wood of the ornate mantel next to his head.

"So, fuck you, Jericho Barrons, and not the way

you like it. Fuck you—as in, you can't touch me. *Nobody* can."

I kicked the table at him. It crashed into his shins. I picked up a lamp from the end table. Flung it straight at his head. He ducked again. I grabbed a book. It thumped off his chest.

He laughed, dark eyes glittering with exhilaration.

I launched myself at him, slammed a fist into his face. I heard a satisfying crunch and felt something in his nose give.

He didn't try to hit me back or push me away. Merely wrapped his arms around me and crushed me tight to his body, trapping my arms against his chest.

Then, when I thought he might just squeeze me to death, he dropped his head forward, into the hollow where my shoulder met my neck.

"Do you miss fucking me, Ms. Lane?" he purred against my ear. Voice resonated in my skull, pressuring a reply.

I was tall and strong and proud inside myself. Nobody owned me. I didn't have to answer any questions I didn't want to, ever again.

"Wouldn't you just love to know?" I purred back. "You want more of me, don't you, Barrons? I got under your skin deep. I hope you got addicted to me. I was a wild one, wasn't I? I bet you never had sex like that in your entire existence, huh, O Ancient One? I bet I rocked your perfectly disciplined little world. I hope wanting me hurts like hell!"

His hands were suddenly cruelly tight on my waist.

"There's only one question that matters, Ms. Lane, and it's the one you never get around to asking. People are capable of varying degrees of truth. The majority spend their entire lives fabricating an elaborate skein of lies, immersing themselves in the faith of bad faith, doing whatever it takes to feel safe. The person who *truly* lives has precious few moments of safety, learns to thrive in any kind of storm. It's the truth you can stare down stone-cold that makes you what you are. Weak or strong. Live or die. Prove yourself. How much truth can you take, Ms. Lane?"

I could feel his mind rubbing up against mine. It was a shockingly sensuous feeling. He was reaching for my thoughts the way I'd hammered at him for his, only he was seducing me into opening my mind, making me blossom like a flower for his sun, beckoning me into one of his memories.

Then I was no longer in the bookstore, a breath away from wanting to kill or—who the hell knew?—kiss Jericho Barrons, I was—

In a tent.

Sawing open a man's chest with a bloody blade.

Drawing back my arm and punching my fist into the bones that protected his heart.

Closing my hand around it.

Ripping it out.

I'd already raped his woman—she was still alive, watching her husband die. As she had watched her children die.

I raised his heart above my face, squeezed it in my fist, let the blood drip—

He was trying to drown me in the scene of

slaughter. Force it on me, graphic detail by detail. But there was more. There was something behind it.

That was what I wanted to see.

I gathered my will, drew back, and launched myself into the scene he was forcing on me. It ripped down the center like a movie screen, revealing another screen behind it.

More slaughter. Him laughing.

I sought that dark glassy lake in my *sidhe*-seer center. I didn't summon what lay in its depths. I merely coaxed a little strength from it. Whatever lay beneath that lake offered it willingly, inflating my mental muscles.

I knifed through screen after screen, until finally there were no more and I went crashing to my knees in a puff of sand in—

A desert.

It is dusk.

I hold a child in my arms.

I stare into the night.

I won't look down.

Can't face what's in his eyes.

Can't not look.

My gaze goes unwillingly, hungrily down.

The child stares up at me with utter trust.

His eyes say, I know you won't let me die.

His eyes say, I know you will make the pain stop.

His eyes said, Trust/love/adore/youareperfect/youwill alwayskeepmesafe/youaremyworld.

But I didn't keep him safe.

And I can't make his pain stop.

Bitterness fills my mouth with bile. I turn my head and

vomit. I never understood anything about life until this moment.

I always sought only my own gain. Mercenary to the core.

If the child dies, nothing will ever matter again, because a piece of me will go with him. Until now I was not aware of that piece. Didn't know it existed. Didn't know it mattered.

Ironic to find it, in the moment of losing it.

I hold him.

I rock him.

He weeps.

His tears fall on my arms and burn my skin.

I stare into those trusting eyes.

I see him there. His yesterdays. His today. The tomorrows that will never be.

I see his pain and it shreds me.

I see his absolute love and it shames me.

I see the light—that beautiful perfect light that is life.

He smiles at me. He gives me all his love in his eyes.

It begins to fade.

No! I roar. You will not die! You will not leave me!

I stare into his eyes for what seems a thousand days.

I see him. I hold him. He is there.

He is gone.

There's a moment, in the dying, of transition. Life to death. Full to empty. There, then gone. Too fast. Come back, come back, you want to scream. I need just one more minute. Just one more smile. Just one more chance to do things right. But he's gone. He's gone. Where did he go? What happens to life when it leaves? Does it go somewhere or is it just fucking gone?

I try to weep, but nothing comes.

Something rattles deep in my chest.
I do not recognize it.
I am no longer what I was.
I look at the others.
None of us are.

The images stopped. I was back in the bookstore. I was shaking. Grief was an open wound in my chest. I was bleeding for the child I'd just lost, bleeding for Alina, for all the people dying out there in this war we'd been unable to prevent.

I jerked, looked up at him. If he thought he was going to get tit for tat, he was wrong.

I was raw. I was badly off balance. If he touched me right now, I might be nice. If he was nice right now, I might touch him.

His face was impassive, his eyes flat black, his hands fisted at his sides.

"Barrons, I—"

"Good night, Ms. Lane."

26

Couldn't we have taken something faster?" I complained, as we skirted abandoned cars and dodged IFPs at what felt like a snail's pace.

Barrons gave me a look. "All the Hunters were busy tonight."

"Well, can you at least step on it?" I groused.

"And end up in another IFP? They're moving, in case you hadn't noticed."

I had, and it seemed highly unfair. Static, they were predictable, but the last two we'd encountered on our way deep into Irish country had been unattached, floating several feet off the ground, drifting wherever the wind carried them. Dodging a stationary IFP was hard enough. Dodging one that was blowing erratically felt like one of those dances you do when you run into someone on the street and both of you keep stepping to the same side, trying to get out of each other's way. Only, in this case, it seemed the floating IFPs *wanted* to dance. Take you in their arms. Swallow you up.

"The last one took us forty minutes to get out of."

Problem was, you couldn't back out of them easily. Once you were inside one, it seemed to shift cunningly, concealing the entry point. You had to fumble around for an exit. "Point," I conceded.

I was bored, restless, and impatient to get to the old woman's cottage. And here we were, lumbering along, taking forever, in the Alpha.

I glanced around the interior of the Hummer and saw a CD case on the backseat. I wondered what Barrons listened to when he was alone. I punched on the audio. Rob Zombie blared:

Hell doesn't love them. The devil's rejects, the devil's rejects . . .

He punched off the audio.

I raised a brow. "Could you be any more trite, Barrons?"

" 'Trite' is merely another word for overdone by the media to the point where the common masses—that would be you, Ms. Lane: *common*—are desensitized by it, most often to their own detriment because they have become incapable of recognizing the danger staring at them from the eyes of a feral animal or down the barrel of a loaded gun."

"I'm not common and you know it." I would never admit he had a valid point. Mirror neurons did funny things to us, made us mentally live things we observed, firing whether we were performing the action ourselves or merely watching someone else perform the action, numbing us bit by bit. But who needed media to desensitize? What was I going to be like after living a few more months of my own life? Numb to everything. "Look at you. All stalky and badass."

"Stalky. Do you think that's a word, Ms. Lane?"

"Who was the child?" I said.

For a moment he said nothing. Then, "You ask absurd questions. What did I feel?"

"Grief."

"What bearing would something as trivial as the child's name or his relevance to my existence have on anything?"

"Maybe it would help me understand you."

"He died. I felt grief. End of story."

"But it's not quite that simple, is it, Barrons?" I narrowed my eyes. "It's not the end of the story."

"Try, Ms. Lane. Just try."

I inclined my head appreciatively. I hadn't even really reached out to test the edges of his mind; still, he'd felt it.

"I let you off easy last night. You punched into my head."

"You invited me. Got all rubby up against my mind."

"I invited you to slaughter. Not to where you went from there. There's a price for that. Don't think you've escaped. I've merely delayed sentencing."

I shivered on a cellular level, refused to identify the emotion behind it. "Try, Barrons," I mocked. "Just try."

He said nothing. I looked over at him. There was a strange tension in his upper lip. It took me a second to realize Barrons was trying not to laugh.

"You're laughing at me," I said indignantly.

"Look at you, all puffed up on yourself. Took a push into my head last night and now you think you're the Shit." He gave me a hard look. It said, *Get in my skin, go as deep as I go, then you can puff about something. Until then, you're feeble, Ms. Lane.* "And, for the record, I could have stopped you."

He could have? He wasn't a boaster. Jericho Barrons had *let* me see his grief? Why? Just what the hell did that mean?

We both saw the floater at the same time.

He yanked the wheel. We barely missed the drifting IFP.

"Those things are dangerous! Where are they coming from? Are they new or are the stationary ones somehow getting cut loose?"

He kept his gaze on the road. "Looks like they're getting cut loose by someone. Probably the Unseelie, just to add to the random chaos."

We drove for a time in silence, occupied with private thoughts. I suspected he was still brooding about the drifting IFPs, but I'd moved on to alternately worrying and being excited about the woman we were on our way to see.

After last night's exhausting events, I didn't stumble to bed until nearly eight in the morning, and then I slept until Barrons pounded on my door at five o'clock this afternoon.

A *sidhe*-seer was waiting downstairs, he told me.

I'd tugged on jeans and a sweatshirt and rushed downstairs, expecting to find Dani.

It was Kat, exuberant with information. They'd found a woman who might talk to us, a woman who could tell us about "unholy doings at the abbey" that had happened twenty-some years ago. They'd stumbled on her by accident while scouring the countryside for survivors. She refused to leave her cottage. Wasn't about to go anywhere near that "be-fouled parcel o' land" and insisted they not breathe a single word to the Grand Mistress about her or she'd seal her lips for good. She'd waved a walking stick forged of purest iron in her gnarled fist and said she knew a thing or two about the Old Ones and was just *foine on me own, so get ye awa!*

"What did she tell you?" I'd demanded.

"Not a blasted thing. She said we had to bring her something to prove we weren't in cahoots with those dark *daoine sidhe* running amuck."

"Like?"

Kat had shrugged. "I'd the feeling she was mean-ing something of the Seelie. We thought of Dani and the sword, but . . ." She trailed off, and I understood her concerns. Of the two of us, I inspired a little more confidence than the impulsive teen. "She seemed afraid we were working with the Unseelie. She seemed to know quite a bit about Fae lore."

I'd been raring to go right then and there.

Convincing Barrons had been the hard part.

He was determined to stay close to the heavily warded bookstore, rooted in his territory, until we'd dealt with the Lord Master.

"But I need to know about the prophecy," I in-sisted, "and whatever she knows about when the Book escaped. Who knows what this woman might be able to tell us?"

"We know all we need to know," he said flatly. "We've got three of the four stones and four of the five Druids."

I gaped. "The five that we need are *Druids*? The

five are people? What the hell? Does everybody know about this prophecy but me?"

"It would appear," he said dryly. "The Keltar, arrogant fucks, believe they are the five Druids: Dageus, Drustan, Cian, Christopher, and Christian. But, Christian's missing and V'lane has the fourth stone. Frankly, Ms. Lane, I think you're the wild card that might make all the rest unnecessary. I'm placing my bets on you."

Unfortunately, I wasn't certain just how wild a card I was. I was afraid there was something in the prophecy about me and it wasn't good. But I wasn't about to tell him that. Instead, I argued that it would be a mistake to pass up any opportunity to learn all we could about the Book. And if this woman knew how it had escaped, who knew what else she might be able to tell us?

Bring the woman here, he said.

Not a chance of moving her, Kat had informed us. Her age was matched only by her stubbornness, cantankerousness, and a pronounced tendency to nod off to sleep without a moment's notice.

So, here we were, making our way to the far edge of County Clare.

Where ninety-seven-year-old Nana O'Reilly was waiting for us.

I'd seen crofters' cottages before, but this one took the cake. Illuminated by the Hummer's headlights, it was a study in whimsy. An uneven stack of field rock, thatch, and moss tumbled across a yard of tiered gardens that, in summer, would yield a profusion of blooms, garnished by fanciful statues and Escher-esque stone fountains. Beyond it, the Atlantic Ocean glistened silver in the moonlight, salting the breeze.

There were no Shades here. The perimeter of the yard was heavily warded.

As we drove over the line of demarcation, I flinched. Barrons had absolutely no reaction. I'd been watching him carefully since the moment our headlamps picked up the faint silvery glow, curious to see if the wards would bother him.

He was the portrait of perfect impassivity.

"Do you even *feel* them?" I asked, irritated.

"I know they're there." Typical Barrons nonanswer.

"Do your tattoos protect you?"

"From many things. From others, no." Another nonanswer.

We got out and made our way up the nearly overgrown flagstone path to the cottage door. It was green, painted with many symbols. The misshapen shamrock was unmistakable. Nana O'Reilly knew of our order. How?

Kat opened the door when I knocked. She'd hurried to the cottage ahead of us, hoping to smooth our way with tea, fresh water, and crates of supplies from town for the old woman.

I peered into the cottage. Candles burned and a brisk fire crackled.

"I'll be getting me own door, I will. I'm no' dead yet!" Nana O'Reilly nudged Kat aside. She wore her gray hair in a long braid over one shoulder. Her face bore the wrinkles of an old sea captain, from nearly a century of living on the shore, and she had no teeth. She gave Barrons a rheumy look and said, "The likes o' ye'll be findin' no bide 'ere!"

With that, she yanked me inside and slammed the door in Barrons' face.

"What kind of likes is that?" I said, the instant the door was closed.

Nana gave me a look that suggested I might just be too stupid to live.

Kat settled the old woman in a chair near the fire and draped a faded quilt of many patterns and fabrics about her shoulders. The blanket looked as if it had been made decades ago from leftover patches of her children's outgrown clothes. "I'll be asking you, too," Kat said curiously. "What likes is that?"

"Air ye daft, lasses? No' our kind."

"We get that, but what *is* he?" I said.

Nana shrugged. "Why would ye care? There's white, and there's not white. Wha' more need ye ken than tha'?"

"But I'm white," I said quickly. Kat gave me an odd look. "I mean, you can see that Kat and I are like you, right? We're not like him." If she could discern people's true natures, I wanted to know mine.

Her rheumy brown eyes fastened on me like muddy leeches. "Ye color yer hair, ye do. Wha's the truth o' it?"

"Blond."

She closed her eyes and went so still that for a

moment I was afraid the old woman had fallen asleep.

Then her eyes snapped open and her mouth parted on a gummy *O* of surprise. "Love o' Mary," she breathed, "I ne'er forget a face. Yer Isla's git! I'd no hae thought to see ye again ere I passed!"

"Git?" I said.

Kat looked stunned. "Daughter," she said.

My mother's name was Isla O'Connor.

I had the unmistakable look of her, Nana told me, in the shape of my face, the thickness of my hair, my eyes, but most of all in my carriage. The way my back flowed into my shoulders, the way I moved, even the angle at which I tilted my head sometimes when I spoke.

I looked like my mother.

My mother's name was Isla O'Connor.

I could have repeated those two thoughts over and over for hours.

"Are you *sure*?" I had a lump in my throat I could barely swallow around.

She nodded. "Countless were the days she an' me Kayleigh played in me gardens. Were yer locks blond, lass, I'd o' been mistaking ye for her haint."

"Tell me everything."

Nana's eyes narrowed. "She carried something, was ne'er wi'out it." Her gaze clouded. "Though later, 'twas lost. Ken ye what it was?"

"From the Seelie?"

Nana nodded, and my eyes widened. Slowly, I

reached inside my coat and pulled out the spear. "My mother carried this?"

Nana's eyes disappeared in nests of wrinkles as she smiled. "I fashed ne'er to see it again! Heard tell 'twas fallen to nefarious hands. Blazes wi' the glory o' heaven, it does. Aye, yer mam carried the Spear of Destiny, and me own dear Kayleigh carried the sword."

"Everything," I said, dropping to Nana's knees by the fire. "I want to know everything!"

Isla O'Connor had been the youngest *sidhe*-seer to ever attain the position of Haven Mistress—spokes-woman for the High Council—in the history of the abbey. Such a gifted *sidhe*-seer had not been born for longer than any cared to recall. The Grand Mistress feared the ancient bloodlines had been too di-luted by reckless and unsupervised unions to again produce such offspring. Just look at those *galló-glaigh* MacRorys and MacSweenys, breeding with the Norse and Picts!

"Gallowglass," Kat clarified for me. "Mercenary warriors of a sort."

No one knew who Isla's father was. My grand-mother, Patrona O'Connor—Nana's face creased in a smile of toothless delight when she said her name; they'd been contemporaries and friends dearer than sisters—had never wed and had refused to divulge his name. She bore Isla late in life and carried the knowledge of her child's father to her grave, which, by the by, was a few miles south if I had interest in paying respects.

Patrona! That was the name Rowena mentioned the day I'd been searching the museum for OOPs and she'd found me in the street. She insisted I had the look of her but was unable to grasp how that could possibly be. She said she would have known. Now I understood why: Rowena had known my grandmother!

"Are there other O'Connors, besides me?"

Nana snorted. "Eire's full 'o 'em. Distant kin. Nary a line as potent as Patrona's."

Rowena said there were no O'Connors left! Had she meant only my direct line? As far as I was concerned, at best she'd misled me, at worst she'd lied.

Although the Grand Mistress had disdained my mother's unproven lineage, Nana continued, there'd been no disputing Isla was the finest *sidhe*-seer any at the abbey had ever encountered. As time passed, she and Nana's granddaughter, Kayleigh, had not only been initiated into the abbey's most private and hallowed circle but were appointed to positions of the greatest power therein.

Life was blessed. Nana was proud. She'd raised her Kayleigh well, trained in the Old Ways.

The old woman's eyes closed and she began to snore.

"Wake her," I said.

Kat tucked the blanket more closely around her. "She's lived nigh a century, Mac. I imagine her bones are weary."

"We need to know more."

Kat cast me a look of rebuke. "I've yet to hear a word about a prophecy or the Book."

"Exactly why we need to wake her!"

"Focus less on your kin and more on our problems," Kat chastened.

It took several minutes of gentle shaking and coaxing, but the old woman finally stirred. She seemed to have no awareness that she'd been asleep and resumed talking as if she'd never stopped.

It was a time of great hope, she said. The six most potent *sidhe*-seers lines began to grow stronger again: the Brennans, the O'Reillys, the Kennedys, the O'Connors, the MacLoughlins, and the O'Malleys. Each house was producing daughters with gifts awakening sooner, developing more quickly.

But things changed and dark days came, days when Nana walked the land and felt the wrongness beneath her feet. The soil itself had been . . . tainted. Some foul thing had roused and was stirring in the belly of the earth. She bid her girls discover the source. Bade them stop it at any cost.

"Are you a *sidhe*-seer, too?" I asked. "Did you once live at the abbey?"

Nana was asleep again. I shook her. It didn't work. She snored on. Kat made the old woman tea. I added a second bag to her mug.

Five minutes later, although her head still nodded dangerously, her eyes were open and she was sipping tea.

She'd no use for the abbey. No care for study. Her bones knew truths. What need had a woman of more than bone-knowing? Learning, she scoffed, confused the bones. Reading blinded the vision. Lectures deafened the ears. Look at the land, feel the soil, taste the air!

"Dark days." I coaxed her to focus. "What happened?"

Nana closed her eyes and was silent so long I was afraid she'd fallen asleep again. When they opened, they glistened with unshed tears.

The two children who'd once played in her garden changed. They became secretive, fearful, exchanging troubled looks. They no longer had time for an old woman. Though she'd been the one to set them on their course, had pointed the way with her bones, they shut her out. They whispered of doings of which Nana had caught only bits and pieces.

Hidden places within the abbey.

Dark temptations.

A book of great magic.

Two prophecies.

"Two?" I exclaimed.

"Aye. One promised hope. One pledged blight upon the earth and more. Both hinged upon a single thing."

"A thing?" I demanded. "Or a person?"

Nana shook her head. She didn't know. Had assumed it was a thing. An event. But it might have been a person.

Kat removed the teacup from the old woman's hand before it spilled. She was nodding off again.

"How was the Book contained in the abbey?" I pressed.

She gave me a blank look.

"Where was it kept?" I tried.

She shrugged.

"When was it brought there and by whom?"

" 'Tis said the queen o' the *daoine sidhe* placed it

there in the mists o' time." A gentle snore escaped her.

"How did it get out?" I said loudly, and she jerked awake again.

"Heard tell 'twas aided by one in the highest circle." She gave me a sad look. "Some say yer mam." Her lids closed. Her face sagged and her mouth fell open.

My hands fisted. My mother would never have freed the *Sinsar Dubh*. And Alina was not a traitor. And I was *not* bad. "Who was my father?" I demanded.

"She's asleep, Mac," Kat said.

"Well, wake her again! We need to know more!"

"Tomorrow's another day."

"Every day counts!"

"Mac, she's weary. We can begin again in the morning. I'll be staying the night. She shouldn't be alone. She should never have been alone this long. Will you be staying, as well?"

"No," Barrons growled through the door.

I inhaled slowly. Exhaled. I was in knots inside.

I had a mother.

I knew her name.

I knew where I came from.

I needed to know so much more!

Who was my father? Why had we O'Connors been getting so much bad press? Blaming my mother, then my sister, now me? It pissed me off. I wanted to shake the old woman awake, force her to go on.

I studied her. Sleep had smoothed the wizened face, and she looked peaceful, innocent, the hint of a smile touching her lips. I wondered if she dreamed of two young girls playing in her gardens. I wanted to see them, too.

I closed my eyes, flexed that *sidhe*-seer place, and found it easy to sip at the edges of her mind. It was, like her bones, weary and without defense.

And there they were: two girls, one dark, one blond, maybe seven or eight, running through a field of heather, holding hands and laughing. Was one of them my mother? I pressed harder, tried to shape Nana's dream and make it show me more.

"What are you *doing*?" Kat cried.

I opened my eyes. Nana was staring at me, looking frightened and confused, hands tight on the arms of her rocking chair. " 'Tis a gift to be given, no' taken!"

I stood and spread my hands placatingly. "I didn't mean to frighten you. I didn't think you'd even feel me there. I just wanted to know what she looked like. I'm so sorry. I just wanted to know what my mother looked like." I was babbling. Anger that she'd stopped me vied with shame that I'd tried.

"Ye ken what she looked like." Nana's eyes drifted closed again. "Yer mam was e'er takin' ye to the abbey wi' her. Search yer memories. 'Tis there ye'll be finding her, Alina."

I blinked. "I'm not Alina."

A soft snore was her only reply.

27

It had been, Barrons said, a grand waste of time, and he wouldn't be escorting me back to see the old woman again.

How could he say that? I exploded. I'd learned the name of my mother tonight! I knew my own last name!

"Names are illusions," he growled. "Nonsensical labels seized upon by people to make them feel better about the intangibility of their puny existences. I am this. I am that," he mocked. "I came from so and so. Ergo I am . . . whatever the blah-blah you want to claim. Bloody hell, spare me."

"You're beginning to sound dangerously like V'lane." I was an O'Connor, from one of the six most powerful *sidhe*-seer lines—*that* mattered to me. I had a grandmother's grave I could visit. I could take her flowers. I could tell her I would avenge us all.

"Irrelevant where you came from. What matters is where you're going. Don't you understand that? Have I succeeded in teaching you nothing?"

"Lectures," I said, "deafen the ears."

We were still arguing hours later, when he pulled the Hummer into the garage behind the bookstore.

"You just don't like that she knew something about what you are!" I accused.

"An old bag of rural superstitions," he scoffed. "Brain-starved by the potato famine."

"Got the wrong century there, Barrons."

He glowered at me, appeared to be doing some math, then said, "So what? Same result. Starved by something. Reading blinds the vision, lectures deafen the ears, my ass."

We both leapt out of the Hummer and slammed the doors so hard it shuddered.

Beneath my feet, the floor of the garage trembled.

The concrete actually *rumbled*, making my shins vibrate, as a sound from something that could only have been born on the far side of hell filled the air.

I stared at him across the hood of the Hummer. Well, at least one of my questions had been laid to rest: Whatever was beneath his garage wasn't Jericho Z. Barrons.

"What do you have down there, Barrons?" My question was nearly drowned out by another swell of hopeless, anguished baying. It made me want to run. It made me want to weep.

"The only way that could ever possibly be any of your business is if it was a book, and one that we need, and it's not, so fuck off." He stalked from the garage.

I followed hot on his heels. "Fine."

"Fiona," he snarled.

"I said 'fine,' not Fiona." I plowed into his back.

"Jericho, it's been too long," a lightly accented, cultured voice said.

I stepped out from behind him. She looked stunning as ever in a hip-hugging skirt, fabulous boots that clung to the shapely lines of her long legs, and a low-cut lace blouse that showcased every voluptuous curve. A long velvet cloak was draped lightly about her shoulders, flapping gently in the night breeze. Blowsy sensuality. Fae on her skin. Expensive perfume. Her flawless skin was paler than ever, more luminous, her lipstick blood-red, her gaze frankly sexual.

My spear was in my hand instantly.

She was flanked by a dozen of the Lord Master's black-and-crimson-clad guard.

"Guess you're not important enough to merit protection from the princes," I said coolly.

"Darroc is a jealous lover," she said lightly. "He does not permit them near me, should they turn my head. He tells me what a relief it is to have a *woman* in his bed, after the bland taste of the *child* he ripped to pieces."

I sucked in a sharp breath and would have lunged, but Barrons' hand closed like a steel cuff around my wrist.

"What do you want, Fiona?"

I wondered if she remembered that Barrons was at his most dangerous when his voice was that soft.

For the barest moment, as she looked at Barrons, I saw unabashed, vulnerable longing in her eyes. I saw hurt, pride, desire that would never stop eating at her. I saw love.

She loved Jericho Barrons.

Even after he'd thrown her out for trying to kill me. Even after taking up with Derek O'Bannion and now the LM.

Even with Unseelie flesh running through her veins, lover to the darkest denizens of the new Dublin, she still loved the man standing next to me and always would. Loving something like Barrons was a pain I didn't envy her.

She devoured his face with tender concern, searched his body with undisguised ardor.

Then her gaze hitched on his hand around my arm, and it emptied instantly of love and burned with fury.

"You have not wearied of her yet. You disappoint me, Jericho. I'd have forgiven a passing fancy, as I've forgiven so many things. But you test my love too far."

"I never asked for your love. I warned you repeatedly against it."

Her face changed, tightened, and she hissed, "But you took everything else! Do you think it works that way? I might have pointed the gun at my head, but *you're* the one who put the bullets in it! Do you think a woman can give a man *everything* while still withholding her heart? We are not made that way!"

"I asked for nothing."

"And gave nothing," she spat. "Do you know how it feels to realize that the one person you've entrusted with your heart has none?"

"Why are you here, Fiona? To show me you have a new lover? To beg to return to my bed? It's full, and always will be. To apologize for trying to destroy the one chance I had by killing her?"

"The one chance you had for what?" I pounced on it immediately. Getting angry at her for nearly killing me hadn't been about me at all but about the fact that I was somehow his one chance at something?

Fiona looked at me sharply, then at Barrons, and began to laugh. "Ah, such delicious absurdity! She *still* doesn't know. Oh, Jericho! You never change, do you? You must be so afraid—" Abruptly, her mouth parted on a sudden inhalation, her face froze, and she sank to the ground, looking startled and confused. Her hands fluttered upward but did not achieve their destination. She crumpled limply to the pavement.

I stared. There was a knife buried deep in her chest, straight through her heart. Blood welled around it. I'd not even seen Barrons throw it.

"I assume she came with a message," he said coldly, to one of the guards.

"The Lord Master awaits that one." The guard nodded toward me. "He said it is her final chance."

"Remove that"—Barrons glanced at Fiona—"from my alley."

She was still unconscious, but she wouldn't remain that way long. Her flesh was laced with enough Unseelie that not even a knife through her heart would kill her. The dark Fae in her blood would heal the injuries. It would take my spear to kill what she was now. Or whatever weapon Barrons had used on the Fae Princess. But his knife sure had succeeded in shutting her up.

What had she been about to say? What didn't I

know that Barrons might be afraid I'd find out? What "delicious absurdity"?

I glanced up at "my wave," the one I'd chosen to carry me through this dangerous sea. I felt like a child plucking daisy petals: I trust him, I trust him not, I trust him, I trust him not.

"And you can tell Darroc," said Barrons, "that Ms. Lane is mine. If he wants her, he can bloody well come and get her."

28

I went straight to both gas fireplaces the next morning, lit them, and turned them up as high as they would go.

I'd had the dream about the beautiful cold woman again. She was alone, something was very wrong with her, but deeper than her physical pain was the suffering in her soul. I'd wept in my dream, and my tears had turned into ice crystals on my cheeks. She'd lost something of such importance that she no longer cared to live.

As usual, I'd woken iced to the bone. Not even a scalding shower had eased the chill. I hate being cold. Now that I'd remembered I'd been having this dream all my life, I also recalled dashing from my bed as a little girl, with frozen feet and chattering teeth, running for the warm comfort of my daddy's arms. I remembered him wrapping me in blankets and reading to me. He'd put on his "pirate voice," although in retrospect I have no idea why, and say, *"Ahoy, matey: There are strange things done in the midnight sun by the men who moil for gold. . . ."*

And as Sam McGee had grown hot enough to sizzle on his funeral pyre, I'd shivered myself warm in my daddy's arms, thrilled by the madness of moiling for gold in the Arctic, dragging the corpse of a friend behind on a sled, to burn on the marge of Lake LaBarge and keep a promise made to the dead.

As I warmed my hands before the fire, I could hear Barrons through the adjoining door, in his study, speaking angrily to someone on the phone.

We'd exchanged a total of eight words last night, after he'd knifed Fiona.

I'd looked up at him as he unlocked the back door, considering all kinds of questions.

He'd pushed the door open and waited for me to walk in, beneath his arm, looking down at me, his gaze mocking.

"What? No questions, Ms. Lane?"

I'd pulled a Barrons and said coolly, "Good night, Barrons."

Soft laughter had followed me up the stairwell. There'd been no point in questions. I wasn't one for exercises in futility.

I heated a cup of water in the microwave behind the counter and added three heaping teaspoons of instant coffee. I opened the utensil drawer. "Damn." I was out of sugar, and there was no cream in the fridge. It's the simple pleasures that have come to mean the most to me.

Sighing, I leaned back against the counter and began sipping bitter coffee.

"Tell that arrogant fuck I said so, that's why," said Barrons. "I need all of you. I don't care what Lor thinks about it."

It seemed he was rallying the troops. I wondered if I would meet the others like Barrons, besides Ryodan. He was determined to have it out with Darroc, get it over with and out of his way. I was perfectly willing to go along with that plan, so long as I was the one who got to bury my spear in the gut of the bastard who'd begun this whole mess, either killed my sister or gotten her killed, and had me raped. I needed one of the dangers in my life gone. The danger I was living with was keeping my hands full enough.

I hoped it happened today. I hoped the LM marched on the bookstore and filled the streets with his Unseelie. I hoped Barrons would line up his . . . whatever they were. I would call on Jayne and his men and the *sidhe*-seers. We would have a battle to end all battles and we would walk away the victors, I had no doubt about it. It wasn't only the dream that had iced me. My resolve was a solid block of it. I was restless as a caged animal. I was sick of worrying about things that might happen. I wanted them to *happen* already.

"No, it's *not* more important than this. Nothing is, and you know that," Barrons growled. "Who the fuck does he think is in charge?" A pause. "Then he can get the fuck out of my city."

My city. I pondered that phrase, wondered why Barrons felt that way. He never said "our world." He always said "your world." But he called Dublin his city. Merely because he'd been in it so long? Or had Barrons, like me, been beguiled by her tawdry grace, fallen for her charm and colorful dualities?

I looked around "my" bookstore. That was what I

called it. Did we call the things of our heart our own, whether they were or not? And if Dublin was his city, did that mean he had a heart, contrary to Fiona's beliefs?

"Nah," I scoffed, and sipped my coffee.

I have no idea how long it flapped on the door before I noticed it.

I would later wonder if someone had walked by and stuck it there while I sipped ignorantly away, eavesdropping on Barrons. Maybe peered in through the tinted glass and looked at me. Smirked or smothered a villainous laugh. I would wonder if it had been Fiona who'd put it there. Would hate her, knowing she would have stood there watching me, relishing my pain.

"Darroc will come," Barrons was saying, as I squinted at the door. "I told Fiona that I have three of the stones, and I know where the fourth is."

He had? When? Had he gone to see her last night while I'd slept? The idea made me feel . . . betrayed.

I skirted the counter and walked slowly toward the front of the store, where the thing flapped in a gentle breeze on the diamond-paned glass of the door. It was the motion that had caught my attention. Who knew how long it might have taken me to find it otherwise.

Barrons said, "It's possible she might make all of it unnecessary. But it's still too soon to tell."

A dozen feet from the door, I recognized it. I looked away, as if, like an ostrich with my head in the sand, I would be safe.

But I wasn't safe.

"It can't be," I said.

I looked back, marched to the door, opened it, and gently removed the tape holding it to the glass.

It was.

I stared at it for a long moment, then closed my eyes.

"The LM's not coming," I told Barrons, stepping into his study. As always, my gaze slid uneasily to the huge mirror that was part of the vast network of Unseelie Silvers: doorway into a hellish no-man's-land of ice and monsters. But my fascination/fear of it held new poignancy today, and new relevance.

"You can't know that," Barrons dismissed.

Seated behind the massive desk, he appeared sculpted from material of the same tension and density, hard with anger.

I gave him a smile. It was that or burst into tears, and there was no way that was happening. "Trouble at home? Boys aren't behaving?" I said sweetly.

"Get to the point, Ms. Lane."

I began to hand him what I'd removed from the front door. My hand trembled. I steeled myself, and when I extended it again, my hand was perfectly steady.

He glanced at the photo. "It's your sister. So?"

Indeed it was. She was laughing, on an open-mouthed smile, standing at the entrance to Trinity College.

"Turn it over," I said tightly.

He flipped it.

"Read it."

"*She was happy,*" he read. "*I love you, Mom and*

Dad. I'll be home as soon as I can. Mac." He paused before continuing. A muscle jerked in his jaw. *"1247 LaRuhe. Fifth Silver on the right. Bring the stones. If you bring Barrons, they both die."* He looked up at me. "He's got your parents. Fuck."

That pretty much summed it up.

"This is a terrible plan," Barrons said for the tenth time.

"You're the one who came up with it," I reminded. "And I agreed. We're not going back now." I continued stuffing things in my backpack.

There was no other way. I'd wanted a confrontation and I was going to get it. Just not the way I'd hoped. "Look, Barrons, you've filled my head with more knowledge about life than anyone else ever has, except my dad. Between the two of you, if I can't survive, I *should* be shot. I *should* be put out of everyone's misery."

"Was that a thank-you, Ms. Lane?"

I thought about it and shrugged. "Yes."

Behind me, he made a strange noise. "That's it. You're not going."

"Because I thanked you? What kind of logic is that?"

"The kind of person that thanks another person never survives. Have you learned nothing?"

"He has my parents."

"If he gets you, he could get the whole world."

"He's not going to get me. I'm going to do exactly what you told me to do. No deviations. No independent decisions. I'll go into the house, snap a photo of whatever destination the Silver shows, and text it to you. Between that and my brand, you'll track me. You'll bring your . . . whatever they are in behind me or get there some other way, and you'll rescue us." And I would kill the LM. Bury my spear to the hilt in his chest. Maybe his eyeball. Stand there and watch him begin to rot. I hoped he died slowly.

"The Silvers are too unpredictable. Something could go wrong even in the brief time you pass from one to the next."

"You wondered if I had the balls. Now you know. Besides, he needs me, remember? He's not going to take any chances."

"Anytime you use the Silvers, you're taking a chance. Especially if you're carrying OOPs. Power provokes change in places of unpredictable power."

"I know. You've told me five times now. I'm to keep my spear hidden and the stones in the pouch."

"With the holes in the prison walls, and Cruce's curse . . . there's no bloody telling what could go wrong. No, Ms. Lane, this just won't work."

"I'm going in, Barrons, with or without your help."

"I could stop you," he said, so softly that I knew he was not only seriously considering it but a breath away from chaining me up somewhere.

I inhaled sharply. "Remember the child dying in your arms?"

His nostrils flared. The thing rattled in his chest.

"Don't make me live it, Barrons. Don't choose my grief for me. You have no right."

"They aren't your biological parents."

"Do you think the heart only follows blood?"

A few minutes later I was preparing to walk out the door, turn right, and head into what had once been the city's biggest Dark Zone.

I knew that by the time I walked the fourteen blocks to 1247 LaRuhe, I'd be dripping sweat, but I was taking no chances. In case the Silver was icy, I'd layered my clothing deep. In case it was dark, I was wearing my MacHalo. In case I had to be there awhile before Barrons broke us out, and in case my parents needed food, I had my pack on my back, stuffed with protein bars, water, Unseelie flesh, and a miscellany of other items Barrons and I had taken turns cramming in. In case the LM insisted on seeing them, I had the three stones in a black pouch covered with delicately shimmering wards. My gun was over my shoulder and my spear under it. I had no intention of needing any of the items I was bringing, but I also had no intention of ever going anywhere without a fully equipped pack again until the last Fae had been wiped from our world. For the tenth time in the past two days, I wished I had V'lane's name in my tongue and wondered again where he was and what had happened to him.

My cell phone was in my palm, ready to snap a photo and transmit it, so Barrons could see the LM's destination in the glass. I glanced down at it. There was something nagging at me and had been ever since he'd told me his plan. There was an inconsistency lurking at the edge of my awareness. A fact that didn't rest comfortably with the others.

"If I understand the Silvers, they all show destinations. And you expect the LM's to show a destination, too. So why does your Silver show a pathway winding through what looks like a graveyard haunted by demons? That's not a destination."

He said nothing.

"You've linked more than two Silvers together, haven't you?" I frowned. "What if the LM has done the same thing? What if his doesn't show a destination, either?"

"He's not adept enough to stack Silvers."

When I get epiphanies, they come hard and fast. "Oh, God, I get it!" I exclaimed. It was no wonder he hadn't wanted to explain the Silvers to me! "The mirror in your study connects to what's beneath your garage! You 'stacked' mirrors to form a passageway filled with demon watchdogs so if anyone found their way into your mirror, they'd never survive the gauntlet you make them run." Instead of one mirror instantly connecting to another, he'd arranged a multitude of mirrors to form a long, deadly corridor. "That's how you get to the three floors beneath the garage. *That's* why I couldn't find the entrance. It's been right under my nose in my bookstore all along!"

"*Your* bookstore?" He snorted. Then he laughed. "Walk out of this with your parents, the stones, and Darroc dead, Ms. Lane, and I'll give you the bloody thing."

I felt suddenly breathless. "Are we talking figurative or literal?"

"Literal. Lock, stock, and barrel."

"Deed and all?" My heart hammered. I loved BB&B.

"To the store. Not my garage or car collection."

"In other words, you'll always be out back, breathing down my neck," I said dryly.

"Never doubt it." He gave me a wolf smile.

"Throw in the Viper?"

"And the Lamborghini."

29

1247 LaRuhe looked exactly the same as it did the first time I saw it, last August.

Six months ago, when I arrived in Dublin, I didn't believe in anything remotely paranormal, had never seen a Fae in my life, and wouldn't have believed one existed for anything in the world.

Then, a mere two weeks later, I'd been standing right where I was now, in the middle of a Dark Zone, watching as the Lord Master released a flood of Unseelie into our world through a gate fashioned from a stone dolmen that had been hidden in a warehouse behind this house.

How quickly my world had changed. Two lousy weeks!

The tall, fancy brick house at 1247 LaRuhe, with its ornate limestone façade, was as out of place in the dilapidated industrial neighborhood as I was in the middle of this whole mess.

Delicate wrought iron fenced in a dirt lawn with three skeletal dying trees. The house's many-mullioned windows were painted black. There was an enormous dirt crater behind the residence. V'lane had not just "squashed" the LM's dolmen—as I'd asked on the day he gifted me with the illusion of playing volleyball with Alina at the beach—he'd blasted it right out of existence, leaving a gaping hole. I regretted not being more specific and asking him to demolish the house, too. Then I wouldn't be standing here, about to enter it again and to step into one of those mirrors I'd found so terrifying the first time I'd seen them. Then again, the LM would merely have sent me to some other awful place, I was sure.

I climbed the stairs, pushed open the door, and stepped into the elegant foyer, my boots rapping smartly on obsidian-and-ivory marble floors. I passed beneath a glittering chandelier, beyond ornate dual staircases and plush furnishings.

I knew that upstairs was the Lord Master's bedroom, with its grand high Louis XIV bed, velvet drapes, sumptuous bathroom, and a fabulous walk-in closet. I knew he wore the finest clothing, the most expensive shoes. I knew he had a taste for the best of everything. Including my sister.

There was no point in delaying the inevitable. Besides, I wanted to get in and get this over with so I could lay claim to *my* bookstore. Barrons had flabbergasted me with his offer. I didn't know what to make of it. Right now he was waiting, back at the bookstore, for my photo. His . . . associates were supposedly closing in behind me. I entered the long, formal parlor, where a dozen large gilt-edged mirrors hung on the walls, and walked through the room, past furnishings Sotheby's and Christie's would have dueled to the death over.

The first mirror on the right was completely black. I wondered if it was shut. It looked dead. I peered at it. The dense blackness suddenly swelled and expanded, and for a moment I was afraid it would explode from its gilt frame, grow like the Blob, and swallow me up. But at the peak of its crest, it thumped loudly, made a squishing sound, and deflated. After a moment it swelled again. Squished. Deflated. I shuddered. It was a giant black heart hanging on the wall, pumping away.

I moved on. The second mirror showed an empty bedroom.

The third was open on a prison cell containing human children. They reached through bars for me with bony, pale arms and imploring eyes. I froze. There were a hundred of them or more crammed into the tiny cell. They were filthy and bruised, with torn clothing.

I had no time for this. I couldn't afford the emotion. I stepped closer to the mirror and turned my palm toward it to snap a picture so that later, after I'd gotten my parents out, I could make Barrons help me find this place in the Silvers and free them. But just as I was about to press the button, one of the children opened his mouth, snapped at me with vicious teeth no human child had, and made a suggestion to me no human child would, and I backed hastily away, cursing myself for allowing emotion to fog my mind.

Dani had said some of the Unseelie were imprisoning children. With that awful thought in mind, I'd looked into the Silver and seen its denizens colored by my fear and worry, which had airbrushed telling clues. If I'd been thinking clearly, I would have noticed the subtle wrongness in the shape of the "children's" heads, the unnatural ferocity in their tiny faces.

I didn't spare a glance for the fourth mirror but walked straight to the fifth. At a slight angle from it, so the LM wouldn't see me doing it, I snapped a picture, sent it to Barrons' cell phone, then slid my phone into my pocket.

Only then did I let the impact of the scene hit me.

We had a definite destination.

He was in *my* living room, at my house, in Ashford, Georgia.

The Lord Master had my mom and dad bound to chairs and gagged, with a dozen black-and-crimson-clad guards standing around them.

The Lord Master was in my hometown! What had he done to it? Had he brought Shades with him? Were Unseelie walking the streets even now, feeding off my friends?

The one place I'd tried so hard to keep safe, and I'd failed!

I'd let V'lane take me there, given in to my weakness, stood outside my own home. Was that the fatal act that drew the Lord Master's attention? Or had he always known and only now decided to make use of it?

In the mirror, across the fifteen or so feet that separated us, my daddy shook his head. His eyes said, *Don't you dare, baby. You stay on that side of the mirror. Don't you dare trade yourself for us.*

How could I not? *He* was the one who'd taught me that the heart had reasons of which reason knew nothing, the only quote of Pascal's I remembered. All the reason in the world couldn't have talked me into turning away now, even if I hadn't had Barrons as backup. Even without a safety net, this was a wire I'd have walked. I might have found out my biological mother's name last night. I might have even begun thinking of myself as Mac O'Connor, but Jack and Rainey Lane were my mom and dad, and always would be.

I walked to the wall. Daddy's eyes were wild now, and I knew, if not for the gag, he'd be roaring at me.

I stepped up, into the Silver.

PART
III

But now we see through a glass darkly and, the truth, before it is revealed to all, face to face, we see in fragments (alas, how illegible) in the error of the world, so we must spell out its faithful signals even when they seem obscure to us and as if amalgamated with a will wholly bent on evil.

—Umberto Eco
The Name of the Rose

30

"Good of you to come," mocked the Lord Master. "Nice hat."

Entering the Silver was like pressing forward into a gluey membrane. The surface rippled thickly when I touched it. When I tried to step into it, it resisted. I pushed harder, and it took considerable effort to force my boot to puncture the silvery skin. I thrust in up to my hip.

Still the mirror pressed back at me with a buoyant elasticity.

For a moment I stood half in each world, my face through the mirror, the back of my head in the house, one leg in the Silver, one leg out. Just when I thought it would expel me with the snap of a giant rubber band, it yielded—sucked me in, warm and unpleasantly wet—and squirted me out on the other side, stumbling.

I'd expected to find myself standing in the living room, but I was in a tunnel of sorts, of moist pink membrane. My living room was farther away than it had looked from outside the mirror. There were forty or so feet between me and my parents. Barrons had been wrong. The LM was more adept with Silvers than he'd thought. Not only was he capable of stacking Silvers, the tunnel hadn't been at all visible from beyond the glass. In tennis-speak, this set went to the LM. But there was no way he was winning the match.

"As if I had a choice." I wiped my face with a sleeve, scrubbing at a thin layer of smelly, slippery afterbirth. It was dripping off my MacHalo. I'd thought about removing it before I'd entered the mirror (it's a little hard for people to take you seriously when you're wearing one), but now I was glad I hadn't. It was no wonder people avoided the Silvers.

You had every choice, my dad's eyes said furiously. *You chose the wrong one.*

My mother's eyes were saying *way* more than that. She began with the mess that was my tousled black hair sticking out from under my "hat," went nearly ballistic over the tight leather pants I was wearing, made short, scathing work of my butchered nails, and by the time she got around to the automatic weapon that kept slipping around my shoulder, banging into my hip, I had to tune her out.

I took a step forward.

"Not so fast," said the Lord Master. "Show me the stones."

I swung my gun forward into my other hand, slipped the pack off my shoulder, opened it, fished out the black pouch, and held it up.

"Get them out. Show them to me."

"Barrons didn't think that was a good idea."

"I told you not to involve Barrons, and I don't give a fuck what he thinks."

"You told me not to *bring* him. I had to involve him. He's the one who had the stones. Have you ever tried to steal anything from Barrons?"

The look on his face said he had. "If he interferes, they die."

"I got your message loud and clear the first time. He won't interfere." I needed to get closer. I needed to be between the LM and his guards and my parents when Barrons and his men arrived. I needed to be in stabbing distance. Barrons planned to reconfigure his Silver to connect to whatever destination the Lord Master was at, but he'd said it would take time, depending on the location. *Stall,* he'd ordered. *Once I get the photo, I'll work on connecting to the other end. My men will come in behind you as soon as I have a lock on the location.*

"Put down the spear, your gun, the pistol in the back of your pants, the switchblade in your sleeve, and the knives in your boots. Kick them all away."

How did he know where all my weapons were?

My mother couldn't have looked more shocked if she'd found out I was sleeping with half the Ashford High football team and smoking crack between touchdowns.

I gave her my most reassuring look. She flinched. Apparently what I considered reassuring lately came off a little . . . savage, I guess. "It's been a rough few months, Mom," I said defensively. "I'll explain it all later. Let my parents go," I told the LM. "I'll cooperate fully. You have my word."

"I do not require your word. I have your last living relatives. Being of such finite duration, humans care deeply about such things. Alina told me her parents died in a car wreck when she was fifteen. Yet another lie. Makes one wonder, does it not? I would never have thought to look for them had you not led me here."

How had I led him here? How had he followed me to Ashford? Could he track V'lane? Was V'lane duplicitous? Working with the Lord Master? "They're not my relatives," I said coolly. "My relatives are dead. When you killed Alina, you wiped out the last of my line, except for me." I was hoping to make my parents' value seem a little less than it really was. It always worked in the movies. "We were adopted."

I snatched a quick look at my mom, even though I knew I shouldn't. Her eyes shimmered with unshed tears. Great. She disapproved of everything about me, and now I'd hurt her feelings. I was batting a thousand.

The Lord Master didn't say a word. Just walked over to my dad and slammed him in the face with his fist. My daddy's head snapped back and blood spurted from his nose. He gave a dazed shake, and his eyes said, *Get out of here, baby.*

"All right!" I shouted. "I lied! Leave him alone!"

The Lord Master turned back to me. "Mortality is the consummate weakness. It shapes your entire existence. Your every breath. Is it any wonder the Fae have always been gods to your kind?"

"Never to me."

"Drop your weapons."

I let my automatic slip to the ground, yanked the pistol from the back of my pants, dropped the switchblade from the cuff of my jacket, and extracted a knife from each boot.

"The spear."

I stared. If I tried to throw the spear the forty feet that separated us, what good would it do? Even if I hit him dead in the heart, he was part human and wouldn't die right away. I had no doubt at least one of my parents would be dead seconds after I'd thrown it, if not both.

Stall, Barrons had said.

I pulled the spear from my holster and slid it from beneath my coat. The moment I uncovered it, it crackled and sparked, shooting jagged white charges into the air. Alabaster, it blazed with almost blinding luminosity, as if drawing power from the Fae realm around it.

I couldn't make my hand let go of it. My fingers wouldn't unclench.

"Drop it *now*." He turned toward my mother and drew back his fist.

I snarled as I flung the spear away from me. It lodged in the wall of the sleek pink tunnel. The fleshy canal shuddered, as if with pain. "Leave. Her. Alone," I gritted.

"Kick away the weapons and show me the stones."

"Seriously, Barrons said not to."

"Now."

Sighing, I withdrew the stones from the pouch and peeled back the velvet cloth they were wrapped in.

The reaction was instantaneous and violent: The

tunnel spasmed, moaning deep in its wet walls, and the floor shuddered beneath me. The stones blazed with blue-black light. The walls contracted and expanded, as if laboring to expel me, and suddenly I was blinded by baleful light, deaf to all but the rushing of wind and water. I squeezed my eyes shut against the glare. There was nothing to hold on to. I clutched the stones, trying to cover them, and nearly lost the velvet cloth to the gale. My backpack banged against my shins and was torn from my grasp.

I howled into the wind, calling for my parents, for Barrons—hell, even for the Lord Master! I felt like I was being ripped in ten different directions. My coat was being torn from my shoulders, rippling in the hard breeze. I struggled to shove the stones back into the pouch.

Abruptly, all was still.

"I told you," I growled, keeping my eyes closed, waiting for the retinal burn to fade, "Barrons advised against it. But did you listen? *No*." There was no answer. "Hello?" I said warily. Still no answer.

I opened my eyes.

Gone was the pink membranous canal.

I stood in a hall of purest gold.

Gold walls, gold floors—I tipped my head back—gold that stretched up as far as I could see. If there was a ceiling, it was beyond my vision. Soaring, towering golden walls to nowhere.

I was alone.

No Lord Master. No guards. No parents.

I looked down, hoping to find my gun, knives, and backpack.

There was nothing but smooth, endless gold floor.

I glanced at the walls, searching frantically for my spear.

There was no glint of alabaster to be found.

In fact, I realized, as I turned in a slow circle, there was nothing on those gold walls at all except hundreds, no, thousands, no—I stared; they went all the way up, vanishing beyond my vision—*billions* of mirrors.

Trying to absorb it, I tasted infinity. I was a minuscule dot on a linear depiction of time that stretched endlessly in both directions, rendering me of utter and absolute inconsequence.

"Oh, shit, shit, shit."

I knew where I was.

The Hall of All Days.

31

I have no idea how long I sat.

Time, in this place, would become an impossible thing for me to gauge.

I sat in the middle of the Hall of All Days—knees tucked up, staring down at the golden floor because looking around made me feel small and vertiginous—trying to take stock of my situation.

Problem: Somewhere out there in the real world, in my living room, in Ashford, Georgia, the Lord Master still had my parents.

I imagined he was seriously pissed off.

It wasn't my fault. *He* was the one who'd insisted I show him the stones. I'd cautioned against it. But fault was as irrelevant as my presence in this vast, indifferent place of all days.

He still had my parents. *That* was relevant.

Hopefully, Barrons was even now speeding his way to them through the reconfigured Silver in his study, and hopefully his comrades were storming in through the mirror at 1247 LaRuhe, and hopefully that slippery pink tunnel that had too closely resembled a portion of the female anatomy for my comfort was still intact and I had merely been expelled by its labor pains, and hopefully within moments my parents would be safe.

That was four too many "hopefullys" for my taste.

It didn't matter. I'd been effectively neutralized. Plucked from the number set and tossed into the quantum hall of variables, none of which computed into the only equation I understood and cared about.

There were billions of mirrors around me. *Billions* of portals. And I had a tough time choosing between fifteen shades of pink.

After a while, I checked my watch. It was stuck at 1:14 P.M.

I slipped off my coat and began to strip, tucking the pouch containing the stones in my waistband. The Hall was too warm for the layers I was wearing. I removed my sweater and long-sleeved knit jersey, and tied them around my waist, then put my coat back on.

I performed an inventory of items on my person.

One knife—an antique Scottish dirk—that the LM hadn't known about, pilfered from the Baubles portion of Barrons Books and strapped to my left forearm.

One baby-food jar full of wriggling Unseelie flesh in my left coat pocket.

Two protein bars tucked into an inner coat pocket, squished.

One MacHalo, still strapped beneath my chin.

One cell phone.

I took inventory of what I didn't have.

No batteries or flashlights.

No water.

No spear.

I stopped there. That was bad enough.

I pulled my cell phone from my back pocket and punched up Barrons' number. I've become so accustomed to his invincibility that I expected it to ring, and when it didn't, I was flabbergasted. Apparently even *his* cell service had dead spots, and if it wasn't going to work somewhere, I could understand it not working here. Even if I'd had V'lane's name, I doubted it would have worked in this place.

My own mind nearly didn't work here. The longer I sat, the odder I began to feel.

The Hall wasn't merely the confluence of infinite doorways to alternate places and times. The many portals made the Hall live and breathe, ebb and flow. The Hall *was* time. It was ancient and young, past and present and future, all in one.

BB&B exuded a sense of spatial distortion from harboring a single Silver in Barrons' study.

These billions of mirrors opening onto the same hall created an exponentially compounded effect, both spatially and temporally. Time here wasn't linear, it was . . . My mind couldn't focus on it, but I was part of it, and I didn't get that at all. I didn't matter. I was essential. I was a child. I was a withered old woman. I was death. I was the source of all creation. I was the Hall and the Hall was me. A tiny bit of me seemed to bleed into every doorway.

Duality didn't begin to describe it. Like this place

itself, I was *all* possibles. It was the most terrifying feeling I'd ever felt.

I tried *IYCGM*.

No service.

I stared at *IYD* for a long time.

Ryodan had said he'd kill me if I used it when I didn't need it.

My first thought was, *I'd like to see him get here and try.* My second thought was that I wouldn't, because then he'd be here, too, and he really might kill me.

I couldn't begin to present a convincing argument that I was dying. I might not like my current situation, but there was no arguing that I was in perfect health, with no apparent threat to my life in the immediate vicinity. Although I seemed to be growing more . . . confused by the moment.

Memories from my childhood had begun to stir in my mind, seeming too vivid and tantalizing for mere memories.

I skipped lightly over them, found one I liked.

My tenth birthday: Mom and Dad had thrown a surprise party for me.

The moment I chose to focus on it, it swelled with dramatic appeal, and there were my friends, laughing and holding presents, real, so real, waiting for me to join them in the dining room, where they were having cake and ice cream. I saw it all happening, right there in the molten gold of the floor I was staring down at. I traced my fingers over the vision. The gold rippled in the wake of my fingertips, and I was touching our dining room table, about to sink into it, slip inside my ten-year-old body in the chair, laughing at something Alina said.

Alina was dead. This was not now. This was not real.

I jerked my gaze away.

In the air in front of me, a new memory took shape: my first shopping trip to Atlanta with my aunts. It had left a serious impression on me. We were in Bloomingdale's. I was eleven. I wandered, staring up at all the pretty things, no longer seeing the gold walls and mirrors.

I closed my eyes, stood, and shoved the cell phone into my back pocket.

I had to get out of this place. It was messing with my mind.

But where?

I opened my eyes and began moving. The moment I did, the memories vanished from the air around me and my mind was clear again.

A thought occurred to me. Frowning, I walked a few yards and stopped.

The memories resumed.

My daddy was cheering at my first ever—and last—softball game. He'd bought me a pink mitt with magenta stitching. My mom had embroidered my name and flowers on it. The boys were laughing at me and my mitt. I ran to catch a ground ball to prove to them how tough I was. It popped up and slammed me in the face, bloodying my nose and chipping a tooth.

I winced.

They laughed harder, pointing.

I manipulated the memory, fast-rewound, caught the ball perfectly, threw out the runner at home plate, and got it there in plenty of time for the catcher to take out the runner at third.

The boys were awed by my ball-playing prowess.

My daddy puffed with pride.

It was a lie, but an oh-so-sweet one.

I began walking again.

The memory exploded into pink-mitt dust and sprinkled the floor.

Stopping in the Hall was dangerous, perhaps even deadly.

My suspicion was confirmed a short time later when I passed a skeleton sitting cross-legged on the floor, leaning back against the gold wall between mirrors. Its posture evidenced no signs of struggle, gave no hint of agony in death. The face of the skull had—inasmuch as a skull could—a peaceful look to its bones. Had it starved to death? Or had it lived a hundred years, lost in dreams? I felt no hunger pangs, and should have, considering all I'd had since yesterday afternoon was coffee, hours ago. Did one even need to eat here, where time wasn't what one expected at all?

I began glancing into the mirrors as I passed.

Some of the things in the mirrors glanced back, looking startled and confused. It seemed some of them could see me as clearly as I could see them.

I was going to have to make a choice, and sooner was probably wiser than later. I was beginning to think gold was the most peaceful, right, perfect color I'd ever seen. And the floor—so inviting! Warm, smooth, I could stretch out and rest my eyes a bit . . . gather my strength for what was certain to be an arduous journey.

First danger of the Hall of All Days: When you can live any day over again in your mind—and live it *right*—why leave at all? I could save my sister here. Save the world. Never know the difference after a while.

Second danger of the Hall of All Days: When anything is possible, how do you choose?

There were tropical vistas of white beaches that stretched for miles, with aqua waves so clear that coral reefs of rainbow hues shimmered through, glinting in the sun, and tiny silver fish leaped and played in the swells.

There were streets of fabulous mansions. Deserts and vast plains. There were ancient reptilian beasts in verdant valleys and postapocalyptic cities. There were underwater worlds and Silvers that opened directly onto open space, black and deep, glittering with stars. There were doorways to nebulae and even one that led straight to the event horizon of a black hole. I tried to fathom the mind that would want to go there. An immortal that had done everything else? A Fae that could never die and wanted to know what it felt like to be sucked up by one? The more I saw in the Hall of All Days, the more I understood that I understood *nothing* about the immortal race that had created this place.

There were mirrors that opened onto images so terrible I looked away the instant I caught a glimpse of what was going on. We've done some of those things. Apparently other beings on other worlds have, too. In one, a man performing a horrific experiment saw me, grinned, and lunged for me. I took off in a mad dash, heart pounding, and ran without stopping for a long, long time. Finally, I glanced behind me. I was alone. I concluded that Silver must have been one-way. Thankfully! I wondered if all the mirrors in the Hall were, or if some of them still worked both ways. If I stepped through one, could I immediately return if I didn't like the world? From what Barrons had told me, unpredictability was the name of the game in here.

How had I gotten to the Hall? What had the stones done to rip me from the tunnel of a set of Silvers and dump me into the vortex of the entire network? Did they work as a homing beacon, and would uncovering them *always* bring me here?

I walked. I looked. I looked away.

Pain, pleasure, delight, torture, love, hate, laughter, despair, beauty, horror, hope, grief—all of it was available here in the Hall of All Days.

There were the surreal mirrors with Dalí-esque landscapes, so similar to his paintings that I wondered if they hadn't been hung here and animated. There were doorways to dreamscapes so alien I couldn't even give name to what I was seeing.

I looked into mirror after mirror, growing more uncertain by the moment. I had no idea if any of the portals actually opened into *my* world at all. Were they different planets? Different dimensions? Once I entered one, would I be committing to a perilous journey through an unbeatable maze?

Billions. There were *billions* of choices. How was I ever going to find my way home?

I walked for what felt like days. Who knows? It might have been. Time has no meaning in the Hall. Nothing does. Tiny me. Huge corridor. An occasional skeleton—the rare human one. Silence except for the sound of my boots on gold. I began to sing. I went through every song I knew, staring into Silvers. Running from some.

Then one stopped me cold in my tracks.

I stared. "Christian?" I exploded disbelievingly. His back was to me as he walked through a dark forest, but the moon in his mirror was bright, and there was no mistaking his build and walk. Those long legs in faded jeans. The dark hair pulled back in a queue. The broad shoulders and confident gait.

His head whipped around. There was a line of crimson and black tattoos down the side of his neck that hadn't been there the last time I'd seen him.

Mac? His lips moved, but I couldn't hear him. I stepped closer.

"Is it really you?"

Apparently he could hear me. Elation and relief battled with anxiety in the gorgeous Scotsman's eyes. He stared at me, leaned closer, looked confused, then shook his head. *No, Mac. Stay wherever you are. Don't come here. Go back.*

"I don't know how to go back."

Where are you?

"Can't you see?"

He shook his head. *You seem to be inside a large cactus. For a moment, I thought you were here with me. How are you seeing me?*

I had to make him repeat it several times. I'm not the best lip-reader. The word "cactus" threw me. I couldn't see a single cactus in the forest. "I'm in the Hall of All Days."

Tiger eyes flared. *Don't stay long! It messes with you.*

"I kind of figured that out." A moment ago, my pink mitt had reappeared in my hand, and I could hear the sounds of the ballpark around me. I began to jog in place. The Hall was not fooled. The mitt remained on my hand. I jogged a tight circle in front of the mirror. Glove and memory vanished.

It's a dangerous place. I was there for a time. I had to choose a Silver. I chose badly. They are not what they seem. What they show you is not where they lead.

"Are you kidding me?" I nearly went ballistic. If I entered a tropical beach, would I end up in Nazi Germany with my highly inconvenient black hair?

The one I chose didn't. I've been jumping dimensions ever since, trying to get to better places. Some of the Silvers are true, some are not. There's no way to tell which.

"But you're a lie detector!"

It doesn't work in the Hall, lass. It only works out of it, and not always. I doubt any of your sidhe-*seer talents work there, either.*

Still jogging a tight circle, I shut my eyes and sought that place in the center of my mind. *Show me what is true,* I commanded. I opened my eyes and looked back at Christian. He still stood in a dark forest.

"Where are you?"

In a desert. He gave me a bitter smile. *With four suns and no night. I'm badly burned. I've had nothing to eat or drink in too long. If I don't find a dimensional shift soon, I'm . . . in trouble.*

"A dimensional shift?" I asked if he meant an IFP and explained what they were.

He nodded. *They abound. But they have no' been abounding here.* "Abooondin'," he'd said. Although the mirror was showing me a perfectly clean, well-rested man, now that I knew what to look for, I could see his exhaustion and strain. More than that, I was picking up a certain . . . grim acceptance? From Christian MacKeltar? No way.

"How bad off are you, Christian?" I said. "And don't lie to me."

He smiled. *I seem to recall saying the same to you once. Have you slept with him?*

"Long story. Answer my question."

That's a yes. Ah, lass. Tiger eyes held mine for a tense, probing moment. *Bad,* he said finally.

"Are you actually even standing there? I mean, up on your own feet?" Was anything I was seeing remotely true?

No, lass.

"Could you stand if you wanted to?" I said sharply.

Not sure.

I didn't waste another moment.

I stepped into the mirror.

32

Some Silvers feel like quicksand. They don't like to let you go.

I expected this one to behave like the one hanging in the LM's house: hard to push into, certain to expel me with a rubbery snap.

It *was* hard to push into, more resistant than the first one, but it proved even more difficult to get out of. Without Christian, I might not have made it.

I found myself trapped inside silvery glue that held my limbs nearly immobile. I kicked and punched and ended up getting so turned around that I had no idea which way was out. Apparently there was only one direction that would work.

Then Christian's hand was on my arm (he *could* stand), and I shoved toward him with all my strength.

The college back home where I take classes part-time has a wind tunnel created by the unique placement of the math building breezeway and the science buildings around it. On especially windy days, it's almost impossible to cut through it. You have to lean forward at a precarious angle as you pass the math building, head ducked, forging ahead with all your might.

I learned the hard way about break points, where either a design flaw or a joke by some pissed-off engineer leaves an "eye" in the breezeway, where the wind abruptly stops. If you're unaware of it and still forging ahead, you fall flat on your face in front of all the math and science geeks—who know about it and loiter in the general vicinity on windy days but don't tell freshmen because that would deprive them of the endless amounts of amusement they get from watching us wipe out, preferably in a short skirt that ends up around our waist.

That was this Silver.

I shoved toward the hand, fighting, pressing with all my might, and abruptly the resistance gave way—and I went flying out of the glass, into Christian, at such velocity that we went rolling and tumbling across sand.

I tried to gasp, but it didn't work. I was in a blast furnace. It was so bright that I couldn't open my eyes; the air was so hot and dry that I couldn't breathe.

I struggled to acclimate and finally sucked down a breath that seared my lungs. I slitted my eyes, got a good look at Christian, and rolled off him.

He was worse than "bad off." He was in serious danger. With his dark complexion, he'd tanned, but there was a cruel redness to it, his lips were cracked, and I could tell by his eyes and skin that he was severely dehydrated. Blisters covered his face.

I whirled around, hoping to find a mirror hanging in the air behind me through which I could drag us to safety.

There wasn't one.

There were, however, hundreds of man-size cactuses, any one of which might have been the one he said I'd appeared to be standing in. Was there a mirror camouflaged inside one of them? It stood to reason that on worlds the Fae wanted to visit unobserved, they'd have had to conceal the Silver in something if there was no place it didn't appear utterly incongruous with the terrain. Or had Cruce's mysterious curse screwed things up?

I wondered if I should try flinging myself into a few of the nearest cactuses, employing the same method Dani had used to try to break through wards, hoping for a two-way portal. The thought held little appeal. She'd gotten nothing but badly bruised for her efforts. The cactuses sported a protective armor of needle-sharp spines.

Squinting, I glanced around.

We were in an ocean of desert.

It had to be a hundred fifteen degrees. No shade anywhere to be seen. Nothing but sand.

I looked up and instantly regretted it. The sky was painfully bright, with four blazing suns. It was whiter than white. It was radioactive white.

"You bloody damned fool," Christian managed through split lips. "Now we'll both be dying here."

"No, we won't. Which . . . uh, cactus did I come through?"

"I've no bloody idea, and those spines are poisonous, so good luck poking around at them."

Damn. Onto plan B, which was basically a wing and a prayer.

I began to remove the black pouch from my waistband, preparing to uncover the stones. Would they return us to the Hall, where we could choose the next portal together? Who knew? Who cared? Anything was better than this. He would die here and so would I.

I rolled close to Christian and pressed against him.

"Och, and now you flirt me up, lass," he said weakly, with a shadow of that killer smile. "When I canna do a thing about it."

"Wrap your arms and legs around me, Christian. Don't let go. No matter what happens, don't let go." Sweat was pouring down my face, dripping from beneath my MacHalo, into my eyes, pooling between my breasts. I was wearing too many clothes, a bike helmet, and a leather coat in a desert.

He didn't question me. Just wrapped his legs around my hips and locked his hands in the small of my back. I prayed he had enough strength to keep his grip. I had no idea what was going to happen, but I didn't expect it to be gentle.

I slid the pouch from between us, loosened the drawstring, and uncovered the tips of the stones. They flared to life, pulsing with blue-black fire.

The terrain responded instantly and violently, just as the pink tunnel did.

The desert began to undulate, and the air was

filled with a high-pitched whine that quickly turned into a metallic-sounding scream. Sand whipped up, stinging my hands and face.

"Are you crazy? What the—" The rest of Christian's words were lost in the howling wind.

The atomic-white sky darkened to blue-black, in dramatic, quick increments. I looked up. The suns were being eclipsed, one by one.

The sand shuddered beneath us. Swells rose, dips formed. Christian and I rolled, down, down, deep into a sandy valley that was still forming as we tumbled. I felt brackets snapping off my MacHalo. I was suddenly afraid the desert would swallow us alive, but the desert didn't want us. That was the whole point, although I didn't know it then.

I struggled to keep my grip on the pouch, clutched it tightly to my chest. Christian's legs were steel around my hips, his hands locked. The temperature dropped sharply.

The desert began to tremble. The tremble became a rumble. The rumble became an earthquake, and, just when I thought we might be shaken to pieces, the ground beneath us sank abruptly, then gave a single gigantic heave and flung us straight up into the air.

As we went soaring into the dark sky, I muttered an apology to Christian. He sort of laughed and muttered back in my ear that he preferred a quick death by falling, with crushed bones and all, to a slow death by dehydration, and at least it was nice and cool finally but maybe, since it seemed the stones had triggered the cataclysmic reaction, I

might try covering them back up and see what happened?

I shoved them in the pouch and crammed it
down the waistband of my pants.

We fell.

I braced for impact.

33

We splashed down into icy water.

I plunged deep. Kicking hard, I surfaced and inhaled greedily. I blinked water from my eyes and saw that we'd fallen into a stone quarry. How lucky. That must mean a terrifying monster with razor-sharp teeth was in the water beneath me, about to snap my legs off, because the gods didn't smile on me—at least not lately or that I was aware of.

And Christian wasn't as bad off as I'd thought, because he was swimming toward shore.

I narrowed my eyes. *Toward* shore, leaving me to my own devices that, as far as he knew, might involve drowning.

I checked to make sure the pouch was still in my waistband and kicked into a breaststroke. I'm a strong swimmer, and I pulled myself out of the quarry just a few seconds after he did. He collapsed hard on the grass-covered bank and closed his eyes.

"Thanks for sticking around to make sure I wasn't drowning." Then I murmured, "Oh, Christian." I touched his blistered face, made sure he was breathing, took his pulse. He was unconscious. It had taken the last ounce of energy he possessed to get himself out of the quarry.

First things first: Were we safe here?

I scanned our surroundings. The quarry was large and deep, overflowing here and there into smaller ponds and pools. It occupied a small corner of a huge valley. Miles and miles of grassy plain were surrounded by moderate mountains with ice-capped crowns. The valley was peaceful and calm. At the opposite edge, animals grazed serenely.

It looked like we were safe, at least for now. I heaved a sigh of relief and struggled out of my wet leather coat. I slipped the pouch containing the stones from my waistband and set it aside. There was no doubt about it: Removing the stones from the spelled pouch made dimensions shift for some reason, but while uncovered, they seem to wreak total havoc on the world around them. The next time we used them, I'd flash them quickly, and maybe we'd get to skip the whole violent expulsion motif and glide at a gentle tempo into the next world.

After a brief hesitation, I stripped down to bra and panties, grateful for the moderate climate. Wet leather sucks. I draped my clothing on nearby rocks to dry in the sun, hoping the leather wouldn't shrink to ridiculous sizes.

Next concern: what to do for Christian. He was breathing shallowly and his pulse was erratic. He'd passed out in the sun, where his burn would deepen. The blisters on his face were crusted and seeping blood. How long had he been in that hellish desert? When had he last eaten? There was no way I could move him. I couldn't even get him out of his wet clothes. I could cut them off, but he'd need them again. Who knew what we might have to face next? He was more heavily muscled than last I'd seen him and, unconscious, he was deadweight. Had he been fighting his way through dimension after dimension since Halloween? Did time pass the same way where he'd been?

Unless it had fallen out, I had a baby-food jar of Unseelie flesh in my coat. I tripped over my own feet in my haste to get to it and unbuttoned pocket after pocket, searching.

"Ow!" I'd found it wriggling wetly in shards of broken bottle, buttoned in an inner pocket. I extracted the flesh carefully from the jar, which must have shattered in my tumble across the sand. Of the seven strips I'd crammed into the tiny container, there were four left. Three of them had wriggled off somewhere. I held the noxious pieces of gray Rhino-boy flesh, picked out slivers of glass, and considered the rapidly healing cuts on my fingers.

Was I healing so well because of the Unseelie I'd eaten in the past? Did it cause permanent changes, as Rowena claimed? Would it do something terrible to Christian? I had no idea what else to do for him. I had only two protein bars, and I didn't know if the water around us was drinkable or contaminated by some deadly-to-humans parasite. I'd never been a Girl Scout, couldn't start a fire with sticks, had no container to boil water in even if I could, and was disgusted to realize I was still, in many ways, remarkably useless.

I hurried back to his side, lay one of the strips on a flat stone, and cut it up into pieces as small as early peas. I pried open his teeth, stuffed the pieces in, and held his mouth and nose closed, hoping the flesh would, in dim-witted Rhino-boy fashion, wriggle toward his stomach, seeking escape.

It did. I wasn't so useless after all!

He gagged, I released my hold on his nose, and his throat muscles convulsed. He gagged again and swallowed involuntarily. He coughed and made a retching sound. Even when you're unconscious, Unseelie meat is revolting.

With a groan, he rolled over onto his side.

I diced another strip, stuffed it into his mouth, and held it closed again. This time he resisted, but his body was still too weak to put up much of a fight.

By the time I got the third strip sliced up and in his mouth, he'd rolled over onto his back again, opened his eyes, and was looking at me. I think he was trying to ask what I was doing, but I clamped his teeth together with one hand on the top of his head and the other beneath his chin. He gagged instead and swallowed again.

The effects of Unseelie flesh on an injured human body are instantaneous and miraculous. As I watched, his blisters disappeared and his color returned to normal, leaving him lightly tanned. The gauntness in his face vanished, and the epidermis on his body plumped everywhere, erasing the damage of dehydration, rebuilding him from the inside out.

Unseelie flesh is potent, and addictive. Even though I was cured of my little obsession with it (did he *really* need that last strip?) I envied what I knew was happening to him: the heady rush of power surging hot through his veins, heightening his hearing, smell, and vision, increasing his strength to Barrons' levels, filling him with a euphoric sense of invincibility and an exquisitely elevated awareness of his own body in relation to its surroundings.

Yes, he was certainly getting better.

Tiger eyes were not only open but moving with unabashed appreciation over the skin bared by my bra and underwear. He pushed my hand off his mouth.

Quickly—and possibly in large part because I was tempted to eat it myself—I knelt over him and shoved the last strip between his lips.

He sat up so fast our heads banged, hard.

I yelped and he spat.

Unseelie flesh went flying from his mouth and flopped on the ground between us.

He looked at the animated piece of meat, then he looked at me, and I'm not sure what he found more disgusting: the smelly gray flesh with oozing pustules, or me, for putting it in his mouth in the first place. It pissed me off, because, even on my worst day, I was preferable to Unseelie flesh. The absence of heat in those amber eyes was downright chilling.

"You might try thanking me," I said stiffly.

He gagged again, cleared his throat, turned, and spat over his shoulder. "What," he said, turning back to me and pointing, "the bloody hell is *that*?"

"Unseelie flesh," I said coolly.

"That's *Unseelie*? You fed me the flesh of a dark Fae?"

"How do you feel, Christian?" I demanded. "Pretty good?" He certainly looked good, sitting there in faded jeans, wet T-shirt straining over his wide shoulders, muscles rippling in his arms as he slicked wet hair back from his face. "No burns, no blisters, no hunger or thirst? Has it occurred to you that I saved your ass?"

"At what cost? What does eating it do to you? Nothing Fae is without price!"

"It *heals* you. Would you rather I hadn't?"

"Big, huge lie in there. There are drawbacks. What are they?" he pushed furiously.

"There are drawbacks to everything," I snapped.

We glared at each other.

"Would you rather I'd let you die?"

"Did you even try anything else first? Or are you all about magic, instant gratification?"

I leapt to my feet and began pacing. "What would you have had me try? Dragging your big body into the shade all by myself so you wouldn't get burned worse? How about figuring out how to start a fire with twigs? No, I have it!" I whirled around and shot him a look. "I should have gone looking for a convenience store for sunblock and aloe gel and then when I found that, set off for a vet so I could find you subcutaneous fluids like my neighbors give their sick cat!"

His mouth twitched. "Nice outfit, Mac."

I bristled. I'd been stomping around in my bra and panties and he found me *amusing* in my underwear? "My clothes are soaked," I growled.

"I was speaking of your—" His gaze shot upward. "Would you be calling that a hat, lass?"

I closed my eyes and groaned. I'd gotten so used to the weight of it on my head that I'd forgotten I was wearing my MacHalo. I unstrapped it, snatched it from my head, scraped off strands of dripping moss, and inspected it for damage. Two of the brackets were broken at the base, and several of the lights had been turned on in our roll down sand dunes, wasting precious batteries. I clicked them off and put the helmet on the rocks near my clothes.

I nodded at the piece of Unseelie lying on the ground between us. "Are you going to eat that?"

"Not for love or money," he said vehemently.

"Well, pick it up and put it in your pocket. You might need it again. Like it or not, it saved your life." No matter how badly I wanted it, I didn't dare impair my *sidhe*-seer abilities. If we encountered anything Fae, my Nulling talents were all I had. We'd have to freeze them and run. Or use the stones again.

"It did something to me. Something . . . wrong." He studied it with distaste, picked it up, drew back his arm, and flung it into the quarry. I heard a splash, a second much larger splash, and a snapping sound, followed by a third splash. Since my back was to the water, I had to interpret what happened from the look on his face. "Something awful-looking ate it?"

Looking mildly shocked, he nodded. "Tell me everything you know about what you just fed me and the effects it has. And as for the loch, lass, I wouldn't recommend swimming in it."

*   *   *

Christian's clothes were soaked, and after a scan of the snow-covered peaks around us, he concluded there was a high probability of a sharp evening drop to frigid temperatures, which meant we needed our clothes dry, fast. As there was no convenient dryer nearby, toasting them in the sun was our only option, so a short time later we were both stretched out, me mostly naked, him completely. He was unself-conscious nude. I had to admit, he had reason to be.

After a quick glance, I'd sought privacy on the other side of the tumble of rocks our clothes were drying on and savored the warmth on my skin. All that was missing was my iPod.

And my parents. And my sister. And any feeling of normalcy or safety. In a nutshell, everything was missing.

I was terrified for Mom and Dad. Since the Silver I'd entered didn't show the tunnel from the outside, what assurance did I have that the destination it did show wasn't also an illusion? What if the LM wasn't holding my parents captive in my own living room but someplace else and I'd sent Barrons on a wild-goose chase with the photo I'd texted?

A wave of frantic helplessness was building inside me, threatening to turn tidal. I didn't dare give in to panic. I had to stay calm and focused and work on moving forward however I could, even if it meant taking baby steps. Right now that meant getting my clothes dry and resting while I had the chance. Who knew what dangers the night—or even the next few hours—might hold?

Christian and I talked while we sunned, our voices carrying easily over the rocks between us. I told him about the effects of eating Unseelie. He questioned me extensively, wanting to know who else had eaten it, exactly what it had done to them, and how long it had lasted. He seemed especially interested in the increased "skill in the dark arts."

"Speaking of dark arts," I said, "what did you guys do the night of the ritual? What happened? What went wrong?"

He groaned. "I take it that means the walls came down anyway. I've been trying to convince myself that my uncles managed a miracle. Tell me everything, Mac. What's happened in the world while I've been stuck here?"

I told him that the walls had crashed completely at midnight, that I'd watched the Unseelie come through, and that the Lord Master and his princes had captured me at dawn. I omitted the rape, being turned *Pri-ya*, and my subsequent . . . er, recovery (no way I was talking to the lie detector about those events), and told him merely that I was rescued by Dani and the *sidhe*-seers. I brought him up to speed on Jayne's efforts, filled him in on what we'd learned about iron, and told him that his family was okay and searching for him. I told him the Book was still loose but withheld the gruesome details of my recent encounter with it.

"How did you come to be in the Hall of All Days?"

I told him about the Lord Master abducting my parents, luring me into the Silver, and insisting that I show him the stones.

"Bloody idiot! Even we know better than to do that, and he was once Fae. It's no wonder the queen appointed us Keltar keepers of the lore. We know more about their history than they do."

"Because they keep drinking from the cauldron and forgetting?"

"Aye."

"Well, at least we have them. Even though the ride's rocky, they help in a pinch."

"Are you daft, Mac?" he said sharply.

"What do you mean?"

"Don't you know what's happening every time you take them out of that pouch?"

"Duh, that's what I was saying. It makes us shift worlds . . . or dimensions, or whatever they are."

"Because the realm we're in is trying to spit us out," he said flatly. "The stones are anathema to the Silvers. Once you remove them from your pouch, the realm detects them and, like an infected splinter, endeavors to expel them. The only reason you go with them is because you're holding on to them."

"Why are they anathema to the Silvers?"

"Because of Cruce's curse."

"You know what Cruce's curse was?" Finally, someone who could tell me!

"I've been wandering worlds in this place for what feels like bloody forever, and I've learned a thing or two. Cruce hated the Unseelie King, for many reasons, and coveted his concubine. He cursed the Silvers to prevent the king from ever entering them again. He planned to take all the worlds inside the Silvers and the concubine for himself. Be king of all the realms. But a curse is an immensely powerful thing, and Cruce cast it into a vortex of un-fathomable power. Like most things Fae, it took on a life of its own, transmuted. Some say you can still hear the words of it, sung softly on a dark wind, ever changing."

"Did he succeed in keeping the king from his con-cubine?"

"Aye. And because those stones you carry were carved from the king's fortress and bear the taint of him, the Silvers reject them, as well. A short time after that, the king was betrayed, he and the queen battled, and he killed the Seelie Queen."

"Was that when the concubine killed herself?"

"Aye."

"Well, if the Silvers are trying to spit us out, then won't they eventually send us back to our world?"

He snorted. "They aren't trying to spit *us* out back to where *we* came from, Mac. They're trying to re-store the natural order of things and spit the *stones* back to where *they* came from."

I inhaled sharply. "You mean every time we use them, whatever realm we're in is trying to send us to the Unseelie prison? What happens? Do they miss?"

"I suspect none of the realms has enough power on its own, so we're being swept toward it, like a broom across a vast floor, through as many dimen-sions as possible."

"Each time we get pushed a little closer?"

"Exactly."

"Well, maybe," I tried hard to be optimistic, "we're a million realms away." Somehow, I didn't think so.

"And maybe," he said darkly, "we're one. And the next time you 'shift' us, we'll end up face-to-face

with the Unseelie King. Don't know about you, but
I'd rather not meet the million-year-old creator of
the worst of the Fae. Some say merely gazing on him
in his true form will destroy your mind."

Some time later, Christian announced our clothes
were dry. I listened to his clothing rustle as he
dressed. When he was done, I got up and moved
toward my clothes, then stopped dead in my tracks,
staring at him.

He gave me a bitter smile. "I know. It started happening shortly after you fed it to me."

I'd seen him nude. I knew he had crimson and
black tattoos on his chest, part of his abdomen,
and up the side of his neck, but the rest of his body
had been unmarked.

It was no longer. Now his arms were covered
with black lines and symbols, moving just beneath
his skin.

"It's spreading down my legs and moving up my
chest," he said.

I opened my mouth but didn't have the faintest
idea what to say. *I'm sorry I fed it to you to save your
life? Do you wish I hadn't? Isn't it better to live to fight
another day, no matter what?*

"It's something to do with the dark-arts part of
it. I feel it surging in me like a storm." He sighed
heavily. "I suspect it's because of what Barrons and I
tried to do on Hallow's Eve."

"And what was that?" I fished.

"Called on something ancient that we should
have let slumber. Invited it. I keep hoping I'll find

him, but once we were sucked into the vortex, we got separated."

I stared. "Barrons got sucked into the Silvers with you on Halloween?"

Christian nodded. "We were both in the stone circle, then it vanished, and so did we. We flashed from one landscape to the next like someone was flipping channels, then suddenly I was in the Hall of All Days, and he wasn't. I may not care for the man, but he knows his dark magic. I've been hoping we can find a way out, if we put both our minds to it."

"Uh, I hate to break it to you, but he already has."

Christian's eyes flared, then narrowed. "Barrons is out? Since when?"

"Since four days after Halloween. And he never said a word about it. He told me you were the only one who vanished that night."

"How the bloody hell did he make it out?"

I gave him a look of helpless exasperation. "How would I know? He never even admitted he'd been here. He lied."

Christian's eyes narrowed further. "When did you have sex with him?"

Uh-oh. The lie detector was staring out at me from those tiger eyes. "It wasn't like I was willing," I prevaricated.

"Lie," he said flatly.

"I wouldn't have done it under any other circumstances." That was the truth, and he could choke on it!

"Lie."

Really? "He made me do it!"

"Major, huge lie," he said dryly.

"You don't understand the situation I was in."

"Try me."

"I hardly think it's relevant to any of our problems." I turned my back on him and began dressing.

"Do you have feelings for him, Mac?"

I dressed in silence.

"Are you afraid to answer me?"

I finished dressing and turned around. Christian was getting a little scary-looking. His eyes were growing inhumanly brilliant, golden. I kept my face a smooth mask. "I'm starved," I told him. "I've got two protein bars. You can have one. And I'm thirsty, but I'd rather not drink from that quarry. And I think we have much bigger problems than my feelings about Jericho Barrons. Or lack thereof. And those animals," I pointed to the far edge of the valley, "look edible to me."

I began to walk.

Unfortunately, we weren't the only ones that thought the sleek, graceful gazellelike creatures looked edible, as we soon discovered in the middle of the valley.

A stampeding herd of thousands of shaggy-furred horned bulls with whiplike tails and wolfish snouts was bearing down on us, hard.

"Do you think maybe they'll just part around us?" I'd seen it happen in the movies.

"I'm not sure it's not *us* they're after, Mac. Run!"

I ran, even though I was pretty sure it was pointless. They were too fast, and we were too far from any kind of shelter.

"Can't you do something Druidy?" I shouted over the nearly deafening pounding of hooves.

He gave me a look. "Druid*ry*," he shouted, "requires preparation, or it can have disastrous results!"

"Well, you're looking all formidable! Surely you can do something with whatever's happening to you!" The black symbols had begun to move up his throat now.

The ground was shaking so hard it was getting difficult to run. It felt like an earthquake creeping up on us.

When I stumbled, Christian moved so quickly that the next thing I knew I was over his shoulder and he was running ten times faster than a normal man. Of course, he was pumped on Unseelie. I raised my head. The herd was too close. We still weren't moving fast enough. The creatures were gaining, snouts snapping, saliva flying. I could practically feel their breath blasting us.

"Use the stones," Christian shouted.

"You said it was too dangerous!"

"Anything's better than dead, Mac!"

I dug into my waistband, pulled out the pouch, and flashed the stones.

Comparatively speaking, it was one of the smoother transitions.

Unfortunately, it deposited us on a fire world.

I flashed the stones again, and the flames on my boots died instantly, because the next world didn't support carbon-based life and there was no oxygen.

I flashed the stones again, and we were underwater.

The fourth time I flashed them, we ended up on the narrow top of a jagged cliff that fell sharply to a bottomless chasm on both sides.

"Put me down," I shouted over the wild gale whipping around us. I was crushed over Christian's shoulder, dripping wet and gasping for breath.

"Here?"

"Yes, here!"

Snorting, he lowered me to my feet but kept his grip tight on my waist. I stared at him. His amber irises were rimmed with black. It was staining inward, like ink clouding water. The strange symbols were licking up over his jaw.

"Just what did you *do* on Halloween?" Why was Unseelie flesh having such a strange effect on him?

He gave me that killer smile, but it wasn't killer charming, it was killer cold. "I chickened out at the last minute, or we wouldn't have failed. We tried to raise the only other power we knew of that had once stood against the Tuatha Dé and held its own. An ancient sect called the Draghar raised it once, long ago. Barrons didn't hesitate. I did. Care to get us off this cliff, Mac?" he snarled.

"What if the next place is even worse?"

"Keep shifting and I'll keep holding on."

A gust of air blasted us. We went stumbling off the edge, into yawning darkness. I opened the pouch as we fell.

A massive vortex exploded around us, black, swirling, tearing at my hair and clothes. I struggled to shove the stones back into the rune-covered bag. I could feel Christian's grip slipping, then his hands were gone and I was alone.

I slammed down onto grassy tundra, on my hands and knees.

I hit so hard, the pouch went flying from my hands. My forehead smacked into the earth and I bit my tongue viciously. I couldn't feel Christian's hands on me anywhere.

Ears ringing from the impact, I lifted my head, dazed.

I stared straight into the eyes of an enormous wild boar with razor-sharp tusks.

34

When you're staring death in the face, time has a funny way of slowing down.

Or maybe, in this realm, it really did move slower, who knows?

All I knew, as I stared into the boar's beady, cunning, hungry eyes—tiny in its cow-size body—was that ever since I'd dropped my cell phone into our swimming pool, I'd begun losing things. One after another.

First my sister. Then my parents and any hope of going home.

I'd tried to roll with the punches, be a good sport. I'd made a new home for myself in a bookstore in Dublin. I'd attempted to make new friends and forge alliances. I'd said good-bye to pretty clothes, my blond hair, and my love of fashion. I'd accepted shades of gray instead of rainbows and finally embraced black.

Then I'd lost Dublin and my bookstore.

Finally I'd lost myself, even my own mind.

I'd learned to use new weapons, found new ways to survive.

And lost those, too.

My spear was gone. I had no Unseelie flesh. No name in my tongue.

I'd found Christian. I'd lost Christian. I was pretty sure he'd ended up being dragged off one way in the vortex, while I'd been sent another.

And now I'd lost the stones, too. The pouch was on the ground, far beyond the boar, drawstring tight. I couldn't even hope for an accidental shift.

The dirk strapped to my forearm wouldn't begin to pierce the animal's scale-plated hide.

And I had to wonder: Was this the whole point? Was it about taking everything from me there was to take? Was that what life did? Made you lose everything you cared about and believed in, then killed you?

Yes, I was feeling sorry for myself.

Fecking A, as Dani would say—who wouldn't at this point?

Fire worlds? Water worlds? Cliffs? What crappy cosmic power was in charge of deciding where the stones sent me next? Were the blue-black slivers of whatever they were so despised by the Silvers that if a realm couldn't spit them all the way back to the Unseelie hell, it would settle for trying to destroy them—therefore, oops, me, too? Was I being deliberately flung into the jaws of danger?

Or, as I'd begun to wonder lately, had the destruction of me begun a long time ago? Hidden in obscured dreams and forgotten memories.

What did I have left?

Nothing.

I crouched, staring furiously across a space of grassy field at a beady-eyed boar that I swore wore an evil smile on its tusked face.

It snorted and pawed the ground.

For lack of anything else to do, I snorted back and pawed the ground myself. Bristled and shot it a look of death.

Beady eyes narrowed. It lifted its heavy-jowled head and sniffed the air.

Was it trying to scent fear? Too bad. There wasn't any rolling off me. I was too angry to be afraid.

Where the hell was everyone when I needed—*oh!* Once before I'd thought myself without options, while I'd still had one left.

As the boar assessed my victim potential, I scowled at it, baring my teeth while easing a hand beneath my coat and into my back pocket.

I slipped out my cell phone. Water poured off it. Would it even work? I snorted inwardly. I was still expecting things to function according to understandable laws, as I crouched here in the *seventh* alternate dimension I'd been in recently. How silly of me.

I flipped it open and laid it on the ground.

The boar ducked its head, readying for the charge.

I didn't dare raise the phone to my ear. I punched buttons as it lay there. First, Barrons, then *IYCGM*, and finally the forbidden *IYD*. This definitely qualified as dying.

I waited. I don't know what for. Some miracle.

I guess I'd been hoping that using *IYD* would do

something like magically transport me to safety at the bookstore. Or Barrons would instantly materialize and rescue me.

I waited.

Nothing happened. Not a damned thing.

I was on my own.

Figured.

The boar dropped its head menacingly. I gazed longingly at the pouch dozens of feet behind it.

It pawed the ground, shifted its haunches. I knew what that meant. Cats do it before they pounce.

I pawed at the ground and gave a deeply enraged snarl. I felt deeply enraged. I shifted my haunches, too.

It blinked beady eyes and grunted thickly.

I grunted back and pawed the ground again.

Standoff.

I had a sudden vision of myself from above.

This was what I'd been reduced to: MacKayla Lane-O'Connor, descended from one of the most powerful *sidhe*-seers lines, OOP detector, Null, once *Pri-ya*, now immune to pretty much all Fae glamour, not to mention possessing interesting healing abilities, on the ground on my hands and knees, dirty, wet, wearing a badly battered MacHalo and singed boots, facing off a deadly wild boar without a single weapon except fury, hope for a better tomorrow, and determination to survive. Wiggling my butt. Pawing the ground.

I felt a laugh building inside me like a sneeze and tried desperately to suppress it. My lips twitched. My eyes crinkled. My nose itched and my gut ached with the need to laugh.

I lost it. It was just all too much. I sat back on my heels and laughed.

The boar shifted uneasily.

I stood up, stared the boar down, and laughed even harder. Somehow, nothing's quite as scary when you're not on your knees.

"Fuck you," I told it. "You want some of me?"

The boar regarded me warily, and I realized it wasn't a mystical creature. It was just a wild animal. I'd heard lots of stories about people in the mountains of North Georgia who'd gotten away from wild animals through sheer bluff and bluster. I had a lot of that to offer.

I took a furious step toward it and shook my fist. "Get out of here! Shoo. Go away. I'm not dying today, you jackass! *GET OUT OF HERE NOW!*" I roared.

It turned and began to slink—inasmuch as a thousand-pound wild boar can—away across the meadow.

I stared, but not because it was retreating.

My last command had come out in layers that were still resonating in the air around me.

I'd just used Voice!

I had no idea whether the boar had been driven away by my lack of fear and threatening bluster or by the power of my words—I mean, really, can you Voice something that doesn't understand English?—but I didn't much care. The point was, I'd *used* it! And it had come out sounding pretty darned huge!

How had I done it? What had I found inside myself? I tried to recall exactly what I'd been feeling and thinking when I shouted at it.

Alone.

I'd been feeling completely and utterly alone, that there was nothing but me and my impending death.

The key to Voice, Barrons had said, *is finding that place inside you no one else can touch.*

You mean the sidhe-*seer place?* I'd asked.

No, a different place. All people have it. Not just sidhe-*seers. We're born alone and we die alone.*

"I get it," I said now.

Regardless of how many people I surrounded myself with, no matter how many friends and family I loved and was loved by in return, I was alone at the moment of being born and at the moment of dying. Nobody came with you and nobody went with you. It was a journey of one.

But not really. Because, in that place, there was *something.* I'd just felt it, when I'd never been able to feel it before. Maybe in the moment of being born and the moment of dying, we're nearer to pure. Maybe it's the only time we're ever still enough to feel that there's something bigger than us; something that defeats entropy; that has always been and will always be. A thing that can't be flipped. Call it what you will. I only know it's divine. And it cares. It was no longer my "comfort zone." It was my truth.

I watched the boar slink off across the field. In a few moments, it would be clear of the pouch of stones, and I would retrieve them. Not that I trusted them much. But they were better than nothing, and I needed them to secure the Book when I got out of here.

I'd just begun to step forward to pick up my cell,

then go for the stones, when an enormous gray beast suddenly exploded in a blur of horns and fangs and talons from nowhere.

I stumbled back.

It slammed into the boar's side, sank fangs into its throat, grabbed its neck, and ripped off its head, spraying blood, taking its kill down between me and the pouch.

Growling, it hunkered over the boar's body and began to eat.

I stared, hardly daring to breathe. If the thing had been standing upright—and it looked as if it could—it would come close to nine feet. It had three sets of sharp, curved horns spaced at even intervals on two bony ridges that ran down each side of its head. The first set was at its ears, the second midway back on its skull, and the final pair sprouted from the rear of its head and curved downward toward its back. Hanks of long black hair tangled around a prehistoric face, with a crested forehead, prominent bones, and deadly fangs. Its hands and feet were lightly webbed with long talons. Its skin was slate gray, smooth as leather. It was massively muscled and obviously male.

I hadn't seen or heard it coming.

I wasn't about to try out-growling it or attempt to use my newfound skill in Voice, which might or might not work on animals. If I was very lucky, I'd get to slink away quietly, without it ever noticing me. Bluffing a boar was one thing. The boar had been a simple animal, one that might have sprung from earth's genetic codes. I didn't need a DNA test to tell me this one hadn't.

I began easing back slowly, barely lifting my feet from the ground. I'd have to come back later for my cell phone and the stones.

Its head snapped up and it looked straight at me, blood all over its face. So much for my hope of slinking off unnoticed.

I held perfectly still, one foot in the air. Bunnies freeze to outwit enemies. Supposedly, bears are deceived by it.

It wasn't fooled. It sat back on its haunches and considered me with cunning, narrowed eyes, as if trying to decide what I might taste like. Rage burned in its gaze, as if it were a lion with thorns permanently embedded in all four paws.

I held my breath. *Eat the boar,* I willed. *I'm lean muscle, not plump pork belly.*

It shifted its body away from the boar toward me, completely dismissing its kill. Shit, shit, shit.

I was its target now.

With no warning whatsoever, it was suddenly on all fours, running straight at me. The thing was preternaturally fast.

I fumbled my dirk from my sheath and dropped into a crouch, heart slamming in my chest.

"STOP RIGHT THERE!" Voice swelled out of me, saturating the air, echoing in a thousand voices. It was formidable, phenomenal, daunting as hell. I couldn't believe I'd made such a noise. Barrons would have been so proud. *"LEAVE ME ALONE!"* I roared. *"YOU WILL NOT HARM ME!"*

Unaffected, the monster kept coming.

I braced myself for impact. There was no way I was going down without a fight. If it stayed on all fours, I'd feint and twist, go for its eyes with my dirk and what was left of my nails. Maybe its male parts. Whatever I had to do to survive.

Half a dozen feet away, the horrific thing stopped so abruptly that it clawed open the earth with its talons. Chunks of sod went flying, narrowly missing my head. Its yellow eyes narrowed to slits, and it snarled.

It was so close to me that I could feel the gust of its hot breath, smell the fresh warm blood on it. I stared at it wildly. It had vertical pupils, expanding and contracting in alien yellow eyes. It bristled with fury, chest heaving in short, rapid pants, as it snarled incessantly.

Shifting its weight forward, it shook its head and snapped its jaws. Saliva and blood sprayed me.

I cringed but didn't dare wipe it away.

Suddenly it rippled into motion, with such smoothly muscled grace that for a bizarre moment I found it . . . beautiful. The thing was a natural-born executioner. It was at the top of its game. Powerful, uncomplicated animal. It had few purposes in life. It had been born and bred to kill, conquer, reproduce, survive. For the duration of that strange moment, I nearly envied it.

It began circling me, taloned hands and feet ripping up tufts of grass and dirt, tossing its head from side to side, yellow eyes burning with bloodlust.

I turned with it, never taking my eyes from its face. I stared into that killing gaze, as if I could hold it at bay with a mere refusal to be cowed. Was this some kind of preslaughter ritual? It hadn't done it to the boar.

It stopped, cocked its horned head, tipped its monstrous face, and . . . *sniffed* in my direction.

What the hell was it doing? I held my breath, hoping I smelled inedible. The fangs—God, those fangs were as long as my fingers!

It didn't seem to like whatever it had smelled. The smell seemed to make it even angrier. It growled long and low, then, without warning, it lunged!

Dirk clenched in my fist, I held my ground. Our actions define us. I would either live or die fighting.

But I didn't get the chance to fight.

At the last second, the monster howled and twisted in midair.

All I saw was a blur of motion. One moment it was launching straight for me, the next it was tearing through the grass, racing back to the boar. As I watched, it sank its fangs into the boar's flesh and, with a violent shake of its head, flayed it open and began to eat, bones crunching, gristle popping.

For a moment, I couldn't move. I was so shaky I wasn't sure my legs would support me. I was too freaked out to process thought.

Mobility returned on the wings of adrenaline.

I darted forward, snatched my cell phone from the ground, and ran like hell.

35

Some time later, I sat in a glade of tall grass and white-barked trees, leaning back against a trunk, trying to get a grasp on my situation. It had taken nearly half an hour for me to stop shaking. I'd wanted to run as far away from the terrifying monster as I could, but I needed those damned stones.

This day had not unfolded remotely as I'd planned. I was having a hard time accepting where I was and what was happening to me.

I'd begun this afternoon with a clear agenda: I'd stepped into a Silver with the perfectly reasonable expectation (oh, God, did that sum up how warped my world had gotten or what?) of stepping out on the other side in my own living room, in my own world, where I would either rescue my parents from the LM's evil clutches, with Barrons' help, or die trying.

Now here I was on some foreign world inside the network of the Silvers, which were—according to Barrons—a place that was virtually impossible to navigate and where one could stay lost forever, being attacked by one predator after another.

I'd been absurdly, dangerously sidetracked. Things had taken such an unprecedented twist that I felt as if I'd slipped down one of Alice's rabbit holes.

It was one thing to watch Fae invade Dublin and try to take over my world, to fight them on my turf. It was entirely another to find myself world-hopping via mirrors and mystical stones, forced to do battle on foreign ground. At least back home, I knew where to get the things I needed, and I had allies to help me. Here, I was screwed.

Events were going on without me back in my world, and I needed to be part of them. I had to get out of here! I had to save my parents, question Nana O'Reilly, get into the Forbidden Libraries, figure out where V'lane was, uncover the prophecy . . . The list was endless.

But I was stuck on one of the worlds in the network of the Silvers, with a terrifying monster between me and stones that I didn't dare leave behind. Not only were they of use here (though risky), but I had to take them back to my world so I could use them there.

If I needed any proof of how difficult the Silvers were to get out of—and survive in—I only had to think of Christian, who'd been wandering lost for two months, and been on the verge of death when I'd found him.

How would I survive two months? How would I survive two *weeks*?

What was happening to my parents?

I punched *IYD* on my cell phone for the hundredth time and, for the hundredth time, nothing happened.

I closed my eyes and rubbed my face. Barrons had gotten out of here.

How? Why hadn't he told me he'd been sucked in with Christian? Why so many lies? Or, as he would call them, "omissions."

I opened my eyes and checked my watch. It was still 1:14. Duh. I took it off and stuffed it into a pocket. The thing was obviously useless here. I was waiting for the monster to finish devouring the boar so I could go get my stones. I thought it had been at least an hour or two, but the sun hadn't moved in the sky at all since I'd sat down, which meant either my sense of time was badly skewed or the days were much longer here than I was used to.

While I killed time, I sorted through my options. The way I saw it, I had three. Once I had the stones back, I could A: start hunting for IFPs, risk entering one, and hope it wouldn't trap me in a desert like the one Christian had gotten stuck in; or B: use the stones and hope that I was really far away from the Unseelie prison and they'd send me back to the Hall of All Days or some other place with mirrors to choose from; or C: stay right where I was and hope that, even though *IYD* didn't work here, Barrons would still be able to track me by my brand. And that the monster would move on and find something else to terrorize and kill. Otherwise, remaining in this area wouldn't even be an option.

Barrons was obviously familiar with the worlds inside the network of Silvers, considering how quickly he'd gotten out. Which seemed to indicate he'd been in here at least once prior to having been sucked in with Christian.

Of all my options, staying put and giving Barrons the chance to track me seemed the most sensible. Once before, I'd discounted his ability to save me, and I didn't want to make the same mistake again.

It had taken him four days to get out.

I'd give him five to find me. But five was the max I would allow, because I was afraid I might start thinking, *Yeah, but what if* today *is the day he comes?* Then I'd be afraid to ever leave. It was imperative I make firm decisions and stick to them.

That resolved, I stoked my courage, stood up, and moved stealthily to the edge of the glade, to see if I could reclaim my stones.

The monster was still eating. It stopped, raised its head, and sniffed. Was it looking at me through the trees?

I dropped to all fours and retreated inch by inch. After I'd put some distance between us, I got up and ran back to my tree.

Why hadn't it killed me? Why had it stopped? Was I inedible? I knew sometimes animals were rabid and killed simply to kill. I'd never seen such fury in an animal's eyes before. One of my friends had been bitten by a rabid dog, and I'd seen it kenneled before it was put down. It had looked more frightened than angry. The gray monster didn't possess one ounce of fear. It was nothing but savagery.

Two more times I slipped through the glade to check. Both times it was still eating and showed no signs of stopping.

I returned to my tree, where I watched the sun crawl across the sky. The day heated up and I stripped off my coat, sweater, and jersey. I made a sling from the jersey, knotted the MacHalo in it, and tied it to a stick, hobo style.

I spent my time alternately worrying about Mom and Dad, trying to convince myself that Barrons had rescued them; Dani being at the abbey and what rash decisions she might make without me there to keep an eye on her; Christian and where he'd gotten off to and hoping he'd found food because I'd never gotten the chance to give him one of my protein bars; and even V'lane, for disappearing and never popping up again.

I couldn't think of a single thing to worry about for Barrons.

I pondered life, trying to make sense of it, wondering how I could ever have grown up believing the world a sane, safe, orderly place.

I was about to push myself up to go check on my stones for the fourth time when I heard a twig snap.

My head whipped around.

The monster was crouched on all fours, no more than twenty feet away from me.

It stared though the tall grass, head hunkered low, yellow eyes glittering.

Was it done with the boar and hungry for *me* now?

I grabbed my hobo stick and coat and shot up the tree so fast I think *I* gouged sod from the earth. Heart in my throat, I flew from limb to limb.

I hate heights as much as I hate confined spaces,

but halfway up I forced myself to stop and look down. Could the monster climb? It didn't look as if it should be able to, with what I estimated had to be four hundred pounds of muscle plus all those talons, but in this world who knew? Especially with the weirdly fluid way it could move.

It was on the ground beneath the tree, on all fours, tearing at the grass where moments ago I'd been sitting.

As I watched, it found my sweater. It pierced it on long talons and raised it to its face.

I gasped. The sweater wasn't the only thing of mine it had. Tied to its rear horns by a leather drawstring was *my* rune-covered bag.

The monster had my stones!

When it finally wandered off—with my sweater knotted around one of its hind legs—I descended the tree. After a long, internal debate with myself, I shrugged and began to follow it.

I was furious at the latest turn of events.

Why had the damned thing picked up my stones, and *how*—with those lethal talons—had it managed to tie the bag to its horns? Wasn't knot-tying pretty damned evolved for a prehistoric-looking beast? And what was the deal with my sweater?

It realized I was following it, stopped, turned around, and looked at me.

My instincts screamed for me to tuck tail and run again, but there was something strange going on here. Although it bristled with fury, it hadn't taken a single step my way.

"Those are my stones and I need them," I tried.

Feral yellow eyes narrowed, unblinking.

I pointed to its horns. "The pouch. It's mine. Give it back."

Nothing. There wasn't a flicker of understanding or anything remotely resembling intelligence in its gaze.

I pointed to my own head and mimed removing a bag and tossing it away. I mimed untying my sweater from its leg to drive my point home. I indulged in a small fit of charades, with many variations on the theme. Nothing. My efforts yielded no more fruit than an interrogation of Barrons would have.

Finally, out of sheer exasperation, I did a little dance, just to see if it would have any reaction at all.

It stood up on its rear legs and began to howl, revealing an alarming number of teeth, then dropped to all fours and lunged at me, over and over again, drawing up short each time, like a dog on a leash.

I went perfectly still.

It was almost as if it wanted to attack me, but for some reason it couldn't.

It stilled, too, growling, watching me carefully with narrowed eyes.

After a moment, it turned and glided away, muscle and madness.

Sighing, I followed it. I had to get my stones.

It stopped, turned around, and snarled at me. It clearly didn't like me following it. Too bad. When it began moving again, I waited where I was for a few seconds, then followed at a more discreet distance. I hoped it had a lair that it would take the stones to, and when it left again to hunt, maybe I could steal them back.

I followed it for hours, through meadows and finally into a forest near a wide, rapidly flowing river, where I lost it among the trees.

Daylight ended with disconcerting abruptness on this world.

The sun had been inching across the sky most of the day, but at roughly five o'clock—or so I assumed by its angle to the planet—the blazing ball plummeted faster than the one in Times Square on New Year's Eve. If I hadn't been squinting up through the trees at that precise moment, trying to decide how much time I had left to find a place to hole up for the night, I'd neither have seen nor believed it.

In the blink of an eye, day was over and it was full, pitch night. The temperature dropped ten sudden degrees, making me grateful I still had my coat.

I hate the dark. Always have, always will.

I fished out my MacHalo, dropped it in my haste, picked it up again, clapped it on my head, and began squeezing on the lights. Since the brackets had snapped off, I moved some of the lights around, wishing I'd made Barrons' version of my creation, without brackets. I'd never admit it to him, but his was more efficient, lighter, and brighter. But, in my defense, it was far easier to improve upon an invention than to actually sit down and invent it. I'd made something from nothing. He'd merely tweaked my "something."

I don't know if I heard it or just sensed its presence, but suddenly I *knew* something was behind me, no more than a dozen feet to my right.

I whipped around and caught it in the harsh white glare of lights on the front of my helmet.

Squinting, it shielded its eyes with an arm.

For a moment, I wasn't sure it was "my" monster. It had darkened like a chameleon from slate gray to coal black, and its eyes were now crimson. I might have mistaken it for something else, a distant cousin to the monster I'd been tracking, except for the pouch of stones tied to its black horns.

It snarled at the lights. Its fangs glistened ebony, long.

I shivered. It looked even more deadly than it had before.

I squeezed off the front light, and it lowered its arm.

What now? Why had it come back? It hadn't seemed to want me to follow it, yet when I'd lost it, it circled back for me. Nothing about it made sense. Might it eventually weary of the pouch banging into the back of its head with every step it took and toss it away? Why did it still have my sweater? How was I going to survive the night? Would it kill me in my sleep? Assuming I ever managed to relax enough to sleep!

If it didn't kill me, would something else? What was nocturnal here? What did I have to fear? Where would I dare try to sleep? Up a tree?

I was starved. I was exhausted and completely out of ideas.

The monster growled and loped from the shadows, passing within a few feet of me, and headed toward the river.

Chilled by such a near brush, I froze and watched my stones go bouncing by.

In another day or two, would I be so despairing and tired and fed up that I might just try to grab the thing's head and wrestle them off it? If enough days passed without it trying to kill me, I could see myself getting desperate enough to risk it.

The monster paused on a mossy bank near the river and looked back at me. It looked at the bank and back at me. It repeated it, over and over.

It might not understand me, but I understood it. It wanted me on that bank for some reason.

I mulled my options. It took all of one second. If I didn't go, what would it do to me? Was there anyplace else I could think of to go? I walked downstream to the bank. Once I was there, it lunged at me and herded me with snapping jaws into the center of the bank.

Then, as I watched in shock and astonishment, it urinated a circle all the way around me.

When it was finished, it rippled sleekly into the night and disappeared.

I stood in the center of the circle of urine still steaming on the ground, and comprehension slowly dawned.

It had marked the earth around me with its scent to repel lesser threats, and I was willing to bet most threats on this world were lesser.

Numb from the day's events, exhausted from fear and physical exertion, I sat down, pulled out the remainder of my protein bar, made a pillow of my coat, then stretched out on the bank, set my MacHalo beside me, and left it blazing.

I chewed slowly, making the most of my meager meal, listening to the soft roar of the river's rapids.

It looked like I was holed up for the night.

I had few expectations that sleep would come. I'd lost everything. I was stranded in the Silvers. My stones were gone. There was a deadly monster collecting my things and pissing circles around me, and I had no idea what to do next. But apparently my body was done for the day, because I passed out with no awareness of having finished my meal.

I woke in the dark heart of the night, pulse pounding, unable to pinpoint what had awakened me. I stared up through the black treetops at two brilliant moons, full in a blue-black sky, and sorted through dream fragments.

I'd been walking the corridors of a mansion that housed infinite rooms. Unlike my cold-place dreams, I'd been warm there. I'd loved the mansion, with its endless terraces overlooking gardens filled with gentle creatures.

I felt it drawing me. Was it somewhere in this realm? Was it the White Mansion the Unseelie King had built for his concubine?

Far in the distance, I heard the howling of wolves as they saluted the moons.

I rolled over, pulled my coat over my head, and tried to go back to sleep. I was going to need all my energy to deal with tomorrow and survive in this place.

Something much closer howled an answer back to those distant wolves.

I shot straight up on my bed of moss, grabbed my dirk, and lunged to my feet.

It was a frightful sound. A sound I'd heard before, back in my own world—beneath the garage of Barrons Books and Baubles!

It was the tortured baying of a thing damned, a thing beyond redemption, a thing so lost to the far side of despair that I longed to puncture my own eardrums so I could never hear such a sound again.

The wolves howled.

The beast bayed back. Not so close this time. It was moving away.

The wolves howled. The beast bayed back. Farther still.

Was there something *worse* than my monster out there? Something like the thing beneath Barrons' garage?

I frowned. That would just be entirely too coincidental.

Was it possible "my" monster *was* the thing from beneath Barrons' garage? "Oh, God," I whispered. Had *IYD* actually worked?

For time uncounted, I listened to the mournful concert, eyes wide, blood chilled. Such desolation, isolation, loss in the thing's cry. Whatever it was, I grieved for it. No living thing should have to exist in such agony.

The next time the wolves howled, the beast didn't bay back.

A short time later I heard terrifying yipping and

the sounds of wolves being slaughtered, one after the next.

Shivering, I lay back down, curled into a tight ball, and covered my ears.

I woke again near dawn, surrounded by dozens of hungry eyes staring at me from beyond the circle of urine.

I had no idea what they were. I could see only powerful shadows moving, stalking, pacing hungrily in the darkness beyond the light from my MacHalo.

They didn't like the scent of the urine, but they could smell me over it, and I obviously smelled like food to them. As I watched, one of the dark shapes pawed a spray of leaves and dirt over the urine.

The others began to do the same.

The black monster with crimson eyes exploded from the forest.

I couldn't make out the details of the fight. My MacHalo was throwing off too much glare. All I saw was a whirl of fangs and talons. I heard snarls of rage, answered by frightened snarls and hisses and screams of pain. I heard some of them go splashing into the river. The thing moved impossibly fast, ripping and slicing through the darkness with deadly accuracy. Chunks of fur and flesh flew.

Some of them tried to run. The monster didn't let them. I could feel its rage. It rejoiced in the kill. It reveled in it, soaked itself in blood, crushed bones beneath its taloned feet.

Eventually I closed my eyes and quit trying to see.

When at last it was silent, I opened my eyes.

Feral crimson eyes watched me from beyond a pile of savaged bodies.

When it began to urinate again, I rolled over and hid my head under my coat.

36

I got up as soon as it was light, gathered my stuff, and picked my way past the remains of mutilated bodies to wash up in the river. Everything, including me, was splattered with blood.

I waded into the shallows, cupped my hands, and drank deeply before washing. I needed water, it was running rapid and crystal-clear, I couldn't build a fire to boil it, and I had to believe that, after all I'd lived through, I was surely slated for a more meaningful death than by waterborne parasite.

After I washed up, I moved into the forest. Finding food was at the top of my to-do list today. Although there was plenty of raw meat lying around, I'd rather not.

I passed corpse after corpse. A lot were small, delicate creatures that couldn't possibly have presented a threat to me. They hadn't been eaten. They'd been killed for the kill.

After about twenty minutes, I realized I was being followed.

I turned. The monster was back, and once again it

was slate gray with yellow eyes. My pouch was still tied to its horns. Tatters of my sweater were knotted around its leg.

"You're IYD, aren't you? It *did* work. You're what Barrons kept beneath his garage, and he sent you to protect me. But you're not the brightest bulb in the box. All you know how to do is kill. Everything but me, right? You keep me alive."

The monster, of course, said nothing.

I was nearly certain of it. After the second mass slaughter, I'd lain awake, waiting for the sun to rise high enough in the sky to go foraging, pondering possibilities. It was the only one that explained why the monster wasn't killing me. When it had first tried to attack me yesterday, it must have smelled Barrons on me. And it was the scent of him that was keeping it at bay. I made a mental note to not wash very well, no matter how dirty I got.

"So, what's the plan? Do you keep me alive until he finds me?"

Was this killing machine what would have shown up on Halloween if I'd dialed *IYD* then? I couldn't see it being any use against the LM and the Fae Princes, but if I'd summoned it during the riots, or even shortly after instead of holing up in the church, it certainly could have cleared my path and led me somewhere safe, where the LM might never have found me.

I examined it. It stared back through matted, bloodied hair. Rage blazed in its gaze, and something wilder, more frightening. It took me a moment to realize it was madness. The thing was one link in a chain away from total insanity.

It *had* to be IYD. There was no other explanation for it. How had Barrons captured the thing? How did he make it obey him? How had he kept it from killing *him*? By mystical means? As usual where Barrons was concerned, I had nothing but questions and no answers. When I was finally back in my own world, he wasn't getting out of answering some. I knew what he kept beneath his garage now, and I wanted to know more.

As I studied its savage face, the eyes deep with psychotic rage, its powerful body built for killing, I realized I was no longer afraid of it. I knew in my bones the thing was not going to kill me. It was going to slaughter and decimate every living thing around me, and piss, and probably collect anything of mine I was careless enough to let get away from me. It might even *want* to kill me, but it wouldn't, because it was IYD and its sole purpose was to make sure I didn't die.

I felt like half the weight of the world had just slid from my shoulders. I could do this. I had a weapon I hadn't known about: a guardian demon. It occurred to me that I didn't even need to retrieve my stones. Barrons could get them when he showed up. There went another quarter of the world off my back.

I got on with my search for food. The monster trailed me most of the time. Occasionally something rustled in the distance, and it would tear off through the trees. I began to hold my ears when that happened. I love animals and hated that it was killing everything. I wished Barrons could have taught it to discriminate.

I found berries in the undergrowth and nuts on low-hanging branches in a grove of slender silvery-barked trees. After I gorged, I gathered them, tying as many of the sweet nuts into my hobo pouch as I could. In a gentle brook, I found fish eggs. A big yuck, but protein nonetheless.

Midmorning, the monster herded me back toward the river, then began snarling and snapping at me, driving me upstream. I figured it had some Barrons-esque agenda.

It "herded" me for several hours. The terrain changed drastically. The forest thickened, the river-bank fell away, and by the time the monster finally let me stop, I was high on top of a sheer rocky cliff that dropped sharply, well over a hundred feet, to whitecapped rapids below. The river no longer tumbled; it roared and crashed, filling the gorge with soft thunder.

I stretched out in a sunny patch on the bank and ate half of my last protein bar. I considered getting up and trying to explore, but I wasn't sure the monster would permit it.

It sniffed the ground around me for a moment, then stalked downstream and sprawled sleek and deadly on the ground. I guessed it was tired from so much killing.

Feeling a little desperate for the sound of a voice, I talked to it. I told it stories about growing up in the South. I told it about all the fine plans I'd had for my life.

I told it how everything had gone so damned wrong and I'd begun losing one thing after another. I told it about the hell of losing my mind and will to the Unseelie Princes and about Barrons bringing me back. I even told it about my recent trip home to Ashford with V'lane, and what I'd learned there, and that I'd begun to fear there might actually be something wrong with me. I told it things I would never have told a sentient being, baring my deepest feelings and worries. It was cathartic to get it all off my chest, even to a dumb beast.

I dozed, too, and woke about a half hour before the sun plummeted to the horizon, cloaking the forest in night.

The monster rose on all fours, stalked over, urinated around me, and melted into the blackness, black on black, with crimson eyes.

I'd been "tucked in" for the night.

I woke several times, startled by one sound or another. Once I ascertained that nothing was lurking beyond my circle, I fell back asleep again.

Near dawn, I was awakened by a storm in the distance, moving closer.

A hundred feet below me, the river swelled to a deafening crescendo of rapids crashing against the sheer walls of the rocky gorge.

The sky crackled with lightning. Thunder rolled, and I braced myself for a drenching, but the storm stayed on the opposite side of the river and passed me by.

It was a violent squall. Thunder cracked and crashed continuously, punctuated by a weird popping, like automatic gunfire. Trees bent low. Rain fell in sheets, soaking the far side of the river. I was grateful I'd been spared.

Finally the storm blew itself out, and I slept.

I wakened to a hand clamped tightly over my mouth and the crushing weight of a body on top of mine.

I fought like a wild thing, punching, kicking, trying to bite.

"Easy, Mac," a voice whispered roughly against my ear. "Be still."

My eyes flared. I knew that voice. It was Ryodan. But I'd been expecting Barrons!

"I've come to get you out of here, but you must do exactly as I say."

I was nodding before he'd even finished speaking.

"It's imperative you make no noise. Whisper when you speak."

I nodded again.

He drew back and looked at me. "Where's . . . the creature?"

"The IYD one?"

He gave me a look but nodded.

"I don't know. I haven't seen it since last night."

"Get your things and hurry. We don't have much time. Darroc's here, too."

"Are you *kidding* me? How the hell does everyone *find* me?" What was I, a big red *X*?

"Shh." He pressed a finger to my lips. "Speak softly." He raised the weight of his body from mine, flipped me onto my stomach, and began searching through my hair. "Hold still. Ah, fuck."

"What?" It came out as a low growl.

"Darroc marked you. He must have done it while the princes had you."

"He *tattooed* me?"

"Right next to Barrons' mark. I can't remove it here. Come."

I rolled over, scrubbing angrily at my scalp. "Where are we going?"

"Not far from here is a—what did Barrons say you call them?—IFP. It will take us to another world, where there's a dolmen to Ireland."

"I thought Cruce's curse corrupted everything."

"The Silvers change. IFPs don't. They're static microcosms."

He grabbed me beneath my armpits, stood up, taking me with him, and set me on my feet.

I clutched his arm. "My parents?"

"I don't know. I came in after you at LaRuhe."

"Barrons?"

"He was trying to get to Ashford, to go after Darroc. I was the only one able to get in before the tunnel collapsed on our end. It took me a while to find you. I found this, too." He tossed my backpack at me. "Your spear's inside."

I could have kissed him! I grabbed my pack and swiftly consolidated possessions, then yanked out my spear and caressed it. Holding it in my hand made me feel like a Travis Tritt song—ten feet tall and bulletproof.

"The creature will attack anything in your vicinity. At the moment, that's me. I can get you out. It can't. It only kills. Remember that."

Ryodan took my hand and led me close to the

river, much nearer the sheer drop of the gorge than I was comfortable with, but I understood why he did it. The crushed-shale edge was soft as sand and made no noise beneath our feet. I looked up at him.

"How did you track me? Do *you* have a mark on me, too?" I whispered.

"I can follow Barrons' mark. Another word and you're going over the edge."

I said no more. If it came down to my survival or his, I was pretty sure he'd choose his. I wondered why Barrons hadn't done anything to keep Ryodan safe from the monster. Given him a Barrons-scented shirt to wear or something.

As if he'd read my mind, he murmured, "It's the tattoo he put on you that keeps you safe from it. No fucking way he's branding me. I came in armed. I hunted it all night through the rain. It ran me out of ammo. It's one clever fuck."

I *had* heard automatic gunfire! "You were trying to kill it?" I breathed, aghast. What a weird paradigm shift. It had been protecting me. Ferociously. Now it was my enemy?

Ryodan gave me a sharp look. "Do you want out of here or not?"

I nodded fervently.

"Then keep your spear handy, shut the fuck up, and hope it doesn't kill me. I'm your way out."

When the monster attacked—and I guess there never really was any doubt in my mind that it would—it did so with the same explosive suddenness with which it had hit the wild boar, blasting out of nowhere, crashing Ryodan to the ground, a fury of fangs and talons.

I watched helplessly as they twisted and rolled, watching for an opportunity to do something. Anything.

The monster was much larger than Ryodan, but Barrons' mysterious brother-in-arms was pretty savage himself. His wristbands sprouted knives and spikes.

As I watched them battle, it speeded up into something very close to Dani's freeze-framing and blurred beyond my vision's ability to follow. I could no longer separate their forms. Ryodan seemed to be every bit as preternaturally agile as the monster.

I was able to snatch only brief glimpses as one or the other flashed into view, momentarily slowed by a wound.

Snarls filled the air as they rolled and fought, battling to the gorge's edge—so near I held my breath and prayed they wouldn't both go over—then back again.

I caught a glimpse of Ryodan, bleeding from dozens of wounds.

Then a flash of my monster, flesh torn, jaws bloody and snapping.

They rolled into a blur again at the river's edge.

I watched, wide-eyed, leaping this way and that, trying to find a moment, an angle, an opportunity to help. I felt strangely torn.

The monster had saved my life repeatedly. It was my savage guardian demon. It had protected me.

But, as Ryodan had pointed out, it could do only that.

It couldn't help me get back home. And it was going to kill my "way home," if it could. Leaving me protected but stranded. I couldn't allow that. I had to get out of here.

I caught another glimpse of Ryodan. The monster was tearing him to pieces!

Then Ryodan must have injured the monster, because it flashed into view and stayed a moment. Before I could blow what might be the only chance I got, I steeled myself, lunged for it, and jammed my spear into its back, right where I figured its heart was, if its internal anatomy was anything like a human's.

It jerked, whipped its head around, and roared at me.

Ryodan seized the opportunity, plunged a knife into its chest, and ripped upward, slicing the monster open from gut to throat.

Its head whipped back around and it shoved Ryodan so hard it drove him to the cliff's edge. As I watched, horrified, he stumbled on the soft shale lip and slipped over the side!

I think I screamed, or maybe I'd been screaming for a while, I don't know; things that day got a little blurred for me.

Ryodan's hands locked around a rock that protruded from the bank. I prayed it was embedded deeply enough in the shale to hold him.

The monster rose to its full height, baying with rage and pain, my spear stuck in its back.

I held my breath as Ryodan inched back up onto the bank. There was so much blood on his face that I could barely make out his eyes. How was he still moving? His cheek was sliced open so deep I could see bone! His chest was a mass of bloody criss-crossed slashes.

The monster staggered then, and I think I must have made a noise. Relief that it was going down? Sorrow? Maybe shame for my part in it? I had a whole mess of emotions going on.

It turned its head and looked straight at me, and there was something in its feral yellow gaze that made me gasp.

For an awful suspended moment, I could have sworn I saw an accusation of betrayal in its gaze, of disbelief at my foul duplicity, as if we'd had some kind of agreement, some unspoken pact between us. It stared at me with reproach; its yellow eyes burned with hatred for my treason. It flung back its head and bayed with desolation and despair, an anguished cry of grief and madness.

I clamped my hands to my ears.

It took a step toward me. I couldn't believe it was still standing, flayed as it was.

When it took a second step, Ryodan managed to stagger to his feet, launch himself onto its back, wrap an arm around its neck—and slit its throat. "Get the bloody fuck *out* of here, Mac," he snarled.

Gushing blood, the beast reached back, dug its talons into Ryodan, ripped him off its back, and flung him straight into the gorge.

"No!" I exploded.

But Ryodan was already gone, falling down, down into the river, a hundred feet below.

37

I stood, staring stupidly at the monster with the flayed body and slit throat.

It was still standing.

I was hot and cold, shaking. I felt like I was in some fevered dream, a nightmare from which I couldn't escape. I could feel myself detaching from the world around me, turning to stone inside, shutting down all emotion.

The monster staggered toward me. Went down on one knee and stared up at me. It shuddered, then collapsed to the earth, facedown.

My spear stuck out of its back.

The forest was silent and still.

As I watched the monster's blood run into the soil, I took distant, unemotional stock of my situation.

Ryodan was dead.

Nothing could have survived that fall—assuming he'd been able to recover from his wounds, which was a pretty far stretch.

The monster was also dead, or very near it and

would be soon, lying in a rapidly growing pool of blood.

I'd lost my way out.

I'd lost my protector, too.

Somewhere in this realm, the Lord Master was hunting me, tracking me by a mystical brand he'd etched on my skull.

Somewhere in this realm was an IFP that contained a dolmen that would take me back to Ireland. Unfortunately, I had no idea which one it was, or in which direction, or how many there were to choose from on this world.

My pouch of stones was still attached to the monster's horns, and the tatters of my sweater were still tied by its sleeves to a leg. When it was dead, I would reclaim the stones. That was a plus of sorts in the ledger of my life, assuming I overlooked that they were really nothing more than a slow boat to hell.

The monster gurgled wetly and seemed to deflate.

I waited a few moments, picked up a stick, took a cautious step forward, and poked it.

There was no reaction. I poked harder, then nudged it with my foot.

I tested the spear in its back, jostling its wound. Again, there was no reaction.

It was definitely dead.

I crouched beside it and had begun to untie my pouch when suddenly its horns softened and melted into a river that flowed past its head, puddling like an oil slick on blood.

I snatched my pouch from its matted hair.

The shape of its head began to change.

Webs and talons vanished.

Matted locks became hair.

I stumbled backward, shaking my head. "No," I said.

It continued to change. Slate-gray skin lightened.

"No," I insisted.

My denial had no effect. It continued to transform. Height diminished. Mass decreased. It became what it was.

What it had been all along.

I began to hyperventilate. Squatting, I rocked back and forth in a posture of grief as old as time.

"No!" I screamed.

I'd thought I'd lost everything.

I hadn't.

I stared at the person who lay dead on the floor of the forest.

The person I'd helped kill.

Now I'd lost everything.

Dear Reader:

I know it's been a wild ride, but it's almost over. *Shadowfever* is the fifth and final installment in the trials and triumphs of MacKayla Lane-O'Connor. And there *will* be triumphs. I've promised that from the beginning.

As I've said on my website and in many interviews, the *Fever* series came to me, fully formed, as I've written it, demanding that I be true to the plot and characters, no matter how difficult parts of it have been to write. Switching from writing third person omniscient point of view that you'll find in my earlier novels to the first person limited point of view in the *Fever* novels was a challenge but one that I've found immensely rewarding. I couldn't have told Mac's story any other way.

The devil is in the details—as is the delight. It's the nuances that make a story rich, compelling, fascinating, that draw us in and make us love, and hate, and hate to love, and love to hate the characters. It's what they choose to quest for; how they mark time; the decisions they make, small and large; the awkwardness of forging bonds; the obvious-to-us-yet-blurred-to-them emotions, doubts, convictions, uncertainties, truths, joys; the beauty of watching them try, fail, try again, fail again, and finally get it right that makes a story—and any life, really—worthwhile. Thanks for joining me on Mac's quest.

Still want more *Fever*? Drop by www.karenmoning .com, where you'll find a message-board forum full of fun, brilliant folks who I sometimes think know the details of my series as well as I do. (Okay, on a tough day, when I can't find my notes, maybe a little better, LOL.) You'll also find a link to the Fever Fan Merchandise Store, where you can buy all kinds of stuff like *Barrons' Babe* or *V'lane's Vixen* tees, Unseelie Sushi Juice mugs, MacHalo stamps, BB&B memorabilia, even your own *Sidhe*-Seers, Inc badge.

There's also a link to BLOODRUSH, the official *Fever* sound track, a collection of songs written and performed by Neil Dover. It's an awesome CD with "Little Lamb," "I Am Not Afraid," plus five new songs and an acoustic reprise. Check out "Sweet Dublin Rain," with Mac's cool rap. For "Taking Back the Night,"—the *sidhe*-seers' anthem—a hundred and fifty fans came in from all over the world to join us in the recording studio in Atlanta, and sing the ending. It was a total blast! The insert contains photos from the studio, a lot of extras, and deleted scenes that aren't available anywhere else.

Mac's hot-pink MacHalo and Barrons' black version—the Z-Lo—have been touring for the past six months, and the pictures are a hoot. You can see where in the world they've both been at www.flickr.com/photos/karenmariemoning. The photos are fantastic, funny, amazing. I love getting the opportunity via photos and e-mail to meet so many of you that I haven't met in person. Thanks for making Mac's adventure such a blast!

Stay to the lights,
Karen

Glossary from Mac's Journal

*AMULET, THE: Unseelie or Dark Hallow created by the Unseelie King for his concubine. Fashioned of gold, silver, sapphires, and onyx, the gilt "cage" of the amulet houses an enormous clear stone of unknown composition. A person of epic will can use it to impact and re-shape reality. The list of past owners is legendary, including Merlin, Boudicca, Joan of Arc, Charlemagne, and Napoleon. Last purchased by a Welshman for eight figures at an illegal auction, it was all too briefly in my hands and is currently in the possession of the Lord Master. It requires some kind of tithe or binding to use it. I had the will; I couldn't figure out the way.

Addendum: The LM still has it, and I think he uses it to help control the Unseelie Princes. He had it with him but didn't try to use it on me. Why? Is he afraid it might not work on me?

BARRONS, JERICHO: I haven't the faintest fecking clue. He keeps saving my life. I suppose that's something.

Addendum to original entry: He keeps a Sifting Silver in his study at the bookstore, and when he walks through it, the monsters retreat from him, just like the Shades do. I saw him carry the body of a woman out of it. She'd been killed, brutally. By him? Or by the things in the mirror? He is at least several hundred years old and possibly, *probably*, way older than that. I made him hold the spear to see if he was Unseelie, and he did, but I found out later from V'lane that the Unseelie King can touch *all* the Hallows (as can the Seelie Queen) and, although I can't fathom why the Unseelie King wouldn't be able to touch his own Book, maybe that's exactly why Barrons thought he *would* be able to touch it. Maybe it evolved into something more powerful than it began as. Also, I can't rule out that he might be some kind of Seelie/Unseelie hybrid. Do the Fae have sex and reproduce? Sometimes . . . I think he's human . . . gone *very* wrong. Other times I think he's nothing this world has ever seen. He's definitely not a *sidhe*-seer, but he sees the Fae as plain as day, just like me. He knows Druidry, sorcery, black arts, is superstrong and fast, and has heightened senses. What did Ryodan mean by his comment about the Alpha & Omega? I've *got* to track that man down!

Addendum to original entry: He admitted he killed the woman he carried from the mirror! I'm pretty sure I figured out where that Silver goes, but I haven't the opportunity to try it yet. I think it connects to the underground floors beneath his garage. I stood in that garage, looking across the hood of the Hummer at Barrons, while whatever he keeps trapped down there bayed. He refused to answer any of my questions about it. (Gee, that's hardly a surprise.)

Addendum to original entry: What he did to bring me back from being *Pri-ya* . . . I can't stop thinking about it. What I saw in his head, the child, the grief, it slays me. Sometimes I wish I didn't have to be anything but a fine beast again. That I could forget again. Everything. And just be.

*CAULDRON, THE: Seelie or Light Hallow from which all Seelie eventually drink, to divest memory that has become burdensome. According to Barrons, immortality has a price: eventual madness. When the Fae feel it approaching, they drink from the cauldron and are "reborn" with no memory of a prior existence. The Fae have a record keeper that documents each Fae's many incarnations, but the exact location of this scribe is known to a select few and the whereabouts of the records to none but him. Is that what's wrong with the Unseelie—they don't have a cauldron to drink from?

CHESTER'S: Ryodan's nightclub, 939 Rêvemal Street. Former gathering place of the rich, bored, and beautiful. Like a cockroach, Chester's would probably survive any fallout. Since Dublin fell, it went underground and now serves an entirely new clientele. Or, rather, serves *us* to an entirely new clientele. Chester's is now the Fae hot spot for preying on humans. The Gray Woman had no interest in her waiter's menu, only her waiter. Ryodan *lets* it happen, right under his nose, watching from high in his glass aerie. Fae worshippers sacrifice themselves left and right for a chance at immortality, and I'm pretty sure it's not even a real chance, just a temporary high. I'm going to shut the place down, one way or another.

COMPACT, THE: Agreement negotiated between Queen Aoibheal and the MacKeltar clan (Keltar = hidden barrier or mantle) roughly six thousand years ago to keep the realms of mankind and Fae separate. The Highland clan of Druids has performed certain rituals and tithed every Samhain (pronounced *Sow-en*, also known as Halloween) to honor the Compact. The walls Queen Aoibheal erected to separate worlds weren't sung into existence with the Song of Making, because the Fae lost it so long ago, but were somehow rigged from a portion of the Unseelie's prison walls and reinforced with blood and oaths. Rigging the new walls that way seriously weakened the prison walls. When our walls came down, *all* the walls came down.

CRUCE: A Fae. Unknown if Seelie or Unseelie. Many of his relics are floating around out there. He cursed the Sifting Silvers. Before they were cursed, the Fae used them freely to travel through dimensions. The curse somehow corrupted the interdimensional channels, and now not even the Fae will enter them. Unknown what the curse was. Unknown what damage it caused or what the risk in the Silvers is. Whatever it is, Barrons apparently doesn't fear it. I tried to get into the Silver in his study. I can't figure out how to open it.

Addendum to original entry: I found out what the curse was! Cruce hated the Unseelie King and cursed the Silvers to keep him from entering them again, so he couldn't get to his concubine. Cruce wanted the concubine and all the worlds inside the Silvers for himself. But the curse went wrong and screwed everything up. Cross-reference with *Silvers*.

CUFF OF CRUCE: A gold-and-silver arm cuff set with blood-red stones; an ancient Fae relic that supposedly permits the human wearing it "a shield of sorts against many Unseelie and other . . . unsavory things" (this according to a death-by-sex Fae—like you can actually trust one).

DANI: A young *sidhe*-seer in her early teens whose talent is superhuman speed. She has to her credit—as she will proudly crow from the rooftops given the slightest opportunity—forty-seven Fae kills at the time of this writing. I'm sure she'll have more by tomorrow. Her mother was killed by a Fae. We are sisters in vengeance. She works for Rowena and is employed at Post Haste, Inc.

Addendum to original entry: Her kills now number nearly two hundred! The kid has no fear.

Addendum to original entry: She's the Shit. She saved me from the LM and his minions. We've become like . . . sisters. I swore I'd never let anybody as close to me as Alina again, but I can't help it. Beneath her toughness is a kid who melts my heart. She's got secrets. I can sense them. And deep emotional scars from things she might never talk about. I hope one day she trusts me. The things we carry inside and refuse to talk about are the things that can end up destroying us. I can no longer even begin to count her kills. She took down an Unseelie Prince!

DARK ZONE: An area that has been taken over by the Shades. During the day it looks like your everyday abandoned, run-down neighborhood. Once night falls, it's a death trap.

Addendum to original entry: They've spread all over the world, now that the walls are down. The huge one next to Barrons Books and Baubles is now empty. They moved on to greener pastures, literally. Other Unseelie are working to restore the power grids the LM took down, because they don't like how quickly the Shades are devouring their potential prey. I'll take all the help I can get to drive the buggers back into the darkness. It buys us more time.

DEATH-BY-SEX FAE (e.g., V'lane): A Fae that is so sexually "potent" a human dies from intercourse with it, unless the Fae protects the human from the full impact of its deadly eroticism.

Addendum to original entry: V'lane made himself feel like nothing more than an incredibly sexy man when he touched me. They *can* mute their lethality if they so choose.

Addendum to original entry: This caste of Fae springs only from royal lines. They can do three things: protect the human completely and give them the most incredible sex of their life, protect them from dying and turn them *Pri-ya*, or kill them with sex. They can sift space.

Addendum: It's hell being *Pri-ya*! But I survived.

DOLMEN: A single-chamber megalithic tomb constructed of three or more upright stones supporting a large, flat horizontal capstone. Dolmens are common in Ireland, especially around the Burren and Connemara.

The Lord Master used a dolmen in a ritual of dark magic to open a doorway between realms and bring Unseelie through.

DREAMY-EYED BOY: Huge question mark. Why does he keep popping up? Who is he? I first encountered him in the streets of Dublin, then in the museum while I was OOP-detecting, then discovered he worked at the Ancient Languages Department with Christian MacKeltar, and now he's bartending at Chester's, Ryodan's infamous den of iniquity. When I was talking to him there, something really weird happened. I saw him in the mirror above the bar and he didn't look the same. It scared me. *Really* scared me. In the mirror, his reflection spoke to me, warned me. He said not to talk to "it."

DRUID: In pre-Christian Celtic society, a Druid presided over divine worship, legislative and judicial matters, philosophy, and education of elite youth to their order. Druids were believed to be privy to the secrets of the gods, including issues pertaining to the manipulation of physical matter, space, and even time. The old Irish *Drui* means magician, wizard, diviner *(Irish Myths and Legends)*.

Addendum to original entry: I saw both Jericho Barrons and the Lord Master use the Druid power of Voice, a way of speaking with many voices that cannot be disobeyed. Significance?

Addendum: Christian MacKeltar descends from a long, ancient bloodline of Druids.

FAE (fay): See also *Tuatha Dé Danaan*. Divided into two courts, the Seelie or light court and the Unseelie or dark court. Both courts have different castes of Fae, with the four Royal Houses occupying the highest caste of each. The Seelie Queen and her chosen consort rule the light court. The Unseelie King and his current concubine govern the dark.

Addendum to original entry. Iron has some kind of effect on them. Weird that on the periodic table, iron is *Fe*.

FIONA: The woman who ran Barrons Books and Baubles before I took over. She was wildly in love with Barrons and tried to kill me by turning out all the lights one night and propping a window open to let the Shades in. Barrons fired her for it—gee, now that I think about it, getting fired for trying to kill me sure feels like underkill. She's hooked up with Derek O'Bannion, and he's got her eating Unseelie. I have a bad feeling that she and I aren't done with each other.

Addendum to original entry: She's working with the LM now. She knows what Barrons is. Barrons killed her before she could tell me. But she was too laced with Unseelie flesh to have died from a mere knife through the heart. Later he went to see her and gave her a message for the LM. They used to be lovers. I don't like her at all.

FOUR STONES, THE: Translucent blue-black stones covered with raised runelike lettering. The key to deciphering the ancient language and breaking the code of the *Sinsar Dubh* is hidden in these four mystical stones. An individual stone can be used to shed light on a small portion of the text, but only if the four are reassembled into one will the true text in its entirety be revealed *(Irish Myths and Legends)*.

Addendum: Other texts say it is the "true nature" of the *Sinsar Dubh* that will be revealed.

Addendum: We have three now. I learned they were chiseled from the walls of the Unseelie King's fortress. They chime hauntingly, disturbingly, when placed together. I think they must make a lesser Song of Making. They are poison inside the network of Silvers because of Cruce's curse. The Silvers reject the Unseelie King and the stones because they bear the taint of his touch. I think V'lane has the fourth.

FREEZE-FRAME: The way Dani moves. She calls it freeze-framing, as she blips from place to place so fast it gives me motion sickness. But what a tactical advantage! The kid rocks.

GLAMOUR: Illusion cast by the Fae to camouflage their true appearance. The more powerful the Fae, the more difficult it is to penetrate its disguise. Average humans see only what the Fae want them to see and are subtly repelled from bumping into or brushing against it by a small perimeter of spatial distortion that is part of the Fae glamour.

GRAY MAN, THE: Monstrously ugly, leprous Unseelie that feeds by stealing beauty from human women. Threat assessment: can kill but prefers to leave its victim hideously disfigured and alive to suffer.

Addendum to original entry: ~~Allegedly the only one of its kind~~ (BIG FAT *NOT;* SEE BELOW!) Barrons and I killed it.

Addendum to original entry: It could sift space.

GRAY WOMAN, THE: The Gray Man's female counterpart. Saw her outside Chester's and later inside. Unlike the Gray Man, she doesn't leave her victims alive. A sifter. No longer consider them singularities. Could be dozens of them.

GRIPPER: Dainty, diaphanous Unseelie that is surprisingly beautiful. Grippers look like the modern media's representation of fairies—delicate, shimmering nude beauties, with a cloud of gossamer hair and lovely features, only they're nearly the size of a human. I named them Grippers because they "grip" us. They can step inside a human's skin and take them over. Once they've slipped inside a person, I can no longer sense them. I could be standing right next to a Gripper inside a person and not even know it. For a while, I was afraid Barrons might be one. But I made him hold the spear.

GUARDIANS, THE: What the Garda have begun calling themselves under Inspector Jayne's leadership as they fight to protect Dublin's remaining citizens. They eat Unseelie and kick serious Fae ass.

HALL OF ALL DAYS, THE: The central hub of the Silvers. Barrons describes it as a quantum travel agency for the Fae, like an airport terminal. The walls and floor are made of pure gold, and it seems to stretch on forever. The walls are covered with billions of mirrors that are portals to other worlds, dimensions, and times. It's a dangerous place. Time feels skewed there, not linear at all, and if you stop moving, you can get lost in memories that begin to play out around you as if they're real. Whatever you think seems to materialize. You have to keep moving. I passed skeletons on the floor. When the Silvers were originally created, all mirrors that were a part of the network (outside the Hall) would immediately deposit you in the Hall of All Days. From there, you could choose your destination. Cross-reference *Silvers*.

HALLOWS, THE: Eight ancient relics of immense power fashioned by the Fae: four light and four dark. The Light or Seelie Hallows are the stone, the spear, the sword, and the cauldron. The Dark or Unseelie Hallows are the amulet, the box, the mirror, and the Book (*Sinsar Dubh*, or Dark Book) (*A Definitive Guide to Artifacts, Authentic and Legendary*).

Addendum to original entry: I still don't know anything about the stone or the box. Do they confer powers that could help me? Where are they? Is it possible the four stones make *the* stone? Correction to above definition, the mirror is actually the Silvers. See *Sifting Silvers* or

Silvers. The Unseelie King made all the Dark Hallows. Who made the light ones?

Addendum to original entry: See the story of the Unseelie King and his mortal concubine, as V'lane told it to me (p. 77, this journal). The king created the Silvers for her to keep her ageless and give her realms to explore. He created the amulet so she could reshape reality. He gave her the box for her loneliness. What does it do? The *Sinsar Dubh* was an accident.

HAVEN, THE: High Council of *sidhe*-seers.

Addendum to original entry: Once selected by popular vote, now chosen by the Grand Mistress for their loyalty to her and the cause. They were the only ones besides Rowena who knew what was being kept beneath the abbey. Some of them died and/or disappeared when the Book escaped twenty-some years ago. How did it happen? I'm twenty-two. *Is it possible my mother was one of them?!!!*

Addendum: Yes, my mother, Isla O'Connor, was one! She was, like Alina and me, immensely gifted. Must find out more!

IFP: Interdimensional Fairy Pothole. These things drive me nuts! When the walls came down on Halloween, parts of Faery splintered into parts of our world, and now, if you're not careful, you can end up walking or driving into one abruptly and without warning. You don't know what's in one until you get inside. They're hard to get back out of. Someone has been "cutting them loose" and they've begun drifting on the wind, making them even harder to avoid. There are IFPs inside the network of the Silvers, too. When Cruce cursed it, the collision of realms caused similarly fractured realities. According to Ryodan, IFPs are static microcosms and can be mapped. Some contain dolmens to our world.

Most contain other IFPs. One can hop from world to world through them. It's pretty much a mess.

IRON: *Fe* on the periodic table. Inspector Jayne discovered that it bothers the Fae. He and his men fashioned bullets from it, lined their helmets with it, and carry it all over their bodies. It can imprison nonsifting Fae. Who knows what massive quantities of it might do to a sifting Fae?

IYCGM: Barrons gave me a cell phone with this number programmed in. It stands for *If You Can't Get Me*. The mysterious Ryodan answers when I call.

IYD: Another of Barrons' preprogrammed numbers; stands for *If You're Dying*.

Addendum: God, I know what it is now!

KAT: I think she'll end up leading the *sidhe*-seers one day, if she lives long enough. I hope she does, because I can't stand Rowena. She's about twenty-five, level-headed, smart, pure-hearted, and is the only one who has consistently kept an open mind and stood up for me. If anything happens to me, trust Kat. And Dani. If I'm dead, go to them for help.

LIBRARIES, THE TWENTY-ONE: Dani knows where they all are, even the forbidden ones, and we got into one, left Kat and her most trusted searching it, but I couldn't get into the other one Dani took me to. Not only was it massively warded, but there was some kind of "guardian" blocking the way that just kept repeating that I wasn't one of them and wasn't permitted there. There's some kind of insurmountable obstacle in the corridor. I summoned V'lane to help me. When he appeared, he hissed at me, contorted in pain, and vanished. I haven't seen him since. I'm getting a little worried.

LORD MASTER: Darroc. My sister's betrayer and murderer! Fae but not Fae, leader of the Unseelie army, after the *Sinsar Dubh*. He was using Alina to hunt it, like Barrons is using me to hunt OOPs.

Addendum to original entry: He offered me a trade: Alina back for the Book. I think he really could do it.

Addendum: Bad enough that he had me turned *Pri-ya*, but now he has my parents!

MACHALO: My invention. Very cool. Hot-pink and covered with lights. It's the ultimate in fashionable Shade protection.

MACKELTAR, CHRISTIAN: Employed in the Ancient Languages Department of Trinity College. He knows what I am and knew my sister! Have no idea what his place in all this is, nor do I know his motives. Will find out more soon.

Addendum to original entry: Christian comes from a clan that once served as high Druids to the Fae and have been upholding the human part of the Fae/Man Compact for thousands of years, performing rituals and paying tithes. He knew Alina only in passing. She'd come to ask him to translate a piece of text from the *Sinsar Dubh*.

Addendum: He disappeared on Halloween, when the Keltars and Barrons performed the ritual to try to keep the walls up. We *both* had a bad night! He got sucked into the vortex that destroyed the stones of *Ban Drochaid*, the sacred stone circle where the Keltar Druids have performed the rites and paid the tithe to uphold the Compact for millennia. I found him trapped in the network of the Silvers.

MALLUCÉ: Born John Johnstone, Jr. On the heels of his parents' mysterious death, he inherited hundreds of millions of dollars, disappeared for a time, and resurfaced as the newly undead vampire Mallucé. Over the next decade, he amassed a worldwide cult following and was recruited by the Lord Master for his money and connections. Pale, blond, citron-eyed, the vampire favors steampunk and Victorian Goth.

MANY-MOUTHED THING, THE: Repulsive Unseelie with myriad leechlike mouths, dozens of eyes, and overdeveloped sex organs. Caste of Unseelie: unknown at this time. Threat assessment: unknown at this time, but suspect kills in a manner I'd rather not think about.

Addendum to original entry: Is still out there. I want this one dead.

Addendum to original entry: Dani bagged the bastard! Could he sift space? Which ones can and can't?

NULL: A *sidhe*-seer with the power to freeze a Fae with the touch of his or her hands (e.g., me). While frozen, a Nulled Fae is completely powerless, but the higher and more powerful the caste of Fae, the shorter the length of time it stays frozen.

O'BANNION, DEREK: Rocky's brother and the Lord Master's new recruit. He wants his brother's spear back, and he wants to kill me for killing his brother. I should have let him walk into the Dark Zone that day.

Addendum to original entry: He's eating Unseelie and has hooked up with Fiona, who's also eating it!

Addendum: Did the Book get him, or was *all* of what happened that night an illusion?

O'BANNION, ROCKY: Ex-boxer turned Irish mobster, and religious fanatic. He had the Spear of Destiny* in a collection hidden deep underground. Barrons and I broke in one night and stole it. His death was the first human blood on my hands. The night we robbed him, Barrons turned out all the exterior lights around the bookstore. When O'Bannion came after me with fifteen of his henchmen, the Shades devoured them right outside my bedroom window. I knew Barrons was going to do something. And if he'd asked me to choose between them or me, I'd have *helped* him turn the lights out. You never know what you'll be willing to do to survive until you get backed into a corner and see what explodes out of you.

OOP: Acronym for *Object of Power;* a Fae relic imbued with mystical properties. Some are Hallows, some aren't.

OOP DETECTOR: Me. A *sidhe*-seer with the special ability to sense OOPs. Alina was one, too, which is why the Lord Master used her.

Addendum to original entry: Very rare. Certain bloodlines were bred for this trait. Rowena's *sidhe*-seers say they've all died out.

ORB OF D'JAI: No clue, but Barrons has it. He says it's an OOP. I couldn't sense it when I held it, but I couldn't sense anything at that particular moment. Where did he get it and where did he put it? Is it in his mysterious vault? What does it do? How does he get into his vault, anyway? Where is the access to the three floors beneath his garage? Is there a tunnel that connects buildings? Must search.

Addendum to original entry: Barrons gave it to me so I could give it to the *sidhe*-seers, to use in a ritual to reinforce the walls on Samhain.

Addendum: Barrons swears it was spiked when he got it. Found entry to the floors beneath his garage—through the Silver in his study!

O'REILLY, KAYLEIGH: One of my mother's friends and also part of the Haven. Something bad happened, and I think my mom and Kayleigh tried to stop it. I think that's when the Book escaped.

O'REILLY, NANA: Nearly a hundred years old, lives by the sea in County Clare, knew my mother! My mother's name is Isla O'Connor. I could say that a thousand times. My mother grew up with Nana's granddaughter, Kayleigh. I think Nana knows what happened when the Book escaped. I need to question her again. Preferably without Kat standing guard.

PATRONA: Mentioned by Rowena, I supposedly have "the look" of her. Was she an O'Connor? She was at one time the leader of the *sidhe*-seer Haven.

Addendum: Patrona was my grandmother!

PHI: Post Haste, Inc., a Dublin courier service that serves as a cover for the *sidhe*-seer coalition. It appears Rowena is in charge.

Addendum: After the Book was lost, Rowena opened branches of this courier service all over the world in an effort to track and reclaim it. It was very clever, really. She has bicycle couriers serving as her eyes and ears in hundreds of major cities. The abbey/*sidhe*-seers have a very wealthy benefactor who funnels funds through multiple corporations. I wonder who it is.

PRI-YA: A human addicted to Fae sex.

Addendum: God help me, I *know*.

RHINO-BOYS: Ugly, gray-skinned Fae who resemble rhinoceroses with bumpy, protruding foreheads, barrel-like bodies, stumpy arms and legs, lipless gashes of mouths, and jutting underbites. They are lower mid-level caste Unseelie thugs dispatched primarily as watchdogs for high-ranking Fae.

Addendum to original entry: They taste horrible.

Addendum to original entry: I don't believe they can sift space. I saw them locked in cells and chained up in

Mallucé's grotto. It didn't occur to me at the time how odd that was, then later I thought maybe Mallucé was somehow containing them with spells. But after Jayne made his comment about imprisoning Fae, I realized that not all Fae can sift, and I'm starting to wonder if only the very powerful ones can. This could be an important tactical edge. Must explore.

Addendum: They have a taste for pretty young human girls and will swap the incredible high of Unseelie flesh for sex. *Ew!*

ROWENA: In charge ~~to some degree~~ of a coalition of *sidhe*-seers organized as couriers at Post Haste, Inc. ~~Is she the~~ Grand Mistress? They have a chapter house or retreat in an old abbey a few hours from Dublin, with a library I *must* get into.

Addendum to original entry: She has never liked me. She's playing judge, jury, and executioner where I'm concerned. She sent her girls after me to take my spear away! I will *never* let her have it. I've been to the abbey but only briefly. I suspect many of the answers I want can be found there, either in the Forbidden Libraries, which only the Haven is permitted to enter, or in their memories. I need to figure out who the Haven members are and get one of them to talk.

Addendum: I'll topple her reign of power yet. She won't let the *sidhe*-seers do their job. She keeps them under lock and key, but I think I've smashed the first cracks in the abbey walls. I think they're going to mutiny.

ROYAL HUNTERS: A mid-level caste of Unseelie. Militantly sentient, they resemble the classic depiction of the devil, with cloven hooves, horns, long satyrlike faces, leathery wings, fiery orange eyes, and tails. Seven to ten feet tall, they are capable of extraordinary speed on both hoof and wing. Primary function: *sidhe*-seer exterminators. Threat assessment: kills.

Addendum to original entry: Encountered one. Barrons doesn't know everything. It was considerably larger than he'd led me to expect, with a thirty- to forty-foot wingspan and a degree of telepathic abilities. They are mercenary to the core and serve a master only so long as it benefits them. I'm not sure I believe they're mid-level, and, in fact, I'm not sure they're entirely Fae. They fear my spear and I suspect are unwilling to die for any cause, which gives me a tactical edge.

Addendum to original entry: I rode one!

RYODAN: Associate of Barrons, and *IYCGM* on my cell.

Addendum: Top on my list of people to track down.

Addendum to original entry: See *Chester's*. This man is one of Barrons' eight, whatever that is. They are all big men, preternaturally fast, most badly scarred, and they ooze something that just . . . isn't human. Ryodan worries me.

SEELIE: The light or "fairer" court of the Tuatha Dé Danaan, governed by the Seelie Queen, Aoibheal.

Addendum: The Seelie cannot touch the Unseelie Hallows. The Unseelie cannot touch Seelie Hallows.

Addendum: According to V'lane, the true queen of the Fae is long dead, killed by the Unseelie King, and with her died the Song of Making. Aoibheal is a lesser royal, who is one of many that has tried to lead the People since.

SEE YOU IN FAERY!: Catchphrase for sycophantic human sex kittens who will trade anything and everything for the high of eating Unseelie flesh. They believe if they eat enough, it will make them immortal and they'll get to go to Faery, too. Said in the most annoyingly chirpy tone possible!!!

SHADES: One of the lowest castes of Unseelie. Sentient but barely. They hunger—they feed. They cannot bear direct light and hunt only at night. They steal life in the same manner the Gray Man steals beauty, draining their victims with vampiric swiftness, leaving behind a pile of clothing and a husk of dehydrated human matter. Threat assessment: kills.

Addendum to original entry: I think they're changing, evolving, learning.

Addendum: I know it is! I swear it's stalking me!

Addendum: They've learned to work together and shape themselves into barriers.

Addendum: They're all over the world now!

SHAMROCK: This slightly misshapen three-leaf clover is the ancient symbol of the *sidhe*-seers, who are charged with the mission to See, Serve, and Protect mankind from the Fae.

SIDHE-SEER (SHE-seer): A person Fae magic doesn't work on, capable of seeing past the illusions or "glamour" cast by the Fae to the true nature that lies beneath. Some can also see *Tabh'rs,* hidden portals between realms. Others can sense Seelie and Unseelie Objects of Power. Each *sidhe*-seer is different, with varying degrees of resistance to the Fae. Some are limited; some are advanced, with multiple "special powers."

Addendum to original entry: Some, like Dani, are superfast. There's a place inside my head that isn't . . . like the rest of me. Do we all have it? What is it? How did we get this way? Where do the bits of inexplicable knowledge that feel like memories come from? Is there such a thing as a genetic collective unconsciousness?

Addendum: In that *sidhe*-seer place in my head is a dark, glassy lake. It scares me.

SIFTING: Fae method of locomotion, occurs at speed of thought. (Seen this!)

Addendum to original entry: Somehow, V'lane sifted me without my awareness that he was even there. I don't know if he was able to approach me "cloaked" somehow, then touched me at the last minute and I just didn't realize it because it happened so fast, or if perhaps instead of moving me, he moved the realms around me. Can he do that? How powerful is V'lane? Could another Fae sift me without me having any advance warning? Unacceptably dangerous! Require more information.

*SIFTING SILVERS, OR SILVERS, THE: Unseelie or Dark Hallow; an elaborate maze of mirrors created by the Unseelie King, once used as the primary method of Fae travel between realms, until Cruce cast the forbidden curse into the silvered corridors. Now no Fae dares enter the Silvers.

Addendum to original entry: The Lord Master had many of these in his house in the Dark Zone and was using them to move in and out of Faery. If you destroy a Silver, does it destroy what was in it? Does it leave an open entry/exit into a Fae realm, like a wound in the fabric of our world? What exactly was the curse and who was Cruce?

Addendum to original entry: Barrons has one and walks around in it!

Addendum: Cross-reference *Hall of All Days*. The way it worked *before* the curse was this: The Hall of All Days was the central airport where you could choose from millions of mirrors that connected to a second mirror on another world, dimension, or time, and travel there. The mirrors were two-way portals at that time, and to return, you just stepped back through them into the Hall. I think they concealed the mirrors on the other worlds in inanimate objects, so only a Fae could find them. The queen sensed the power of the Silvers, which the king had created for his concubine. To allay her suspicions that he was still keeping the mortal the queen despised, he had to give her the main part, including the Hall, but he kept a portion separate, where he built the White Mansion on a hill for his concubine.

The way it works *now,* since Cruce cursed it: Everything is screwed up. The mirrors in the Hall multiplied exponentially and now number in the billions. They are no longer two-way, the places they show as destinations aren't necessarily where they deposit you, and the worlds connected by the Silvers have all been badly splintered with IFPs. Cruce messed up billions of worlds, dimensions, and times. However, they are, as Barrons puts it, navigable if one knows what one is doing and has the necessary Druid arts at his disposal. It seems Barrons has been in the Silvers quite a bit. Usually, one mirror connects directly to the next. When you look in that Silver, it shows its destination. But sometimes people (like Barrons and the LM) "stack" Silvers, forming tunnels to create space to force the person (i.e., me!) stepping in to drop their weapons and show the ransom, or, in Barrons' case, so he can litter the corridor to his garage with killing demons who won't let anyone through. Don't strain your brain trying to understand the Silvers. I don't think anyone does. Just expect the unexpected.

SINSAR DUBH, **THE** (she-suh DOO): Unseelie or Dark Hallow belonging to the Tuatha Dé Danaan. Written in a language known only to the most ancient of their kind, it is said to hold the deadliest of all magic within its encrypted pages. Brought to Ireland by the Tuatha Dé during the invasions written of in the pseudo-history *Leabhar Gabhåla,* it was stolen along with the other Dark Hallows and rumored to have found its way into the world of man. Allegedly authored over a million years ago by the Dark King of the Unseelie (*A Definitive Guide to Artifacts; Authentic and Legendary*).

Addendum to original entry: I've seen it now. Words cannot contain a description of it. It is a book, but it lives. It is aware.

Addendum: The Beast. Enough said.

Addendum: How the feck am I supposed to contain the thing? Is this a joke?

*SPEAR OF LUISNE, THE: Seelie or Light Hallow (a.k.a. Spear of Luin, Spear of Longinus, Spear of Destiny, the Flaming Spear). The spear used to pierce Jesus Christ's side at His crucifixion. Not of human origin, it is a Tuatha Dé Danaan Light Hallow and one of few items capable of killing a Fae—regardless of rank or power.

Addendum to original note: It kills *anything* Fae, and if something is only part Fae, it kills part of it horribly.

*SWORD OF LUGH, THE: Seelie or Light Hallow, also known as the Sword of Light, capable of killing Fae, both Seelie and Unseelie. Currently, Rowena has it and dispatches it to her *sidhe*-seers at PHI as she deems fit. Dani usually gets it.

Addendum: Saw it. It's beautiful!

Addendum: Stole it from Rowena and gave it to Dani permanently.

TABH'RS (TAH-vr): Fae doorways or portals between realms, often hidden in everyday human objects.

Addendum: I think they're actually Silvers, like the cactus on the desert world where I found Christian, only apparently I can't see them. Sure could use a *sidhe*-seer who could!

"TAKING BACK THE NIGHT": Song Dani and I made up, now the *sidhe*-seer international anthem.

TUATHA DÉ DANAAN, OR TUATHA DÉ (TUA day dhanna or Tua DAY) (See *Fae,* above): A highly advanced race that came to earth from another world, comprising the Seelie and Unseelie.

UNSEELIE: The dark or "fouler" court of the Tuatha Dé Danaan. According to Tuatha Dé Danaan legend, the Unseelie have been confined for hundreds of thousands of years in an inescapable prison. Inescapable, my ass.

UNSEELIE PRINCES: Death, Pestilence, Famine, and War. According to the LM, one of them was killed eons ago, and Dani killed another, which means only two remain. Then who was the fourth at the church? The LM claims it wasn't him and that there was no fourth. Did I just imagine it? There are memories from those earliest hours, even days that are terribly blurry.

V'LANE: According to Rowena's books, V'lane is a Seelie Prince, the light court, member of the queen's High Council, and sometimes consort. He is a death-by-sex Fae and has been trying to get me to work for him on behalf of Queen Aoibheal to locate the *Sinsar Dubh.*

Addendum: He gave me Georgia back! When the walls came down, he protected my parents and preserved Ashford. He restored power and order to the entire state for me. Our relationship is changing, now that I am immune to his death-by-sex Fae eroticism. Are we becoming equals? I'm worried about him. Why did he disappear from the abbey? Why did he look so pained?

VOICE: A Druid art or skill that compels the person it's being used on to precisely obey the letter of whatever command is issued. Both the Lord Master and Barrons have used this on me. It's terrifying. It shuts down your will and makes you a slave. You stare helplessly out from your own eyes and watch your body doing things your mind is screaming at you *not* to do.

I'm trying to learn it. At least to be able to resist it, because otherwise I'll never be able to get close enough to the Lord Master to kill him and get vengeance for Alina.

Addendum: I can resist *and* use it now! Funny the steel you find inside when it's either that or die. But Barrons was right: The student and teacher lose the ability to use it on each other. Proficiency cancels it out.

WARD: Just learning about these. They're all over outside the Forbidden Libraries. I can pass through most of them for some reason. I don't know why. It's either one of my *sidhe*-seer talents or something I acquired through all my struggles. They're tricky things.

Z-LO: Barrons' version of the MacHalo. Black. Lighter, brighter, and more efficient, but I'm not about to tell *him* that.

*Denotes a Light or Dark Hallow.

Recipes from Dublin
Mac's Favorite Unseelie Dishes
Perfect for meals or quick snacks on-the-go!

IRISH SODA BREAD

(Great for in pockets on-the-go!)

4½ cups flour
2 Tbsp. sugar
1 tsp. salt
1 tsp. baking soda
4 Tbsp. butter
1 cup raisins

1 cup diced Unseelie
(the more finely you dice it, the harder it is for it to move)
1 large egg, whisked
2 cups buttermilk

Preheat oven to 425 degrees.

Sift together 4 cups flour, sugar, salt, and baking soda into large mixing bowl.

Using pastry cutter, cut butter into flour mixture until it resembles coarse crumbs, then stir in raisins. Add diced Unseelie, making certain it doesn't wriggle back out of the bowl.

Add beaten egg and buttermilk until dough is too

stiff to stir. Dust hands with flour and gently knead dough just enough to form rough ball. DO NOT OVERKNEAD, as this will make the bread tough. Place dough on lightly floured surface and shape into round loaf.

Place dough in lightly greased cast-iron skillet. Score top with an X to open the loaf so center cooks well. Bake until golden brown, about 40–50 minutes. Bread is done when toothpick or knife inserted into center comes out clean.

TRADITIONAL IRISH STEW

1 cup Unseelie, cubed
1 Tbsp. olive oil
Parsley, bay leaf, thyme,
   rosemary
1 lb. potatoes
2 cups finely shredded
   cabbage

1 sweet Vidalia onion,
   chopped
10 small white onions
1½ cups diced celery
1½ cups peas
Salt and pepper to taste
Fresh chopped parsley

Heat Unseelie in lightly oiled pan. (Enjoy how miserable it seems to make it!) Add enough water to cover. Bring to a boil and add parsley, bay leaf, thyme, and rosemary. Lower heat and simmer.

Peel potatoes and cut into eighths if large, quarters if medium.

Add potatoes, cabbage, onion, small onions, and celery. Simmer 20–30 minutes, then add peas. Simmer

an additional 20 minutes or until potatoes are tender.
Season to taste and garnish with fresh parsley.

BUTTERMILK/STRAWBERRY SCONES

❦

(My personal favorite!)

2½ cups all-purpose
    flour
2 Tbsp. sugar
1½ tsp. baking powder
½ tsp. baking soda
½ tsp. salt

½ cup cold butter, cubed
1 cup buttermilk
1 egg
¾ cup sliced strawberries,
    well drained
½ cup Unseelie chunks

Preheat oven to 400 degrees.

Line large baking sheet with parchment paper.

In large bowl, whisk together flour, sugar, baking
powder, baking soda, and salt. Using pastry cutter,
cut in butter until the mixture resembles coarse
crumbs. In a separate bowl, whisk buttermilk and
egg and pour over the dry mix. Stir (minimally!) with
fork to make loosely formed dough. With a wooden
spoon, gently mix in strawberries and Unseelie
chunks.

With lightly floured hands, form ball of dough. On
floured surface, knead *gently*, no more than ten times.

Pat into a 10-by-8-inch rectangle. Cut into 4 squares, then cut each diagonally in half to make 8 triangles. Place on sheet and bake on center rack of oven until golden, 15–18 minutes.

I like to glaze them a few minutes before they're done with butter and sprinkle them lightly with raw sugar!

TEA, AKA FINGER*, SANDWICHES

(As served to Inspector Jayne)

1 8-oz. package cream cheese, softened

1 cup Unseelie, diced

3 hard-boiled eggs, finely chopped

½ cup celery, finely chopped

Half a medium onion, finely diced

¾ cup finely chopped Georgia pecans

Dash rosemary

Dash garlic

Salt and pepper to taste

1 loaf fresh-baked bread, sliced, with crusts removed.

Add all ingredients to softened cream cheese and mix well. Spread on bread and cut into desired shapes.

An invaluable advantage of this recipe is its thick consistency, which keeps the Unseelie from wriggling too much. Non-cream-cheese-based tea sandwiches have the unfortunate penchant for crawling off the serving platter. (Unseelie sticks well in peanut butter sandwiches, too.)

Or toe, or arm, or whatever parts you've got.

Another great thing about this recipe is that the only thing you have to cook is the hard-boiled eggs, and if you're in a hurry, you can omit them.

SHEPHERD'S PIE

❦

(One of Inspector Jayne's favorites)

2 lbs. potatoes, peeled
  and cubed
2 Tbsp. sour cream
1 large egg yolk
½ cup heavy cream
1 Tbsp. olive oil
2 cups Unseelie, cubed
Salt, pepper, and garlic
  powder to taste
1 carrot, peeled and
  chopped

1 sweet Vidalia onion,
  chopped
2 Tbsp. unsalted butter
2 Tbsp. all-purpose flour
1 cup beef broth
2 tsp. Worcestershire
  sauce
½ cup peas
2 Tbsp. chopped fresh
  parsley leaves

Preheat oven to Broil/High.

Boil potatoes in salted water until tender. Drain and place in bowl; put aside. Mix sour cream, egg yolk, and cream. Add to potatoes and mash to desired smoothness.

Place large skillet on medium-high heat. Add oil and Unseelie cubes and season to taste with salt, pepper, and garlic powder. Add carrot and onion and cook for 5 minutes, stirring frequently.

In a saucepan over medium heat, melt butter and add flour. Whisk in broth and Worcestershire sauce. Thicken gravy and add to meat and vegetables. Add peas.

Fill casserole dish with meat and vegetable mixture, and spoon potatoes over meat. Season potatoes to taste and broil 6 to 8 inches from top of oven, until evenly browned. (You may need to cook covered so the Unseelie doesn't slither up the sides and end up on the bottom of the oven.) Garnish with chopped parsley.

Acknowledgments

Many thanks to my fabulous editor, Shauna Summers, whose keen insights, unflagging enthusiasm, and support have been such a big part of bringing this series to life. You're a dream editor, Shauna! Thanks to Jessica Sebor for staying on top of the details and for keeping track of me as I move all over the country. I know it hasn't been easy. Thanks to Bantam Dell's fabulous marketing, art, and sales departments for all your hard work and energy. Thanks also to the brilliant Genevieve Gagne-Hawes for reading and critiquing the first drafts of all the *Fever* books. You're an amazing woman, and my thanks are long overdue! Also, to my agent, Amy Berkower, and the good people at Writer's House who do the behind-the-scenes work that isn't immediately recognized. I see and appreciate all of it!

Thanks to the Moning Maniacs, who make the message boards at karenmoning.com such a fun place, sharing your passion for life, love, and books. Our drop-of-a-hat get-togethers mean so much to me. Thanks to the talented fans who designed the artwork at the Fever Fan Merchandise Store, and to the "precinct captains" who managed their leg of the MacHalo World Tour. You're the best!

Thanks to Leiha Mann, whose talents are so

many and diverse that I can never list them all: manager, innovator, coordinator, photographer, mover and shaker, and maker of grand events. I'm continually astounded at how much person is packed inside that tiny frame!

Finally, a special thanks to my husband, Neil, who is the first person to hear Mac's escapades every morning and the last person I talk to about them every night. From brainstorming to editing, to writing the songs and recording the sound track, you've enriched the *Fever* world, and my life, in so many ways! It's pure joy creating with you.

To all the people who've devoted their time, energy, creativity, and insight to the *Fever* world—thanks!

Want more Mac?

Read on for never-before-published
bonus material from your favorite author . . .

⊛ A deleted scene from *Dreamfever*

⊛ An interview between Karen Marie
Moning and Jericho Barrons

Deleted Scene from *Dreamfever*

This was written before Faefever *was finished, as a sort of aiming-at-emotion in the future. By the time I began writing* Dreamfever, *I no longer liked it. I have few actual "deleted" scenes but I have a lot of notes and small sketches like this.*
—KAREN MARIE MONING

"You're not the only fucking one that got branded!" Barrons slammed his fist into the wall behind my head. Bits of plaster dusted my shoulders.

Oh, really? I wasn't the only one walking around with a mark on me I didn't want? Our gazes locked and I jerked. Was he *letting* me see this, or had intimacy given me a window into his soul. As if he had one. He deserved no less. He hadn't done it to save me. He'd had sex with me because it was the only way he could continue using me. He'd had sex with me to steal my services back from his enemies at Camp Pri-ya.

And for the first time since the morning he'd gotten up and walked out, leaving me painfully, horrifically aware of both who I was and where I was—in Jericho Barron's lust-drenched bed on the verge of begging him not to leave me *while in full possession of my senses*—I could see that it hadn't left him nearly as untouched as I'd thought. As he'd led me to think.

I searched his face. Beneath his left eye, a tiny muscle contracted, smoothed, contracted again. That minute betrayal was Barron's equivalent of a normal person having a full-blown hissy fit. Oh, no, *far* from untouched. Had he stood outside my door as I'd stood outside his, fists at his sides, lips drawn back? Did it have him as bad as it had me? Was it eating at him, gnawing at him with the same sharp vicious little teeth that wouldn't let me sleep?

Yes, it was. I could see the rage of insatiable, uninvited lust in every line of that dark, stoic face that had once been too subtly etched for me to read. I wasn't the only one lying awake at night, fevered with memories, tossing, turning, soaking my sheets, burning up—not for Fae sex, but him, damn it all to hell, *him*.

Remembering being too naked in body and soul, trembling with need. Backing to him, a wild animal. Later, straddling him, holding him down and demanding more and *more* because Jericho Barrons couldn't be depleted. Of anything. Whatever he was. He was without limit.

He hadn't erased the Fae Princes' marks—he'd burned his own into them until I could no longer discern the shape of the marks they'd left. He'd scarred their scars out of me with a bigger scar. The bastard. And if I'd managed to carve up some part of him in return—

"*Good*," I said, hard and low. "Welcome to my world, Barrons. I hope it hurts like hell." His hand was on my throat and my back was to the wall. I couldn't breathe. I didn't need to. He was touching me. Two enormous magnets, repelling and attracting; a manifest of nature, not a matter of will at all. The air between us crackled with energy. Did I smell flesh burning?

"Good?" he said softly, and staring into those black eyes was like staring down the shadowy, demon-littered corridor of the Unseelie mirror in his study. "You think it's *good* to have something like me obsessed with you? My dear, dear, bloody idiotic, suicidal Ms. Lane, you have no fucking idea what's gotten the scent of you in its nostrils, what has the taste of you in its blood, or you'd run. You'd run for what little remains of what you think of as your life."

He whirled, long black coat fluttering, out the door, and was gone.

I stared into the deepening twilight into which he'd disappeared. Nightfall was painting the stone walkway one of those new Fae shades that hadn't existed before the walls had come crashing down around our ears; a dreamy silvery violet, spider-webbed with moonbeams that was eerily beautiful. I shivered. I hated the new colors. They were . . . somehow just . . . wrong.

I shook it off.

Obsessed, Barrons had said.

I smiled. Good.

Interview with
Jericho Barrons

It's me, KMM, and I'm at Barrons Books & Baubles where I'll be interviewing Jericho Barrons today.

I choose my seat with care, sitting on the chesterfield sofa Mac usually occupies. It tickles me to sit where she usually sits. There's a bottle of pink polish on the table next to me, and two fashion magazines. The gas fireplaces are on. I feel as if Mac might have just left, when the truth is she hasn't been here for quite a while. Barrons moves a chair close to me and sits so near our knees almost touch. If I move, they will. I battle the urge to move. Before I begin the interview, I glance around my bookstore with pleasure. I see the parts of it that aren't fully realized, the opaqueness in certain areas that I've not committed to the page in comprehensive detail. It occurs to me that perhaps I should finish painting the mural five floors up, maybe add a few chairs. Barrons makes a sound of impatience. I know that sound well. I open my laptop and begin.

Karen Marie Moning: Let's start things off with the question we all want the answer to: What are you, Jericho Barrons?

Jericho Z. Barrons: At the moment, hungry.

He gives me a look that makes me want to feed him whatever he wants.

KMM: That's not what I mean and you know it.

JZB: I've been informed I'm a "lefty." Does that help?

I refuse to look at his crotch to see where his package is. He's doing to me what he does to Mac all the time: trying to distract and evade with sex. But I know every mistake Mac has made, and I'm not falling for it. I will get answers.

KMM: Are you the Unseelie King? I say coyly.

JZB: Don't you think I'd be able to touch my own bloody book if I was?

He sounds cross.

KMM: You answered my question with a question, not an answer, Barrons. Are you the Unseelie King: yes or no? I push.

His eyes narrow. I refuse to squirm in my chair. I'm the author. I created him. I don't need to squirm. As if he read my mind, he says:

JZB: You think you created me don't you?

KMM: I did create you, I say dryly.

Perhaps there's a touch of conceit in my voice. If I created him then I can control him and if I can control a man like Barrons, then I must be one hell of a woman.

JZB: Has it occurred to you that perhaps I created you?

I go blank for a moment. I've always been more than a little perturbed by Zhuangzi's conundrum of whether Chuang Chou was a man dreaming he was a butterfly or a butterfly dreaming he was a man. I suspect reality is a bit less tangible, more frighteningly malleable to fiction writers.

JZB: Or perhaps, *he exploits my hesitation instantly,* I stroll by your bedroom window at night, whisper my tale to you and let you believe it is fiction. Allow you to suffer the delusion that you're in charge.

Mockery shimmers in his dark gaze and for a moment I'm transfixed. I don't think I put small gold flecks in his eyes. Where did they come from?

KMM: *I shake off the thrall and say,* Get over yourself, Barrons. No doubts. I created you.

JZB: Really. Then why the bloody hell are you asking me what I am? *The Sahara could be no dryer than his voice.*

I stare. Why am I? The answer comes swiftly. Because— try though I might to convince myself otherwise—I've long suspected I don't have any control over Barrons, and never had. He has parted with his secrets only if and when he felt like it—and that hasn't been often. Still, I'm the author. I do too know what he is. I set my laptop aside and stand, bristling with irritation and indignation.

KMM: That's it, Barrons. You pushed me too far. I'm going to tell them everything, right now. I'm going to spill it all. Tell them every sordid detail about what you are, what you did, and what you want.

He stands, too. He towers over me. I did not write him that tall and I know it. And I certainly didn't write him that attractive. I gave him flaws. Where are they? And where did his tattoos go? The ones on his left arm are gone now, and there's something new on his neck. Is it moving? He smiles and I know I didn't write that smile. Death smiles like that.

JZB: Really, *he says softly and I shiver because I know—after all, I created him—that soft from Barrons is dangerous.* And risk that I created you, and if you become too much of a nuisance I'll kill you off? Are you ready to die, Ms. Moning? You know what happens to unwanted, irksome characters. *He touches my cheek. Electricity sizzles under my skin. He traces a finger down* *my jaw, stopping at my jugular.* You are swift becoming unwanted.

I stare up at him, appalled to realize I want to be wanted by Jericho Barrons. I want to touch him. I want him to touch me. I want him to look at me with lust. I'm baffled by this. Like Fae creations, can a fictional character take on a life of its own? Change without the author's consent? Do I really know who and what he is? Is it possible he's been masquerading all along, deceiving even his own creator? The lines of reality blur around me.

KMM: I do, too, know what you are, I insist.

JZB: Bored now. Where's Mac?

KMM: I'm the one asking the questions.

JZB: I said, "Where's Mac?"

Unbelievable! He Voiced me! The bastard actually Voiced me!

KMM: At Chester's with Ryodan, I grit, where I left her when I came here to interview you.

His hand is suddenly around my throat and I can't breathe. My toes barely touch the floor.

JZB: If she fucks him you die.

He releases me, and I collapse onto the sofa. With a blur of movement, and the slam of the front door, Jericho Barrons is gone.

Eventually, I collect myself. I'm not sure why I bother, but I stop to turn off both gas fires on the way out, as if it's all so real that a backdraft might burn my fictional bookstore down. As I'm leaving, I glance up, and do a double take. The mural is complete!

I stop and turn slowly. Sure enough, right where I wanted them, sit two plush, red velvet chairs.

I didn't put them there.

CHECK OUT

BloodRush: The Official Fever Soundtrack

and get a **FREE** DOWNLOAD of "JERICHO RAIN"

at KarenMoning.com

If you're dying to know what happens to Mac, don't miss the upcoming installment in Karen Marie Moning's "addictively dark, erotic and even shocking"* series.

SHADOWFEVER

by

Karen Marie Moning

Coming soon from Delacorte Press

*Publishers Weekly